Books by Jonathan Kellerman

FICTION

ALEX DELAWARE NOVELS

Guilt (2013)
Victims (2012)
Mystery (2011)
Deception (2010)
Evidence (2009)
Bones (2008)
Compulsion (2008)
Obsession (2007)
Gone (2006)
Rage (2005)
Therapy (2004)
A Cold Heart (2003)
The Murder Book (2002)
Flesh and Blood (2001)

Dr. Death (2000)
Monster (1999)
Survival of the Fittest (1997)
The Clinic (1997)
The Web (1996)
Self-Defense (1995)
Bad Love (1994)
Devil's Waltz (1993)
Private Eyes (1992)
Time Bomb (1990)
Silent Partner (1989)
Over the Edge (1987)
Blood Test (1986)
When the Bough Breaks (1985)

OTHER NOVELS

True Detectives (2009)
Capital Crimes (with Faye Kellerman, 2006)
Twisted (2004)
Double Homicide (with Faye Kellerman, 2004)
The Conspiracy Club (2003)
Billy Straight (1998)
The Butcher's Theater (1988)

GRAPHIC NOVELS

Silent Partner (2012)   *The Web* (2013)

NONFICTION

With Strings Attached: The Art and Beauty of Vintage Guitars (2008)

Savage Spawn: Reflections on Violent Children (1999)

Helping the Fearful Child (1981)

Psychological Aspects of Childhood Cancer (1980)

FOR CHILDREN, WRITTEN AND ILLUSTRATED

Jonathan Kellerman's ABC of Weird Creatures (1995)

Daddy, Daddy, Can You Touch the Sky? (1994)

GUILT

JONATHAN KELLERMAN

GUILT

AN ALEX DELAWARE NOVEL

DOUBLEDAY LARGE PRINT HOME LIBRARY EDITION

BALLANTINE BOOKS

NEW YORK

Published in the United States by Ballantine Books,
an imprint of The Random House Publishing Group,
a division of Random House, Inc., New York.

BALLANTINE and colophon are registered trademarks
of Random House, Inc.

ISBN 978-1-62490-077-8

Printed in the United States of America

This Large Print Book carries the
Seal of Approval of N.A.V.H.

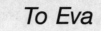

To Eva

Special thanks to Clea Koff,
Terri Porras, Miguel Porras, and
Randy Ema

GUILT

CHAPTER

1

All mine!

The house, the life growing inside her.

The husband.

Holly finished her fifth circuit of the back room that looked out to the yard. She paused for breath. The baby—Aimee—had started pushing against her diaphragm.

Since escrow had closed, Holly had done a hundred circuits, imagining. Loving every inch of the place despite the odors embedded in ninety-year-old plaster: cat pee, mildew, overripe vegetable soup. Old person.

In a few days the painting would begin and the aroma of fresh latex would bury all that, and cheerful colors would mask the discouraging gray-beige of Holly's ten-room dream. Not counting bathrooms.

The house was a brick-faced Tudor on a quarter-acre lot at the southern edge of Cheviot Hills, built when construction was meant to last and adorned by moldings, wainscoting, arched mahogany doors, quarter-sawn oak floors. Parquet in the cute little study that would be Matt's home office when he needed to bring work home.

Holly could close the door and not have to hear Matt's grumbling about moron clients incapable of keeping decent records. Meanwhile she'd be on a comfy couch, snuggling with Aimee.

She'd learned the sex of the baby at the four-month anatomical ultrasound, decided on the name right then and there. Matt didn't know yet. He was still adjusting to the whole fatherhood thing.

Sometimes she wondered if Matt dreamed in numbers.

Resting her hands on a mahogany

sill, Holly squinted to blank out the weeds and dead grass, struggling to conjure a green, flower-laden Eden.

Hard to visualize, with a mountain of tree trunk taking up all that space.

The five-story sycamore had been one of the house's selling points, with its trunk as thick as an oil drum and dense foliage that created a moody, almost spooky ambience. Holly's creative powers had immediately kicked into gear, visualizing a swing attached to that swooping lower branch.

Aimee giggling as she swooped up and shouted that Holly was the best mommy.

Two weeks into escrow, during a massive, unseasonal rainstorm, the sycamore's roots had given way. Thank God the monster had teetered but hadn't fallen. The trajectory would've landed it right on the house.

An agreement was drawn up: The sellers—the old woman's son and daughter—would pay to have the monstrous thing chopped down and hauled away, the stump ground to dust, the soil leveled. Instead, they'd cheaped out, paying a tree company only to cut down the sycamore, leaving behind a massive horror of deadwood that took up the entire rear half of the yard.

Matt had gone bananas, threatened to kill the deal.

Abrogate. What an ugly word.

Holly had cooled him off by promising to handle the situation, she'd make sure they got duly compensated, he wouldn't have to deal with it.

Fine. As long as you actually do it.

Now Holly stared at the mountain of wood, feeling discouraged and a bit helpless. Some of the sycamore, she supposed, could be reduced to firewood. Fragments and leaves and loose pieces of bark she could rake up herself, maybe create a compost pile. But those massive columns . . .

Whatever; she'd figure it out. Meanwhile, there was cat-pee/overripe-soup/mildew/old-lady stink to deal with.

Mrs. Hannah had lived in the house for fifty-two years. Still, how did a person's smell permeate lath and plaster? Not that Holly had anything against old people. Though she didn't know too many.

There had to be something you could do to freshen yourself—a special deodorant—when you reached a certain age.

One way or the other, Matt would settle down. He'd come around, he always did.

Like with the house, itself. He'd never expressed any interest in design, all of a sudden he was into *contemporary.* Holly had toured a ton of boring white boxes, knowing Matt would always find a reason to say no because that was Matt's thing.

By the time Holly's dream house materialized, he didn't care about style, just a good price.

The deal had been one of those warp-speed magical things, like when the stars are all aligned and your karma's perfectly positioned: Old lady dies, greedy kids want quick cash and contact Coldwell and randomly get hooked up with Vanessa, and Vanessa calls Holly before the house goes on the market because she owes Holly big-

time, all those nights talking Vanessa
down from bad highs, listening to Vanessa's nonstop litany of personal issues.

Toss in the biggest real estate slump
in decades and the fact that Holly had
been a little Ms. Scroogette working
twelve-hour days as a P.R. drone since
graduating college nine years ago and
Matt was even tighter plus he'd gotten
that raise plus that IPO they got to in-
vest in from one of Matt's tech buddies
had paid off, and they had just enough
for the down payment and to qualify for
financing.

Mine!

Including the tree.

Holly struggled with a balky old brass
handle—original hardware!—shoved a
warped French door open, and stepped
out into the yard. Making her way
through the obstacle course of felled
branches, death-browned leaves, and
ragged pieces of bark, she reached the
fence that separated her property from
the neighbors.

This was her first serious look at the
mess, and it was even worse than she'd

thought: The tree company had sawed away with abandon, allowing the chunks to fall on unprotected ground. The result was a whole bunch of holes—craters, a real disaster.

Maybe she could use that to threaten a big-time lawsuit unless they carted everything away and cleaned up properly.

She'd need a lawyer. One who'd take it on contingency . . . God, those holes were ugly, sprouting thick, wormy masses of roots and a nasty-looking giant splinter.

She kneeled at the rim of the grossest crater, tugged at the roots. No give. Moving to a smaller pit, she dislodged only dust.

At the third hole, as she managed to tug loose a thatch of smaller roots, her fingers brushed against something cold. Metallic.

Buried treasure, aye aye, pirate booty! Wouldn't that be justice!

Laughing, Holly brushed away soil and rocks, revealed a patch of pale blue. Then a red cross. A few more strokes and the entire top of the metal thing came into view.

A box, like a safe-deposit box but larger. Blue except for the red cross at the center.

Something medical? Or just kids burying who-knew-what in an abandoned receptacle?

Holly tried to budge the box. It shimmied but held fast. She rocked it back and forth, made some progress but was unable to free the darn thing.

Then she remembered and went to the garage and retrieved the ancient spade from the stack of rusty tools left behind by the sellers. Another broken promise, they'd pledged to clean up completely, gave the excuse that the tools were still usable, they were just trying to be nice.

Like Matt would ever use hedge clippers or a rake or a hand edger.

Returning to the hole, she wedged the spade's flat mouth between metal and dirt and put a little weight into the pry. A creak sounded but the box only budged a tiny bit, stubborn devil. Maybe she could pop the lid to see what was inside . . . nope, the clasp was held tight by soil. She worked the spade some more, same lack of progress.

Back in the old days she would've borne down hard. Back when she did Zumba twice a week and yoga once a week and ran 10Ks and didn't have to avoid sushi or carpaccio or latte or Chardonnay.

All for you, Aimee.

Now every week brought increasing fatigue, everything she'd taken for granted was an ordeal. She stood there, catching her breath. Okay, time for an alternative plan: Inserting the spade along every inch of the box's edges, she let loose a series of tiny, sharp tugs, working methodically, careful not to strain.

After two go-rounds, she began again, had barely pushed down on the spade when the box's left side popped up and it flew out of the hole and Holly staggered back, caught off-balance.

The spade fell from her hands as she used both arms to fight for stability.

She felt herself going down, willed

herself not to, managed to stay on her feet.

Close call. She was wheezing like an asthmatic couch potato. Finally, she recovered enough to drag the blue box onto the dirt.

No lock on the latch, just a hasp and loop, rusted through. But the rest of the box had turned green from oxidation, and a patch worn through the blue paint explained that: bronze. From the weight, solid. That had to be worth something by itself.

Sucking in a lungful of air, Holly jiggled with the hasp until she freed it.

"Presto-gizmo," she said, lifting the lid.

The bottom and sides of the box were lined with browned newspaper. Resting in the nest of clippings was something wrapped in fuzzy cloth—a satin-edged blanket, once blue, now faded mostly to tan and pale green. Purplish splotches on the satin borders.

Something worth wrapping. Burying. Excited, Holly lifted the blanket out of the box.

Feeling disappointed immediately because whatever was inside had no serious weight to it, scratch doubloons or gold bars or rose-cut diamonds.

Laying the blanket on the ground, Holly took hold of a seam and unfurled.

The thing that had been inside the blanket grinned up at her.

Then it shape-shifted, oh God, and she cried out and it fell apart in front of her eyes because all that had held it together was the tension of the blanket-wrap.

Tiny skeleton, now a scatter of loose bones.

The skull had landed right in front of her. Smiling. Black eyeholes insanely *piercing.*

Two minuscule tooth-thingies on the bottom jaw looked ready to bite.

Holly sat there, unable to move or breathe or think.

A bird peeped.

Silence bore down on Holly.

A leg bone rolled to one side as if by its own power and she let out a wordless retch of fear and revulsion.

That did nothing to discourage the

skull. It kept *staring.* Like it knew something.

Holly mustered all of her strength and
screamed.

Kept screaming.

CHAPTER

2

The woman was blond, pretty, white-faced, pregnant.

Her name was Holly Ruche and she sat hunched atop a tree stump, one of a dozen or so massive, chain-sawed segments taking up a good portion of the run-down backyard. Breathing hard and clutching her belly, she clenched her eyes shut. One of Milo's cards rested between her right thumb and forefinger, crumpled beyond recognition. For the second time since I'd arrived, she waved off help from the paramedics.

They hung around anyway, paying

scant attention to the uniforms and the coroner's crew. Everyone standing around looking superfluous; it would take an anthropologist to make sense of this.

Milo had phoned the EMTs first. "Priorities. It's not like there's any emergency to the rest of it."

The rest of it was an assortment of brown bones that had once been a baby's skeleton, scattered on an old blanket. Not a random toss, the general shape was of a tiny, disarticulated human body.

Open sutures in the skull and a couple of dental eruptions in the mandible made my guess four to six months, but my Ph.D.'s in the wrong science for that kind of prophecy. The smallest bones— fingers, toes—weren't much thicker than toothpicks.

Looking at the poor little thing made my eyes hurt. I shifted my attention to details.

Beneath the blanket was a wad of newspaper clippings from 1951 lining a blue metal box around two feet long. The paper was the L.A. *Daily News,* defunct since 1954. A sticker on the side of the box read *Property Swedish Benevolent Hospital and Infirmary, 232 Central Avenue, Los Angeles, Ca.*—an institution just confirmed by Milo to have shut down in '52.

The homely, squat Tudor house fronting the yard looked to be older than that, probably from the twenties when so much of L.A. had taken shape.

Holly Ruche began crying.

A paramedic approached again. "Ma'am?"

"I'm fine . . ." Swollen-eyed, hair cut in an off-kilter bob mussed by nervous hands, she focused on Milo, as if for the first time, shifted to me, shook her head, stood.

Folding her arms across her occupied abdomen, she said, "When can I have my house back, Detective?"

"Soon as we finish processing, Ms. Ruche."

She regarded me again.

Milo said, "This is Dr. Delaware, our consulting psychologist—"

"Psychologist? Is someone worried about my mental health?"

"No, ma'am. We sometimes call Dr. Delaware in when—"

"Thanks but I'm fine." Shuddering, she glanced back to where she'd found the bones. "So horrible."

Milo said, "How deeply was the box buried?"

"I don't know—not deep, I was able to pull it up, wasn't I? You don't really think this is a real crime, do you? I mean a new one. It's historical, not for the police, right? The house was constructed in 1927 but it could've even been there way before, the land used to be bean fields and grapevines, if you dug up the neighborhood—any neighborhood— who knows what you'd find."

She placed a hand on her chest. Seemed to be fighting for oxygen.

Milo said, "Maybe you should sit down, ma'am."

"Don't worry, I promise I'm okay."

"How about we let the paramedics take a look at you—"

"I've already been looked at," she said. "By a real doctor, yesterday, my ob-gyn, everything's perfect."

"How far along are you?"

"Five months." Her smile was frigid. "What could possibly not be okay? I own a gorgeous house. Even though you're *processing* it." She hmmphed. "It's *their* fault, all I wanted to do was have them get rid of the tree, if they hadn't done it sloppy, this would never have happened."

"The previous owners?"

"The Hannahs, Mark and Brenda, it was their mother's, she died, they couldn't wait to cash out . . . hey, here's something for you, Detective . . . I'm sorry, what'd you say your name was?"

"Lieutenant Sturgis."

"Here's something, Lieutenant Sturgis: The old woman was ninety-three when she died, she lived here for a long time, the house still smells of her. So she could easily have . . . done that."

"We'll look into it, Ms. Ruche."

"What exactly does *processing* mean?"

"Depends on what else we find."

She reached into a jean pocket and drew out a phone that she jabbed angrily. "C'mon, answer already—oh, I got you. Finally. Listen, I need you to come over . . . to the house. You won't believe what happened . . . what? No, I can't—okay, soon as the meeting's finished . . . no, don't call, just come over."

She hung up.

Milo said, "Your husband?"

"He's an accountant." As if that explained it. "So what's *processing*?"

"Our first step will be bringing some dogs in to sniff around, depending upon what they come up with, maybe a below-ground sonar to see if anything else is buried down there."

"Else?" said Holly Ruche. "Why would there be anything else?"

"No reason, but we need to be thorough."

"You're saying my home is a graveyard? That's disgusting. All you've got is some old bones, there's no reason to think there's more."

"I'm sure you're right—"

"Of course I'm right, I own this place. The house *and* the land."

A hand fluttered to her abdomen. She massaged. "*My* baby's developing perfectly."

"That's great, Ms. Ruche."

She stared at Milo, gave out a tiny squeak. Her eyes rolled back, her mouth went slack, she pitched backward.

Milo and I both caught her. Her skin was dank, clammy. As she went limp, the paramedics rushed over, looking oddly satisfied.

I-told-you-so nods. One of them said, "It's always the stubborn ones. We'll take it from here, Lieutenant."

Milo said, "You sure as hell will," and went to call the anthropologist.

CHAPTER

3

Liz Wilkinson had just finished a lecture at the U., would be over in twenty. Milo went to make more calls and I sat with Holly Ruche.

All vital signs fine per the EMTs, but she needed to rest and get down some fluids. They gave me custody of the Gatorade squeeze bottle, packed up and left for an emergency call near the 405 freeway.

The first time I offered the bottle to Holly she clamped her mouth and shook her head. The second time, her lips parted. Several sips later, she smiled and lowered her right hand until it rested atop my left. Her skin had warmed. She said, "I feel much better . . . you're a psychologist for victim aid?"

"I do what's needed, there's no set routine."

"I guess I am a victim. Of sorts."

"It had to be rough."

"It was horrible. Do you think he's going to dig up my entire yard?"

"He won't do anything unnecessary."

"That sounds like you're covering for him."

"I'm judging from experience."

"So you work with him a lot."

"I do."

"Must be . . . ooh." She winced, touched her belly. The black jersey of her top puffed. "She's moving like crazy—it's a girl."

"Congratulations."

"Girls rule." She grinned. "I'm looking forward to having a little BFF." Another grimace. "Wow, she's being really hyper . . . oh, my . . . that one smarted a bit, she's kicking me in the ribs."

I said, "First baby?"

"You can tell?" she said. "I'm coming across like an amateur?"

"Not at all. You're young."

"Not that young," she said. "I'm thirty-one."

"That's young."

"My mother had me when she was eighteen."

"That's younger."

She laughed, grew serious. "I didn't want that."

"Starting so young."

Her eyes shifted upward. "The way she did it . . . but I always knew I wanted it."

"Motherhood."

"Motherhood, house, yard, the whole domestic-goddess thing . . . it's going to be great." Looking past me, she took in the crime scene techs studying the tree segments. They'd arrived fifteen minutes ago, were waiting for Liz Wilkinson, had placed a white cloth over the blue box. The fabric had settled into an oblong; a deflated ghost costume.

Holly Ruche said, "I can't have them turning my property into a disaster zone

or something. I know it's not much right
now but I have plans."

Not a word about the tiny bones. I
wondered why a married woman would
avoid the plural form.

"It was all coming together," she said.
"Then that crazy tree had to—"

Movement from the driveway caused
us both to turn. A man around Holly's
age, skinny-but-soft, bald and bearded,
studied the felled tree before heading
over. He wore a long-sleeved blue shirt,
gray slacks, brown shoes. Beeper on
his belt, iPhone in his hand, aviator sunglasses perched atop his clean head.

"Hey," she said.

"Hey," he said.

His wedding ring matched hers. Neither of them took the greeting beyond
that. He had one of those faces that's
allergic to smiling, kept several feet between himself and Holly, looked put-
upon.

She said, "Matt?"

His attention shifted to the hand she'd
continued to drape over mine.

I stood, introduced myself.

He said, "A doctor? There's a problem, health-wise?"

"She's doing well, considering."

"Good. Matt Ruche. She's my wife."

Holly said, "Doctor as in psychologist. He's been giving me support."

Matt Ruche's eyes narrowed. "Okay."

His wife flashed him a broad, flat smile. "I'm feeling much better now. It was crazy. Finding it."

"Had to be . . . so when can we clean up?"

"Don't know, they'll tell us."

"That sucks."

"They have to do their job, Matt."

He touched his beeper. "What a hassle."

"The stupid tree fell down," said Holly. "No way could anyone—"

"Whatever." He glanced at his phone.

I turned to leave.

Holly Ruche said, "Hold on, one sec."

She got to her feet. "Do you have a card, Dr. Delaware?"

I found one. Matt Ruche reached to take it. She beat him to it. He flushed clear up to his scalp. Shrugging, he began texting.

Holly gripped my hand with both of hers. "Thanks."

I wished her good luck just as Liz Wilkinson strode into the yard, carrying two hard-shell cases. She had on a pantsuit the color of bittersweet chocolate; same hue as her skin, a couple of tones lighter. A white coat was draped over one arm. Her hair had been straightened recently and she wore it loose and long. She saw me, waved, kept going.

Someone must've prepped her because she headed straight for the tarp, put on the coat, tied her hair back, gloved up, stooped, and drew the cloth back deftly.

"Oh, look at this poor little thing."

The bones seemed even smaller, the color of browned butter in places, nearly black in others. Fragile as lace. I could see tiny nubs running along the chewing surfaces of both jaws. Un-erupted tooth buds.

Liz's lower lip extended. "Buried under the tree?"

I pointed out the hole. Liz examined the blue box.

"Swedish Hospital? Never heard of it."

"Closed down in '52. What do you think the box was originally used for?"

"Maybe exactly this," she said.

"A morgue receptacle?"

"I was thinking something used to transfer remains."

"The baby died a natural death in the hospital and someone took the body?"

"Bodies don't stay in hospitals, they go to mortuaries, Alex. After that, who knows? Regulations were looser back then."

I said, "The box is solid brass. Maybe it was intended to transfer lab specimens and someone thought iron or steel increased the risk of oxidation."

She returned to the skeleton, put on magnifying eyeglasses, got an inch from the bones. "No wires or drill holes, probably no bleach or chemical treatment, so it doesn't appear to be a teaching specimen." She touched the tooth buds. "Not a newborn, not with those mandibular incisors about to come through, best guess is four to seven months,

which fits the overall size of the skeleton. Though if the baby was neglected
or abused, it could be older . . . no frac-
tures or stress marks . . . I'm not seeing
any obvious tool marks—no wounds of
any sort . . . the neck bones appear to
be intact, so cross out strangulation . . .
no obvious bone malformations, either,
like from rickets or some other defi-
ciency . . . in terms of sex, it's too young
for sexual dimorphism. But if we can
get some DNA, we can determine gender and possibly a degree of racial origin. Unfortunately, the backlog's pretty
bad and something this old and cold
isn't going to be prioritized. In terms of
time since death, I can do some carbon
dating but my gut tells me this isn't
some ancient artifact."

I said, "The box was out of active use
in '52, those newspaper clippings are
from '51, and the house was built in '27.
I know that doesn't determine the time
frame—"

"But it's a good place to start, I agree.
So rather than go all super-tech from
the get-go, Milo should pull up real es-

tate records, find out who's lived here, and work backward. He identifies a suspect, we can prioritize DNA. Unless the suspect's deceased, which is quite possible if we're talking a sixty-, seventy-year-old crime. That's the case, maybe some relative will cooperate and we can get a partial."

A deep voice behind and above us grumbled, "Milo has begun pulling up real estate records. Afternoon, Elizabeth."

Liz looked up. "Hi, didn't see you when I came in."

Milo said, "In the house making calls."

And taking the detective walk through the empty space. His expression said that nothing obvious had come up. "So what do you think, kid?"

Liz repeated her initial impressions. "Not that you need me for any of that."

He said, "Young Moses needs you, I appreciate your input."

Detective I Moe Reed was her true love. They'd met at a swamp full of corpses.

She laughed. "Moses appreciates

me, too. Say hi when you see him, which is probably before I will."

She stood. "So what else can I do for you?"

"Take custody of the bones and do your wizard thing. If you need the box, you can have it, otherwise it's going to the crime lab."

"Don't need the box," she said. "But I'm not really sure I can tell you much more."

"How about age of victim?"

"I'll get it as close as I can," she said. "We can also x-ray to see if some sort of damage comes up within the bones, though that's unlikely. There's certainly nothing overt to indicate assault or worse. So we could be talking a natural death."

"Natural but someone buried it under a tree?" He frowned. "I hate that—*it.*" His shirt had come loose over his paunch. He tucked it in, hitched his trousers.

Liz said, "Maybe covert burial does imply some sort of guilt. And no visible marks doesn't eliminate murder, asphyxiating a baby is way too easy. And it's not rare in infanticides."

"Soft kill," he said.

She blinked. "Never heard that before."

"I'm a master of terrible irony."

CHAPTER

4

Milo and I returned to Holly Ruche. Her husband was gone.

She said, "He had a meeting."

Milo said, "Accountant stuff."

"Not too exciting, huh?"

Milo said, "Most jobs are a lot of routine."

She scanned the yard. "I'd still like to know why a psychologist was called in. Are you saying whoever lived here was a maniac?"

"Not at all." He turned to me: "You're fired, Doc."

I said, "Finally."

Holly Ruche smiled for half a second.

Milo said, "That woman in the white coat is a forensic anthropologist."

"The black woman? Interesting . . ." Her hands clenched. "I really hope this doesn't turn out to be one of those mad-dog serial killer things, bodies all over the place. If that's what happens, I could never live here. We'd be tied up in court, that would be a disaster."

"I'm sure everything will turn out fine."

"Just one little teensy skeleton?" she snapped. "That's fine?"

She looked down at her abdomen. "Sorry, Lieutenant, it's just—I just can't stand seeing my place overrun with strangers."

"I understand. No reason to stick around, Holly."

"This is my home, my apartment's just a way station."

He said, "We're gonna need the area clear for the dogs."

"The dogs," she said. "They find something, you'll bring in machinery and tear up everything."

"We prefer noninvasive methods like

ground-penetrating radar, air and soil analysis."

"How do you analyze air?"

"We insert thin flexible tubing into air pockets, but with something this old, decomposition smells are unlikely."

"And if you find something suspicious, you bring in machines and start ripping and shredding. Okay, I will leave but please make sure if you turned on any lights you turn them off. We just got the utilities registered in our name and the last thing I need is paying the police department's electrical bill."

She walked away, using that oddly appealing waddle pregnant women acquire. Hands clenched, neck rigid.

Milo said, "High-strung girl."

I said, "Not the best of mornings. Plus her marriage doesn't seem to be working too well."

"Ah . . . notice how I avoided telling her how you got here. No sense disillusioning the citizenry."

Most homicides are mundane and on the way to clearance within a day or two. Milo sometimes calls me on "the interesting ones."

This time, though, it was a matter of lunch.

Steak, salad, and scotch to be exact, at a place just west of Downtown. We'd both spent the morning at the D.A.'s office, he reviewing the file on a horrific multiple murder, I in the room next door, proofreading my witness statement on the same killings.

He'd tried to avoid the experience, taking vacation time then ignoring messages. But when Deputy D.A. John Nguyen phoned him at midnight and threatened to come over with cartons of week-old vegan takeout, Milo had capitulated.

"Sensible decision and don't even think of flaking on me," said Nguyen. "Also ask Delaware if he wants to take care of his business at the same time, the drafts just came in."

Milo picked me up at nine a.m., driving the Porsche 928 he shares with his partner, Rick Silverman. He wore an unhealthily shiny gray aloha shirt patterned with leering sea lions and clini-

cally depressed angelfish, baggy, multi-
pleated khakis, scuffed desert boots.
The shirt did nothing to improve his indoor pallor, but he loved Hawaii so why
not?

Solving the multiple had taken a lot
out of him, chiefly because he'd nearly
died in the process. I'd saved his life
and that was something neither of us
had ever imagined. Months had passed
and we still hadn't talked about it. I figured it was up to him to broach the
topic and so far he hadn't.

When we finished at the court building, he looked anything but celebratory.
But he insisted on taking me out for a
seventy-buck sirloin-T-bone combo and
"all the Chivas you can tolerate, boy-o,
seeing as I'm the designated wheel-
man."

An hour later, all we'd done was eat
and drink and make the kind of small
talk that doesn't work well between real
friends.

I rejected dessert but he went for a
three-scoop praline sundae drowned in
hot fudge syrup and pineapple sauce.
He'd lost a bit of weight since facing

mortality, was carrying maybe two forty on his stilt-legged seventy-five inches, most of it around the middle. Watching him maximize the calories made it tempting to theorize about anxiety, denial, masked depression, guilt, choose your psychobabble. I'd known him long enough to know that sometimes gluttony was a balm, other times an expression of joy.

He'd finished two scoops when his phone signaled a text. Wiping his chin and brushing coarse black hair off his pockmarked forehead, he read.

"Well, well, well. It's good I didn't indulge in the firewater. Time to go."

"New case?"

"Of sorts," he said. "Bones buried in an old box under an older tree, from the size, a baby."

"Of sorts?"

"Sounds like an old one so probably not much to do other than trace ownership of the property." Tossing cash on the table, he got up. "Want me to drop you off?"

"Where's the property?"

"Cheviot Hills."

"No need to drive all the way to my place then circle back."

"Up to you," he said. "I probably won't be that long."

Back at the car, he tucked the aloha shirt into the khakis, retrieved a sad brown tweed sport coat from the trunk, ended up with a strange sartorial meld of Scottish Highlands and Oahu.

"A baby," I said.

He said nothing.

CHAPTER

5

Seconds after Liz Wilkinson left with the bones, Moe Reed beeped in.

Milo muttered, "Two ships passing," clicked his cell on conference.

Reed said, "Got all the deed holders, El Tee, should have a list for you by the time you get back. Anything else?"

"That'll do it for now, Moses. Regards from your inamorata."

"My what?"

"Your true love. She was just here."

"Oh," said Reed. "Yeah, of course, bones. She have anything to say?"

"Just that she thinks you're dreamy."

Reed laughed. "Let's hope she holds that thought 'cause we're going out tonight. Unless you need me to work late or something."

"Not a chance," said Milo. "This one won't earn overtime for anyone."

Reed was waiting outside Milo's office, holding a sheaf of paper and sipping from a water bottle. His blond hair had grown out a couple of inches from the usual crew cut, his young face was pink and unlined, belying his old-soul approach to life. Massive muscles strained the sleeves of his blue blazer. His pants were creased, his shoes spit-shined. I'd never seen him dress any other way.

"Just got a call, El Tee, got to run. Blunt force trauma DB in a bar on Washington not far from Sony Studios."

"Go detect."

"Doesn't sound like much detection," said Reed. "Offender's still at the scene, patrol found him standing on top of the bar yelling space demons made him do it. More like your department, Doc."

"Not unless I've offended someone."

He laughed, hurried off. Milo unlocked his door.

One of Milo's lieutenant perks, negotiated years ago in a trade-off deal with a criminally vulnerable former chief of police, is his own space, separate from the big detective room. Another's the ability to continue working cases, rather than push paper like most lieutenants do. The new chief could've abrogated the deal but he was smart enough to check out Milo's solve stats and though he amuses himself with chronic abuse of "Mr. So-Called Hotshot" he doesn't fix what isn't broken.

The downside is a windowless work space the size of a closet. Milo is long-limbed and bulky and when he stretches he often touches plaster. When he's in a certain mood the place has the feel of an old-fashioned zoo cage, one of those claustrophobic confinements utilized before people started thinking of animals as having souls.

He sank down into his desk chair, setting off a tirade of squeaks, read the list, passed it over.

Holly Ruche's dream abode was a thirty-one-hundred-square-foot single-family residence situated in what was then the Monte Mar-Vista Tract, completed on January 5, 1927, and sold three months later to Mr. and Mrs. Jacob Thornton. After ten years, possession passed to the Thorntons' daughter, Marjorie, who unloaded the property thirteen months later to Dr. and Mrs. Malcolm Crowell Larner.

The Larners lived there until 1943, when the deed was transferred to Dr. and Mrs. George J. Del Rios. The Del Rioses resided at the property until 1955, after which possession shifted to the Del Rios Family Trust. In 1961, ownership passed to the Robert and Alice Hannah Family Trust and in '74 Alice Hannah, newly widowed, took sole possession, a status that had endured until sixty days ago when her heirs sold to Mr. and Mrs. Matthew Ruche.

Initial purchase price: forty-eight hundred dollars. Holly and Matt had gotten a recession bargain at nine hundred forty thousand dollars, with a down payment of a hundred seventy-five thousand and the remainder financed by a low-interest loan.

Milo jabbed the list twice. "*Dr.* Larner to *Dr.* Del Rios. The time frame works, that box came from a hospital, and a shady white-coat fits with swiping medical equipment for personal use."

I said, "I'd start with the period of those newspaper clippings—post-'51. That narrows it to the Del Rioses' ownership."

"Agreed. Let's see what we can learn about these folk."

He plugged in his department password and typed away, chewing a cold cigar to pulp. Official databases yielded nothing on Dr. George Del Rios other than a death certificate in 1947, age sixty-three, natural causes. A search for other decedents with the same surname pulled up Del Rios, Ethel A., DOD 1954, age sixty-four, cancer, and Del Rios, Edward A., DOD 1960, age forty-five, vehicular accident.

"I like Edward A. as a starting point," he said. "The trust sold the house a year after he died, so there's a decent chance he was George and Ethel's boy and inherited the place."

I said, "A boy in his thirties who George and Ethel might've worried about, so they left the house in trust rather than bequeathed it to him outright. And even though the trustee didn't get it until '55, a son could have had access to the property before then, when Mama was living there alone."

"She goes to bridge club, he digs a little hole."

"Maybe their lack of faith was due to lifestyle issues."

"Eddie's a miscreant."

"Back then a well-heeled miscreant could avoid stigma, so 'vehicular accident' might've been code for a one-car DUI. But some stigmas you'd need to take care of yourself. Like a socially embarrassing out-of-wedlock birth."

He said, "Eddie's married and the mother's someone other than wifey? Yeah, that would be blush-inducing at the country club."

"Even if Eddie was a bachelor playboy, burying a social inconvenience could've seemed like a grand idea."

He thought. "I like it, Alex, let's dig dirt on this charmer. Pun intended."

He searched for obituaries on all three family members. Dr. George J. Del Rios's was featured in the *Times* and the *Examiner.* He'd been an esteemed, certain-to-be-missed cardiologist on staff at St. Vincent Hospital as well as a faculty member at the med school where I sometimes taught. No final bio for his widow. Nothing on her at all.

Father Edward Del Rios, director of the Good Shepherd Orphanage of Santa Barbara, had perished when a bus ferrying children from that institution to the local zoo had veered off Cabrillo Boulevard on July 6, 1960. Several of the children had been injured, a few seriously, but all had recovered. The priest and the bus driver hadn't been so lucky.

The *Santa Barbara News-Press* covered the crash on its front page, reporting that "several of the terrified youngsters describe the driver, Meldrom Perry, suddenly slumping over the wheel leading to the bus going out of control. The children also report that 'Father Eddie' made an heroic attempt to gain control of the vehicle. Both Perry, 54, of Vista, and Father Del Rios, just days from his 46th birthday, perished after being thrown free of the bus. But the man of God's valiant attempts may have pre- vented an even worse disaster. An in- vestigation has begun into allegations that Perry suffered from a prior heart condition, a fact known to the bus char- ter company, an outfit with previous vi- olations on record."

"Some playboy," said Milo. "Poor guy was a damn hero."

I said, "He lived in Santa Barbara so the house was probably rented out dur- ing his ownership."

"And try finding a tenant. Okay, time to canvass the neighborhood, maybe some old-timer will remember that far back."

"There's another reason the house could've been left in trust: Father Eddie was in charge but he had siblings."

"Seeing as he was Catholic?"

"Seeing as most people have sib- lings. If you can access any trust docu- ments, they'll list who else benefited."

◆

It took a while, but an appendix stashed in the bowels of the tax rolls finally yielded the data.

Two brothers, one sister, all younger than Father Eddie. Ferdinand and Mary Alice had passed away decades ago in their sixties, consistent with the genetic endowment bestowed by their parents.

The baby of the family, John Jacob Del Rios, was listed as residing in Burbank. Age eighty-nine.

Milo looked up his number and called. Generally, he switches to speaker so I can listen in. This time, he forgot or chose not to do so and I sat there as he introduced himself, explained the reason for calling as an "occurrence" at John J. Del Rios's old family home, listened for a while, said, "Thank you, sir," and hung up.

"Sounds young for his age, more than happy to talk about the good old days. But it needs to be tomorrow, he's entertaining a 'lady friend.' He also let me know he'd been on the job."

"LAPD?"

"Sheriff."

He typed some more. Commander

John J. Del Rios had run the Sheriff's Correctional Division from 1967 through 1974, retired with pension, and received a citation from his boss for distinguished service. Further cyber-snooping pulled up a ten-year stretch at a private security firm. After that, nothing.

Milo made a few calls to contacts at the tan-shirts. No one remembered Del Rios.

I said, "Entertaining a lady friend? Maybe he's our playboy. He'd have been in his twenties, prime time for an active sexual life."

"We'll check him out tomorrow. Eleven a.m. After his golf game."

"Golf, women, the good life," I said. "A good long life."

"The priest dies young, the hedonist thrives? Yeah, I love when justice prevails."

CHAPTER

6

The following morning, I picked Milo up on Butler Avenue and Santa Monica, just north of the West L.A. station.

The bones had made the morning news, print and TV, with Holly Ruche's name left out and the neighborhood described as "affluent Westside." Milo was carrying a folded *Times* by his side. He wore a lint-gray suit, algae-green shirt, poly tie the color of venous blood. The sun wasn't kind to his pockmarked face; that and his size and his glower made him someone you'd cross the street to avoid.

He appreciates the value of publicity as much as any experienced detective. But he likes to control the flow, and I expected him to be angry about the leak. He got into the Seville, stretched, yawned, said "Top of the morning," thumbed to the editorial pages. Scanning the op-ed columns, he muttered cheerfully: "Stupid, stupid, stupid, and big surprise . . . *more* stupid."

Folding the paper, he tossed it in back.

I said, "Any tips come in from the story?"

"Nothing serious, so far. Moe and Sean are working the phones. The good news for Mr. and Mrs. Ruche is the dogs turned up nothing else, ditto for radar and sniff-tubes. Nothing remotely iffy in the house, either, so looks like we've got a lone antique whodunit, not a psycho cemetery."

He stretched some more.

I said, "You're okay with the leak."

"That's like saying I'm okay with earthquakes. What's my choice?"

He closed his eyes, kept them shut as I got on the 405. By the time I was over the hills and dipping down into the Valley and the 101 East, he was snoring with glee.

Burbank is lots of things: a working-to middle-class suburb, host to film lots and TV studios, no-nonsense neighbor to the mansions and estates of Toluca Lake where Bob Hope, William Holden, the Three Stooges, and other luminaries established a celebrity outpost that avoided the Westside riffraff.

The city also also butts up against Griffith Park and has its own equestrian center and horse trails. John Jacob Del Rios lived just northeast of the park, on a street of ranch houses set on half-acre lots. Paddocks were visible at the ends of driveways. The aroma of well-seasoned equine dung seasoned the air. A shortage of trees helped the sun along and as noon approached, the asphalt simmered and a scorch, like that of an iron left too long on wool, melded with the horse odors.

Del Rios's residence was redwood-sided, shingle-roofed, fronted by a marine-buzz lawn. An old wagon wheel was propped to the left of the door. A white Suburban with utility tires was parked at the onset of the driveway, inches behind a horse trailer. No paddock in view but a corral fashioned from metal piping housed a beautiful black mare with a white diamond on her chest. She watched us approach, gave two short blinks, flicked her tail.

I took the time to get a closer look. She cocked her head flirtatiously.

Glossy coat, soft eyes. Years ago, I'd take breaks from the cancer wards and ride up at Sunset Ranch, near the Hollywood sign. I loved horses. It had been too long.

I smiled at the mare. She winked.

Milo said, "C'mon, Hopalong, time to meet John Wayne."

The man who answered the door was more Gregory Peck than Duke: six five, and patrician, with a shelf of deeply cleft chin, a well-aligned arrogantly tilted nose, and thick hair as snowy as well-beaten egg whites. His eyes were clear blue, his skin clear bronze veneered by a fine mesh of wrinkles, his build still athletically proportioned save for some hunching of the shoulders and widening of the hips. Nearing ninety, John J. Del Rio looked fifteen years younger.

He wore a blue-and-white mini-check long-sleeved shirt, navy slacks, black calfskin loafers. The blue-faced steel Rolex on his left wrist was chunky and authoritative. Rimless, hexagonal eyeglasses gave him the look of a popular professor. Emeritus for years, but invited back to campus often.

Or one of those actors hired by health insurance companies to play Elderly-but-Fit on their scam commercials.

He proffered a hand larger than Milo's. "Lieutenant? J. J. Del Rios, good to meet you. And this is . . ."

"Dr. Alex Delaware, our consulting psychologist."

"I was a psychology major, myself, at Stanford." To me: "Studied with Professor Ernest Hilgard, I assume you've heard of him."

I said, "Of course."

He turned back to Milo. "I read about your 'occurrence' this morning. Least I'm assuming that's the case you're working. Is it?"

Milo said, "Yes, sir."

"Box of baby bones. Sad. The article said they were probably old, I figure you're here to pinpoint a likely offender using property tax rolls. Am I right?"

Milo smiled.

John J. Del Rios said, "Can't fault you for that approach, makes sense. But if it's an old 187, why the psych angle?"

Milo said, "Cases that are out of the ordinary, we find the input helpful."

"Psychological autopsy?"

"Basically. Could we come in, sir?"

"Oh, sure," said Del Rios. "No sense keeping you in the heat."

He waved us into a lime-green, beam-ceilinged front room cooled by a grumbling window A.C. Burnt-orange carpeting was synthetic, spotless, firm as hardwood. Blocky oak furniture from the seventies, the kind purchased as a suite, was placed predictably. Horse prints clipped from magazines were the concession to art. The only sign of modernity was a wall-mounted flat-screen, hung carefully so no wires showed. A pass-through counter led to a kitchen devoid of counter equipment. The house was clean and orderly, but ripe with the stale-sweat/burnt-coffee/Old Spice tang of longtime bachelorhood.

J. J. Del Rios headed for an avocado-colored fridge. "Something to drink? I'm having a shot of grape juice. Virgin Cabernet, if you will." He gave a bark-like chuckle. "Too early for my one-a-day booze infusion but the antioxidants in grape skin are good for you, you don't even need the alcohol." He brandished a bottle half full with magenta liquid. "Good stuff, no added sugar."

"Water'll be fine, sir."

" 'Sir.' Been a while since I heard that from someone who meant it." Another low, clipped laugh. "Don't miss the job but there was a nice order to it, everyone knowing their place."

"You ran the jail division."

"Big fun," said Del Rios. "Keeping lowlifes locked up, making sure they knew they weren't living at the Hilton."

"How long did you do it?" said Milo.

Del Rios returned with two waters in one huge hand, juice in the other. We all sat.

"What's this, small talk to gain rapport? If you know I ran it, you know for how long."

Milo said, "Didn't dig that deep, sir."

Del Rios snorted that off. "Tell me about your bones."

"Infant," said Milo. "Half a year old, give or take."

"That was in the paper."

"That's what we know so far."

"You've narrowed down the time frame to when my family owned the place?"

"Yes, sir."

"How?"

"Afraid I can't get into that, sir."

Del Rios smiled. "Now I'm not liking the 'sir' so much."

Milo smiled back.

The warmth generated by the exchange might've heated a baby gnat.

Del Rios said, "No sense drawing this out. My family had nothing to do with it but I can't tell you none of the tenants did. Nor can I give you a name, I have no idea who rented the place, stayed completely out of it."

"Out of real estate?"

"Out of anything that got in the way

of having fun." Del Rios drank grape juice. Smacked his lips, dabbed them with a linen handkerchief. The resulting magenta stain seemed to fascinate him.

Milo said, "We've narrowed the time frame to the period your mother lived in the house."

"And what period might that be?"

"Nineteen fifty to '52."

"Well," said Del Rios, "I'm sure you think you're clever. Problem is you're wrong. After Dad died in '47, Mom did live there by herself, but only until she was diagnosed with both heart disease and cancer." The seams across Del Rios's brow deepened. "She was a devout woman, talk about a one–two punch from a benevolent God. It happened winter of '49, right after the two-year anniversary of Dad's death. She hung on for four years, the last two were a horror show, the only question was which disease would get her first. We tried having her stay in the house with a nurse but that got to be too much and by the spring of 1950 she was living with my brother Frankie, his real name was Ferdinand, but he hated it so he

had us call him Frank. He and his wife
lived in Palo Alto, he was in medical
residency back then, orthopedics. That
lasted until the beginning of '52, when
Mom had to be put in a home near
Stanford. During her last year, she was
basically vegetative, by '54 she was
gone. Before she moved up north with
Frankie and Bertie, she put the house
in trust for the four of us. But none of
us wanted to live there, it reminded us
of dead parents. Frankie was living in
Palo Alto, my sister Mary Alice was
studying medicine in Chicago, and I,
the rotten kid, the dropout, was in the
marines and couldn't care less. So Eddie—the oldest one, he was a priest—
hired a management company and we
rented it out for years. Like I said, I can't
tell you who any of the tenants were.
And everyone else is dead, so you're
out of luck, son."

"Do you remember the name of the
management company?"

"Can't remember something I never
knew in the first place," said Del Rios.
"I'm trying to tell you: I had no interest
in anything but fun. To me the damn

house was a source of moolah. Each
month I'd get a check from Eddie for
my share of the rent and promptly blow
it. Then Eddie died in a bus accident
and the three of us got rid of the place,
can't even tell you who bought it, but
obviously you know."

He finished his grape juice. "That's
the full story, my friend. Don't imagine it
makes you happy but I can't change
that."

Milo said, "It clarifies things."

Del Rios removed his glasses. "A man
who sees the bright side? Funny, you
don't give that impression."

He stood. We did the same.

Milo said, "Thanks for your time,
Chief."

At the door, Del Rios said, "When I figured out what you were after, the thought
that my family was under suspicion annoyed me. Even though if it was my
case, I'd be doing the same thing. Then
I realized I couldn't help you and I started
feeling for you, son. Having to dig that
far back." Winking. "So to speak. So
here's one more tidbit that's probably

irrelevant but I don't want you thinking
J.J.'s not simpatico with a fellow officer.
Before my brother Eddie became a
priest, he was a car nut, an early hot-
rodder, into anything with four wheels
and a big engine. He even got Dad to
buy him a Ford coupe that he souped
up and drag-raced. Anyway, one day
Eddie and I were having lunch in the
city. He was working as an assistant
priest at St. Vibiana on Main Street, this
was before he got transferred to Santa
Barbara. During the time Mom was already living with Frankie. Anyway, Eddie
says, 'Johnny, I drove by the house a
few nights ago, making sure the man-
agers were getting the lawn cut better
than the last time, and you won't believe what was parked in the driveway.
A Duesie.' "

I said, "A Duesenberg."

"In the flesh," said Del Rios. "The
metal. It didn't mean much to me, I
didn't care about cars, still don't, but
Eddie was excited, going on about not
just a Duesenberg but one with the big
chrome supercharger pipes coming out
of the side, apparently that's a big deal.

He informs me this is the greatest car ever built, they were rare to begin with, twenty years later they're a treasure. He tells me a car like that would've cost more new than the house did, he's wondering how the tenant could have that kind of money, his best guess is she's got a rich boyfriend. Then he blushes, shuts his mouth, remembering he's a priest, no more gossip. I laughed like hell, told him he should get himself a hot rod on the sly, it bothers him he can confess about it. Meanwhile he can lay rubber right in front of the church, worst case the cardinal has a stroke. He laughed, we had our lunch, end of topic. Okay?"

"Female tenant."

"That's what he said," said Del Rios. "*She*. A woman fits with a baby. A rich boyfriend fits with an unwanted baby. What do you think, son?"

"I think, sir, that you're still at the top of your game."

"Always have been. Okay, good, now you have to get out of here, got a hot date and at my age getting ready is a production."

CHAPTER

7

As I drove back to the city, Milo called a DMV supervisor to find out how far back car registrations ran.

"Inactive records are deleted after a few months, Lieutenant."

"What about paper archives?"

"Nothing like that, sir."

"No warehouse in Sacramento?"

"No such thing, Lieutenant. What exactly are you looking for?"

Milo told her.

She said, "With a subpoena, we could give you a list of currently registered Duesenbergs. That German?"

"American," he said.

"Really? I lived in Detroit, never heard of them."

"They haven't been manufactured for a long time."

"Oh," said the supervisor. "A historical vehicle. Would a list of current regs help?"

"Probably not, but if it's all I can get, I'll settle."

"Send me the proper paper and it's all yours, Lieutenant."

He hung up. I said, "Auburn, Indiana."

"What about it?"

"It's where Duesenbergs were built. Back in the day, cars were manufactured all over the country."

"My home state," he said. "Never knew that. Never saw anything exotic."

"You wouldn't unless you had rich friends. When Duesenbergs came out, they cost the equivalent of a million bucks and Father Eddie was right, they're prime candidates for the greatest car ever made. We're talking massive power, gorgeous custom coachwork, every screw hand-fashioned."

"Listen to you, amigo. What, you were once a gear-head?"

"More like a fantasizing kid." Who'd memorized every make and model because cars represented freedom and escape. Mentally cataloging all that information was a good time-filler when hiding in the woods, waiting out a drunken father's rage.

Milo tapped the tucked-leather passenger door. "Now that I think about it, this is kind of a classic buggy."

My daily ride's a '79 Seville, Chesterfield Green with a tan vinyl top that matches her interior leather. She rolled out of Detroit the last year before GM bloated the model beyond recognition, is styled well enough to help you forget she's Caddy froufrou over a Chevy II chassis. She loves her third engine, is dependable, cushy, and makes no unreasonable demands. I see no reason to get a divorce.

I said, "Bite your tongue. She thinks she's still a hot number."

He laughed. "So how many Duesenbergs were made?"

"I'd guess hundreds, not thousands.

And chrome pipes means it was super-charged, which would narrow it down further."

"So getting that subpoena might be worthwhile . . . but then I'd need to backtrack the history of every one I find and the most I can hope for is some guy who visited the woman who lived in the house maybe at the time the baby was buried."

I said, "There could be a more direct way to identify her. If Father Eddie noticed the car, other neighbors probably did. Anyone who was an adult back then is likely to be deceased, but in nice neighborhoods like Cheviot, houses get passed down to heirs."

"A kid who dug cars," he said. "Okay, can't postpone the legwork any longer. You have time?"

"Nothing but."

We began with properties half a mile either way from the burial site, encountered lots of surprise but no wisdom. Returning to the Ruche house, Milo knocked on the door, rang the bell, checked windows. No one home.

I followed him to the backyard. The yellow tape was gone. The holes where air-sniffing tubes had been inserted were still open. The chair where Holly Ruche had sat yesterday had been moved closer to the felled tree sections and a woman's sweater, black, size M, Loehmann's label, was draped over one of the massive cylinders. A few errant blond hairs stood out on the shoulders. Beneath the chair, a paperback book sat on the dirt. What to expect during pregnancy.

I said, "She came back when everyone left, wanting to check out her dream."

He said, "Location, location, location . . . okay, let's ask around some more about the car. Haystacks and needles and all that."

Expanding the canvass another quarter mile produced similar results, initially. But at a house well north, also Tudor but grander and more ornately trimmed than Holly and Matt's acquisition, a small, mustachioed man in his sixties holding a crystal tumbler of scotch said,

"A Duesie? Sure, '38 SJ, blue over blue—navy over baby."

His mustache was a too-black stripe above a thin upper lip. The few hairs on his head were white. He wore a bottle-green velvet smoking jacket, gray pin-striped slacks, black slippers with gold lions embroidered on the toes.

Milo said, "What else can you tell us about it, sir?"

"Gorgeous," said the man. "True work of art. I saw it in . . . '50, so we're talking a twelve-year-old car. But you'd never know. Shiny, kept up beautifully. Those chrome supercharger pipes coming out the side were like pythons on the prowl. All that menace and power, I'm telling you, that was one magnificent beast."

"Who owned it?" said Milo.

The man shook his head. "I tried to get her to tell me, she'd just smile and change the subject."

"She?"

"Eleanor," said the man. "Ellie Green. She lived there—that brick place pretending to be this place, that's where the Duesie used to park. Right in the driveway. Not often, just once in a while. And always at night but there was a porch light so you could see it. Down to the color. Looking back, it had to be a boyfriend of hers, but I was a kid, five years old, it was the car that interested me, not her personal life. I'd never seen anything like it, asked my father about it. He knew everything about everything when it came to cars, raced at Muroc before the war."

He grinned. "Then he married my mother and she civilized him and he went to work selling Packards downtown. He's the one who filled me in on the Duesie. That's how I know it was a true SJ. Because he told me it wasn't one of those where someone retrofitted the pipes, this was the real deal."

"He never mentioned whose it was?"

"Never asked him," said the man. "Why, what's up? I saw all the commotion yesterday. What happened at that place?"

"Something was found there. What can you tell us about Ellie Green, sir?"

"She babysat me. Back before I started school, I was always sick. My parents got tired of never going out, so they hired her to watch over me. Couldn't have been fun for her, I was a runty piece of misery, had scarlet fever, bad case of the mumps, measles even worse, could throw up at will and be-lieve me, I did when the devil told me to." He laughed. "At one point they thought I had diphtheria but it was just some nasty flu. But Ellie was always patient."

"How old was she?"

"Hmm . . . to a kid everyone looks old. Probably thirty, give or take? Why're you asking about her? What was found over there? I asked one of your guys in uniform but all he said was *an incident.*"

Milo said, "Some bones were dug up in the backyard. It was on the news, Mr.—"

"Dave Helmholtz. I avoid the news. Back when I was a stockbroker I had to pay attention, now I don't. Bones as in human?"

"Yes, sir. A complete human skeleton. A baby."

"A baby? Buried in the backyard?"

Milo nodded.

Helmholtz whistled. "That's pretty grotesque. You think Ellie had something to do with it? Why?"

"We don't know much at all at this point, Mr. Helmholtz, but there's indication the bones were buried during the early fifties. And the only information we picked up about that period was that a Duesenberg was sometimes parked at the house."

"Early fifties," said Helmholtz. "Yup, that could certainly fit when Ellie was here. But why in the world would she bury a baby? She didn't have any kids."

"You're sure?"

"Positive. And I never saw her pregnant. Just the opposite, she was skinny. For back then, I mean. Today she'd be what's expected of a woman."

"How long did she live there?"

"She babysat me for close to a year."

"Did she have a day job?"

"Sure," said Helmholtz. "She was a nurse." He smoked, tamped, smoked some more. "Mom made a big deal about that—'a trained nurse.' Because I pulled a snit about being left with a stranger. I was a cranky runt, mama's boy, afraid of my own shadow. Trained nurse? What did I care? The first time Ellie came over, I hid under the covers, ignored her completely. She sat down, waited me out. Finally I stuck my head out and she was smiling at me. Bee-*yoot*iful smile, I'm talking movie-star caliber, the blond hair, the red lips, the smoky eyes. Not that I care much about that, I kept ignoring her. Finally I got hot and thirsty and came out and she fetched me something to drink. I had a fever, that year I always had a fever. She put a cold compress on my forehead. She hummed. It soothed me, she had a nice voice. She was a nice person. Never tried to force anything, real re- laxed. And a looker, no question about that."

I smiled. "You didn't care about her looks, you were concentrating on the Duesenberg."

Helmholtz stared at me. Broke into laughter. "Okay, you got me, I had a crush on her. Who wouldn't? She was nice as they came, took care of me, I stopped being upset when my parents went out."

"Obviously, someone else thought she was nice."

"Who's that?"

"The owner of the Duesenberg."

"Oh," said Helmholtz. "Yeah, Mr. Lucky Bastard." He laughed some more. "That's what Dad called him. Looking back it makes sense. Some rich guy wooed her, maybe that's why she left."

I said, "She never gave you any indication at all who he was?"

"I asked a couple of times, hoping maybe she'd figure out I loved the car, was angling for a ride. All she did was smile and change the subject. Now that I think about it, she never talked about herself, period. It was always about me, what I wanted, what I needed, how was I feeling. Pretty good approach when you're working with a spoiled little brat, no? I can see her doing great as a nurse."

He brightened. "Hey, maybe Lucky Bastard was a rich doctor. Isn't that why girls became nurses back then? To hook up with M.D.s?"

Milo said, "Is there anything else you can tell us about her?"

"Nope. I turned six, got miraculously better, went to school, made friends. Don't know exactly when Ellie moved out but it wasn't long after and instead of the Duesenberg we got a Plymouth. Big family with a Plymouth station wagon the color of pea soup. Talk about a comedown."

I said, "Could you estimate how many times you saw the Duesenberg?"

"You're trying to figure out if she was entertaining some regular visitor, something hot and heavy going on? Well, all I can say is less than a dozen and probably more than half a dozen."

"At night."

"So how did a five-year-old see it? Because that five-year-old was a disobedient brat who'd sneak out of the house through the kitchen in the middle of the night and walk over to see the car. Sometimes it was there, sometimes it wasn't. The last time I tried it, I ran into my father. He was standing on the sidewalk in front of Ellie's house, looking at the car, himself. I turned to escape, he saw me, caught me. I thought he'd whack me but he didn't. He laughed. Said, yeah, it's fantastic, Davey, can't blame you. That's when he told me the model. 'Thirty-eight SJ. And what the pipes meant, the advantage of supercharging. We stood there together, taking in that monster. It was one of those—I guess you'd call it a bonding thing. But then he warned me never to leave the house without permission or he *would* tan my hide."

Helmholtz smiled. "I always felt he thought I was a sissy. I guess he didn't punish me because he assumed I was out there being a guy."

We continued up the block. No one else remembered Ellie Green or the Duesenberg.

Back at the station, Milo ran her name. Nearly two dozen women came up but none whose stats fit the slim blonde who'd lived at the bone house in 1951. He repeated the process with *Greene, Gruen, Gruhn,* even *Breen,* came up empty. Same for death notices in L.A. and the neighboring counties.

I said, "She worked as a nurse and

the box came from the Swedish Hospital."

He looked up the defunct institution, pairing it with *Eleanor Green* and the same variants. A few historical references popped up but the only names were major benefactors and senior doctors.

He said, "Helmholtz could be right about Lucky Bastard being a medical honcho. Maybe even someone George Del Rios or his two M.D. kids knew and Ellie Green came to rent the house through personal referral."

"Rich doctor wanting a stash pad for his pretty girlfriend," I said. "For partying or waiting out her pregnancy."

"Helmholtz never saw her pregnant."

"Helmholtz was a five-year-old, not an obstetrician. If she moved in before she started babysitting him, she could have already delivered."

"Rich doctor," he said. "Insert 'married' between those two words and you've got one hell of an inconvenience. Problem is, Ellie seems to have disappeared."

"Like her baby," I said.

"Lucky Bastard making sure to clean up his trail?"

"The baby was only found by chance. If her body was concealed just as skillfully, there'd be no official death notice."

"Nasty . . . wish I could say it felt wrong."

He got up, paced. "You know anyone who'd remember Swedish Hospital?"

"I'll ask around."

"Thanks." He frowned. "As usual."

CHA...

up...

The baby was...

whole body was...

fully there'd be...

"Nasty..."

wrong..."

He got up, paced. "You know anyone

who d...bers Sydian Hospital?"

"I'll ask around.

"Thanks." He frowned. "As usual."

CHAPTER

8

Milo's request to find an old-timer got me shuffling the reminiscence Rolodex. The first two people I thought of turned out to be dead. My third choice was in her late eighties and still training residents at Western Pediatric Medical Center.

Salome Greiner picked up her own phone.

"Hi, Sal, it's Alex Delaware."

"Well, well," she said. "What favor does Alex Delaware need?"

"Who says I need anything?"

"You don't write, you don't call, you

don't even email or text or tweet." Her cackle had the dry confidence of someone who'd outlived her enemies. "And yes, I am still alluring but I don't see you asking me on a hot date. What do you need?"

"I was wondering if you remembered Swedish Hospital."

"That place," she said. "Yes, I remember it. Why?"

"It's related to a police case."

"You're still doing that," she said.

"At times."

"What kind of police case?"

I told her about the bones.

She said, "I read about it." Chirps in the background. "Ahh, a page, need to run, Alex. Do you have time for coffee?"

"Where and when?"

"Here and . . . let's say an hour. The alleged emergency won't last long, just a hysterical intern. A man, I might add. Roll that in your sexist cigar, Sigmund."

"I'll be there," I said, wondering why she didn't just ask me to call back.

"Meet me in the doctors' dining room—you still have your badge, no?"

"On my altar with all the other icons."

"Ha," said Salome. "You were always quick with a retort, that's a sign of aggressiveness, no? But no doubt you hid it from patients, good psychologist that you are."

Western Pediatric Medical Center is three acres of gleaming optimism set in an otherwise shabby section of East Hollywood. During the hospital's hundred years of existence L.A. money and status migrated relentlessly westward, leaving Western Peds with patients dependent on the ebb and flow of governmental goodwill. That keeps the place chronically broke but it doesn't stop some of the smartest, most dedicated doctors in the world from joining the staff. My time on the cancer ward comprised some of the best years of my life. Back in those days I rarely left my office doubting I'd done something worthwhile. I should have missed it more than I did.

The drive ate up fifty minutes, parking and hiking to the main building, another ten. The doctors' dining room is in the basement, accessible through an unmarked door just beyond the cafeteria steam tables. Wood-paneled and quiet and staffed by white-shirted servers, it makes a good first impression. But the food's not much different from the fare ladled to people without advanced degrees.

The room was nearly empty and Salome was easy to spot, tiny, nearly swallowed by her white coat, back to the wall at a corner table eating cottage cheese and neon-red gelatin molded into a daisy. A misshapen sludge-colored coffee mug looked like a preschool project or something dreamed up by the hottest Big Deal grad of the hippest Big Deal art school.

Salome saw me, raised the mug in greeting. I got close enough to read crude lettering on the sludge. *To Doctor Great-Gramma.*

A blunt-nailed finger pinged ceramic. "Brilliant, no? Fashioned by Number Six of Generation Four. She just turned five, taught herself to read, and is able to add single digits."

"Congratulations."

"The Gee-Gees are entertaining, but

you don't get as close as with the grand-
children. More like diversion from senil-
ity. Get yourself some coffee and we'll
chat."

I filled a cup and sat down.

"You look the same, Alex."

"So do you."

"You lie the same, too."

Dipping her head, she batted long
white lashes. I'd seen a photo from her
youth: Grace Kelly's undersized sib. Her
eyes were still clear, a delicate shade of
aqua. Her hair, once dyed ash-blond,
had been left its natural silver. The cut
hadn't changed: jaw-length pageboy,
shiny as a freshly chromed bumper,
bangs snipped architecturally straight.

Born to a wealthy Berlin family, she
was one-quarter Jewish, which qualified her to enroll in Dachau. Escaping
to New York in the thirties, she worked
as a governess while attending City
College night school, got into Harvard
Med, trained at Boston Children's where
she did research on whooping cough.
At thirty, she married a Chaucer scholar
who never made much money but
dressed as if he did. Widowed at fifty,

she raised five kids who'd turned out well.

"Down to business," she said. "Tell me more about that skeleton."

I filled in a few more details.

"Ach," she said. "A fully formed baby?"

"Four to six months old."

"Intact."

"Yes."

"Interesting," she said. "In view of the rumors about that place."

She returned to her cottage cheese. It took me a moment to decode her remark.

"It was an abortion mill?"

"Not exclusively, my dear."

"But . . ."

"If you were a girl from a well-to-do family who'd gotten into a predicament, the talk was Swedish could be exceptionally discreet. The founders were well-meaning Lutheran missionaries, seeking to help the poor. Over the years, any religious affiliation was dropped and priorities changed."

"They went for-profit?"

"What else? One thing they *didn't* have was a pediatrics department. Or a conventional maternity ward. So I really can't see how a baby would ever come in contact with the place."

I described the blue box, asked if she knew what it was.

"I've never heard of such a thing. We wrap our bodies in shrouds, then bag them. Typically, mortuaries pick them up, there'd be no reason to use solid brass containers."

"Maybe it was designed for something else and whoever buried the baby improvised."

"Hmm," she said. "Yes, why not—how about storage for tissue samples? A precaution when dealing with infectious material. Back in those days all kinds of nasties were rampant—TB, polio. My old friend, pertussis. I don't see bronze serving any particular antiseptic purpose but someone could've had a theory."

"Makes sense. Did you know any of the staff?"

"My work was always here."

Not really an answer. I said, "But you know quite a bit about the place."

She smiled. "It's not only psychologists who know how to listen."

"Who did the talking?"

"A friend of mine attended there briefly."

"Why only briefly?"

She used her fork to section a perfect cube of Jell-O. "I'd imagine something drew his attention elsewhere."

"Was he bothered by what went on?"

She speared the Jell-O, ate, drank tea. "I can't remember what was related to me back in the Jurassic era."

"I'll bet you can, Salome."

"Then you lose the bet."

"Was it the abortions?"

Carving and piercing another cube, she withdrew the tines slowly. Red liquid oozed onto her plate. "I don't need to tell you, Alex. Those were different times. In any event, I can't see any direct link between Swedish Hospital and a full-term baby."

I said, "Eleanor Green."

The fork wavered. She put it down. "Who's that?"

"A pediatric nurse. She lived in the house where the bones were found."

"If you already have a name, why all the circumlocution? Go and track her down."

"She seems to have disappeared."

"Nurse on the run." She chuckled. "Sounds like a bad movie."

I said, "The friend who told you about Swedish—"

"Is gone, Alex. Everyone from my wanton youth is gone, leaving me the last woman standing. That's either my triumph or cause for clinical depression, take your pick."

"No peds, no ob-gyn," I said. "Besides abortions, what brought in the profit?"

"My guess would be the same kinds of things that bring it in now. Procedures—radiology, short-term surgery."

"Were the attending physicians from any particular part of town?"

She stared at me. "I appreciate your persistence, darling, but you're pressing me for data I simply don't have. But if we're still in a betting mood, I'd wager against Watts or Boyle Heights." She took hold of the fork, speared the abandoned Jell-O. Savored. "How have things been going for you, my dear? Doing anything interesting other than police work?"

"Some court work," I said.

"Custody?"

"Custody and injury. One more question, Sal: Did your friend ever mention a doctor who drove a Duesenberg?"

She blinked. "That's a car."

I said, "It's a very expensive car, made in the thirties and forties."

"I've never been much for automobiles, Alex. A fact that greatly distressed my boys when they wanted fancy-shmancy wheels and I insisted on no-frills functionality." She looked at her watch. "Oops, need to get going."

Standing on tiptoes, she pecked my cheek hard, marched away, stiff-shouldered, stethoscope swinging.

I called her name but she never broke step.

CHAPTER

9

Milo said, "Abortion mill. Plenty of those, back then."

I said, "This one served wealthy families."

"Good business model." He speared a massive forkful of curried lamb, studied the outsized portion as if daring himself. Engulfed, chewed slowly.

We were at Café Moghul, a storefront Indian restaurant on Santa Monica near the station. The bespectacled woman who runs the place believes Milo is a one-man strategic defense system and treats him like a god in need of gastric tribute.

Today, the sacrificial array was crab and chicken and the lamb, enough vegetables to fill a truck garden. The woman came over, smiling as always, and refilled our chai. Her sari was hot pink printed with gold swirls and loops. I'd seen it before. More than once. Over the years, I've seen her entire wardrobe but I have no idea what her name is. I'm not sure Milo does, either.

"More of anythIng, LIeutenant?"

"Fine for the time being." He snarfed more lamb to prove it, reached for a crab claw.

When the woman left, he said, "Anything else?"

"That's it."

"I go with Dr. Greiner's logic. No reason for a baby to be linked to a place like that. Same for Ellie Green, seeing as she worked with kids. Anyone with access to medical equipment coulda gotten hold of that box."

I said nothing.

He put the claw down hard enough for it to rattle. "What?"

"When I asked Salome if she recalled a doctor who drove a Duesenberg, she tensed up and terminated the conversation and walked out on me."

"You touched a nerve? Okay, maybe Duesie-man was the guy who worked at Swedish and he was more than a friend and she didn't want to get into details with you. Was Greiner married back then?"

"Yes."

"Happily?"

I thought about that. "Don't know."

"Kids?"

"Five."

"What was her husband like?"

"He wrote books about Chaucer."

"Professor?"

"Never got his Ph.D."

"How'd he earn a living?"

"He didn't."

"Real alpha male, Alex. So she was the breadwinner. So a fellow doc with hot wheels coulda been appealing. She doesn't want to dredge all that up, so she terminates the tête-à-tête."

"Why have a tête-à-tête in the first place?" I said. "Why not just talk over the phone?"

"She bothers you that much," he said.

"I'm not saying Salome did anything criminal. I do think she knows more than she let on."

"Fine, I respect your intuition. Now, what do you suggest I do about it?"

I had no answer, didn't have to say so because his phone began playing Debussy. Golliwog's Cakewalk.

He slapped it to his ear. "Sturgis . . . oh, hi . . . really? That was quick . . . okay . . . okay . . . okay . . . yeah, makes sense . . . could be . . . if I need to I'll try it . . . no, nothing else from this end. Thanks, kid."

Clicking off, he snatched up the crab claw, sucked meat, swallowed. "That was Liz Wilkinson. She dates the bones consistent with the clippings. No new evidence of trauma, internal or external, not a single deformity or irregularity. She didn't find any marrow or soft tissue but will ask DOJ to try to get DNA from the bone tissue. Problem is between budget cuts and backlog, this is gonna go straight to the bottom of the pile. If I want to speed it up, she suggested I ask Zeus to descend from Olympus. Only thing that'll motivate him is if the media continue to cover the case. And Liz just got a call from a *Times* reporter."

"The press contacts her but not you?"

"When did you hear me say I wasn't contacted?" His tongue worked to dislodge food from a molar. Placing the crab claw on a plate piled with empties, he scrolled his phone through a screen of missed calls. The number he selected was from yesterday afternoon.

"Kelly LeMasters? This is Lieutenant Milo Sturgis returning your call on the bones dug up in Cheviot Hills. Nothing new to report, if that changes, I'll let you know."

He returned to his food.

I said, "So we forget about Swedish Hospital."

"I don't see it leading anywhere, but feel free to pursue. You come up with

something juicy, I'll say it was my idea
in the first place."

An innocuous chime sounded in my
pocket. My phone's turn to join the conversation.

Milo said, "The ringtone era and
you're living in a cave?"

I picked up.

"Hi, Doctor, Louise at your service.
Just took one from a Holly Ruche. She
said no emergency but to me she
sounded kind of upset so I thought I'd
be careful."

"Thanks, Louise."

"All these years talking to your patients," she said, "you pick things up.
Here's her number."

I walked to the front of the restaurant,
made the call.

Holly Ruche said, "That was quick.
I'm sorry, I didn't mean to bother you."

"No bother. What's up?"

"Is there anything new on the . . . on
what happened at my house?"

"Not yet, Holly."

"I guess these things take time."

"They do."

"That poor little thing." Sharp intake

of breath. "That *baby.* I was all about myself, didn't even think about it. Now I can't stop thinking about it. Not that I'm OCD or anything."

"It's a tough thing to go through, Holly."

"But I'm fine," she said. "I really am . . . um, would you have time to talk? Nothing serious, just one session to clear things up?"

"Sure."

"Oh," she said. "Well, thank you. I couldn't do it tomorrow. Or the day after."

"What works for you, Holly?"

"Um . . . say in three days? Four? At your convenience."

I checked my calendar. "How about three days, one p.m.?"

"Perfect. Um, could I ask what your fee is?"

"Three hundred dollars for a forty-five-minute session."

She said, "Okay. That'll work. Seeing as it's only once. Where's your office?"

"I work out of my home." I told her the address. "Off of Beverly Glen."

"You must have fantastic views."

"It's nice."

"Bet it is," she said. "I'd have loved something like that."

CHAPTER

10

There are many reasons I became a psychologist. Some I understand, some I'll never even be aware of.

One motive I think I do get is the urge to protect, to make up for the abandonment that ruled my childhood. It's a trait that usually fits the job well, earning patient gratitude and delusions of godliness.

Sometimes I get heavy-handed, offering armor-plate when a thin sweater will do. That's why figuring out how much to tell Robin about the bad stuff has always been an issue. I've learned to include her, but I'm careful about the details.

On this one, I didn't even know how to start.

Robin's an only child. Her mother's a difficult woman, emotionally stingy, self-centered, competitive with her daughter. The loving parent was her dad, a master carpenter. He taught her what he knew about wood and the joy of craft, died when Robin was young. Now she works with power tools, doesn't take well to being smothered by testosterone, no matter how well intended.

For all the support I got from my older sister, I might as well have been a singleton. Mom was too up and down mood-wise to be of use when Dad drank and went hunting for prey. I learned to value solitude because alone meant safe. Inherently a friendly child, I learned to be sociable and genuinely empathic, but more often than not any group of people makes me feel alienated.

Two people like that and you can see how it would take time to work out Relationship 101.

I believe Robin and I have done a pretty good job. We've been together for a long time, are faithful without strain, love each other madly, press each other's erotic buttons. All that bliss has been ruptured twice by breakups, neither of which I understand fully. During one separation, Robin got pregnant by another man. The pregnancy and her time with him ended badly. I've worked with children my entire adult life but have never been a father. Robin and I haven't talked about that in ages.

I hope she doesn't spend too much time wondering.

I drove home thinking about tiny bones, a life barely lived, a nurse who could be anything between saint and monster. I still hadn't figured out what to divulge when I reached the top of the old bridle path that snakes up to our property.

To look at the house, free of trim or artifice, high white stucco walls sliced into acute angles where the trees don't shroud, you'd think emotionally distant people live here. The original structure, the one I bought for myself as soon as

I had a bit of money, was tiny, rustic, all wood and shingle and quirk and creak. A psychopath burned it down and when we rebuilt we were looking for change, maybe a fortress.

Inside, matte-finished oak floors, comfortable, slouchy furniture, and art biased toward pretty rather than politics combine to warm things up. The square footage isn't vast but it's more than two people and one small dog need, and my footsteps echo when I cross the living room and head up the skylit corridor to my office.

Robin's truck was parked out front but no sign of her in the house, so she was out in her studio, working. I postponed a bit, checking email, paying bills, scanning news sites and reassuring myself that the world continued to spin with all the logic of a grand mal seizure.

By the time I poured a mug full of coffee in the kitchen and walked down to the garden where I stopped to feed the koi, I was still unresolved about what to say.

"Baby bones," I told the fish. "Don't even know if it was a boy or a girl."

They slurped in gratitude.

I was dawdling by the water's edge when the door to the studio opened. Blanche, our little French bulldog, trotted toward me, twenty pounds of blond charm and Zen-serenity. The breed tends to be stubborn; Blanche isn't, preferring diplomacy to artillery. She nuzzled my pant leg, snorted coquettishly. I rubbed her head and she purred like a cat. She'd rolled on her back for a belly tickle when Robin emerged, fluffing her mass of auburn curls and brushing sawdust from her favorite red overalls.

Mouthing an air kiss as she hurried toward me, she arrived smiling, planted a real smooch on my lips. Her breath was sweet with cola, the black T-shirt under the overalls fragrant with wood dust. Spanish cypress, a material that holds on to its perfume for centuries. The feather-light flamenco guitar she'd been working on for weeks.

I kissed her back.

She said, "What's the matter?"

GUILT   101

"Who says anything?"

She stepped back, studied me. "Honey?"

"What was the tell?"

"The shoulders," she said. "It's always in the shoulders."

"Maybe it's just a kink."

Taking my hand, she guided me toward the house. Blanche trotted at our side, checking me out every few seconds. Between the two of them, I felt like a patient. As we reached the door, Robin said, "The new case?"

I nodded.

"Especially bad?"

"Maybe."

She put her arm around my waist. When we got in the kitchen, I offered her coffee.

"No, thanks, just water." She fetched a bottle from the fridge, sat down at the table, propped her perfect chin in one hand. Chocolate eyes were soft, yet searching. Her lips parted. The slightly oversized central incisors that had turned me on years ago flashed into view.

I filled a second mug, joined her. "A baby. A baby's skeleton."

She winced. "That must have been terrible for everyone involved."

She stroked my fingers.

I told her everything.

When I was through, she said, "One of the girls at that hospital changed her mind and had her baby? Gave it to that nurse to take care of and something went wrong?"

"Could be."

"*Wrong* doesn't have to mean a crime, Alex. What if the poor little thing died by accident? Or from a disease and it couldn't be buried legally because officially it didn't exist?"

A new tremolo colored the last three words.

She said, "A thing; *it.* Can they do DNA, find out the sex?"

"Theoretically." I told her about the case's low priority.

She said, "Every generation thinks it invented the world, no one cares about history."

"Are you sorry I told you?"

"Not at all." She stood, got behind me, kneaded my shoulders. "You are one block of iron, darling."

"Oh," I said. "Perfect. Thanks."

"Full-service girlfriend." She worked on my muscles some more, stepped away, unsnapped the overalls, let them fall to the kitchen floor. The black T-shirt and a navy blue thong contrasted with smooth, tawny skin. She stretched, flexed each lovely leg. I stood.

"I'm filthy, hon, going to shower off. After that, we can figure out what to do about dinner."

I was waiting when she emerged from the bathroom, armed with a few restaurant suggestions.

She unpeeled her towel, folded it neatly, stood there naked. Holding out a hand, she led me to the bed. "Time for you to be a full-service boyfriend."

Afterward, she ran her nails lightly over my cheek. Bobbled my lips with the side of an index finger the way kids do when they're goofing. I let out a high-pitched moan, did a fair imitation of a leaky drain. When we both stopped laughing, she said, "How are you doing now?"

"A lot better."

"High point of my day, too. How about Italian?"

CHAPTER

11

I'd heard nothing new about the bones for two days when the *Times* ran a follow-up piece.

The article was stuck at the bottom of page 15, trumped by water issues and legislative ineptitude, a shooting in Compton, the usual petty corruption by various civic employees. The byline was Kelly LeMasters, the reporter Milo had belatedly called.

The coverage boiled down to a space-filling rehash ending with the pronouncement that "A priority request to analyze the bones for DNA at the state Department of Justice lab is LAPD's best hope for yielding fresh information on a decades-old mystery."

The newspaper was in Milo's hand when he rapped on my door at ten a.m.

I said, "Pleasant surprise."

He strode past me into the kitchen, flung the fridge door open, did the usual bear-scrounge, and came up with a rubbery-looking chicken leg that he gnawed to the bone and a half-full quart of milk that he chugged empty. Wiping the lacto-mustache from his nearly-as-pale face, he thrust the *Times* piece at me. "Compelling and insightful, call the Pulitzer committee."

I said, "Pulitzer was a tabloid shlock-meister."

He shrugged. "Time heals, especially with money in the ointment." He flung the article onto the table.

I said, "So you spoke to LeMasters."

"Not quite. I spoke to His Grandiosity's office begging for DOJ grease. That was yesterday afternoon. Next morning, voilà."

"The chief leaks?"

"The chief plays the press like a harmonica. Which is fine in this case because everything's dead-ended. Social Security can't turn up records of our Eleanor Green, and I can't find dirt on Swedish. Even the oldest vice guy I know doesn't remember it, one way or the other. So if they were breaking the law, they were doing it discreetly."

He got up again, searched the pantry, poured himself a bowl of dry cereal. Midway to the bottom, he said, "The bones aren't why I'm here. I never really thanked you for last year."

"Not necessary."

"I beg to differ." He flushed. "If ensuring my continuing survival doesn't deserve gratitude, what the hell does, Alex?"

"Chalk it up to the friendship thing."

"Just because I didn't get all sentimental doesn't mean I'm not aware of what you did." Deep breath. "I've been thinking about it every damn day."

I said nothing.

"Anyway." He used his fingers to grasp the last few nuggets of cereal. Drawing his big frame to its feet a second time, he loped to the sink, washed the bowl. Said something I couldn't hear over the water.

When he turned off the spigot, I said, "Didn't catch that."

"The T word, amigo. Gracias. Merci. Danke schoen."

"You're welcome."

"Okay . . . now that we've got that out of the way . . . how're Robin and the pooch? She working out back?"

"Delivering a mandolin."

"Ah."

His jacket pocket puffed as his phone squawked.

Moe Reed's pleasant voice, tighter and higher than usual, said, "New one, boss."

"I could use something fresh, Moses."

"It's fresh all right," said Reed. "But I'm not sure you'll like it."

"Why not?"

"More bones, boss. Same neighborhood. Another baby."

A city worker, part of a crew planning a drainage ditch at the western edge of

Cheviot Hills Park, had spotted the scatter of white.

Unruly toss, strewn like trash, barely concealed by bushes. What might pass for dried twigs at a distance was an assortment of tiny skeletal components.

This baby appeared even smaller than the one unearthed in the Ruches' backyard. The skull was the size of an apple. Some of the bones were as thin as drinking straws and some of the smallest—the phalanges of the hand—were thread-like.

These remnants were clean-looking. Silvery white, luminous in the sunlight.

I thought: Scrubbed clean, maybe polished. *Prepared*?

The orange-vested laborer who'd found them was a huge, muscular guy named George Guzman who kept dabbing tears.

Moe Reed stood next to him, pad in hand. His expression said he'd been offering continuous sympathy, wasn't sure he liked that gig. At Reed's other side stood Liz Wilkinson, impassive but for soft searching eyes, tool cases on the ground next to her, white coat draped over one arm. Ready to have a go at the skeleton but waiting for the coroner's investigator to release the victim for further analysis.

The C.I. hadn't shown up yet. Neither had the crime scene techs, but Liz had gloved up in anticipation. She stood right up against Moe, hips pressed against his. Hard to say who was supporting who.

Guzman stared at the white bones and sniffled.

Reed's mouth twisted. "Okay, thanks, sir."

"For what?"

"Calling us."

"There was a choice?" said Guzman. He took another look. "Man."

Reed said, "You can go, now."

Guzman said, "Sure," but he lingered. Reed prompted his exit by pointing at the yellow tape.

Guzman said, "Sure, sure," took a step, stopped. "I'll never forget this. We just had one."

"One what, sir?"

"Baby." The word came out strangled.

"George Junior. We waited a long time for him."

"Congratulations," said Milo.

Guzman looked at him.

Reed said, "This is my boss, Lieutenant Sturgis. Sir, Mr. Guzman is our first arriver. He called it in."

Guzman said, "I'm always here first. Since we started the job, I mean."

"What's the job?" said Milo.

"Making sure water doesn't collect and ruin the roots of all those trees." Guzman pointed. "We need to check out the entire area, taking samples of what's below, then if we need drains, we put 'em in. Few years ago it was done wrong, flooded the archery field."

"It's your job to get here before anyone else?"

"No, no, not officially," said Guzman, "but that's what happens, I make it at seven ten, fifteen, the other guys not till seven thirty. 'Cause I take my wife to work, she waitresses at Junior's on Westwood. I drop her off, she gives me coffee, I drive a couple minutes and I'm here."

Guzman's eyes drifted back to the

bones. "I thought it was a squirrel or something. Dead animals, we see plenty of that. Then I got close and . . ." He blinked. "It's definitely human?"

Everyone turned to Liz Wilkinson. She said, "Unfortunately."

"Damn," said Guzman, biting his lip. His eyes misted.

Milo said, "Appreciate your help, sir. Have a nice day."

His prompt was more directive than Reed's, a nudge to Guzman's elbow that got the giant in motion. Guzman plodded toward the tape, ducked under with effort, walked several yards, and joined another group of orange-vests hanging near a yellow city truck. The group stayed there, listening as Guzman regaled them.

Milo said, "There's one who likes attention. You pick up anything about him that fills your nostrils, Moses?"

"Kind of a crybaby," said Reed, "but nothing overtly creepy."

"Run him through, anyway."

"Already done, boss. Clean."

"Good work, kid, that's why you get

the big bucks. Any anthropological impressions, Liz?"

Wilkinson said, "By its size, this child
might be younger than the first. The
teeth will help me judge but I haven't
inspected them because the way the
skull's positioned the mouth is in the
dirt."

"We'll get you access soon as the
C.I. okays it." To Reed: "Any word from
the crypt?"

"Held up in traffic. Best guess is
within the hour."

"What about Crime Scene?"

"They should've been here already."

Milo turned to Liz. "You were notified
by the crypt crew?"

She smiled. "By Moe."

Reed fidgeted.

Milo laughed. "Anything for a date,
Detective Reed?"

"I'll take what I can get."

Liz said, "I think that's a compliment."

Milo said, "Anything else of a scientific nature, Dr. W?"

"These bones look considerably
fresher than the first, so you could have

a fairly recent crime. But that could also be the result of cleaning or bleaching. From what I can see so far, they appear totally de-fleshed. As to how that was done, I'm a bit puzzled. The most common methods would be mechanical—scraping—or chemical—corrosives, boiling—or a combination of both. But all that seems to be lacking here."

"How can you tell?"

She let go of Reed's hand, walked closer to the bones. "Don't tattle on me to the crypt folk, Milo, but I crouched down and had a good close look." She held up a gloved hand. "Then I put these on and touched several of the bones because the freshness intrigued me. I was careful not to move anything, there was no disruption of the crime scene. But I wanted to see how they responded to tactile pressure. I also used a magnifying loupe and couldn't find any of the tool marks you'd get from scraping, or the pitting and cloudiness you'd get from a corrosive bath. More important, the bones felt relatively rigid, as firm as an infant skeleton could be, and with boiling you'd expect them to turn at least a bit rubbery. Especially the smaller bones, those could be as pliable as cooked noodles. It's possible there's a new chemical able to do the job without leaving traces but I haven't heard of it. Maybe something'll turn up in the analysis."

"De-fleshed," said Milo, "but no sign of trauma. So maybe this one *is* a lab specimen, Liz. Some sick wiseass reads about the first case, decides to prank us with a medical souvenir he buys on the Internet."

"Anything's possible but I don't think so. For the same reason as with the first: You'd expect holes for wires."

Milo went over to the bones, squatted, a Buddha in a bad suit. "Almost like plastic, with that shine."

I said, "Is it possible they were coated with something that's obscuring the tool marks?"

Liz said, "I thought about some kind of lacquering but it would have to be super-thin because normal anatomical irregularities are visible."

Milo said, "Call the C.I. again, Moses, get a fix on ETA."

Reed complied. "Half an hour, minimum."

"Wonderful."

I said, "Sick joke or murder, with the dump being so close to the first bones, this reeks of copycat."

Milo inhaled, gut heaving. "Two in Cheviot Hills. Can't remember the last time we had a murder here."

Liz said, "The distance to the Ruche home is less than a mile—point nine three to be exact."

Milo smiled. "Geography's in your job description?"

Reed said, "She clocked it 'cause I asked her."

"You did me a favor, honey. Distracted me from thinking about two dead babies." Ungloving, she took out her phone, walked a few feet to the side.

Milo said, "Moe, soon as the techies and the crypters get here, you and I are heading back to the office to run a search on missing infants. Meanwhile, call Sean. I'll be wanting him to canvass the neighborhood."

Moe left a message for Binchy.

Liz returned. "Just spoke to one of my old profs. He's never seen a specimen without wires and he's not aware of any lacquer that's commonly used. But no one knows everything so I'll stay on it. One bright spot: If these are relatively fresh, DNA's likely. Speaking of which, what's the status with the first set? DOJ hasn't instructed me to send them yet."

"Start the paperwork, kid."

Reed's phone rang. He said, "Hey, Ess-man, whusup? *What?*"

As he listened, his hand tapped the butt of his service gun. When he clicked off, his face was tight. "You're not going to believe this, they just found another."

Liz said, "Another *baby*?" Her voice caught. All pretense of scientific detachment ripped away like a dangling scab.

Reed said, "Another DB, adult female, gunshot wound, right here in the park, the southern edge."

Milo's face was as animated as a frozen chuck roast. He waved a uniform over.

"Keep this area tight, Officer. No one but the techies and the C.I. gets in."

"Yessir. That mean you're finished here?"

"Not even close."

The woman was late twenties to early thirties, dark-haired, medium height, slightly heavy at arms, hips, and ankles. She lay on her right side, the front part of her body shaded by shrubbery. Her dress, short-sleeved and knee-length, was patterned in a pale green mini-paisley with old-fashioned cap sleeves.

One leg rested atop the other, a position that almost resembled peaceful sleep. No disruption of clothing, no obvious sexual posing, but Milo pointed out faint pink rings around her wrists

that were probably the residuals of being bound.

A rubber-soled brown loafer encased
her right foot. Its mate lay a couple of
feet away to the north. Her hair was
trimmed short enough to expose the
nape of her neck. The bullet hole was a
red-black mini-crater at the junction of
cranium and spine.

A single shot, fired at close enough
range to leave light stippling, entering
the medulla oblongata and cutting off
the respiratory functions marshaled by
the lower brain.

What the papers like to call execu-
tion-style, but there are all sorts of ways
to execute someone and what this
wound and the wrist marks said was a
killer in total control leaving nothing to
chance.

The two uniforms guarding the scene
said she'd been spotted by a jogger.
Her bare foot, clean and white amid the
greenery, had been the attention-getter.

No jogger in sight. Milo didn't comment on that as he explored the edges
of the scene.

Even without her foot protruding, the

woman would've been noticed soon enough. This part of the park was relatively secluded but could be reached by any number of pathways or a simple walk across rolling lawn, followed by a brief pass through a planting of gum trees. The jogging trail was a well-worn rut that paralleled the park's southern border. Where the body lay, the trail veered especially close, maybe three feet away.

Intending for her to be found? A methodical killer eager to show off?

Milo kept looking at the woman. I forced myself to do the same. Her mouth was agape, eyes half open, filmed like those of a hooked fish left too long on deck. Crusts of dried blood leaked from her ears, nose, and mouth. That and the size of the bullet hole said a small-caliber slug had bounced around her brain like a pinball.

No purse, no jewelry, no I.D. Whatever bare skin was visible was free of tattoos, scars, distinguishing marks.

I spotted additional blood speckling dirt, leaves, a rock. No need to point it out; Milo crouched like a silverback gorilla, examining one of the larger splotches.

He moved to a spot just north of the woman's legs and pointed. A broken chain of footprints appeared to lead up to the body. A second series pointed in the opposite direction.

Large, deep impressions for both. The same person, a heavyweight. The tracks revealed none of the corrugations you'd see with an athletic shoe or a hiking boot, just your smooth heel-sole imprint lacking trademark or label or idiosyncrasy.

Both sets of prints vanished as soil gave way to grass. Tough park turf had sprung back hours ago, concealing the killer's entrance and exit.

Milo circled a couple more times, wrote something down in his pad, showed me a pair of depressions in the grass, slightly to the left of the corpse.

Shallow indentations, as if two weighted bowls had been placed there. Easy to miss but hard to ignore once you saw them. The resilient lawn had tried but failed to mask them completely.

I said, "On her knees."

"Has to be," he said. "Then he shot her and she fell over."

"Or was pushed."

"No bruising or dirt on her face."

"He could've cleaned her off before he arranged her."

"You think she looks posed? He didn't put that other shoe on."

"It was dark, maybe he didn't notice."

He crouched, took out his flashlight despite ample sun, aimed the beam between her teeth.

Victim on her knees, check for oral rape.

I said, "Anything?"

"No obvious fluid but I am seeing little white specks on her gums."

He showed me.

I said, "Looks like fabric. Bound *and* gagged."

He waved the uniforms over. Both were young, male, clean-featured, with gym-rat swaggers. One was sandy-haired and freckled, the other had a dark buzz cut and suspicious brown eyes.

"You guys check for casings?"

Sandy said, "We did, sir, nothing."

Milo did his own search, took his time but came up empty-handed. Careful shooter or a revolver.

The uniforms had returned to their original positions. He waved them back. "Who called it in?"

"Like we said, the jogger," said Sandy. "A girl."

"Where is she?"

Buzz said, "We got her information and let her go home. Here you go, sir."

Milo took the paper. "Heather Goldfeder."

Sandy said, "She lives just a few blocks away. With her parents."

"We talking a minor?"

"Barely a major, sir. Eighteen last month, she was pretty traumatized."

"Who made the judgment to let her go?"

The cops looked at each other. Buzz said, "Sir, it was a joint decision. She's maybe five two, hundred pounds, so she's obviously not the offender."

Milo said, "Teeny toon."

"Student at SMC, sir. She was really distraught."

Milo said, "Thanks for the psychological profile."

"Sir," said Buzz, "she told us she runs
here three times a week, never saw your
victim before. Ever."

Sandy said, "Sir, if we did something
wrong by letting her go, we're sorry.
She was totally emotional, we made the
judgment that babysitting her would
distract our attention away from what
needed to be done."

"Which was?"

"Securing the scene, sir."

Milo ushered me several yards away.
"Everyone's a damn therapist. So what
does a real shrink have to say about
this one being connected to the new
bones?"

I said, "Two bodies in the park, same
approximate time?"

He nodded. "So what do we have,
Mommy and Baby?"

"If so, Baby died first. Days or weeks
or months ago."

"Maybe Mommy got blamed for that
by Daddy?"

"That would be a good place to start."

"On the other hand, if Daddy's so devoted, why would he dump his kid's bones?"

I thought about that. "We could be talking about someone with serious psychiatric issues—paranoia, an active delusional system that got kicked up by the baby's death. That could also explain the bones being preserved. He elevated them to an object of worship—some sort of icon. It also fits with leaving them in the park on the night he killed the person he deems responsible. This is what *she* did, this is what *I* did to *her.*"

"Some nutter de-fleshing his own kid's skeleton? What's next, he walks into traffic with an AK?"

"Delusional doesn't have to mean a raving lunatic," I said. "There's nothing disordered about the woman's murder, so you could be dealing with someone who keeps it under wraps pretty well."

"Till he doesn't." He phoned Reed, found out the coroner's investigator had arrived, done a quick visual, authorized Liz to take possession of the bones, and left. The crime scene techs were doing their thing but had turned up nothing, so far.

Returning to Sandy and Buzz, he said, "We're heading back to the other scene. You stay here."

"How is that one, sir?" said Sandy.

"What do you mean?"

"The other scene. We heard bones over the radio. Whose?"

"Someone dead."

Sandy flinched.

Buzz said, "They have something to do with each other? Have to be, no?"

Milo rocked on his heels. He spoke between clenched jaws. "Here's what has to be: Guard this scene as if it was your best set of barbells. Don't let anyone but the C.I. and the C.S. crew within fifty yards of the body—make that a hundred. Stand right there. Don't wander off. Don't answer any questions. Of any sort. From anyone. At any time. If you're considering thinking, don't do that, either."

Buzz stood straighter. "Sir. We're all about proper procedure."

Milo saved his laughter until we were well away. Not a pleasant sound, quick and harsh as a gunshot.

Liz Wilkinson stood just outside the perimeter of the bone-dump. A team of three crime scene techs had nailed up an inner cordon on stakes, was photographing, bagging and tagging. Moe Reed stood near enough to observe, far enough to avoid getting in their way.

Liz said, "Got some new data for you. The front of the face exhibits no breakage or damage of any sort. No erupted teeth on either jaw, the buds are barely visible, I'm estimating age at around two months. And Alex, you were right about the bones being coated. When I got up close I could smell beeswax, it's got a distinct aroma. My father collects antique tea caddies and he uses it to shine them up. So maybe we're dealing with another type of collector. Some sort of fetishist."

Milo repeated the enraged-father theory.

She said, "A father preserving his own child's bones?" She looked at me.

I said, "You know the drill: Anything's possible."

"God, I hope that's not how it turns out. These past few days are already testing my detachment mettle."

"If there were faint tool marks could they be spotted under the wax?"

"I think so but I'll find out when I get them magnified. I'll x-ray every single one, maybe we'll get lucky and internal damage due to disease will show up, or a subtle injury. The nice thing—God, that sounds horrible—is that fresh infant skeletal remains have the best chance of yielding genetic material."

Milo said, "Fresh, as opposed to the first ones."

"DNA's been extracted from eons-old tissue so I'm guardedly optimistic on those, as well."

"That like nervously calm?"

She grinned. "Kind of. Anyway, Mommy and Baby should be easy enough to verify."

"Good," said Milo. "I like answers."

CHAPTER

13

Milo and I drove back to his office, where he searched missing persons for a match to the dead woman. By three p.m., twenty-eight possibilities had surfaced. By six, each lead had fizzled. An initial foray into one of the national data banks proved fruitless but there were other lists. So many women unaccounted for.

My phone rang. Service operator letting me know that Holly Ruche had canceled her appointment.

"Any reason given?"

"No, Doctor, but she did sound kind

of tense. You'd think that would be a bad time to cancel, huh?"

I agreed and amended my date book.

Milo was staring at a phone-photo he'd taken of the dead woman. He said, "Even if her main squeeze doesn't miss her, someone will. Time to go back to the media. Starting with that reporter." He checked the blue-bound murder book he'd begun on the old bones, found what he was looking for. "Kelly LeMasters, you're my new girlfriend. And that's saying a lot."

He punched numbers, barked, "Sturgis, call me." Moments later, his office phone rang.

I said, "That was quick."

"The old charm kicking in." He switched to speaker.

Deputy Chief Maria Thomas said, "How's it going on the two you picked up today?"

"Just started, Maria."

"Run the details by me." Not sounding the least bit curious.

He gave her basics.

She said, "How are you planning to I.D. your adult vic?"

"The usual way."

"Meaning?"

"Our pals in the press. Just left a message for the *Times* reporter."

"What message?"

"To call me back."

"When she does," said Thomas, "undo it."

"What?"

"Tell her you were just touching base on the old one, don't give her anything on the new ones."

"Why would I touch base without new info?"

"Figure something out."

"What's going on, Maria?"

"You know the answer."

"Actually, I don't."

"Think."

"Edict from on high?"

"An administrative decision has been made."

"Why?"

"Can't get into that, nor can I advise you how long it'll be operative."

"On the first bones you couldn't wait to play *Meet the Press*. In fact, you did it without letting me—"

"Flexibility," said Thomas, "is the hall-mark of good management."

"What the hell changed?"

"Nothing changed. The cases aren't the least bit similar."

"Exactly, Maria. The first one *was* ancient history. With these new ones I might actually get a lead by going public."

"Or not," said Thomas.

"What's the risk?"

"As I said, the cases are structurally different. The first bones were perceived as a human-interest story. Historical, quaint, however you want to put it."

"A dead baby is quaint?"

"No one likes a dead baby, Milo, but the consensus is that we probably don't have a *murdered* baby, are most likely dealing with natural causes, some sort of extreme grief reaction. The consensus is also that lacking media input you'd never close it, but that with media exposure you had a minimal chance. Obviously, that hasn't panned out, so much for good press for the department."

"This is about P.R.?"

"Have you seen the latest city council budget proposals?"

"I avoid smut."

"Some of us don't have that luxury and trust me, it's bad, we're talking across-the-board slash-and-burn like I've never seen before. Given that, some touchy-feely closure on a poor little baby would've been nice."

"That doesn't answer my first question, Maria. Why a blackout on the new ones? Closing real murders is gonna make us look even better."

"Whatever," she said. "Meanwhile, do not talk to the *Times,* or anyone else in the media."

"How do I I.D. my adult victim, let alone a sack of bones?"

"Did your adult victim appear homeless or otherwise a lowlife?" said Thomas.

"No, and that's exactly why I figured—"

"If she's not a throwaway, someone will report her missing."

"So I wait."

"You do your job and obey directives."

"Whose secret are we keeping, Maria?"

"Stop whining. Some things are better left unsaid."

"Not in my business."

"We're in the same business."

"Are we?" he said.

She snickered. "It didn't take long, did it? The outrage, the self-righteousness, the lonely warrior tilting against windmills."

"Who's tilting? I just want to—"

"Listen and listen well because I'm only going to explain it one more time: There's a strong desire among those responsible for the decisions that govern your professional life to avoid getting lurid with this particular case at this particular juncture."

"Lurid as in . . ."

"Yuck-stuff," she said. "As in more baby bones start popping up all over the place because psychotics get stimulated by coverage. Go ask your shrink friend, he'll tell you about that kind of thing."

"Yuck-stuff," he said, "that just hap-

pens to take place in a high-end neighborhood. A dead woman and baby
bones in Nickerson Gardens would be
a whole different story."

"Discussion over," said Thomas.

Click.

Milo swiveled and faced me. "You're
an ear-witness. That actually happened."

I said, "Your point about which neighborhood got to her. May I?"

As I pulled my chair up to his computer, he rolled his back to give me
room.

A check of *viprealestate.net* sub-
headed *cheviot hills* pulled it up in nano-
seconds.

Last year, Maxine Cleveland, a recently retired county supervisor, had
purchased a "thirteen room Mediterranean manse" on an oversized lot on
Forrester Drive in the "leafy upscale
district of Cheviot Hills."

A onetime public defender long considered hostile to cops, Cleveland had
morphed into a law-and-order stalwart
following the chief's endorsement of her
reelection and some well-placed fund-

raisers arranged by the chief's retired-anchorwoman wife.

Cleveland and her labor-lawyer husband had only lived in the Cheviot house for seven months before putting it up for sale. Both had accepted jobs in D.C., she as an assistant attorney general, he as chief counsel for the Occupational Safety and Health Administration.

Cleveland's first assignment would be heading a task force on financial shenanigans in the banking arena and the real estate website wondered if she could be objective, given a drop in the value of her investment due to the recession. An economic slump brought on, in part, by Wall Street's addiction to junk mortgages.

I said, "Toss in two DBs a short hop away and it won't be much of a broker's carousel."

"Idiots," he growled. "Okay, go home, no sense sitting and watching me type."

I moved out of the way and he bellied up to his keyboard. Entering his password, he logged onto NCIC. The screen froze. He cursed.

I said, "What about the jogger—Heather Goldfeder?"

"What about her? My resident geniuses said she didn't know the victim."

"She didn't know the victim but the way the bones and the body were dumped suggests a bad guy familiar with the park. She runs there regularly so it's possible she's seen something or someone she doesn't realize is relevant. A man casing the area or loitering near the jogging path."

He loosened his tie, yanked it off. "I was going to get to her once I finished with missing persons."

His phone rang again. Kelly LeMasters sounding excited about "touching base."

Instead of picking up, he sat there and listened as LeMasters emphasized her interest in the old bones, offered an additional cell number, and hung up.

"Okay," he said, "let's do it."

"Do what?"

"Check out little Heather."

"You changed your mind."

"I hate typing."

◆

He phoned the Goldfeder home. Heather's father picked up, Milo introduced himself then listened for a while.

"Yes, I know that had to be difficult, Mr. Goldfeder . . . *Doctor* Goldfeder, sorry . . . yes, I'm sure it was. Which is one reason I'm calling you. We happen to have an expert psychologist and he's available to offer some crisis . . ."

He hung up shaking his head.

I said, "No-go?"

"Quite the contrary, definite yes-go. 'About time you people considered the human factor.'"

"Thanks for calling me an expert."

"Onward."

CHAPTER

14

I pulled up in front of the Goldfeder home at ten the following morning. Going it alone because Milo felt "the pure psych angle would work best."

The two-story Spanish Colonial was three blocks south of the dead woman's dump site. Two white Priuses shared the driveway with an identically hued Porsche Cayenne SUV. One of the hybrids bore a Santa Monica College decal on the rear window. That vehicle was dust-streaked, its interior a jumble of paper, empty bottles, rumpled clothing. The other two were spotless.

I climbed a geranium-lined walkway to a stout oak door, raised a brass lion's-head knocker and let it drop gently onto the wood. The man who answered wore green surgical sweats, baggy in most places but snug around bulky shoulders and lifter's arms. Fifty or so, he had thinning dark hair, a small face conceding to gravity, a gray goatee more stubble than beard.

"Dr. Delaware? Howard Goldfeder." The hand he offered was outsized, smooth at the palms, pink around the cuticles from frequent washing. I'd looked him up last night: ENT surgeon with a clinical professorship. Same for his wife, Arlene, Department of Ophthalmology.

Heather's Facebook page had showed her as a pixie-faced cutie nearly overwhelmed by a storm cloud of dark hair. The page was thinly utilized, with only a smattering of friends. Favorite activities: running, more running. Phys. ed. major at SMC.

"Doctor," I said.

"Howard's fine."

"So is Alex."

"Given the context, I'll stick with Howard and Dr. Delaware."

"What context is that?"

"You're here to work, I'm here as Heather's dad. Speaking of which, how about we get things straight from the outset: Are you here to counsel my daughter about finding a corpse or to pry information out of her for the police? I'm asking because I thought it was a little weird for that lieutenant to offer the services of a psychologist out of the clear blue. Also, I did a little checking and you're a serious guy, we're both faculty crosstown. Why would someone with your credentials work for the cops? Do you have some sort of research project going on?"

I said, "I work with them, not for them, because I find it satisfying. In terms of your main concern, which is understandable, Lieutenant Sturgis would love any new information but my focus is going to be on Heather's well-being. How's she doing?"

Howard Goldfeder studied me. "Okay, I guess."

"You have your doubts?"

"She can be a high-strung kid. C'mon in."

"Anything else I should know before I talk to her?"

"My opinion is she exercises too much."

The living room was vault-ceilinged, furnished in overstuffed chenille, suede, and brass-accented mahogany. A U-shaped staircase rose to a landing. Rails, risers, and newel posts gleamed. The furniture looked as if it was rarely used, every pillow plumped and dimpled, as if styled for a photo shoot. Persian rugs lay as flat as if they'd been stenciled onto the wide-plank floor. Mullion windows sparkled, fireplace tools glinted. If dust was present, it was hiding in fear.

Howard Goldfeder said, "My wife's working, she's an eye surgeon. I'll go get Heather; if you need me, I'll be in my study. How long do you figure this will take?"

"Probably no more than an hour."

"I can handle that."

I said, "What did Heather tell you about finding the body?"

"She was running," said Goldfeder. "Like she usually does. Every day, rain or shine, she's out the door between seven and nine, depending on her class schedule, does her six miles religiously. Sometimes she ups it as high as ten a day."

"Rigorous."

"That's just morning, her afternoon run's another three, four. That she does at the track at school."

"Was she a high school athlete?"

"Not even close, couldn't get her involved in anything extracurricular, she started after she graduated." His lips pursed. "Obviously, you're wondering if she's got an eating disorder and honestly, we don't think so. She doesn't take in a lot of calories, true, and she's vegan, I'm always on her to get more iron. But she's always been a small eater and we have plenty of meals together so we can tell what she's ingesting. In terms of bingeing and bulimia, there's absolutely no sign of that. Her teeth are as perfect as the day her braces came off and I had her pediatrician look at her electrolytes just in case

I was missing something and she's in peak condition. Yes, she's on the thin side, but she's always been that way, just like my wife and my wife's entire family. My side's all the fatties, which is why I need to watch."

Patting a flat abdomen. "Make yourself comfortable."

"In terms of finding the body—"

Goldfeder's meaty shoulders drooped. "That was some drawn-out answer to a simple question, huh? I guess I'm not too concerned with a onetime thing like the body. It's the general stuff that concerns me. Like the fact that she's incredibly compulsive about her running but with everything else she slacks off totally. I won't even tell you her GPA, it's clearly way below what she's capable of. That's why she's at SMC instead of the U."

"Not much for academics."

"Never reads, never shows any interest in—but she's a good kid . . . never had a boyfriend, either. Never dated. Ever. I guess we should be grateful she's never gotten into any sort of trouble

with boys . . . but now that she's in college . . . also, she doesn't share much."

"About?"

"What's going on with her, her feelings. Her life. She used to share, everything's lip service, now. Love you Daddy,
love you Mommy, then she's off by herself."

"But her mood's okay."

"She seems happy to me," said Goldfeder.

"So she likes her privacy."

"I guess, but I can't stop wondering
if she's holding back. She's an only
child, we put a lot into her—this all probably sounds neurotic, maybe it is, I don't
know."

I said, "Sounds like parental concern."

"I guess I should stop being a pain—
you'll meet her, you be the judge. Okay,
back to your question: She didn't say
much about what happened yesterday,
just that she was running and saw it.
She could tell right away it was dead
from the color and the blood, some flies
were already there. She said that freaked
her out the most, the flies, the noise
they made. She felt light-headed but

she didn't faint, she kept her wits about her, called 911 and stuck around. Overall, I'd have to say I'm proud of how she handled it."

"You should be."

"Basically, she's a *great* kid . . . I'll go get her."

The girl who preceded him down the stairs seconds later had lopped off most of her hair since posting her Facebook shot, massive mane giving way to a crew cut. Her features were delicate and symmetrical. Huge, deep blue eyes connoted wonder.

She smiled and waved as she bounced down on stick-legs, seemed to take flight only to alight with grace. I thought: *Tinker Bell.*

Her father worked to keep up with her.

When she reached the bottom, she kissed his cheek. "Go back to work, Daddy, I'm fine."

"I've got paperwork to do in the study."

"Oh, Daddy. *Really.* He looks like a nice man. I don't need a chaperone."

"I'm not trying to be one, baby, there are bills to be paid."

"So organized." She giggled. "Okay, go to your study but close the door."

"I intended to."

"Sure you did."

Howard Goldfeder's reply was inaudible as he headed up the hall. Looking back for a second, he shut his door.

Heather said, "He's protective 'cause he loves me," and sat down perpendicular to me. She had on an oversized, sleeveless white blouse, khaki shorts, flat sandals. Skinny limbs but none of the ropy dehydration of severe anorexia. Lovely teeth, as her father had claimed. No evidence of breast development but the shirt would hide a less-than-generous bust.

"Well," she said, "my therapy begins."

I laughed.

"What's funny?" she said.

"You're pretty organized yourself."

"Oh, I'm not, trust me, I'm a total slob."

"Your dad tells me you're quite a runner."

"What he means is I'm a freak. My

mother thinks so, too, 'cause I like to get down at least three hundred miles a month, more if I have time."

"Impressive."

"They think it's nuts. Like an OCD thing, even though they bugged me to do sports in high school. Even though she's at the gym six times a week and he's there like three, four times, lifting weights and hurting himself all the time. I run 'cause I'm good at it. First time I tried I could go five miles without even breathing hard. I thought it would take time but it was easy. Felt amazing. Still does. When I run, it's like I'm flying, nothing else makes me feel that way. That's why I switched from Spanish to P.E. I want to be a coach or a personal trainer."

"Makes sense."

"So," she said. "What should we talk about?"

"Whatever you'd like."

"Would you like me to talk about yesterday?"

"If you want."

"What do *you* want?" she said. "Being with the police."

"I'm not here as a police representative."

"Then what?"

"To make sure you're okay after what happened."

"Okay? Sure I'm okay. It was a great experience, seeing a dead person, let's do it again tomorrow."

She looked at the carpet. "Will talking to you help with my dreams?"

"You're having nightmares?"

"Just last night. First I saw her face, then it kind of blended into a skeleton. Then I saw babies, tons of babies, with teensy little faces, all looking at me. Like they needed help. Then *they* turned into skeletons, it was like a mountain of skeletons."

"Babies," I said.

"Babies turning into skeletons. They told me about the skeleton across the park and it probably got stuck in my brain. Don't you think?"

"Who's they?"

"The two cops that showed up. They said there'd been another case across the park, a baby skeleton, maybe it was connected to the woman. Till then I was

holding out pretty good. But a baby?
Just thinking about it freaked me out."

She smiled broadly. Burst into tears.

I fetched tissues from a spotless
powder room left of the front door,
waited until she'd composed herself.

"Wow," she said. "I really thought I
was okay. Guess I wasn't."

"Crying doesn't mean you're not okay,
Heather. Neither does dreaming. Yesterday was a lot to deal with."

"It's weird," she said. "Seeing her
again. It's not like I knew her but now I
feel I kind of do. Like finding her made
us . . . connected us. Like her face will
be with me forever. Who was she?"

"We don't know yet."

"She looked like a nice person."
Laughing. "That's a stupid thing to say."

"Not at all, Heather. You're searching
for answers. Everyone is."

She sat there for a while, shredding
the tissue, letting flecks fall to the im-
maculate rug. "I saw the hole in her
head. She was shot, right? I asked the
cops but they wouldn't tell me."

"She was," I said. "How'd the topic of
the baby come up?"

"Soon after they finished asking me questions one of them got a call on his doo-what, his radio, then he hung up and the two of them started discussing something. They looked nervous so I asked them what's up. They didn't want to tell me but I cried and bugged them. Because that always works with my parents. Finally they told me. Was it *her* baby?"

"We don't know."

"Don't you think it was? Why would both of them get killed the same time in the park? Nothing ever happens in the park. I've been running for months and the worst thing I ever saw was a coyote, that was way back when I first started. Just standing there, all bony and hungry-looking. I screamed and it ran away."

"Spotting the body was a lot tougher."

"The flies," she said. "That was the grossest. At first I thought it was one of those dummies in the department store—a manikin." Giggle. "They should call it a womanikin, right? She had one bare foot and that's what got my attention, real pale, almost like plastic. Then

I saw the rest of her, then I heard the flies." She sighed. "I guess someone had to find her."

"Keeping your wits about you and calling 911 took presence of mind."

"Actually my first thought was to book as fast as I could, but then I thought what if someone's still around and they try to shoot *me*? So I took a second to look around, check out the area, figure out the best escape route. The park was so quiet and that kind of made it even freakier. A nice morning, the sky was blue, and she's just *lying* there. When do the cops think they'll know who she is?"

"There's no way to tell, Heather."

"That sucks. So . . . my dreams don't mean I'm a head-case?"

"Your brain's using sleep to take in what happened and give your mind time to integrate. And yes, talking about it can help. Because one way or the other people need to express themselves."

She finished destroying the tissue. Deliberately sprinkled the fragments onto the floor. "Is this talk totally secret?"

"Absolutely."

"No one finds out? Not the cops? Not my parents?"

"You have total confidentiality."

"What if I want you to say something to someone?"

"Your choice."

"I'm in control."

"Yes."

"That's . . . interesting."

She got up, spent a long time gathering the shredded tissue, found every single speck, threw the collection out in the powder room. When she returned, she remained on her feet. Her mouth was tight. "So . . . can I get you something to drink?"

"No, thanks."

"You're sure?"

"I'm fine."

"Okay . . . I guess that's it. Thanks for talking to me."

I said, "Your question about confidentiality."

"What about it?"

"So far you haven't told me anything your parents and the cops don't already know."

She turned her back on me. Gave a half turn, reversed it. Rotated a bit more and revealed a tight-jawed profile.

"No, I haven't," she said.

I sat there.

She said, "I like girls, okay? Like that Katy Perry song, I kissed one and it was more than cherry ChapStick that made me do it? Now I'm in love with someone and that gives me *good* dreams."

She faced me. "Do you think I'm weird?"

"Not in the least."

"*They* will. The cops will."

"Can't speak for your parents but the cops won't know or care."

"It's no one's business anyway, Doctor. Just mine and Ame— I don't want my parents to know. Ever."

"I can understand that."

"But that's not realistic, is it?" she said. "I'm their kid."

"You're an adult, Heather. What you tell them is your decision."

"Ha," she said. "I mean the part about being an adult. Like I'm even close."

"Legally you are."

"So if my birthday was next month instead of last month, I'd still be a kid and you could tell them?"

"It can get complicated," I said. "But I'd never tell them, anyway."

"Why not?"

"It's your personal business."

"But now I am an adult. Cool." Giggle. "I guess that sucks if it means I have to pay for stuff."

She turned serious. Touched her cropped hair. "I cut it all off last month. I feel like wearing boy clothes but I don't have the guts. Think I can get away with boy clothes like in a cute way? So they'll think it's just a fashion thing?"

"Keep it subtle enough? Sure."

"Like what?"

"Don't show up in a business suit and a tie. And I'd forget the pencil mustache."

She laughed. "You seem okay but no offense, I don't think I need you. I already started therapy with someone at student counseling. She's a total dyke—compared with her, I'm Super-Femme."

"I'm glad you've found someone you trust."

"I don't know if I trust her yet. But maybe, we'll see. So anyway, thanks for trying to help me."

"Thanks for being open to it."

"Honestly," she said, "the only reason I agreed to talk to you was Dad and Mom were bugging me to do it, saying they were finally getting something from their tax dollars. I try to do what they ask if it's only a small hassle. No offense."

"Picking your battles."

"That way I can do what I want when it's important."

"Sounds like a good strategy." Same one I'd used throughout my childhood. Up to the day I turned sixteen and bought an old car and began my escape from Missouri.

She said, "You think it's okay to play them like that?"

"You're not playing them, you're being selective."

"Sometimes I wonder if I should just be honest—this is who I am, deal."

"One day you may be able to do that."

"That's kind of scary," she said.

"One day it may not be."

A creak came from up the hall. The door to Howard Goldfeder's study opened and he stuck his head out.

Heather said, "I'm fine, Daddy."

"Just checking."

"Thank you, Daddy."

He didn't budge.

"Daddy."

He went back inside but the door remained ajar. Heather trotted over, pushed it shut, returned. "Do me a favor, Dr. Delaware. Before you leave tell him I look normal. So he doesn't think I need some Beverly Hills shrink."

"Will do," I said.

"You don't think I need that, right?"

"You're the best judge of that."

"Are you saying I'm screwed up but you don't want to piss me off?"

"Everything you've told me says you're reacting normally. The fact that you're already in therapy says you know how to take care of yourself."

"What about my running?"

"Sounds like you like to run. So do I."

"That's it?"

"Do you eat normally?"

"Yes."

"Do you binge and gag yourself in secret?"

"No."

"In general, do you think life's going okay?"

"Yes."

I shrugged.

She said, "Are you like . . . super-supportive to everyone?"

"I don't read minds, Heather, so all I can go on is what you tell me and what I observe about you. If there's some se-cret problem you're not telling me about, I could be missing something. But so far you're not setting off any alarms."

"Okay . . . do you like talk directly to the police?"

"Not about what patients tell me—"

"No, no, that's not what I meant," she said. "I'm talking about crimes. Like if someone tells you something and *wants* you to tell the cops, what do you do, just get on the phone?"

"You bet."

"And then the police come to see that person?"

"Sometimes," I said. "But the police

can't force anyone to talk to them. Even a suspect."

"Like on TV. You have the right to remain silent."

"Exactly."

She sat back down. "Okay. I have something. It's probably not important, I was going to call them, then I said why bother, it's probably nothing. Then I wasn't sure if I was doing a wrong thing. But since you're here, anyway . . ."

She exhaled. "It's *not* some big clue or anything but the night before, I was near the park. Pretty close to where I found her but outside the park, on the other side of the fence."

"On the street."

"I wouldn't think anything about it, but with what happened . . . I mean it was so close. If you could walk through the fence, you'd be right there in seconds."

Her right hand tugged at the fingers of her left. "I was with someone. Parked in my car. My parents were out late, a party in Newport Beach. I figured it would be a good time to . . . then I chickened out of using the house so we went driving and we parked. Not that we were doing anything, we were just talking." She colored. "Kissing a little, that's it. Just hanging out, it was nice. Until someone drove by and slowed down. Then they drove away and came back and slowed down again. Like they were checking us out. We got the frick out of there. Think we were in danger?"

"I think you were smart to be careful."

"I figured I should tell the cops," she said. "But the person with me can't . . . she's got commitments, okay? This could screw things up."

"I understand."

She punched the arm of her chair. "I'm *trying* to do the right thing but I also need to do the right thing for her."

"I don't see a problem with that, Heather."

"You promise she won't get hassled?"

"She doesn't need to get involved at all if you know everything she does."

"I do, I was in the driver's seat, had a better view."

"Then I don't see any need for her to be interviewed."

"I need to be interviewed?"

"At the most Lieutenant Sturgis will follow up with a phone call and have you repeat what you just said to me so he can have an official statement."

"That's it? You promise?"

"I do."

"I don't mind talking, it's just Amelie—I care about her."

"So you want me to pass this along to Lieutenant Sturgis?"

"I guess."

"I need you to be sure."

"Fine, I'm sure."

"Is there anything else you want to say about the car that checked you out?"

"Not a car, an SUV, that's all I know, I don't know brands."

"Can you recall any details?"

"It wasn't the same as my dad's SUV, his is a Porsche, this was bigger. Higher up."

"What about color?"

"Dark, can't tell you a color."

"Unusually high? Like it had been raised?"

"Hmm," she said. "Maybe . . . yes, I'd

say so. I definitely felt we were being looked down on—oh, yeah, it had shiny rims."

"Did you see who was inside?"

"No, it was dark and honestly, we didn't want to know, we just got out of there."

"What did the SUV do?"

"It didn't follow us," she said. "Maybe it stayed there, I don't know. Which would be weird, when the next morning . . ."

"Someone checking out the park."

"I mean you can see right through the fence, it's not wood, it's just chain link. Do you think I'm making a big deal out of nothing?"

"One pass might be someone driving by, Heather. Coming back a second time's more troublesome. Whatever the intention, you were right to leave."

"Oh, man . . . city full of freaks. I don't know if I'll ever step foot in the park again."

"What time did this happen?"

"Late," she said. "Like one a.m. I know 'cause I called my parents at twelve forty-five, they were just about to leave, I figured we had half an hour more. But after the SUV freaked us out, I drove her to her car and went home."

"Any chance you saw even part of the SUV's license plate?"

"Uh-uh."

"Anything else you remember?"

"No," she said. "Oh, one more thing: The police guy can call me but use my personal cell, not the landline where they pick up."

I copied down the number.

Howard Goldfeder emerged from his office. "How we doing?"

"We're doing great, Daddy."

He said, "Doctor?" As if his daughter hadn't spoken.

I said, "She's terrific."

Goldfeder said, "I could've told you that."

Heather smiled, hiding it from him but allowing me a glimpse of her satisfaction.

CHAPTER 15

Milo cursed. "Geniuses. They give a witness info then let her leave the scene before I have a chance to talk to her."

"It could work in your favor," I said. "Hard to keep secrets with that level of professionalism, so Maxine Cleveland's squeeze play may be exposed. You ever touch base with that reporter?"

"We keep missing each other, wink wink. Meanwhile, no one's reported my vic missing."

"Maybe she hasn't been gone long enough."

"Always the optimist," he said. "The

prelim from the coroner just came in. She's had good dental care, maybe orthodontia. Her blood's clean, no booze, drugs, or disease, and her body's free of needle marks, scars, iffy tattoos, or any other sign of a rough life. Dr. Rosenblatt said she looked like someone who shouldn't have ended up on his table. And yeah, I know that's politically incorrect but truth is truth, right?" He pounded his hand with his fist. "Someone has to be looking for her."

He gulped a big chunk out of the egg bagel I'd just turned down. A bag that had once held a dozen mixed leaned against his computer. The crumbs of the jalapeño and the onion that he'd finished littered his desktop. "In terms of LeMasters, it's all I can do not to call her and leak but when the air turns brown and the fan gets filthy, you know who the brass will be chasing down."

"Want me to call her?"

"Oh, yeah, *that* would be subtle. So little Heather and her girlfriend got spooked by a dark SUV—not a Porsche—no info on the tags, no view of the driver. That narrows it to half the vehicles on the Westside."

"Even without more info, it's interesting, no?"

"Somebody casing the park? Hell, yeah."

The egg bagel disappeared down his gullet. He washed it down with cold coffee from the big detective room. We were in his office, the tiny space humid from poor ventilation and discouragement. I'd arrived just before noon, honoring his early-morning request for a "sit-down." He'd sounded anxious. I'd been there for a quarter hour, still had no idea exactly what he wanted.

He brushed crumbs into his wastebasket. "One pass by the SUV might not mean much but coming back a second time's a bit more ominous. But ominous doesn't mean it's connected to my murders, there are all kinds of night-crawlers out at that hour. And showing himself that openly doesn't fit an offender who picks up his casings, leaves nothing serious behind."

"Or he used a revolver and got lucky."

"Hey," he said, "you're supposed to

see the good in everyone. Yeah, that's possible but the overall picture's organized, you said so yourself. Someone like that's planning a shoot-and-dump, he's gonna advertise his presence the night before to a coupla jumpy girls?"

"True," I said.

"Don't do that."

"What?"

"Agree so readily. It scares me."

"Keep living, you'll have plenty of opportunity for terror."

He grinned, stretched, pushed lank black hair off his mottled forehead, sank as low as the chair would allow. "This guy's an exhibitionist, right? Showing off his work, look how clever I am. Having a grand old time."

"He could be bragging," I said. "Or his message is something not so obvious. Specific to his mode of thinking."

"He's crazy?"

"Not to the point where he can't function, but his mind's probably a scary place. Whatever his motive, it's personal."

"Woman and child, a family thing? Yeah, I know we talked about that but

I'm having my doubts, Alex. I just can't see a father processing his own kid's bones then strewing them like garbage. Speaking of which, Liz Wilkinson called me just before you got here, totally beating herself up. Apparently, there's a technique for cleaning bones that she missed."

He pulled two sheets of paper out of his printer. One contained a pair of split-frame photos: on the left, half a dozen small, glossy, hard-shelled brown insects, to the right a single, spiky, caterpillar-type creature.

The second sheet was an order blank for "high-grade, mite-free dermestid beetles" from a lab supply company in Chicago.

I said, "Flesh-eating bugs?"

"Flesh, hair, wool carpeting, any sort of animal matter, wet, dry, or in between. Not bone and teeth, because the little buggers' jaws can't handle anything that hard, but anything short of that. The adults like to snack, but it's the larvae—the ones with the whiskers—that are the serious gourmets. Set 'em loose and they can munch a bear skull sparkling clean within twenty-four hours, inflict no damage on the skeleton. Which is exactly why taxidermists and museums and scientists use 'em to spruce up specimens. Liz called it anthro for dummies, said two babies in a row probably clouded her judgment."

He swung his feet onto the desk. "Does the use of creepy-crawlies spark any ideas?"

I said, "Set the beetles, then wax and buff? It's starting to sound ritualistic."

"Beetles and *bees*wax," he said. "Maybe I should be looking for a deranged entomologist."

"Or one of those guys who like to mount heads over the mantel. Her I.D. was missing, same for jewelry, if she was wearing any."

"Trophy-taking."

"Maybe not in the sense of a sexual sadist evoking a memory," I said. "If that was his aim, he'd have held on to at least some of the bones. Family or not, this one's rooted in intimacy and specific to these victims. Can purchasers of the beetles be traced?"

"If only," he said. "They're legal and not protected like toxic chemicals so anyone can buy them. No way could I get a subpoena that broad."

"You could narrow the search," I said.

"How?"

"Order your two geniuses not to leak the information then sit back as the tips pour in."

He started with laughter, ended with a coughing fit. When he recovered, he said, "How do you see the first bones fitting in, if at all?"

"Reading about them could have been the trigger that got our bad guy to dump his bones nearby."

"And shoot and dump the woman the same night. What, he got a message from God? Time to take out the garbage?"

"Or hearing about the first bones jelled things for him," I said. "Maybe he'd been holding on to them, trying to achieve mastery by transforming them. That didn't work. Or it did. Either way, he had no further use for them."

"I still can't get past a father doing that to his own kid."

"We could be dealing with a stepfather or a boyfriend. Maybe even someone who thought the baby was his until he learned differently and grew enraged. Infanticide's not that rare among primates and that includes us. One of the most frequent motives is eliminating another male's offspring. Our offender may have believed that getting rid of the baby would solve his problems, he'd be able to forgive her, move on. That didn't happen so he got rid of her, too. Flaunted both victims as a final flourish: Now I'm the master of my own destiny. And by leaving the bodies in proximity he made sure they were connected: This is what she did, this is why she died."

"So why not leave her right next to the bones?"

"Don't know," I said.

"Guess."

"By placing his kills at opposite ends of the park he could've been symbolically laying claim to the entire area. Or I'm over-interpreting and it was a simple matter of expediency: He got distracted or alarmed by someone."

"You guess pretty fast."

"Used to get into trouble in school for that."

"Thought you were Mr. Straight A."

"That annoyed the teachers even more."

This time he produced a complete laugh. "A stepdad, yeah, I like that. But holding on to the bones and fooling with them, you see Mommy going along with that?"

"Who says Mommy knew?"

"She has a baby one day, next day it's gone?"

"What if he forced her to give it up for adoption? As a condition of staying together. Told her he'd handle it and took care of business in a horrible way. Even if she suspected, she could've been too passive or guilty or frightened to do anything about it. Back when I worked at the hospital I can't tell you how many cases I saw where mothers stood by as stepfathers and boyfriends did terrible things to their children, including torture and murder. Any word on the DNA?"

"Maria Thomas emailed an hour ago,

wanting me to know she got it priori-tized. Like I'm supposed to feel grateful for her allowing me to do my job. Looks like under a week for basic analyses but fancy stuff will take longer."

He took out a cold cigar, propped it between his index fingers. "You ever feel you've had enough of the garbage I send your way?"

"Nah, keeps life interesting."

"Does it?"

"Why the question?"

"Just wondering." He got up, opened the office door, stood gazing out to the corridor, his back to me. "What about Robin? She's okay with it?"

All these years, first time he'd asked.

"Robin's fine."

"And the pooch?"

"Perfectly content. So are the fish. What's going on, Big Guy?"

Long silence.

Then: "What you did for me . . . I'm not gonna forget it."

That sounded more like complaint than gratitude.

I said, "Let's not forget the times you saved my bacon."

"Ancient history."
"Everything ends up as history."
"Then we die."
"That, too."
We both laughed. For lack of any-
thing else.

CHAPTER

16

The new murders had nudged the first set of bones off Milo's screen. But I couldn't let go of the baby in the blue box. Kept thinking about Salome Greiner's tension when I'd asked about a Duesenberg-driving doctor.

DMV kept no records of old registrations but a car that rare and collectible couldn't be hard to trace.

Back home, I went straight to my office. The Auburn Cord Duesenberg Club in Indiana had a museum, an online store, and an energetic members forum.

A woman answered the phone, sounding cheerful. I told her what I was looking for and she said, "You're in California?"

"L.A."

"The top Duesenberg expert is right near you, in Huntington Beach."

"Who's that?"

"Andrew Zeiman, he's a master restorer, works on all the serious cars, here's his shop number."

"Appreciate it."

"Was a Duesie involved in a crime?"

"No," I said, "but it might lead to information about a crime."

"Too bad, I was hoping for something juicy. Lots of colorful characters owned our babies—Al Capone, Father Divine, Hearst—but nowadays it's mostly nice people with money and good taste and that can get a little routine. Good luck."

A clipped voice said, "Andy Zeiman."

I began explaining.

He said, "Marcy from ACD just called. You want to locate an SJ for some sort of criminal investigation."

Statement, not a question. Unperturbed.

I said, "If that's possible."

"Anything's possible. Date and model."

"We've been told it was a '38 SJ, blue over blue."

"SJ because it had pipes, right? Problem is you can put pipes on anything. Real SJs are rare."

"Aren't all Duesenbergs?"

"Everything's relative. Total Duesenberg production is four hundred eighty-one, SJs are less than ten percent of that. Most were sold on the East Coast until '32, then the trend shifted out here because that's where the money and the flamboyance were."

"Hollywood types."

"Gable, Cooper, Garbo, Mae West, Tyrone Power. Et cetera."

"How about we start with the real SJs. Is there a listing of original owners?"

"Sure."

"Where can I find it?"

"With me," said Zeiman. "What year

does your witness think he saw this supposed SJ?"

"Nineteen fifty, give or take."

"Twelve-year-old car, there'd be a good chance of repaint, so color might not matter. Also, it wasn't uncommon to put new bodies on old chassis. Like a custom-made suit, altered to taste."

"If it helps to narrow things down, the owner may have been a doctor."

"Give me your number, something comes up I'll let you know."

Seven minutes later, he called back. "You might have gotten lucky. I've got a blue/blue Murphy-bodied Dual Cowl Phaeton ordered by a Walter Asherwood in '37, delivered November '38. Murphy body with later enhancement by Bohman and Schwartz. Both were L.A.-based coachbuilders."

"The car started out on the West Coast."

"Yup. Walter Asherwood held on to it until '43, when he transferred ownership to James Asherwood, M.D. Nothing else in the log fits, so it's either this one or your person didn't see a real SJ."

"Where did the Asherwoods live?"

"Can't give you the address because for all I know family members are still living there and we respect privacy."

"Can you give me a general vicinity?"

"L.A."

"Pasadena?"

"You can fish but I won't bite," said Zeiman. "You've got a name, that should be sufficient."

"Fair enough," I said. "Can you tell me who owns the car, now?"

"One of our members."

"Did he or she buy it from Dr. Asherwood?"

"There's a complete chain of ownership but that's all I can say. Why do you need the current owner, anyway?"

"We're trying to trace a dead baby's mother."

"What?"

"The car was seen parked in the driveway of a house where an infant was buried decades ago. The bones were just dug up."

"Dead baby?" said Zeiman. "So we're talking murder."

"That's not clear."

"I don't get it, either it's murder or it's not."

I said, "Depends on cause of death."

"Hold on," he said. "My wife mentioned something about that, she'd heard it on the news. Made her cry. Okay, I'll make some calls."

"Thanks for all the help."

"Most interesting request I've had since two months ago."

"What happened two months ago?"

"Shifty Mideastern type walks into my shop, flashing cash, wants me to build a Frankencar out of retools that he can sell as genuine to a sucker in Dubai. I said no thanks, phoned the Huntington Beach cops, they told me intent's no felony, until a crime was committed there's nothing they can do. That felt wrong to me so I tried the FBI, they didn't even return my call. At least you do your job. So I'll help you."

It took just over an hour to hear back from Zeiman. By then I'd made progress on my own.

A search of *38 duesenberg dual cowl*

phaeton murphy body had produced three possibilities. The first was a "barn find" up for auction in Monterey. The once-sleek masterpiece had been the victim of a 1972 engine fire during careless storage in Greenwich, Connecticut. Hobbled by engine rot, char scars, metastatic rust, and a broken axle, it was deemed "ripe for restoration to show condition" and estimated to fetch between six and eight hundred thousand dollars. The auction company's catalog presented a history that included a California stint, up north, under the stewardship of a Mrs. Helen Bracken of Hillsborough. But subsequent owners included neither Walter nor James Asherwood and the original color, still in evidence through the blemishes, was claret over scarlet.

Candidate number two, a black beauty, due to go on the block in Amelia Island, Florida, had accumulated a slew of awards during a pampered life. Five owners: New York, Toronto, Savannah, Miami, Fishers Island.

Bingo came in the form of a car that

had taken first place at the Pebble Beach Concourse d'Elegance ten years ago, a gleaming behemoth benefiting from a six-year frame-off restoration by Andrew O. Zeiman.

Program notes from the award ceremony noted that care had been taken to replicate the car's original cerulean/azure paint job as well as the "precise hue of its robin's egg blue convertible roof, now replaced with modern but period-reminiscent materials."

The proud owners were Mr. and Mrs. F. Walker Monahan, Beverly Hills, California. A winners' circle photo showed them to be mid-sixtyish, immaculately turned out, flanked by a burly, white-bearded man. Andrew Zeiman was clad, as was Mr. Monahan, in a straw Borsalino, a navy blazer, pressed khakis, conservative school tie.

I had my eyes on Zeiman's photograph when the phone rang. "It's Andy again." Low-tech Skype. "You must be one of those fortunate sons, maybe we should hit the blackjack tables."

"The case resolves, I might just take you up on that."

"The current owners agreed to talk to you. They're good people."

"Do they remember the Asher-woods?"

"Talk to them," said Zeiman.

CHAPTER
17

Researching the person you're trying to influence is a handy tool when peddling gewgaws, pushing con games, and practicing psychotherapy.

The same goes for witness interviews; before reaching out to the F. Walker Monahans of Beverly Hills, I searched their names on the Web.

Mister sat on the board of two banks and Missus, a woman named Grace, occupied similar positions at the Getty, the Huntington, and the volunteer committee of Western Pediatric Medical Center.

The hospital affiliation made me wonder if she'd be the link to Dr. James Asherwood.

A search of his name pulled up nothing but a twelve-year-old *Times* obituary.

Dr. James Walter Asherwood had passed away of natural causes at his home in La Canada–Flintridge, age eighty-nine. That placed him at forty or so during the period Ellie Green had lived at the house in Cheviot Hills. Easily feasible age for a relationship. For unwanted fatherhood.

Asherwood's bio was brief. Trained at Stanford as an obstetrician-gynecologist, he'd "retired from medicine to pursue the life of a sportsman and financier."

The *Times* hasn't run social pages in a while and being rich and wellborn no longer entitles you to an obit. At first glance, nothing in Asherwood's life seemed to justify the paper's attention, but his death was the hook: "A lifelong bachelor, Asherwood had long voiced intentions to bequeath his entire estate to charity. That promise has been kept."

The final paragraph listed beneficiaries of Asherwood's generosity, including several inner-city public schools to which Asherwood had bequeathed a hangarful of vintage automobiles. Western Peds was listed midway through the roster, but unlike the cancer society, Save the Bay, and the graduate nursing program at the old school across town, the hospital wasn't singled out for special largesse.

Fondness for the nursing school because he remembered one particular RN?

Had ob-gyn skills meant detour to a career as an illegal abortionist? Did dropping out of medicine imply guilt? A legal concession as part of a plea deal?

Lifelong bachelor didn't mean loveless. Or childless.

Doctor to financier. Moving *big* money around could mean the ability to purchase just about anything, including that most precious of commodities, silence.

No sense wondering. I called the F. Walker Monahans.

◆

A beautifully inflected female voice said, "Good evening, Doctor, this is Grace. Andy told us you'd be phoning."

No curiosity about a psychologist asking questions on behalf of the police. "Thanks for speaking with me, Mrs. Monahan."

"Of course we'll speak with you." As if a failure to cooperate would've been unpatriotic. "When would you care to drop by?"

"We can chat over the phone."

"About cars?" Her laugh was soft, feline, oddly soothing.

"About a car once owned by Dr. James Asherwood."

"Ah, Blue Belle," she said. "You do know that we've sold her."

"I didn't."

"Oh, yes, a month ago, she'll be shipped in a few weeks. Immediately after Pebble Beach we were besieged with offers but refused. Years later, we're finally ready. Not without ambivalence, but it's time to let someone else enjoy her."

"Where's she going?"

"To Texas, a natural gas man, a very

fine person we know from the show circuit. He'll pamper her and drive her with
respect, win-win situation for everyone."

"Congratulations."

"We'll miss her," said Grace Monahan. "She's quite remarkable."

"I'll bet."

"If you'd like to pay your respects before she leaves, that can be arranged."

"Appreciate the offer," I said. "If you
don't mind, could we talk a bit about
Dr. Asherwood?"

"What, in particular, would you like to
know?"

"Anything you can tell me about him.
And if you're familiar with a woman he
knew named Eleanor Green, that would
be extremely helpful."

"Well," she said, "this is a person
we're going to discuss and that de-
serves a more personal setting than the
phone, don't you think? Why don't you
drop by tomorrow morning, say eleven?
Where are you located?"

"Beverly Glen."

"We're not far at all, here's the address."

"Thank you, Mrs. Monahan."

"You're quite welcome."

Board seats and ownership of a multi-million-dollar show car had led me to expect residence in Beverly Hills' uppermost echelons. A manse at the northern edge of the flats, or one of the mammoth estates nestled in the hillocks above Sunset.

The address Grace Monahan gave me was on South Rodeo Drive, a pleasant but low-key neighborhood well away from the try-too-hard glitz and glassy-eyed tourism of the twenty-four-karat shopping district.

The numbers matched a nondescript, two-story, not-quite-Colonial apartment building on a block of similar structures, shadowed by the white marble monument on Wilshire that was Saks Fifth Avenue.

Monahan: 2A. A once-wealthy couple who'd fallen on hard times? The real reason for selling the blue Duesenberg?

I climbed white-painted concrete steps to a skimpy landing ringed by three units. The wooden door to 2A was open but blocked by a screen door. No entry hall meant a clear view into a low, dim living room. Music and the smell of coffee blew through the mesh. Two people sat on a tufted floral sofa. The woman got up and unlatched the screen.

"Doctor? Grace."

Five and a half feet tall in spangled ballet slippers, Grace Monahan wore a peach-colored velvet jumpsuit and serious gold jewelry at all the pressure points. Her hair was subtly hennaed, thick and straight, reaching an inch below her shoulder blades. Her makeup was discreet, highlighting clear, wide brown eyes. The Pebble Beach photo was a decade old but she hadn't aged visibly. Nothing to do with artifice; smile lines and crow's-feet abounded, along with the inevitable loosening of flesh that either softens a face or blurs it, depending on self-esteem at seventy.

The duration and warmth of Grace Monahan's smile said life was just grand in her eighth decade. One of those women who'd been a knockout from birth and had avoided addiction to youth.

She took my hand and drew me inside. "Do come in. Some coffee? We get ours from Santa Fe, it's flavored with piñon, if you haven't tried it, you must."

"I've had it, am happy to repeat the experience."

"You know Santa Fe?"

"Been there a couple of times."

"We winter there because we love clean snow—have a seat, please. Anywhere is fine."

Anywhere consisted of a pair of brocade side chairs or the floral sofa where her husband remained planted as he continued watching a financial show on the now muted TV. Still canted away from me, he gave an obligatory wave.

Grace Monahan said, "Felix."

He quarter-turned. "Sorry, just a second."

"Felix?"

"A sec, sweetie, I want to see what Buffett's up to, now that he's a celebrity."

"You and Buffett." Grace Monahan completed the three steps required to

transition to a tiny kitchenette. She fiddled with a drip percolator.

I sat there as Felix Walker Monahan
attended to stock quotes scrolling along
the bottom of the screen. Above the
numbers, a talking head ranted mutely
about derivatives. Watching without
sound didn't seem to bother Felix
Monahan. Maybe he was a good lip-
reader. The same tolerance applied to
TV reception that turned to snow every
few moments. The set was a convex-
screened RCA in a case the size of a
mastiff's doghouse. Topped by rabbit
ears.

The room was warm, slightly close,
filled with well-placed furniture, old, not
antique. Three small paintings on the
walls: two florals and a soft-focus portrait of a beautiful, round-faced child.
Great color and composition and the
signature was the same; if these were
real Renoirs, they could finance another
show car.

The blowhard on the screen pointed
to a graph, loosened his tie, continued
to vent. Felix Walker Monahan chuckled.

His wife said, "What can you get out of it without hearing it?"

"Think of it as performance art, sweetie." He switched off, swiveled toward me.

Unlike his wife, he'd changed a lot since Pebble Beach: smaller, paler, less of a presence. Scant white hair was combed back from a wrinkled-paper visage that would've looked good under a powdered wig or gracing coinage. He wore a gray silk shirt, black slacks, gray-black-checked Converse sneakers sans socks. The skin of his ankles was dry, chafed, lightly bruised. His hands vibrated with minor palsy.

He said, "Jimmy Asherwood, fine man. Better than fine, first-rate."

"Did you buy the Duesenberg from him?"

He grinned. "Even better, he gave it to us. To Gracie, actually. She was his favorite niece, I lucked out. When I met her I knew nothing about cars or much else. Jimmy's collection was quite the education."

His wife said, "I was his favorite niece because I was his only niece. My father was Jack Asherwood, Jimmy's older brother. Jimmy was the doctor, Dad was the lawyer."

Felix said, "If Jimmy had twenty nieces, you'd still be his favorite."

"Oh, my." She laughed. "I already give you everything you want, why bother?"

"Keeping in practice for when you finally say no."

"Scant chance—here's coffee."

"Let me help you," he said.

"Don't you dare be getting up."

"Oh, boy," he said. "Starting to feel like a cripple."

"The difference, Felix, is that cripples remain crippled while you can be up and around soon enough. *If* you follow orders."

"Hear, hear," he said. To me: "Had surgery five weeks ago. You don't want to know the details."

Grace said, "He certainly *doesn't.*"

"Let's just say plumbing issues and leave it at that."

"*Felix.*"

He rotated his arm. "They cored and bored me, like an engine. Roto-Rooter wasn't picking up their messages so I had to go to a urologist."

"*Fee-lix!* TMI."

"What's that mean, sweetie?"

"Don't play innocent with me, young man. The grandkids always say it when you're overdoing."

"Ah," he said. "Too Many Issues."

"Exactly." She brought a silver tray holding three coffees and a box of cookies. "Pepperidge Farm Milano Mints, Doctor. Cream?"

"Black's fine."

Pouring, she sat down next to her husband. They lifted their cups but waited until I'd sipped.

I said, "Delicious. Thanks."

Felix said, "Here's to another day aboveground."

"So dramatic," said Grace, but her voice caught.

I said, "Nice paintings."

"They're all we have room for, I don't like crowding, art needs room to breathe." She sipped. "In Santa Fe we have oodles of wall space but not being there much of the year we don't like to hang anything too serious."

"In S.F., we patronize the local artists," said Felix. "Nice level of talent but not much in the way of investment."

"Life's about more than compound interest, dear."

"So you keep telling me."

I said, "Have you lived here long?"

"Ten years."

"Bought the building fifteen years ago," said Felix. "Followed it up by buying the rest of this side of the block."

"There you go again," said Grace. "Making like a tycoon."

"Just citing facts, sweetie." Working to steady his hand, he put his cup down. Bone china rattled. Coffee sloshed and spilled. His lips moved the same way Milo's do when he wants to curse.

Grace Monahan bit her lip, returned to smiling at nothing in particular.

Felix Monahan said, "The original plan was to tear the entire block down and build one big luxury condo but the city proved obdurate so we kept the block as is and went into the landlord business. The last thing on our minds was actually moving here, we had a fine Wallace Neff on Mountain Drive above

Sunset. Then our daughter moved to England and we said, what do we need thirty rooms for, let's downsize. The house sold quickly, those were the days, caught us off-guard and we hadn't found a new one. This apartment was vacant so we said let's bunk down temporarily."

Grace said, "We found out we liked the simplicity and here we are."

"Tell him the real reason, sweetie."

"Convenience, darling?"

"Walking distance to shopping for someone who's not me. By the way, Neiman phoned. They're prepared to offer you a daily chauffeur if strolling three blocks proves too strenuous."

"Stop being terrible, Felix." To me: "I buy only for the grandkids. We're in our post-acquisitional stage."

I said, "Perfect time to sell the car."

Felix said, "On the contrary, perfect time to keep it. And all the others. One day the entire collection will go to a deserving museum, but Blue Belle is taking her leave because we believe cars are to be driven and she's gotten too valuable for that." His eyes softened. "She's lovely."

I said, "Dr. Asherwood was a generous man."

"*Generous* doesn't do him justice," said Grace. "Uncle Jimmy was selfless and I mean that literally. Nothing for himself, everything for others. He left every penny to charity and no one was resentful because we respected him, he'd given us so much during his lifetime."

"I read about the donations in his obituary."

"His obituary doesn't begin to describe it, Dr. Delaware. Well before Jimmy passed he was giving away money and things."

I said, "I used to work at Western Pediatric and I noticed the hospital on the list of beneficiaries. Did he attend there?"

"No," she said, "but he cared about the little ones." Scooting back on the couch, she sat up straight. "Why are you curious about him?"

Her voice remained pleasant but her stare was piercing.

Know the person you want to influence. The real reason *she'd* wanted a face-to-face.

I said, "Did you read about a baby's skeleton being dug up in Cheviot Hills?"

"That? Yes, I did, tragic. What in the world would Jimmy have to do with such a thing?"

"Probably nothing," I said. "The burial date was traced to a period when a woman named Eleanor Green lived in the house."

I waited for a reaction. Grace Monahan remained still. Felix's hand seemed to shake a bit more.

He said, "You think this woman was the mother?"

"If we could learn more about her, we might find out," I said. "Unfortunately, she seems to be somewhat of a phantom—no public records, no indication where she went after moving. Dr. Asherwood's name came up because his Duesenberg was spotted parked in her driveway on more than one occasion."

Grace said, "Eleanor Green. No, doesn't ring a bell." She turned to her husband.

"Hmm . . . don't believe so."

His palsy had definitely grown more pronounced. Her fingers had stiffened.

She said, "Sorry we can't help you, Doctor. Jimmy knew lots of women. He was an extremely handsome man."

She crossed the room to a low bookshelf, took out a leather album, paged through and handed it to me.

The man in the scallop-edged black-and-white photo was tall, narrow, fine-featured, with a downy pencil mustache under an upturned nose and pale, downslanted eyes. He wore a cinch-waisted, pin-striped, double-breasted suit, black-and-white wingtips, a polka-dot handkerchief that threatened to tumble from his breast pocket, a soft fedora set slightly askew. He'd been photographed leaning against the swooping front fender of a low-slung, bubble-topped coupe.

"Not the Duesenberg, obviously," said Felix Monahan. "That's a Talbot-Lago. Jimmy brought it over from France immediately after the war. It was decaying in some Nazi bastard's lair, Jimmy rescued it and brought it back to life."

Grace said, "He was barely out of med school when he enlisted, was assigned to an infantry unit as a field surgeon, served in the Battle of the Bulge, raided Utah Beach. He was injured on D-Day, earned a Purple Heart and a host of other medals."

"A hero," said Felix. "The real deal."

Grace said, "Now, would you like to see Blue Belle? She's downstairs in the garage."

As smooth a dismissal as any I'd heard. I said, "She's here?"

"Why not?" said Felix. "A garage is a garage."

"Is a garage," said Grace. "To paraphrase Alice B. Toklas."

I said, "I'd love to see the car but could we talk a bit more?"

"About what?"

"Your uncle's medical practice."

"There's nothing to talk about. After his wounds healed, he delivered babies."

"Then he quit," I said.

"No," she said, "he retired. Quitting implies a character flaw. Jimmy left medicine because his father, my grand-

father Walter, was ill and his mother, my
nana Beatrice, was terminal. Someone
had to take care of them."

"Jimmy had no wife or children."

Quick glances passed between them.

"That's true," said Grace. "If you ask
me why I'll tell you I don't know, it was
none of my business."

"Never met the right woman," said
Felix. "That would be my guess."

"That's not what he's after, darling.
He's looking for dirt on poor Jimmy."

"Not at all, Mrs. Monahan."

"No?" she said. "You work with the
police, they dig dirt—granted it's generally for a good cause. You've been involved in over a score of very nasty
cases, have probably come to see the
world as a terrible place. But that doesn't
apply to Jimmy."

A score. Serious research on her part.

I said, "I'd like to think I keep a pretty
balanced view of the world."

Rosy spots radiated through her
makeup. "Forgive me, that was rude.
It's just that I adored Uncle Jimmy.
And—I confess to being a bit of a snoop
myself, Dr. Delaware. After you called, I

inquired about you at Western Peds. We donate there. Everyone had good things to say about you. That's why we're talking." She caught her breath. "If that offends you, I'm sorry."

"Girl Scout heritage," said Felix. "Be prepared and all that."

"Brownie," she corrected. "But yes, I do respect a logical plan. As I'm sure you do, Dr. Delaware. But trust me, Jimmy led a quiet, noble life and I can't have his name sullied."

"Mrs. Monahan, I'm sorry if I—"

"Actually," Felix broke in, "it's Doctor Monahan."

"No, it's not!" she snapped.

He flinched.

She said, "Sorry, darling, sorry," and touched his hand. He remained still. "Forgive me, Felix, but all this talk about Uncle Jimmy has made me edgy."

He said, "Nothing to forgive, sweetie." To me: "She doesn't like tooting her own horn but she *is* a doctor. Full M.D., trained and qualified. Women's medicine, same as Jimmy."

"Not to be contentious," she said, "but a doctor is someone who doctors.

I never practiced. Got married during my last year of residency, had Catherine, said I'd go back but I never did. There was more than a bit of guilt about that, I felt I'd let everyone down. Especially Jimmy because it was he who'd written a personal letter to the dean, back then women weren't exactly welcomed with open arms. After I decided to eschew medicine, it was Jimmy I talked to. He told me to live my life the way I wanted. In any event, if you need me to tend to your ills, you're in trouble. Now, since you probably have no serious interest in seeing Blue Belle—"

"I do."

"Don't be polite, Dr. Delaware, we don't force our enthusiasms on anyone."

"Never seen a Duesenberg," I said. "I'd be foolish to pass up the opportunity."

Felix Monahan stood with effort. "I'll take him, sweetie."

"Absolutely not," said Grace. "I can't have you—"

"I'm *taking* him. *Darling*."

"Felix—"

"Grace, I have yet to convince myself I'm a fully functional human being but if you could pretend it would be an enormous help."

"You don't need to prove anything—"

"But I do," he said in a new voice: low, flat, cold. "I most certainly do."

He walked toward the door, slowly, overly deliberate, like a drunk coping with a sobriety test.

Grace Monahan stood there, as if daring him to continue. He opened the door and said, "Come, Doctor."

She said, "Hold his arm."

Felix Monahan turned and glared. "Not necessary. *Sweet*heart."

He left the apartment. I followed.

Grace said, "Men."

I trailed Felix Monahan down the stairs to the sidewalk, sticking close and watching him sway and lurch and intentionally ignore the handrail.

Midway down he tripped and I reached out to steady him. He shook me off. "Appreciate the offer but if you do it again, I might just acquaint you with my left jab."

Laughing but not kidding.

I said, "You boxed?"

"Boxed, did some Greco-Roman wrestling, a bit of judo."

"I get the point."

"Smart man."

When we reached the street, he continued south, turned the corner at Charleville, and entered the alley behind his building. Six garages, one for each unit, each furnished with a bolt and a combination lock.

The third garage was secured with an additional key lock. Keeping mc out of view, Monahan twirled, inserted a key, stood back. "Slide it up, I'm smart enough to know my limitations."

The door rose on smooth, greased bearings, curved inward and upward, exposing two hundred square feet of pristine white space filled with something massive and blue and stunning.

A gleaming vertically barred grille stared me in the face. The radiator cap was a sharp-edged V aimed for takeoff.

The car was huge, barely fitting into the space. Most of the length was taken

up by a hood fashioned to accommo-
date a gargantuan engine. Headlights
the size of dinner plates stared at me
like the eyes of a giant squid. Hand-
sculpted, wing-like fenders merged with
polished running boards topped by
gleaming metal tread-plates. A side-
mounted spare matched four wide-wall,
wire-wheeled tires. The car's flanks
were fluid and arrogant.

"Supercharged," said Felix Monahan,
pointing to a quartet of chrome pipes
looping out of a chrome-plated grid.
Thick and sinewy and menacing as a
swarm of morays. "We're talking zero to
sixty in eight seconds in the thirties."

I whistled.

He went on: "She cruises at one oh
four in second gear and that's without
syncromesh. Max speed is one forty,
and back when she was born you were
lucky to get fifty horsepower out of a
luxury car."

"Unbelievable," I said.

"Not really, Doctor. What's unbelievable is how a country that could create
this can't come up with anything better

than plastic phones that die in six months. Put together by peasants living on gruel."

I'd come to see the car in the hope that I might pry more info from him. But the Duesenberg's beauty held me captive. The paint, a perfect duet of convivial blues, was a masterpiece of lacquer. The interior was butter-soft, hand-stitched leather whose pale aqua hue matched the spotless top. More artisanal metalwork for the sculpted dashboard. The rosewood-and-silver steering wheel would've looked dandy on a museum pedestal.

Even silent and static, the car managed to project an aura of ferocity and mastery. The kind of queenly confidence you see in a certain type of woman, able to work natural beauty to her advantage without flirting or raising her voice.

I said, "Thanks for giving me the opportunity."

Felix Monahan said, "You can thank me by dropping the whole notion of Jimmy Asherwood being some sort of criminal. A, he isn't, and B, I don't like anything that upsets my wife."

"No one's out to—"

He stopped me with a palm. "That woman you mentioned—Green—I can't tell you about her because I don't know her and I'm sure that applies to Grace. However, I did know Jimmy and there's zero chance he fathered that baby or had anything to do with its death."

"Okay."

"That doesn't sound sincere."

"I—"

"When Grace inquired about you, she was told you're quite the brilliant fellow, had a promising academic career that you traded, for some reason, for immersing yourself in the lowest elements of society—hear me out, I'm not judging you, as Jimmy told Grace, everyone should live their own life. But now I see you as intruding on Grace's life and that worries me because of something else your former colleagues said: You never let go."

I kept silent.

He said, "Close the garage."

◆

After he locked up, he faced me. His eyes were slits, and the tremor in his hands was mimicked by quivers along his jawline.

"Mr. Monahan, I'm—"

"Listen carefully, young man: Jimmy didn't father that child or any other. He was incapable."

"Sterile?"

"Grace doesn't know. But I do, because Jimmy was like an older brother to me and he could confide in me in a way he couldn't with Grace because I was able to keep my emotions in check. He and I used to motor together, drive out to where he stored his cars, pick one on a whim and go hit some great, dusty roads. One day we were out in his '35 Auburn Boattail Speedster. Motoring in Malibu, up in the hills, in those days it was brush and scrub. The Auburn chewed up the asphalt, glorious thing, Jimmy and I took turns behind the wheel. We stopped for a smoke and a nip—nothing extreme, a taste from the hip flask and a couple of fine Havanas at a spot where the ocean was visible. Jimmy seemed more relaxed than I'd ever seen him. Then all of a sudden, he said, 'Felix, people think I'm homosexual, don't they? Because I like art and going to the ballet and have never married.' What do you say to something like that? The truth was he was right. Jimmy was regarded as what was then called 'sensitive.' Apart from cars, his interests were feminine."

"The paper described him as a sportsman."

"The paper relied on information provided by Grace. The only sport I ever saw Jimmy engage in was a spot of polo in Montecito and not much of that. Now, there's nothing wrong with liking *Die Fledermaus,* but combine that with his never marrying—never showing interest in women—it was a reasonable conclusion. But what I said was, 'Jimmy, that's rot.' To which he said, 'You're not a fool, Felix. You never wondered?' I said, 'Your business is your own, Jimmy.' To which he replied, 'So you believe it, too.' I protested and he laughed that off, stood and proceeded to unbuckle his belt and lower his trousers and his shorts."

His eyes clamped shut. "Terrible sight. He'd been mangled. Shrapnel fly-off from a land mine on D-Day. Larger pieces and he'd have been sheared in two, fortunately he survived. However, the shards that did find their way into his body left hideous scars on his legs. And nothing much in the way of man-hood."

"Poor man."

"When I saw it, Dr. Delaware, I couldn't help myself, I cried like a baby. Not my style, when my *mother* passed I held myself in check. But Jimmy like that?"

Long sigh. "He pulled up his trousers and smiled and said, 'So you see, Felix, it's not for lack of interest, it's for lack of equipment.' Then he took a long swallow from the flask—emptied it—said, 'You drive home.'"

Monahan placed both hands to his temples. "Jimmy was a man's man. And you need to honor that and vow to not repeat this to anyone because if Grace ever learned the truth and that I was the one who told you, it would destroy her and do irreparable harm to my marriage."

"I promise, Mr. Monahan. But there's something you need to consider: The lieutenant I work with is honorable and discreet, but he's also extremely persistent and left to his own devices he may eventually trace the car back to Jimmy, as I did. I have credibility with him and if I'm allowed to give him some basic details, it's unlikely you'll ever hear from him."

"Unlikely," he said. "But you can't guarantee."

"I'm being honest, Mr. Monahan."

"You're a psychologist, sir. Your allegiance should be building people up, not tearing them down."

"I agree."

"What would you like to tell this policeman?"

"That Jimmy was a good man whose war injuries prevented him from fathering a child. That most of his life seems to have centered around good deeds."

"Not most," said Felix Monahan. "All. A purer soul never walked this earth."

His eyes swept over my face, thorough as a CAT scanner. "I choose to consider you a man of honor."

"I appreciate that."

"Show your appreciation by doing the right thing."

CHAPTER

18

A call to the development office at Western Peds added focus to Dr. James Asherwood's generosity. Back in the sixties he'd endowed a small fund for the neonatal ICU.

Special concern for problem newborns on the part of a man unable to father children. A man who worked obgyn at a place where covert abortions were standard operating procedure.

How that connected to a baby buried under a tree eluded me.

That night the big blue Duesenberg didn't appear in my dream but a cream-colored Auburn Boattail Speedster did. No reason to believe Jimmy Asher-wood's had been that color but I'd pulled up images on the Web, supplied my own script and scenery.

In the dream, Asherwood and a young Felix Monahan, who bore a striking re-semblance to me in my twenties, roared up a series of dusty, sun-splotched canyons that snaked through the Santa Monica Mountains.

The ride ended with a smoke and a nip from a silver flask at a spot where the ocean grew vast. Then a return ride that felt more like aerial gliding than mo-toring.

When Asherwood dropped me at the dingy apartment building on Overland that had housed me during starving-student days, he tipped his fedora and saluted and I did the same and I as-sured him I'd never betray him.

His smile was blinding. "I trust you, Alex."

The following morning Milo dropped in at nine o'clock.

Robin had left early for a trip to Tem-

ecula, visiting an old Italian violin-maker
who'd finally retired and was parting
with maple, ebony, and ivory. I was sitting at the kitchen table reviewing a
custody report that had a decent chance
of being read because the judge was a
decent human being. Blanche curled at
my feet relishing the shallow sleep of
dogs, snoring gently. She sensed Milo's
presence before the door opened, was
up on her feet waiting for him.

He said, "Ah, the security system,"
patted her head, placed his attaché
case on the table, and sat down.

No fridge-scavenge. Maybe he'd
eaten a big breakfast.

"Time for current events, class." Out
of the case came a rolled-up newspaper. The masthead read:

The Corsair
*The voice of Santa Monica
College*

A pair of articles shared the front
page: a feature on renewed interest in
the benefits of high colonics and "SMC

Student Plays Crucial Role in Westside Murder."

Heather Goldfeder's headshot was accurately elfin. The slant was her "extreme bravery after coming across a hideously slain homicide corpse as she trained for a marathon in Cheviot Park. 'What made it worse,' said the SMC freshman, 'was this wasn't the first murder in my neighborhood, a little baby skeleton was also found in the park and there was also another baby dug up real close to where I live. Though I heard that one was real old.'"

I said, "Let's hear it for freedom of the press. Maria know yet?"

"She woke me at six, was spewing like I've never heard her. I told her it hadn't come from me, she said she didn't believe me, I said feel free to waste time investigating. Then she started in on how it was my responsibility to muzzle my witness and I said last I heard gag orders came from judges."

He put the paper away. "The one who's *really* got steam coming out of her ears is that *Times* gal, LeMasters.

She left a message an hour ago using naughty words and accusing me of allowing *this* august publication to scoop her, probably because I have a kid who goes there."

He went to the fridge, searched a top shelf.

I said, "Any tips come in?"

"Nothing serious yet, and I don't think there will be unless Flower Dress's picture goes public. Still waiting to hear back from Maria on that."

He tried a lower tier. "What's with you guys, no leftovers?"

"We've been eating out."

"Not even a doggie bag? Oh, yeah, that's not a dog, it's an alien princess who won't touch her foie gras unless it's been consecrated by a celebrity chef. Am I right about that, mademoiselle?"

Blanche trotted up to him, cocked her head to the side.

Grumbling about his back, he bent low to rub behind her ears. She rolled over and exposed her belly. He murmured something about "Entitlement."

She purred. "Nice to see my charm transcends gender."

I said, "She's a happy girl. Had lamb chop leftovers last night."

"Don't gloat, Dr. De Sade." He foraged some more, returned with a half pint of cottage cheese and a bottle of KC Masterpiece Original Barbecue Sauce that he glurped directly into the container, concocting a mélange that evoked something you'd find at a shotgun homicide.

Three tablespoons later: "Got the DNA results on everything. Nothing in the old bones, too degraded, but plenty in the new bones: The baby's mommy had some African American heritage so Flower Dress wasn't her. So much for the mother-child-bad-daddy theory. Any suggestions?"

"Nothing that would make you feel better."

"Try me."

"Take away the family angle and you could have an offender who murders all kinds of people for motives you won't understand until you catch him."

"A pleasure killer," he said. "Gets off

on amateur taxidermy. I was hoping you wouldn't say that, knew you would." His eyes dropped to the cottage cheese container. He downed another spoonful of clotted red soup. First time I'd seen him grimace after ingesting anything.

Dumping the mixture in the trash, he drank water from the tap. "So what's my plan, just wait and hope this nutcase screws up on the next one?"

"You could put the park under surveillance."

"You think he'd actually go back?"

"Nothing succeeds like success."

"Well," he said, "the best I can do for surveillance is a couple of additional drive-bys per shift by sector cars. I know 'cause I've already asked, great minds and all that . . . maybe I'll do an all-nighter . . . God, I'm hungry, how long will it take you to defrost a steak? Or a roast? Or half a cow?"

His phone chirped Ravel's "Bolero." He picked up, flashed a V. "That's great, sir, I apprec—" The victory sign wilted as he listened for a long time.

He put the phone down and drank more water at the sink.

I said, "His Godliness ranting?"

"Lower the volume, it woulda been a rant. 'Well, Sturgis, looks like your fucking victim is gonna be a fucking reality star for fifteen fucking minutes so get a decent fucking photo of her fucking dead face because you've got one fucking shot at this. And you better fucking be able to do something with it because I just swallowed a whole lot of fucking bullshit from a fucking piece-of-shit politician who's got fucking White House connections.'"

I said, "When will the photo run?"

"Tonight at six. If I get my fucking ass in gear." He smiled. "I believe I will."

Ten-second flash at the tail end of the news. Three hours later, Milo phoned, exuberant. "Her name's Adriana Betts and she's originally from Boise. A cousin from Downey saw it and recognized her, called Adriana's sister back in Idaho, the sister called me, emailed a photo. She's flying down tomorrow, I booked Interrogation B at the Butler Avenue Hilton."

"Did the sister have anything interesting to say about Adriana?"

"Wonderful person, not an enemy in the world, how could this happen, why do bad things happen to good people."

That got me thinking about Jimmy Asherwood and I was hit with a strange, aching sympathy for a man I'd never known.

"Alex? You there?"

"Pardon?"

"I asked if you can make it tomorrow for the sister and you didn't answer. Three p.m."

"Yes," I said.

"My favorite word."

CHAPTER

19

No DNA was needed to link Helene Johanson's chromosomes to those of Adriana Betts.

Four years older than Adriana, Helene had a pleasant, square face, solid build, and chestnut hair that made her a near-twin to her sister. Watching her step into the interview room was unsettling: a dead woman come to life.

The match didn't extend to style. Adriana had been found wearing a loose dress and budget shoes, both tagged by the coroner as "Walmart, made in China." Helene's preferences ran to designer jeans with rhinestone accents, a formfitting black ribbed top under a fringed caramel suede jacket, snakeskin cowboy boots. Her nails were polished rose-pink. The diamond studs in her ears looked real. So did the Lady Rolex on her left wrist and the Gucci bag from which she pulled out a silk, lace-edged handkerchief.

HAJ monogram on one corner. She took in the room, dried a corner of one eye.

Milo said, "Thanks for getting here so quickly, Ms. Johanson. I'm sorry it had to be for such a terrible reason."

Helene Johanson said, "I'm sure you hear this all the time but I can't believe this is real."

"I hear it often, ma'am, but that doesn't make it any less true. Are you able to talk about Adriana?"

"I'm here," she said, with no conviction. "I guess it's better than watching the bulls get castrated."

"Pardon?"

"We ranch beef cattle outside of Bliss. Red and Black Angus for the organic market. This is the week some of the boys become less-than-boys. The noise and the smell are terrible, I always leave. But I'd rather be doing that than *this*." She slapped the handkerchief on the table. "Lieutenant, what happened to my *sister*?"

"What we know so far is she was shot in a park."

"During the day?"

"At night, ma'am."

"That makes absolutely no sense," said Helene Johanson. "What would Adriana be doing in a park at night? Did she make a wrong turn into a slum or something?"

"Actually, it's a very nice neighborhood. A place called Cheviot Park. Did Adriana ever mention it?"

"No, she didn't mention L.A., period. Why would she? She lived in San Diego."

"Really," said Milo. "When did she move there?"

"Around a year ago. Before that, she was a year in Portland. Why would she be in a park in L.A.?"

"Did she know anyone here?"

"Not that she ever mentioned."

"What brought her to San Diego?"

"Same thing as Portland," said Johanson. "A job. Babysitting. Not like a teenager doing it part-time, a real job, working for a family. She loved it. Loved children." Her face crumpled. "Now she'll never have any of her own—can I call my husband?"

"Sure," said Milo.

She took a while to locate her cell in her purse, speed-dialed, spoke to "Danny" and cried.

When she hung up, Milo said, "Ms. Johanson, anything you can tell us about Adriana will be helpful. The kind of person she was, who her friends were."

"The kind of person she was . . . is a good person. A wonderful person. There wasn't a mean cell in Adriana's body. She was kind and sincere. Very religious. We were brought up Methodist but she went for something more intense. Religion was important to her. She taught Sunday school. Preschoolers—she *always* loved the little ones."

"In terms of her friends—"

"Her church group. Even before she

switched. She always hung with the good kids."

"Who'd she hang with in California?"

She twisted a diamond stud. "I guess this is the point where I tell you we weren't close. And feel crappy about it. The entire flight I was thinking of why I didn't pay Adriana more attention. Even if she didn't ask for it, I should've included her more . . . I'm sorry, I don't know. Don't know much about her life since she left Idaho."

"Why'd she leave Portland?"

"The people she worked for couldn't afford her. Adriana had grown attached to the little boy but there was no choice."

"Did she get her jobs through an employment agency?"

"Couldn't tell you."

Milo said, "Do you have her address? In Portland, as well, if you recall."

Head shake. "Sorry."

"What about a phone number?"

"All she gave me was her cell." She scrolled her own phone, read off the number. Not committed to memory; the sisters hadn't talked often.

Milo said, "Did she tell you anything about her San Diego employers?"

"They were doctors—medical professors."

I said, "At UC San Diego?"

"All she told me was one of them did research on cancer, Adriana was impressed by that. But I can't tell you if it was the husband or the wife."

"Was she happy with the job?"

"Adriana was happy about everything, she was a happy person—oh, here's something, the little girl was adopted. Korean or Chinese, some kind of Asian." Her eyes brightened. "Oh, yeah, her name was May, Adriana said she was adorable."

"How long ago did you have that conversation?"

Helene Johanson's eyes wandered. "Too long ago. Right after she started."

Milo said, "This may sound like a stupid question, ma'am, but did Adriana have any enemies?"

"No, everyone loved Adriana. And I can't see her falling in with a bad crowd, that wasn't her. She liked quiet things, reading, crocheting—she'd make blankets for her church friends' babies."

"What about her personal relationships?"

"With men?"

"Yes."

"She had a boyfriend in high school. Dwayne Hightower, his family farmed a big spread near where Danny and I run our Angus. Great family, everyone thought Dwayne and Adriana would be married after high school graduation. Then Dwayne got himself killed in a tractor accident and Adriana never wanted to date." She sniffled. "All those years doing for others. It's so unfair."

"I'm sorry, ma'am."

"When Dwayne died, it's like Adriana pulled away. Drew into herself. But then she came out of it and it was the same old Adriana, cheerful, happy, helping others."

"Resilient," I said.

"You bet."

"But no interest in dating."

"It wasn't for lack of guys trying. Then they stopped, I guess they got the message."

"Was there anyone in particular who might've felt rejected?"

"One of those crazy stalker things? No way."

"Would your parents have any additional—"

"They're gone," she said. "Cancer, both. Danny thinks it was the radon in the basement and I think he might be right. Because Mom and Dad went within nineteen months of each other and there was definitely radon, Danny had it measured. So we'd know if our kids could be safe. They didn't find a lot but there was some. I wanted Adriana to sell the house and keep all the money. Danny and I sell every pound of meat we raise and we're also getting good money for bones and skin and renderable fat. So I wanted Adriana to get the house but she said it belonged to both of us by right, she wouldn't take extra."

"What happened to the house after Adriana moved to Portland?"

"We sold it, by the time taxes and the mortgage were paid, there really wasn't much left."

I said, "Any reason Adriana took jobs outside of Boise?"

"She told me it was time to travel, see what was out there. I said, why don't you go all the way, do something crazy, check out Europe? Danny and I love to travel, we cruise, last year we saw the coast of Italy, it was amazing." She smiled. "I guess the West Coast was adventure enough for Adriana." She bit her lip. "Now I guess I have to look? To identify her?"

"That won't be necessary, Ms. Johanson."

"No?"

"We know who she is."

"Oh, okay, so how does it work? Do I take her back with me?"

"Eventually but not quite yet, Ms. Johanson."

"She's being autopsied?"

"Yes, ma'am."

"When will that be finished?"

"Within a few days."

"Then what?"

Milo said, "You'll be informed and given a list of local undertakers who can help you through the process. They'll take care of everything."

"I guess I'll bury her next to Mom and Dad . . . there's a space. Two, one for each of us."

I said, "No other sibs?"

"Nope, just Adriana and me . . . I'll tell her pastor, I'm sure he'll want to do some kind of memorial."

Milo said, "Could we have his name, please?"

"Pastor Goleman. Life Tabernacle Church of the Fields. Any recommendations for picking an undertaker, Lieutenant Sturgis?"

"They're all good, ma'am."

"Six of one, half dozen of the other? Okay, I guess I'll fly back, you tell me when I can have my sister."

"Do you need a ride to the airport?"

"No, I reserved a car and driver for all day."

"When's your flight?"

"Whenever I want." She looked away. "I'm leaving from Van Nuys, we own a small plane—a tiny little jet, you can't even stand up in it, nothing fancy. We use it for business, visiting the various cattle auctions and semen dealers and whatnot."

"Makes sense," said Milo.

"Efficient. That's what Danny says, though between us, I think he just wanted his own plane. I thought I'd be bringing Adriana back with me, talked to the pilot about there being room in the hold, he said there was." She swiped at her eyes. "I guess I'll be going home alone."

CHAPTER
20

Adriana Betts's cell phone registration traced to an address in Portland but her recent billing had gone to a Mailboxes Galore in a La Jolla strip mall. Milo began the paperwork for subpoenaing the records, then tried the mail drop.

The clerk said, "Let me check . . . here we go, Betts. Closed three months ago."

"Any idea why?"

"We don't ask."

"She leave a forwarding?"

"Let me check . . . nope, just a close-down."

"Was she all paid up?"

"To the day," said the clerk. "That's pretty cool."

"What is?"

"Someone being honest."

I said, "La Jolla makes sense if she was working for two doctors. Big medical town. And a pair of physicians would be less likely to run out of nanny money."

"Med school's a big place," he said. "You have any contacts?"

"A few in Pediatrics, but the sister said cancer research so I'd try Oncology first."

"Sister didn't know much, did she? Maybe Adriana didn't want her to. Why would a church girl need a P.O.B.?"

I said, "Church girl with a secret life?"

"She didn't die pretty."

An outraged activist might call that blaming the victim. Anyone with homicide experience would call it logic.

He read off the Portland address on the cell registration. "Let's talk to these people, first."

◆

Susan Van Dyne worked as a reference librarian at the Multnomah County Library, Main Branch. Bradley Van Dyne was in human resources at a start-up software company. Both had Facebook pages that showed them as bespectacled towheads with an interest in snow sports. Their only child was a three-year-old named Lucas, already wearing glasses. In one of several posted photos, Adriana Betts could be seen holding the boy on her knee.

Everyone smiling, Adriana's grin the widest. She had on the same dress she'd died in. Lucas grasped her finger with a tiny hand. Child and nanny appeared in love. So far, I believed everything Adriana had told her sister.

The Van Dynes' number was listed. They gasped in unison when Milo told them about the murder.

"My God, my God," said Susan. "Adriana was a gem. We so regretted having to let her go."

"Why did you?"

Bradley said, "Lost my job, couldn't afford her anymore. When the HR department gets reamed, you know the company's terminal. And guess what? They bellied up ten days after I got my pink slip."

Susan said, "With Bradley staying home it didn't make sense."

"I became Mr. Mom," said Bradley. "Not my finest hour, I'm finally bringing in a paycheck again. Poor Adriana, I can't believe anyone would hurt her. Was it a random thing? 'Cause it's not like she traveled the fast lane."

"No partying?" I said.

"Her? She made us look like night-lifers and trust me, we're not."

Susan said, "She had her evenings to herself but never went out. All she wanted to do was read and watch TV and crochet. She made three lovely blankets for Lucas. Oh, God, he'd be so sad if he knew."

Milo said, "Did Adriana have any friends?"

"None that we ever met."

Bradley said, "She actually told me her best friend was Lucas."

Susan said, "She and Lucas really bonded. She had great instincts, could get down and play at his level. He still asks about her. Letting her go wasn't easy."

"How'd she react to that?"

Bradley said, "No drama, it was like she'd expected it. I'd been bitching for a while about the company having problems."

Susan said, "To tell you the kind of person she was, we offered her an extra month's severance. She refused to take it, said we needed it to tide ourselves over."

I said, "That's pretty close to saintly."

Bradley said, "You could describe her as saintly. That's why it doesn't make sense, someone killing her."

Susan said, "Maybe not, Brad."

"What do you mean?"

"Saints get martyred."

"Oh," he said. "Yeah, I guess so."

I said, "Any idea who'd want to martyr Adriana?"

"Of course not," said Susan. "We haven't been in touch for over a year."

"Do you know who she went to work for?"

"Of course," she said. "The Changs."

"You know them?"

"No, but Adriana gave us their address so we could forward mail. They're doctors."

"Better financial bet," said Bradley.

Milo said, "Did she get much mail for forwarding?"

"Actually, not a single piece. Even when she lived here it was just junk—coupons she gave to us. Oh, yeah, she also got occasional correspondence from her church back in Idaho."

Susan said, "Tabernacle Something. I guess she was a fundamentalist. But it's not like she was heavy-handed, some kind of Jesus freak."

"Did she find a church in Portland?"

"She went every Sunday," she said. "Ten to noon, that's the only time she left for any stretch. Can't tell you where the church was, though, because we never asked and she never said."

"Anything else you think would help us?"

Bradley said, "Sue?"

Susan said, "No, sorry."

Milo said, "How about the address in La Jolla?"

Susan said, "Hold on, I'll find it."

Seconds later, she was reading off the P.O.B. Milo had just called.

He gestured obscenely. "One more question: Did you find Adriana through an agency?"

"Nope," said Bradley, "through an ad we ran in the paper."

"It wasn't as risky as it sounds," said Susan. "We ran a background check through a friend, he does security for one of the hotels. He said she came up absolutely spotless."

"Could we have his name?"

Silence. "That's absolutely necessary?"

"There's a problem, ma'am?"

"Well," said Susan, "actually, he's not a friend, he's my brother and I'm not sure he's allowed to freelance with the hotel account."

"I promise not to get him in trouble, Ms. Van Dyne, just want to find out anything I can about Adriana."

"Okay. Michael Ramsden. Here's his number."

"Appreciate it and if you think of anything, here's mine."

"It really makes no sense," said Bradley. "Whoever did this has to be mentally ill or something."

"Absolutely," said Susan. "Adriana was so stable, Lucas adored her. I am *not* going to tell him what happened."

Michael Ramsden was caught off-guard by the call from Milo.

He said, "Who?"

"Adriana Betts."

"Never heard of her."

"Hmm," said Milo. "So I guess your sister lied."

"Hold on—let me switch to another phone." Moments later: "Are we talking the housekeeper?"

"Susan said you backgrounded her."

"All I did was the basics, nothing anyone couldn't do online, so I'd appreciate your not making a big deal of it."

"Doing it on company time."

"Coffee-break time," said Ramsden. "My personal laptop, my sister was satisfied. You're saying someone killed this girl?"

"Yes."

"Whoa," said Ramsden. "Well, there was nothing in her record to suggest that might happen."

"Spotless?"

"That's what the computer said."

A scan of the UCSD med school faculty revealed that Donald Chang, M.D., was a fellow in vascular surgery and Lilly Chang, Ph.D., worked in Oncology as a cell biologist. He was in the operating room. She answered her extension.

"Adriana? Oh, no, that's terrible. In L.A.?"

"Yes, Doctor."

"Well," she said, "I suppose that might explain it."

"Explain what, Dr. Chang?"

"Her flaking on us," she said. "At least that's what we assumed. Not at the outset, mind you. Our initial worry was something had happened to her, because she'd always been so reliable, never even went out at night. Then about three months ago she said she was meeting a friend for dinner and never came back. We called the police, checked E.R.'s, were really worried. When she didn't answer her phone we figured she'd bailed and got pretty irate, I have to tell you. Both of us work all day and now there was no one for May. We complained to the agency and they gave us a discount on her replacement."

"What about her car?"

"She didn't have one, used the bus or walked. Obviously that would restrict her but as I said, she wasn't much for going out."

"Until she was," said Milo.

"Well, yes," said Lilly Chang. "I'm so sorry to hear what happened to her. It happened in L.A.? That's where she went?"

"Did she ever talk about L.A.?"

"Never," said Lilly Chang.

"What agency did you get her from?"

"Happy Tots. They were highly apologetic."

"What happened to Adriana's personal effects?"

"The little she had we boxed and stored. It's still there because, frankly, we forgot about it."

"We'd like to come down and pick up the boxes."

"Sure, they're just sitting in our storage unit. There really wasn't much."

"How about we come down today?"

"This evening would be okay, I guess. After seven thirty, I've got meetings until six thirty, want to put May to bed myself."

"No problem, Doctor. While we're there, if we could chat a bit more with you and your husband that would be great."

"There really isn't anything to chat about."

"I'm sure, Doctor, but this is a homicide and we need to be thorough."

"Of course. But if you want Donald, it'll have to be even later—no earlier than nine, probably closer to ten."

"He keeps long hours."

"Long would be good," said Lilly Chang. "More like infinite."

Milo phoned Happy Tots Child Care Specialists, spoke to a woman named Irma Rodriguez who sounded as if she was wrestling with abdominal pain.

"That one," she said. "She sure fooled us."

"About what, ma'am?"

"Thinking she was reliable. What trouble's she gotten herself into?"

"Death," said Milo.

"Pardon?"

"She was murdered."

"Oh good Lord," said Rodriguez. "You're kidding."

"Wish I was, ma'am. How'd Adriana come to register with you?"

"She phoned us, emailed references from her previous employers, was lucky the job with the Changs came up right then. That's a good solid job, I was p.o.'d at Adriana for treating them so shabbily."

"What was Adriana like?"

"Well," said Rodriguez, "usually I meet applicants face-to-face but with the quality of her references and the perfect background check, I figured she'd be okay."

"Who supplied the references?"

"Hold on."

Several moments of dead air before she returned. "Only one but it was good.

Mr. and Mrs. Van Dyne from Portland, Oregon. Someone killed her, huh? You just never know."

I called Robin, told her I'd either be home late or spend the night in San Diego, explained why.

She said, "A nanny. Everything seems to revolve around little ones."

"Seems to," I said, picturing a paper-doll chain of tiny skeletons.

"If you do come home tonight, wake me, no matter how late."

"You're sure?"

"Positive. I miss your feet in the bed. The way you end up in some weird position and I'm stretching and groping to find you."

"Love you."

"That's another way of saying it. Whoever drives, be careful."

We left the station at five fifteen. Rather than brave rush-hour freeway traffic, Milo took surface streets to Playa Del Rey, where we had dinner at a dockside Italian place with C décor and A food.

He said, "Leave the driving to moi,
you can have wine, Mr. Wingman."

We both drank coffee and by seven
thirty I was feeling keyed up but no
clearer on who'd want to kill a near-
saintly woman. Once we got on the 405
South, Milo turned quiet and I picked
up my messages.

Holly Ruche had phoned at six, apol-
ogizing for canceling and wanting another appointment. I left her a message
saying okay. A hundred and ten minutes
later, we rolled into La Jolla.

CHAPTER

21

Donald and Lilly Chang lived a brief stroll from the UCSD campus in a massive, gated complex called Regal Life La Jolla. Four-story brown-and-beige apartment blocks were surrounded by Torrey Pines. So was most of the beach town, where land didn't nudge blue Pacific.

Gorgeous place, warm night. A lot more temperate than Portland though I doubted Adriana Betts had weather on her mind when she'd moved.

Searching for the right kind of job: caring for other people's little treasures.

I knew all about that.

Milo rolled up to the Regal Life guard-house. No need to flash the badge, Lilly Chang had left his name. We parked in a visitors' area, walked past fountains, flagstone roundabouts, perfect palms and pines and coral trees, precise sections of velvet lawn.

It took a while to locate the building but we got buzzed through the security door immediately.

A redheaded, exuberantly freckled woman wearing enormous blue-framed eyeglasses, a black T-shirt, and baggy green linen pants responded to Milo's knock. Her feet were bare. The shirt read *I May Look Lazy but on a Cellular Level, I'm Quite Busy.*

"Hi, I'm Lilly, c'mon in. Donald's showering, he'll be right with you."

Dr. Lilly Chang was five six and lanky with a loose walk that caused her ginger mop of hair to shudder as she led us into her living room.

Despite the exterior luxe, the apartment was small, white, generically bland, a status unrelieved by the obligatory granite kitchen outfitted with the requisite brushed-steel appliances. What passed for a Juliet balcony offered an oblique view of a brown wall. The furniture looked as if it had been rescued from a dorm. The sole artwork was a poster featuring a cartoon human brain. The legend beneath the drawing read *Software: Sometimes You Don't Have to Buy It.*

No need for paintings or prints; the walls were pretty much taken up by photos of a beautiful almond-eyed baby with blue-black hair. In some of the shots, May Chang had been propped up for a solo pose. Her reaction to stardom ranged from stunned disbelief to glee. In other pictures, she sat on Lilly Chang's lap or that of a balding Asian man who looked close to forty.

A white plastic baby monitor breathed static from atop a black plastic end table. Above the table hung the largest portrait of May, gilt-framed.

Lilly Chang said, "I know, we're a bit too in love."

I said, "She's adorable. How old is she?"

"Twenty-two months. She's our joy."

She fingered the hem of the T-shirt. One of those smooth-faced women whose age was hard to determine. My guess was early thirties.

"Please, sit," she said. "How was your drive?"

Milo said, "Piece of cake."

"My parents live in L.A., I try to see them every five, six weeks. Sometimes it can get pretty hairy." She smiled. "Though I guess you guys could use your siren to speed through."

Milo said, "That would be nice but unfortunately it's a big no-no."

"Figures," she said. "Can I get you some coffee or juice?"

"No, thanks, Dr. Chang."

"Lilly's fine."

I said, "Where do your parents live?"

"Sherman Oaks. I was the original Valley Girl." Showing teeth. "Gag me with a spoon. Fer sure." She turned grave. "So we're here to talk about poor Adriana. I'm still integrating the news, it's so dreadful."

"It is," said Milo.

"May I ask where it happened?"

Milo said, "Cheviot Park."

"Wow," she said. "My family used to go there for Fourth of July fireworks. It always seemed like a safe place."

"It generally is."

"Wow," she repeated. "After we spoke I tried to think if there was anything I could remember that might help you. The only thing I came up with, and it's probably nothing, is four, five months ago, Adriana came with us on a trip to see my parents. We offered her the day off but she said she didn't need it, just in case Donald and I wanted to go out to dinner she'd be available to babysit."

I said, "Your parents couldn't baby-sit?"

"Of course they could. I sensed that Adriana wanted to come along so I said sure. My mother had cooked dinner so we stayed in. When Adriana heard that, she asked if we minded if *she* went out. To meet a friend for dinner. I know I told you over the phone that she didn't have friends but I was thinking of down here and the L.A. thing slipped my mind. Anyway, we said sure, go have fun. She made a call and soon after someone picked her up and she was gone for a

couple of hours. Now I'm wondering if
her real reason for tagging along was
she'd planned on a date."

Milo said, "A man picked her up?"

"No idea, all I can tell you is it was a
red car and the only reason I remember
that was the color shined through the
lace curtains over the picture window. I
do remember thinking, *Pretty flashy for
Adriana, maybe she's got a secret boyfriend.* But then she never went out
again. And I mean never."

I said, "What was her mood when
she returned?"

"Normal," she said. "Not upset, not
ecstatic. She was always kind of quiet.
To tell the truth, I wasn't paying attention because I was exhausted and
dreading two more hours on the freeway. Donald had been on call and he
was just zonked out and Adriana didn't
have a license. So I was stuck with the
driving."

"You did a great job," said a voice
from the doorway.

Since being photographed with his
daughter, Donald Chang had shaved
his head and grown a drooping mus-

tache. Broad-shouldered and slim-hipped, he had taut skin and bright black eyes. I revised my age estimate a few years downward.

We shook hands. His skin barely touched mine. Surgeon's caution. I'd anticipated that and was careful not to squeeze. Milo's touch was even lighter, a bare graze of fingertips. Courtesy of all those years living with Rick, whose name for the policy was "Don't scratch the Stradivarius."

Donald Chang sat next to his wife, placed a hand on her knee.

"Terrible about Adriana," he said. "She was a really nice person. Not the most social person, but I don't mean that in a weird way. I just never saw her desirous of any prolonged interaction with anyone but May."

Lilly said, "Except for that time in Sherman Oaks."

"What time?"

"When we were with my folks and she went out?"

"Oh," said Donald. "That is true. But it never happened again, did it?"

She shook her head.

I said, "She enjoyed her time with May but wasn't much for adult conversation."

"I wouldn't imply immaturity from that," said Donald. "She was a serious person. But yes, she definitely preferred to be with May and the moment May was asleep, she'd retire to her room."

Lilly said, "Not to evade housework, during the day she managed to clean and straighten up beautifully. Even though that's not what she was originally hired for, the plan was to get a maid twice a week."

Donald said, "Adriana insisted it wasn't necessary, the place isn't big, she could handle everything. We offered to pay her whatever we were going to pay the maid but she refused. We didn't want to take advantage of her and insisted she get something extra. Finally, she agreed to an additional hundred dollars a week. Which was a huge bargain for us. So when she considered her day over and went into her room, that was fine."

Lilly said, "Right from the get-go, she was great with May, but we were careful anyway, installed hidden baby cams. Watching the recordings reassured us. She couldn't have been more patient or loving or attentive."

Milo said, "Do you have the recordings?"

"Sorry, everything was uploaded to my computer at work and once I was confident Adriana was okay, I deleted the file and got rid of the system."

Donald said, "We removed the cameras when Adriana was out walking May. We didn't want her discovering them, thinking we hadn't trusted her. Though, of course, we hadn't. Trust needs to be earned."

I said, "And Adriana earned it."

"In spades," said Lilly. "She was a gem."

Same term Susan Van Dyne had used.

Donald said, "For someone like that to be murdered is astonishing. Do you have any idea who did it?"

"Not yet, Doctor," said Milo. "What else can you tell me about her?"

Donald turned to his wife. She shook her head.

I said, "Where did she sleep?"

"In the spare bedroom."

"Could we see it?"

"There's nothing of hers left in there, it's all the current nanny's stuff and she's sleeping in there."

"How's the new nanny working out?"

"She's nice," said Lilly.

I said, "But no Adriana."

"Corinne's pleasant, May seems to be attaching to her. But Adriana had something special. A real kid person."

Donald said, "Corinne's also not much for cleaning, now we do bring a maid in once a week."

I said, "Did Adriana talk about herself?"

"Not really," said Lilly. "She wasn't rude but she had a way of . . . I guess *deflecting* would be the right word."

"How so?"

"With ambiguous answers, then changing the subject. 'Oops, there's a stain on the counter,' and she'd get busy cleaning. I wondered if her personal history was painful, maybe a past relationship that had hurt her."

Donald stared at her. "Really?"

"Yes, darling."

He said, "I always thought she was just shy. What specific evidence of being hurt did you pick up?"

She smiled. "No evidence at all, it was just a feeling."

I said, "Did you pick up signs of her worrying about anything?"

Lilly thought. "Like depression?"

"Depression, anxiety, or just plain worry."

"No, I couldn't say that, she wasn't moody at all. Just the opposite, she was even-tempered, never raised her voice. I just felt she wanted her privacy and I respected that."

"Unemotional," said Milo.

"No, I wouldn't say that, either. Her default mood was . . . *even* is the best word I can come up with. Going through her day, pleasant, never complaining. Once in a while—infrequently—I'd catch her with a remote look on her face. Like she was remembering something troubling. But, honestly, it was nothing dramatic."

I said, "She lost a fiancé to a farm accident."

"Oh, my. Well, that could be it, then."

Donald put his arm around Lilly's shoulder. "Honey, you're an emotional detective. I'm impressed."

A beep sounded on the monitor. Both Changs turned to the machine.

Silence.

"Back to sleep," said Donald, crossing his fingers.

Lilly said, "That's really all I can tell you about Adriana. Would you like to collect her belongings?"

Donald said, "So to speak."

Milo said, "Not much in the way of worldly possessions?"

"Let's put it this way, guys. Everything fit into two boxes and one of them's small. That's not much of a life, is it?"

CHAPTER
22

Donald Chang took us down in the elevator to a parking garage filled with vehicles save for a section cordoned by a mesh gate. Behind the mesh was a wall lined with storage lockers.

Chang unlocked the gate and one of the lockers and stood back. "The two in front are Adriana's, everything else is our stuff."

Milo drew out a cardboard wardrobe and a carton of the same material, around two feet square. Both boxes had been sealed cleanly with packing tape and neatly labeled *Adriana Betts's Belongings.*

Chang said, "Can't tell you what's in there, Lilly packed. Do you want to go upstairs to look at them?"

"Thanks, but we'll take them back to L.A."

"Forensic procedure and all that? Makes sense. Good luck, guys."

Milo gave him a card. "In case you or your wife remember something."

Chang tugged a mustache end. "I don't want to demean the dead but my opinion is Adriana was a bit odder than you just heard from Lilly."

"How so, Dr. Chang?"

"My wife sees the good in everyone, puts a gloss on everything. The way I perceived Adriana she was a total loner, no life at all other than caring for May and cleaning like a demon."

I said, "Except for that one time the red car picked her up."

"Yes, that would be the exception, but outliers don't necessarily say much, do they?"

Milo said, "When she got back from the date she looked okay."

"Nothing stood out but bear in mind that neither of us was psychoanalyzing Adriana, our priority was that May stay calm during the drive home."

Another mustache tug. "I certainly don't want to put Adriana down just because she stuck to herself, lots of the people I worked with in computer sciences at Yale were like that. And I'm not complaining about her work, as Lilly said Adriana was a dream employee, great with May. But once in a while, I wondered about her."

"Wondered about what?"

"Her being too good to be true. Because I've observed people like that— the ones who come across totally dedicated to the job, single-minded, no outside life. Sometimes they're fine but other times they end up cracking. I've seen it on high-pressure wards, your saintly types can turn out to be horrid."

I'd learned the same lesson working my first job as a psychologist: the plastic bubble unit on the Western Peds cancer ward where I finally figured out the most important question to ask prospective hires: *What do you do for fun?*

Milo said, "So you were waiting for the shoe to fall, huh?"

"No, I'm not saying that, Lieutenant. Not even close, I liked Adriana, was pleased with the order she brought to our lives. I'm just a curious person." He smiled. "Maybe overly analytic. I didn't want to say any of this in front of Lilly. She was totally enamored of Adriana, hearing about the murder was pretty traumatic for her. I know she looked fine to you but two hours ago she was sobbing her heart out. It's an especially soft heart, my wife likes to believe in happy endings."

I said, "You're a bit more discriminating."

"Maybe I'm just a distrustful bastard by nature, but when Adriana flaked on us—what we thought was flaking—Lilly was surprised but I wasn't."

Milo said, "You figured something stressed her out."

"I figured she was like everyone else: Something better comes up, you bail." Chang smiled again, wider but no warmer. "That's a California thing, right?"

◆

We placed the boxes in the back of the unmarked and headed back to L.A.

Milo swerved into the carpool lane and kept up a steady eighty-five per, jutting his head forward, as if personally cutting through wind resistance.

At Del Mar, he said, "Adriana goes on her one and only date with someone in a red car. So maybe the SUV little Heather saw isn't relevant. Hell, what's to say any of it's relevant?"

I said, "Something drew Adriana to that park."

"Something drew her to L.A., amigo. I'd say a better gig but bailing on the Changs for extra dough doesn't sound in character."

"A friend in need might have lured her. Someone with a baby."

"It was Mama in a red car, not a date?"

"Mama in a red car who called Adriana for help because something scared her. If those fears were justified, Adriana could have lost her life because she got too close to the situation."

"Bad Daddy."

"Major-league monster Daddy who murdered the mother of his child and the child, held on to the baby's skeleton as a psychopathic trophy. That ended when he read about the bones in Holly Ruche's backyard and decided to ditch his collection nearby. Mom had already been taken care of and Adriana, suspicious after her friend disappeared, followed him. Unfortunately, he spotted her."

He drove for a while. "Charming scenario. Too bad I've got nada to back any of it up."

"You've got Adriana's personal effects."

"There was anything juicy in those boxes, the Changs—being trained observers—would've noticed and said something."

"That's assuming they snooped."

"Everyone snoops, Alex."

"Not busy people."

"Okay, fine. I'll burn some incense to the Evidence Gods, pray a hot lead shows up in the boxes. I was a less pro-*fessional* detective, I'd pull into the next truck stop and do an impromptu forensic."

"Everything goes straight to the lab?"

"Hell, no," he said. "Finders keepers, but I'm doing it by the book."

We got off the freeway at Santa Monica Boulevard at 1:36 a.m. For all its rep as a party town, most of L.A. closes down early and the streets were dark, hazy, and empty. That can stimulate the creepers and the crawlers but Milo's police radio was calm and back at the station the big detective room was nearly deserted, every interview room empty.

He used the same room where Helene Johanson had cried, dragged in an additional table and created a work space. Spraying the surfaces with disinfectant, he gloved up, used a box cutter to slit the wardrobe open, emptied the contents.

Clothing. More clothing. A peer at the bottom evoked a disgusted head shake. He examined the garments anyway.

A couple more bland dresses similar to the one Adriana Betts had died in, two pairs of no-nonsense jeans, seven nondescript blouses, cotton undergarments, T-shirts, a pair of sneakers, black flats, cheap plastic sunglasses.

"No naughty secret-life duds, amigo." He sniffed the garments. "No secret-life perfume, either. Adriana, you wild and crazy kid." Shutting his eyes for several moments as if meditating, he opened them, repacked the clothes, sealed the box and filled out a lab tag.

The smaller box yielded a hairbrush, a toothbrush, antacid, acetaminophen, a blue bandanna, and more garments: two pairs of walking shorts and a wad of white T-shirts. Milo was about to put everything back when he stopped and hefted the shirts.

"Too heavy." Running his hands over each tee, he extracted a shirt from the middle of the stack and unfolded. Inside was a brown leatherette album around six inches square, fastened by a brass key clasp.

"Looky here, Dear Diary." He pressed his palms together prayerfully. "Our Father Who Art in Heaven, grant me something evidentiary and I'll attend Mass next Sunday for the first time in You know how long."

The clasp sprang free with a finger-tap. A pulse in his neck throbbed as he opened the book.

No diary notations, no prose of any sort. Three cardboard pages held photographs moored by clear plastic bands.

The first page was of a teenage Adriana Betts with a boy her age. Bubbly cursive read:

Dwayne and Me. Happy Times.

Dwayne Hightower had been a huge kid, easily six six, three hundred, with a side-of-beef upper body and thick, short, hairless limbs. His face was a pink pie under coppery curls, his smile wide and open as the prairie. He and Adriana had posed in front of hay bales, barns, a brick-faced building, and a green John Deere tractor with wheels as tall as Adriana. In each shot, Hightower's heavy arm rested lightly on Adriana's shoulder. Her head reached his elbow. She clung to his biceps. Their

smiles were a match in terms of inno-
cence and wattage.

The following page began with more
of the same but ended with shots from
Dwayne Hightower's funeral. Adriana in
a black dress, her hair tied back severely. Wearing the cheap sunglasses
from the wardrobe.

The final page was all group shots:
Adriana and several other young adults
in front of a red-brick church. The edi-
fice that had backdropped her and
Dwayne. Had they planned to wed
there?

Not a single tattoo, body pierce, or
edgy hairdo in sight. These pictures
could've dated from the fifties. Heart-
land America, unaffected by fad or fashion.

In some of the shots, a portly white-
haired man in his sixties wearing a suit
and tie stood to the left of the group.

In most of the pictures, Adriana,
though not particularly tall, had positioned herself at the back. Not so in the
last three, where she posed front-cen-
ter, next to the same person.

Young black woman with short,

straightened hair and a heart-shaped face. Extremely pretty and graceful despite a drab smock that could've come out of Adriana's closet.

A single chocolate dot in a sea of vanilla.

The bones in the park had yielded African American maternal DNA.

I didn't need to say anything. Milo muttered, "Maybe." Then he pointed to the older man in the suit. "Got to be the pastor, whatever his name is."

"Reverend Goleman," I said. "Life Tabernacle Church of the Fields."

He turned to me. "You memorize everything?"

"Just what I think might be important."

"You figured the church might be important? Why didn't you say so?"

"There's *might* and there's *is*," I said. "No lead before its time."

"You and that party wine from when we were kids—the Orson Welles thing."

"Paul Masson."

"Now you're showing off."

I reexamined the photos that included the black woman. "Adriana stands nearer to her than she does to anyone else. So let's assume a close relationship."

"The pal in the red car?"

"What we've heard about Adriana says she had a moral compass, would never have bailed on the Changs without a good reason. Helping a good friend might qualify."

"If she was murdered because she knew too much, why dump the bones near her and risk the association?"

"He's a confident guy."

"Talk about a poor choice for your baby's daddy. And that leads me back to the problem I had before. Child abuse, even murder, something rage-related, happens all the time. But I'm still having trouble seeing anyone, even a psychopath, taking the time to clean and wax his own offspring's bones then tossing them like trash."

I have no trouble seeing anything and that turns some nights hellish. I said, "You're probably right. The first step is I.D.'ing this woman."

He looked at his watch. Close to three a.m. "Too early to rouse Reverend Goleman in Idaho." Separating the photo album from the cartons, he dropped it into an evidence bag. We carried both boxes to the big D-room, where he secured them in a locker. Returning to his office, he wrote an email to the crime lab. Leaning back in his chair, he yawned. "Go home, sleep late, kiss Robin and pet the pooch. Have a nice breakfast tomorrow morning."

"You're not going home."

"There's a sleeping room near the holding cells. I may just bunk out so I can be ready to phone Boise in four hours. Hopefully a devout fellow like the Rev will be cooperative."

"Speaking of devout," I said, "where will you be attending Sunday Mass?"

"What? Oh, that. I said evidentiary, not suggestive."

"Driving a tough bargain with the Almighty?"

"He wouldn't respect me otherwise."

CHAPTER

23

I slipped into bed just after three thirty a.m., careful not to rouse Robin.

She rolled toward me, wrapped her arms around my neck, murmured, "Morning."

"Not enough morning. Go back to sleep."

One of her eyes opened. "Anything new?"

"I'll tell you about it when we wake up."

"We're awake now." She propped herself up.

I gave her a rundown.

She said, "Mothers and babies," sighed and slid away from me, was breathing evenly within seconds. Sometimes she talks in her sleep when she's upset. This time she remained silent until daybreak. I knew because I watched her for a long time.

An internal prompt woke me at seven a.m. I should've been wiped out; instead I was hyped, eager to know what Milo had learned from the Right Reverend Goleman. I waited for him to call and when he hadn't by seven thirty, I took a robotic run, showered, shaved, brought coffee out to Robin in her studio.

No saw buzz or hammer percussion as I approached. Maybe she'd dozed less soundly than I'd thought, didn't trust herself with sharp things.

She was sitting on her couch, Blanche a little blond pillow under her arm, studying a beautiful book showcasing a collection of vintage guitars. One man's monomania. I'd bought it for her last Christmas.

I said, "Inspiration?"

"Aesthetics. You get any decent sleep?"

"Sure," I lied.

"Hear from Big Guy?"

"Not yet."

I held out the mug. She said, "Let's go outside," and we sat near the pond, tossing pellets to the koi and drinking coffee and not saying a thing.

Eleven minutes of uneasy serenity before I heard from Big Guy.

For someone who hadn't slept at all, Milo sounded chipper.

"The bad news: Reverend Goleman is away from the office. The good news: He's right here in SoCal, attending a convention in Fullerton. We're meeting at my office at noon."

"He give you the name of Adriana's friend?"

"Yes," he said, "but it's complicated. See you when the sun's high?"

"Wouldn't miss it."

I arrived a few minutes early, encountered Milo as he was locking up his office. "According to Goleman, the friend is Qeesha D'Embo. Unfortunately, that doesn't match anything in the data-bases."

"Alias? She was hiding something?"

"Maybe—this looks like our clergy-type."

A tall rotund man accompanied by a smallish female officer headed our way.

Milo said, "I'll take it from here, Offi-cer," and shook Goleman's hand. Gole-man's suit was plaid, deep blue with a pale pink crosshatch. His white hair was shorter than in the church photos, cropped nearly to the skin at the sides, bristly and uncooperative on top. Heavy build but hard-fat, no jiggle when he moved. One of those thick sturdy men built for hours behind the plow.

"Thanks for meeting with me, Rever-end."

"Of course," said Goleman. His voice was deep and mellow, easy-listening at sermon time. He reached out to grip my hand. His paw was padded and cal-lused, just firm enough to be sociable.

Milo led him to the same interview room, minus the extra table.

When Goleman sat, he overwhelmed

the chair. He tugged up his trousers, revealed high-laced work boots.

"Something to drink, Reverend?"

Goleman patted his belly. "No thanks,
Lieutenant, I had breakfast at the hotel
including way too much coffee. Big buf-
fet and I overdid it with the huevos ran-
cheros. As usual."

Milo said, "Know what you mean."

Goleman smiled faintly. "It's tough for
us big guys with healthy appetites. I
don't even make resolutions anymore
because I'm weary—and wary—of failing my Savior." He began crossing a
leg, changed his mind, planted his foot
back on the linoleum. "I'm in despair
over Adriana. She was a wonderful girl,
not a mean bone in her body. I say that
as more than her pastor. I knew her
personally. She dated my nephew."

"Dwayne."

Goleman's lips folded inward. "You
know about Dwayne."

"He came up in the course of trying
to learn about Adriana."

"Terrible, terrible thing," said Goleman. "Farmwork's always dangerous
but when it actually happens . . . I have

no doubt Dwayne and Adriana would've married and raised wonderful, warm-hearted children." His voice caught. "Now it's Adriana we're mourning. Do you have any idea who did this?"

"No, Reverend."

"This is the kind of ordeal that tests one's faith and I'm not going to tell you I passed with flying colors. Because when I heard about Adriana from her sister—wanting me to conduct the ser-vice—I couldn't dredge up an ounce of faith."

Milo said, "Bad stuff can do that, Reverend."

"Oh, it can, Lieutenant. But that's the point of faith, isn't it? Believing when everything's rolling along hunky-dory is no challenge." Goleman massaged double chins. "And now you've implied Qeesha might be in trouble."

"I didn't find any record of any Qee-sha D'Embo."

"I'm not surprised," said Goleman.

"You figured it for an alias?"

"Qeesha was always quite secretive, Lieutenant, and given her circumstances I can't say I blamed her. She came to us two years ago as part of a group of fire survivors, a conflagration in New Orleans. Poor, desperate people who'd survived Katrina only to see their homes go up in flames. Several churches in our city collaborated to take some of them in and we got Qeesha. She was a lovely girl. Hardworking when it came to church activities. And the fire's not all I was referring to as her circumstances. Not only had she lost her mother and her house, she was forced to run from someone who'd terrorized her."

"Terrorized her how?"

"Domestic violence," said Goleman. "One of those stalking situations. This fellow—she only referred to him by his first name, Clyde—had become ob-sessed with her, wouldn't take no for an answer. Mind you, I never heard this from Qeesha. Adriana told me after I voiced my concerns about Qeesha's reluctance to talk about her ordeal, sug-gested bottling everything up might not be the best idea, perhaps counseling would help. Adriana explained to me that Qeesha was dealing with more than the fire, was too overwhelmed to handle counseling."

I said, "Instead, she confided in Adriana."

"Adriana opened her home to Qeesha, they grew close very quickly. Inseparable, really, it was rare to see one without the other, Adriana was our best preschool teacher and Qeesha served as her aide. They were terrific with the little ones. Then one day Qeesha didn't arrive with Adriana and Adriana told me she'd moved to California."

"Running from Clyde?"

"I don't know, Lieutenant. Adriana seemed to be surprised herself. Apparently, Qeesha had moved out in the middle of the night without explanation."

Same thing Adriana had done with the Changs. "How long ago was this?"

"Qeesha was only with us for a short while—I'd say a couple of years ago, give or take."

"Reverend," said Milo, "when a homicide occurs, we need to ask all sorts of questions. You just said Adriana and Qeesha grew inseparable. Could there have been more than friendship?"

"Were they lovers?" said Goleman. "Hmm, never considered that. There were certainly no signs. And we do have gay people in our church, there wouldn't be any official stigma. Though I'm sure some of our parishioners might look askance. But no, I never saw that. Not that I'm an expert."

"What kind of church is it?"

"Nondenominational, fairly fundamentalist in terms of how we read Scripture. And yes, I do have my personal views on homosexuality but I keep them to myself because our emphasis is on faith, prayer, careful study of both Testaments with an emphasis on textual exegesis, and, most important, good works. We're a community of doers."

"Charity," said Milo.

"Charity implies one person doing a favor for another, Lieutenant. Our view is that the giver gets as much out of the gift as the taker. I'm sure that sounds self-righteous but in practice it works out quite well. All of our members tithe and most everyone takes on some kind of good work. We're not a wealthy tab-

ernacle but we do our best to provide
shelter and sustenance to the needy."

Milo nodded. "Back to Clyde, if we
might?"

Goleman said, "The only thing I can
tell you other than his first name—and I
must say I found it appalling—is that
he's a police officer."

"From New Orleans."

"Adriana never specified but I assumed that to be the case. She told me
that contributed to Qeesha's fear: Clyde
was a law officer, she felt he could get
away with anything."

"Was there any indication Clyde had
located Qeesha?"

"No, sir," said Goleman. "May I assume from your questions that you believe she's also been a victim?"

"The investigation has just begun so
we don't believe anything, Reverend.
Did Qeesha have a vehicle?"

"No, she—all the New Orleans people—arrived with virtually nothing."

"Did Adriana drive?"

"Of course. Why do you ask?"

"Because she didn't drive in California."

"Really," said Goleman.

"Really."

"Well, I can't explain that, Lieutenant. What she drove in Boise was Dwayne's truck. His parents—my sister and brother-in-law—insisted Adriana have it. But when she left to take the job in Portland, she insisted on returning it to Nancy and Tom and left on Greyhound. Truth is, my sister never wanted to see the truck again. Dwayne's high school sticker was still on the rear window and Adriana hadn't cleaned out his personal effects from the glove compartment. But Adriana insisted."

I said, "Why'd Adriana leave Boise?"

"She never told me," said Goleman. "I assumed she'd had enough."

"Of what?"

"Grief, memories. A life that needed changing."

CHAPTER
24

Milo and Goleman exchanged cards and Goleman extracted a promise from Milo to let him know "once you've solved it."

As we watched him barrel away, Milo said, "Optimism of the righteous." We returned to his office, where he called Delano Hardy's home number in Ladera Heights.

Milo's initial partner at West L.A., Hardy had retired a few months ago. The department's logic back then was a pairing of outsiders: gay D with black D. The partnership had worked well until Del's wife pressured him not to spend his days with "someone like that."

That same wife answered.

"Martha, it's Milo. Del around?"

"Milo, how nice." Her voice was Karo syrup. "He's out gardening. How've *you* been doing?"

"Great, Martha."

"Well, that's *good.* Everything just coasting *along*?"

"The usual, Martha."

"That's really good, Milo. Hold on."

Del came on. "What's the occasion?"

"High intrigue in New Orleans. You garden?"

"Yeah, right. I'm weeding her flower beds, big-time fun," said Hardy. "The old country, huh?" He'd moved to California as a teen but had grown up in one of the parishes swept away by Katrina. The division had passed around the hat for some of his relatives. I kicked in a couple hundred bucks, received a personal call from Del. I'm sure he did the same in response to Milo's thousand-dollar donation.

"So what can I help you with, Big Guy?"

Milo explained about Qeesha D'Embo and a scary cop named Clyde.

Hardy said, "Only connection I might conceivably still have is Uncle Ray—not my real uncle, my godfather Ray Lhermitte, did patrol with Daddy, worked his way up to captain. But he's a lot older than us kids, Milo. For all I know he's passed."

"This point, I'll take anything, D.H. Got a number for him?"

"Hold on, I'll go find it. You want, I can prime the pump by calling him first."

"Thanks."

"I should be thanking you," said Hardy.

"For what?"

"Letting me pretend I'm half useful. This retirement business is like dying on your feet."

Eighteen minutes later, a call came in from Commander Raymond Delongpre Lhermitte (Retired). In a bass voice that alternated between rasp and molasses, Lhermitte said, "Tell me why you need this, son."

Milo obliged.

"Okay," said Lhermitte. "You present

your case well. Problem is, we've been dealing with some pretty bad corruption issues here. Hurricane agitated it, the waters are still roiling, and even though I'm off the job I have no desire to stir up more."

"Me neither, sir."

"But you're working a whodunit so to hell with anything else."

"That's true."

"As it should be," said Lhermitte. "Fact is, I shouldn't even care, I'm growing orchids and shooting nutria for sport, but I can't break the bonds. To the department as well as to my beautiful, crazy city. Never found a better place to live but sometimes it seems we've irritated the Almighty."

"Gotta be rough," said Milo.

"So," said Lhermitte, "this girl was one of the fire survivors? That was a bad one, started in a hotel and took down an entire block of old wood buildings. What was that name again?"

"Qeesha D'Embo."

"Sounds African-phony to me, son. No, afraid I'm not aware of anyone by that name."

"Wouldn't expect you to know every-one, sir."

"I know a lot of people," said Lher-mitte. "Including Clyde Bordelon."

"A cop?"

"Unfortunately, son. Ugly piece of psychology, I'd like to think the regs we got in place now he'd never have gotten hired. But who knows, nothing's per-fect."

"He's still on the force?"

"No, he's lying under dirt. Shot with his own poorly maintained service gun in the backyard of his own poorly main-tained house."

"When?"

"Coupla years ago. Still an open case."

"Any suspects?"

"Too many suspects, son. Nasty indi-vidual that he was."

"What kind of nasty?"

"Clyde was what's known as an indi-vidual of loose morals. By that I don't mean transgressions of a sexual nature, though if you told me Clyde had con-gress with a herd of cocaine-blinded goats I wouldn't gasp in amazement because bottom line, the man was amoral, rules just didn't apply to him. But the sins the *department* suspected were of a monetary nature: payoffs, bribes, hijacking cigarette and liquor trucks, consorting with the criminal element on a variety of projects. So you can see what I mean about a plethora of suspects."

"Any of them stand out?"

"A girl," said Lhermitte. "A dancer, not a church-girl. But her name wasn't Qeesha, it was Charlene Rae Chambers."

"By dancer—"

"I mean stripper. Her stage name was CoCo. Like the dress designer. Pretty little thing, not one of ours, she was a Yankee, came up from somewhere in New York to work the pole at the Deuces Wild. One of Clyde's favorite after-hour spots. After she started there it became his only after-hour spot."

"Obsessed?"

"You could say that."

"Why was she the prime?" said Milo.

"Because she was the last person seen with Clyde when he was alive and talk was he'd stalked her, wouldn't take no for an answer. Despite her claim of being bothered, witnesses have her getting into his car that night and riding away. It took a while for our detectives to talk to her. So many suspects and all. By the time they reached her it was too late for a GSR and she had an alibi. Clyde took her straight home, she showered and slept for eight hours. Her roommate, another dancer, verified it."

"Not exactly ironclad."

"Oh, there's a good chance she did it," said Lhermitte. "Or had someone else do it for her. Matter of fact, I'd bet on her being responsible. Two days after she was interviewed, she was gone, no forwarding."

"I'd like to send you a picture of Qee-sha—"

"Then you'd have to do it by what my grand-babies call snail mail. Got no computer, no fax machine, only one phone in the house, a rotary, as old as me, made of Bakelite. Tell you what, though, I'll make a call and see if someone still on the job can help you."

"Appreciate it, sir. Did Charlene actually live in the fire zone?"

"Don't know if she did or she didn't," said Lhermitte. "I'll ask about that, too."

"Thank you, sir."

"Pleasure's all mine."

By the time a New Orleans detective named Mark Montecino had emailed asking for Milo's fax number, Milo had already pulled up two NCIC mug shots of Charlene Rae Chambers, female black, brown and brown, five four, one oh two. A DOB that would make her twenty-seven.

Her record was unimpressive: five-year-old bust for soliciting prostitution, four-year-old bust for battery on a peace officer, both filed at a precinct in Brooklyn. Dismissal on the first, four days in jail for the second.

"Couldn't have been heavy-duty battery," he said.

Even disheveled and wild-eyed with fright, Charlene Chambers had photographed pretty.

I said, "She looks scared."

"That she does."

His fax beeped. Out slid a solicitation mug shot from New Orleans. Now she was beautiful and more composed than during her previous arrests. On the paper Mark Montecino had written, *She didn't live near the fire.*

Milo ran her through the data banks. She'd never paid taxes or registered for Social Security in New York, Louisiana, Idaho, or California. No driver's license, no registered vehicle, red or otherwise.

"Running away," he said, "but not because she was scared of Clyde. She was worried she'd be collared for his murder. Church folk in Idaho were charitable so she took advantage. An opportunity came up here in L.A., and she was gone."

I said, "I know it's a stereotype but New Orleans and voodoo aren't strangers and waxy bones sounds like something that could be part of a hex."

"Let's find out," he said, turning back to his screen. "First time in a long time *I'm* not feeling hexed."

CHAPTER
25

Websites on New Orleans voodoo pulled up nothing about waxed infant skeletons. The closest match was a Day of the Dead offering to the ancestral spirit Gede that sometimes included bones.

Milo looked up the date of the rite. "November first. Months off."

I said, "People improvise."

"Some local whack concocted his own private sacrifice?"

"Making it up's a lot easier and more lucrative than studying theology, Big

Guy. Do-it-yourself religion's the SoCal way."

"Another Charlie Manson. Wonderful."

"To a devout woman like Adriana, black-arts worship would've been the worst kind of heresy. But Qeesha could have been attracted to an occult group because it reminded her of her time in New Orleans. If it started to bother her and she wanted out and told Adriana about it, I'm betting Adriana would've jumped at helping her."

"It was Qeesha picking her up in that red car."

"Doesn't sound as if unregistered wheels would be a problem for Qeesha."

"Coupla old friends trying to escape the zombie horde."

I said, "What if Qeesha's involvement with the horde included getting pregnant? With Daddy being a loony warlock who ended up killing her and the baby? Adriana went looking for them, paid for her loyalty."

"Adriana bailed on the Changs three months ago but she got shot a few days ago. What happened during the interim, Alex? Are we talking about a patient bunch of freaks? Because there's no evidence she was confined. Zero signs of abuse on her body and those lig marks were relatively fresh."

"Maybe she was careful, snooping around without showing herself. Until she did."

He rubbed his face. "A picture just flashed in my head."

"Black-robed ghouls chanting ominously in the moonlight?"

"You're getting a little scary, dude."

"You don't know?"

"Know what?"

"Ph.D.'s in psych," I said. "The state grants us a license to mind-read."

"What am I thinking now?"

"You're back in Bizarro World with no damn leads."

"Oh, man," he said. "This case ever closes, we're definitely playing the stock market."

His desk phone jangled.

Dr. Clarice Jernigan said, "New lab result. Your victim Adriana Betts was dosed up before she was shot. Nothing

illegal, her blood showed high concen-
trations of diphenhydramine. Your basic
first-generation antihistamine, what they
put in Benadryl."

"How much is high, Doc?"

"Not a lethal dosage but enough to
sedate her profoundly or put her out
completely."

"She was knocked out first, then
shot."

"That's the sequence, Milo. To me it
says a calculated offender operating in
a highly structured manner. Seeing as
her murder is probably related to that
infant skeleton, we're obviously dealing
with someone who operates on a different psychiatric plane. Have you spoken to Delaware recently?"

I said, "Right here, Clarice."

"Hi, Alex. I'm thinking a sociopath
with some looseness of thought around
the edges, or someone downright deranged who manages to keep his crazi-
ness under wraps. Not necessarily
schizophrenic but maybe an isolated
paranoid delusion. Make sense?"

"It does, Clarice. I'm also wondering

if we've got a killer who lacks physical strength."

"He uses a downer to incapacitate her? Sure, why not? What's your take on the baby?"

"Beyond cruel."

"Sorry I asked."

After she hung up, Milo said, "Lack of physical strength. As in female?"

"Ray Lhermitte pegs Qeesha as a likely murderer. What if she acquired a taste for power and became a cult queen?"

"No warlock," he said, "a nasty little witch. *That's* turning it a whole new way. You're saying she killed Adriana? What's the motive? And why bring Adriana back to L.A. to do it?"

"Could've been something religious," I said. "Uncomfortable truths about the cult. Adriana was outraged, threatened to go to the cops. That could explain the diphenhydramine. A relatively humane way to eliminate a former friend."

"Then why shoot her in the head? Why not just poison her straight out?"

I had no answer for that.

He said, "Qeesha as Devil Spawn. We keep jumping around like frogs on a griddle. Sit around long enough, we can probably come up with another hundred scenarios."

He stood, hitched his trousers. "One way or the other, I need to look for Ms. D'Embo aka Chambers aka God-Knows-Who-Else."

I said, "If she's driving unregistered wheels she could wrongly assume that's another layer of security."

"So focus on the car, maybe it's stolen."

"Starting with people who frequent the park."

"And there's restricted parking at night, so check for citations. Yeah, I like it, it's damn close to normal police work."

Moe Reed and Sean Binchy reported nothing fruitful from the canvass of park employees, patrons, and nearby residents. Both would re-inquire about red cars and dark SUVs.

While Milo checked the grand theft

auto file I stepped into the hall and phoned Holly Ruche.

She said, "I hope you're not mad at me. For canceling."

"I'm sure you had a good reason."

"I—I'll explain when I come in. If you'll take me."

"No problem."

"Just like that? Do you have time to-morrow?"

I checked my book. "Eleven a.m. works."

"Wow," she said. "You're not that busy, huh?"

"Looking forward to seeing you, Holly."

"I'm so sorry. That was bratty."

"How's the house going?"

"The house?"

"Remodeling."

"Oh," she said. "Nothing's really hap-pening . . . I'll tell you everything tomor-row. Eleven, right?"

"Right."

"Thanks again, Dr. Delaware. You've been incredibly tolerant."

◆

I returned to Milo's office. He said, "No vehicles were ticketed that night. These are the theft stats, not as bad as I expected."

He showed me his notes. Sixteen thousand GTAs in the city of L.A. over the past year. The three-month total was three thousand, eight hundred fifty-four. Of those, six hundred thirty-three were red. Westside red GTAs numbered twenty-eight. Ten of those had been recovered.

Milo got on the phone and questioned the detectives assigned to the eighteen open cases. Seven were suspected insurance scams, all from a section of Pico-Robertson, with the reporting individuals members of a small-time Ukrainian gang. Of the remaining eleven cars, one was a four-hundred-thousand-dollar Ferrari lifted from the Palisades, the other a comparably priced Lamborghini taken in Holmby Hills, both deemed improbable choices for the car Lilly Chang had seen because of their conspicuousness and the engine noise they'd generate.

The D handling the exotics was a

woman named Loretta Thayer. She said, "If your witness didn't hear a roar that set off the Richter scale it wasn't one of those. Same for a red Porsche Turbo I just picked up that's not in the files yet."

Milo said, "Spate of red hotwheel heists?"

"Interesting, no?" said Thayer. "My hunch is they're going to the same collector overseas, probably Asia or the Mideast."

"Toys for some oil sheik's twelve-year-old to roll around the desert in."

"At that age," said Thayer, "I was happy to have roller skates."

Milo emailed photos of Charlene Chambers/Qeesha D'Embo to Thayer and two other detectives, asked them to show the images to their victims.

Thayer called back an hour later. "Sorry, no recognition."

"That was fast."

"Protect and serve, Lieutenant. It helps being on the Westside, everyone's got a computer or an iPhone, I reached them electronically."

No calls back from the other D's for

the next half hour. Milo worked on some
overdue files and I read abstracts of
psych articles on his computer.

He looked at his watch. "More I think
about it, more of a waste of time the
car angle seems. It could be unregistered but not stolen. Or Lilly Chang re-
members wrong and it wasn't even
red—hell, maybe it was a scooter. Or
an RV. Or a horse and buggy."

I said, "Power of positive thinking."

"Wanna hear positive? Time for
lunch."

"The usual?"

"No, I'm craving vegan. Just kidding."

We drove to a steak house a mile
west of the station, sawed through a
couple of T-bones, and drove back to
his office where he picked up replies
from the remaining auto theft detectives. None of their victims recognized
Qeesha but a D II named Doug Groot
said, "It's possible one of my victims
lied."

"Why do you think that?"

"The usual tells," said Groot. "Looking everywhere but *at* me, too quick on
the draw, like he'd rehearsed it. Also, he

just gave me a feeling from the beginning. The car was a nice one, BMW 5 series, all tricked out, only a couple of years old, low mileage. But he didn't seem that bugged about having it boosted. Made the right speech but no emotion—again, like he'd rehearsed."

"Insurance thing?" said Milo.

"He filed with his carrier the day after I interviewed him."

"When did it happen?"

"Nineteen months ago."

"What were the circumstances?"

"Taken from his driveway sometime during the night," said Groot. "It's not impossible, his building's got an open carport. But supposedly he'd left it locked with the security system set and I talked to the neighbors and no one heard any alarm go off. He seemed so hinky I actually ran a check on him. But he had no obvious ties to any scammers, no record of anything."

"What's this solid citizen's name?"

"Melvin Jaron Wedd, like getting married but two 'd's."

"This guy really twanged your antenna, huh?"

"You know what it's like, El Tee. Sometimes you get a feeling. Unfortunately none of mine led anywhere. The car's never shown up."

"Loretta said nice red wheels might be going to the Mideast."

"Two-year-old Bimmer's nice," said Groot, "but probably not nice enough for that. Mexico or Central America, maybe. For all I know it's being used to ferry around Zeta hit men."

"What line of work is Wedd in?"

"Something showbizzy. Can I ask what your curiosity is about the car and this Chambers woman?"

"She might be a really bad girl," said Milo. "Or a victim. Or neither and I'm spinning my wire wheels."

Groot chuckled. "The job as usual. You want to follow up with Wedd?"

"Might as well."

"Here's his info."

Milo copied, thanked Groot, clicked off. Seconds later, he'd pulled Melvin Jaron Wedd's driver's license.

Male white, thirty-seven, six two, one ninety, brown, brown, needs corrective lenses.

Wedd's photo showed him with a pink, squarish face, smallish eyes, thin lips, a dark spiky haircut. He'd posed in a black V-necked T-shirt. Black-framed glasses gave him the hipster-geek look of any other Westside guy working a Mac at a Starbucks table.

"Doesn't look like a warlock," said Milo.

I said, "More like Clark Kent at leisure."

He ran Wedd through the banks just in case something had popped up since Groot's search. No criminal record, a scatter of parking tickets, the most recent thirty months ago. All paid in a timely fashion.

Then he switched to the DMV files and said, "Well, looky here."

Wedd's new registered vehicle was a black Ford Explorer, purchased brand-new, three weeks after the theft of the red BMW. "Be interesting if he jacked it way up and stuck on fancy rims."

He shifted to the Web, called up an image of an Explorer enhanced that way, sent the picture to Heather Goldfeder, and asked if it resembled the SUV she'd seen.

Seconds later: *cud b cant say 4 sure how r u.*

He sent back a happy face emoticon.

Her instant response: *me 2 xoxoxo.*

◆

The landline and cell phone Groot had given for Wedd were unresponsive to Milo's calls. No message machine on either.

He said, "A fellow who likes his privacy. Let's invade it."

The address was an apartment west of Barrington and just north of Wilshire. Officially Brentwood, but not what you thought of when someone said Brentwood.

Quarter-hour drive from the station under the worst circumstances. Circumstances were favorable: i.e., Milo's leaden foot. We made it in eight.

CHAPTER

26

Back in the fifties, someone thought it was a nifty idea to erect a two-story box with the top floor cantilevered over a concrete carport, the entire structure slathered with pimply aqua stucco, the squat, expressionless face embellished by a five-foot starburst spray-painted gold and the proclamation *Dawn-Lite Apts* in that same gaudy tint.

Several decades later someone thought restoring the dingbat to its original glory was historical preservation.

As we pulled up to Melvin Jaron Wedd's building, a white-garbed painter was regilding the star, his compadre patching thin spots of aqua.

Milo said, "Misdemeanor, maybe a felony."

I said, "You don't like midcentury?"

"Depends on the century."

"Didn't know you were into architecture, Big Guy."

"Rick is. I imbibe through osmosis."

We got out and inspected the carport from which the BMW had been lifted. Six stalls, one occupied by a dusty brown Acura. No tenant names, not even a unit number. The mailbox at the foot of the grubby stairs that led up to the second story listed J. Wedd as residing in 3.

Each apartment was accessed through an open landing. Number 3 was ground-floor rear. Cheap vertical blinds blocked the single window. A dead plant in a terra-cotta-colored vinyl pot squatted near the door. So did several piles of junk mail. Milo pushed a button. The resulting buzzer sounded like flatulence.

No answer. He tried again. Rapped hard with detective-callused knuckles.

The door to the adjoining unit opened

and a dreadlocked head emerged, bleached-blond with dark roots. Matted strands trailed to a black-shirted shoulder. The face below the hair was bronze, seamed, craggy, hazed by three days of dark stubble. Sagging eyes were wary. A bass voice said, "Police, right?" and the eyes turned friendly.

Milo said, "Yes, sir."

"My brother's a cop." Six feet of sun-damaged sinew stepped out onto the landing. The black shirt was a body-conscious tee that said *Think: It's Not Illegal Yet.* Below that, baggy shorts printed with leaping dolphins ended at knees enlarged by random bumps. Bare feet sported ragged nails and more protrusions. Calcium deposits, your basic surfer knots.

He looked around thirty-five, accounting for sun damage. A thumb hooked toward Melvin Jaron Wedd's door. "He do something?"

"We're here to talk to him."

"He hasn't been here for days."

"Any idea where he's gone?"

"He's gone all the time. Obviously, he's got somewhere else to crash."

"When's the last time you saw him, Mister . . ."

"Robert Sommers." Cornrow grinned crookedly, as if his name provided unceasing amusement. "The last time was . . . a couple of weeks ago? I'm not good with time. Except for the tide tables."

"Chasing waves?" said Milo.

"Whenever I can," said Sommers.

"Follow the big ones?"

Sommers grinned. "Not to Peahi or anything like that, I'm only Laird Hamilton in my dreams. My folks have a place in Malibu, sometimes I bunk down with them." Wider grin. "Dump some laundry, too. Mom claims she still misses me."

"Nice to have that kind of freedom."

"I'm a Web designer so I'm flexible."

"We heard Wedd does something in show business."

Sommers huffed. "That could mean he's part of a catering crew."

"How long have you been living next to him?"

"I've been here around three years, he moved in later, maybe two, two and a half. I don't have problems with him, he keeps to himself. Not your friendly type, though. He'll never be the first to say hi and when he answers it's like he's being forced to do it. Guess that makes him your basic loner. My brother says that can be a danger sign but I can't say anything weird goes on here."

Milo said, "Your brother a detective?"

"Malibu Sheriff, rides a cruiser up and down PCH. One time he stopped me, made like he was going to ticket me. Revenge for all those times I kicked his ass."

Milo said, "You got a warning instead."

Sommers flexed a muscle and laughed. "More like I warned him."

"Do you recall when Mr. Wedd's car was stolen?"

"So that's what you're here about. What, you recovered it?"

"Not yet."

"Oh," said Sommers. "That little Bimmer was sweet, I wouldn't replace it with a Monstro-mobile."

"The Explorer."

"Explorer all ghettoed up with crazy wheels, black paint job, black windows."

"What kind of crazy wheels?" said Milo.

"Big," said Sommers, drawing a wide circle with his hands. "Chromed, reversed, had to be serious cash. And the whole thing's jacked up. Maybe he's got hydraulics to lowride it, never seen him do it, but people get crazy with their cars."

"Big wheels, jacked and black," I said. "Pretty macho."

"My ex-girlfriend says you're secure in your masculinity, you don't need to pimp your wheels." Sommers laughed. "But maybe she was just making me feel good about my turdmobile."

"Brown Acura?"

"That's a nice way to put it," said Sommers. "Used to be my parents' cleaning lady's. She got a new one, I glommed El Crappo. You guys suspect Clark of a rip-off, like an insurance scam?"

"Clark?"

"He looks just like Clark Kent plus

dude's attitude is kind of . . . I guess you'd say self-righteous."

I said, "Takes himself seriously."

"Jump in the phone booth and save Metropolis," said Sommers.

"Who does he hang out with?"

"No bros but lots of girls. Mostly I hear them rather than see them."

"Thin walls."

Sommers laughed. "Not that, at least that would be entertaining. More like they talk, wake me up. Like it's the morning and I'm hearing chick voices. I keep flexible hours because I have clients in Asia, try to catch Z's whenever I can. When he's here it's like Chick Central. And chicks *talk*."

Milo clucked sympathetically as he drew out a photo of Charlene/Qeesha. Any hint the image was a mug shot had been removed. Still, she didn't look happy to be posing.

"Robert, ever see this girl with Wedd?"

"Not for a while."

"But you have seen her."

"Sure," said Sommers. "I remember her because she was the only black chick. Also, she was pregnant, like out to here, I'm like whoa, Clark thinks he's a superhero but he forgot the condom. I kinda felt sorry for her because she was in and out a lot—more than the others. And he's playing around with other chicks when she's not here."

"When's the last time you saw her?"

"Hmm . . . maybe a half year ago? It was a while."

"You ever see any conflict between them?"

Sommers said, "You know, one time, guess it was the last time, I heard the door slam and I looked out the blinds and saw her leaving, she's walking real fast. But he didn't go after her and I didn't hear them hassling, so I don't know, is that conflict—is that like from a mug shot?"

Milo said, "It is, Robert."

"She's a criminal type? Her and Clark are doing car scams together?"

"She was here more than the others?"

"Definitely. Most of the chicks you saw them once, twice." Sommers twirled a dread. "The black chick I saw maybe . . . six times, seven times?"

I said, "He's into one-night stands."

"Guess so." He snorted. "Playah Clark."

Milo showed him a picture of Adriana Betts.

"Her I never saw. She part of the scam gang? Looks kinda shady." His hand gathered up several clumps of hair. "More I think about it, more I'm pretty sure she was pissed at him—the black chick. Walking fast, like she couldn't wait to get away from him. Maybe it was hormones, you know? Baby hormones. That happened to my girlfriend when she was with child. The bigger she got, the grumpier she turned, kind of hellish."

"You have a kid?"

"Nope, she terminated. Her decision, she'd rather go to law school." Sommers shrugged. "I thought it might be cool. Being a daddy. But she had to do what she had to do."

CHAPTER
27

Milo gave his card to Sommers, asked him to call if Wedd showed up.

Sommer said, "Sure, but like I said, he's not here too much."

We tried the remaining four apartments in Wedd's building. No answers at the first three units. A woman came to the fourth door towing an I.V. line on wheels. Something clear and viscous dripped into her veins. Her hair was a gray tangle, one shade darker than her face.

"Sorry . . ." She paused for breath. "I never leave . . . don't know anyone."

"He lives downstairs in Three," said Milo. "Had his car stolen a while back."

"Oh . . . that." Her jaws worked. She could've been any age from fifty to eighty. "People were . . . surprised."

"Why's that, ma'am?"

She inhaled twice, braced herself in the doorway. "At nights . . . the lights are . . . super-bright."

"Anyone trying to break into a car would be conspicuous."

"Yes . . . funny."

She labored to smile. Succeeded and hinted at the beautiful woman she'd once been. "It . . . happens."

We returned to the unmarked. Milo put the key in the ignition but didn't start up.

"Groot's instincts were good, the Bimmer's a likely scam and Clark Kent's shaping up like a bad boy with a second pad. Think he's the daddy?"

I said, "He's got women coming in and out constantly, but Qeesha's the only one seen more than once or twice. That says beyond casual and the last time Sommers saw her, she was conspicuously pregnant and looked angry. Maybe because Wedd wanted her to terminate? If she was pressing Wedd for money, it could've motivated the car scam: He finds her wheels, gets her temporarily out of his hair, uses the insurance money for his own new drive. A pimped-up SUV just like Heather saw at the park that night."

"At the park 'cause he's doing advance work, taking care of business. Qeesha hassled him, he killed her and the baby. Ditto Adriana, because she knew too much. Clark's sounding like a *real* bad boy." He frowned. "With no criminal record."

"The timing works," I said. "Qeesha left Idaho a couple of years ago, plenty of time to hook up with Wedd, get pregnant. What I find interesting is Adriana didn't follow her to L.A. but she did leave home, right around the same time. Reverend Goleman suggested she needed a life change. Meeting Qeesha, seeing her independence, might've inspired Adriana. She'd run the day care at the church. She found child-care work with the Van Dynes, then the

Changs. San Diego's close to L.A. so it's not illogical she and Qeesha would reconnect. Maybe that post office box of hers was her own bit of naughty intrigue, allowing the two of them to correspond in secrecy. Allowing her vicarious entry to Qeesha's world without actually participating. But four, five months ago that changed when Qeesha called for help and Adriana went down to L.A. with the Changs—a break of her usual routine. That's the same time Sommers saw Qeesha pregnant and unhappy. What if Qeesha sensed she was in danger—she'd seen something frightening in Wedd's attitude—and wanted support? Or a witness?"

He looked over at the building. The painters had paused, were sitting at the curb eating burritos. ". . . Those bugs. Wax. If Wedd's our guy, he's something other than human." Head shake. "All those women, he's got some kind of charisma going."

"Women who aren't seen more than once or twice."

He stared at me. "Oh, no, don't get imaginative. Too early in the day."

He started the car but kept it in Park. His left hand gripped the steering wheel. The fingers of his right hand clawed his knee. He rubbed his face.

I said, "Sorry."

"No, no, now it's *my* head's going in bad directions. What if the baby wasn't unwanted, Alex? What if it was wanted in a bad way? Literally. For some kind of nut-cult ritual."

His normal pallor had leached to an unhealthy off-white. I felt my own skin go cold.

He said, "Dear God in Heaven, what if that poor little thing was *farmed.*"

CHAPTER

28

A woman stood near the entrance to the division parking lot. Tall, lanky, long-legged with frizzy yellow hair, wearing a maroon pantsuit with shoulder pads a couple of decades too big, she consulted a piece of paper as she checked out entering vehicles. A badge was clipped to her lapel.

I said, "Department bean counter?"

Milo said, "Your tax dollars at work." He rolled up behind a black-and-white and a blue Corvette that was someone's civilian ride. Both cars passed the frizzy-haired woman's scrutiny. When

Milo pulled up to the keypad, she looked at him, waved the paper.

"Lieutenant Sturgis?" She approached the driver's side.

Milo said, "Another survey? Not today," began rolling the window up.

"Don't do that!" Her protest was more screech than bellow. Her pantsuit was the color of pickled beets, some fabric that had never known soil or harvest. She wore glasses framed in pale blue plastic, rouge that was too bright, lipstick that wasn't bright enough. Had one of those rawboned bodies that abhor body fat. Nothing masculine about her, but nothing feminine, either.

She pressed a hand on the half-rolled window. Picture on her badge; I was too far to read the small print. She showed Milo the paper in her hand: On it was a full-page, color photo of him.

He said, "Never seen the guy."

"C'mon, Lieutenant."

He rolled down the window. "What can I do for you?"

"You could stop avoiding me." She unclipped the badge, showed it to him. "Kelly LeMasters, L.A. *Times.*"

Milo didn't oblige her with a response.

She said, "That's the way it's going to be? Fine, I'll grovel for every crumb. Even though I shouldn't have to 'cause I'm with the paper of record and I've been calling you all week on those skeletons and you've been shining me on like I'm your ex-wife filing for more spousal support."

She smiled. "Or in your case, ex-husband."

Milo said, "A comedian."

"Anything that works," said Kelly Le-Masters. Her tone said she was used to rejection. But not inured to it.

A car pulled up behind us. Large black man at the wheel of a brand-new Chevy unmarked. Dark suit, white shirt, red tie. Scowl of impatience. Horn-beep.

Milo said, "That's a captain behind me, so I'm going to pull into the lot. It has nothing to do with avoiding you."

"You couldn't avoid me if you wanted to, I'll be right here when you come walking out."

True to her word, she hadn't budged a foot. Looking at me, she said, "This is the psychologist. He advise you to shine me on?"

"No one's shining you on. Sorry if it came across that way."

"Ma'am bam thank you *not,*" she said. "What, you're allergic to cooperation?" She looked me over, top-to-bottom. "Good angle, grizzled homicide cop and dashing shrink." Blue eyes shifted back to Milo. "Delete *grizzled,* insert *rumpled.*"

He reached for his tie, lying crookedly across his paunch. The reflexive move cracked up Kelly LeMasters. She slapped her knee with glee. Long time since I'd seen anyone do that. Not since my last drive through the Ozarks.

Milo said, "Glad to be amusing."

Kelly LeMasters said, "See? You're human. Have your vanities like everyone else. So why in the world would you refuse to cooperate with me? I could make you famous. At least temporary-famous and that's pretty cool, no?"

"Thanks but no thanks."

"Playing hard to get? Why run from stardom, Milo Sturgis? In addition to being a sexual-preference pioneer, for

which you've never received just credit,
you're darn good at what you do. According to my sources, over the past
twenty years you've closed proportion-
ately more murders than any other detective. And yet no one really knows
about the totality of your accomplish-
ments because you refuse to maintain
any sort of media presence. Sure, you
pop up from time to time, giving pithy
little quotes. But more often than not
you let some boss-type get the credit
for your work."

"Aw shucks."

"Fine, you're the gay Jimmy Stewart
but why shut me out on these baby
cases? What is it? My breath?"

She leaned close, exhaled noisily.
"See? Minty fresh?" I was favored with
a second blast of herbal aroma. "Back
me up on that, Doctor."

Milo and I laughed.

"See," she said, "I'm a funny girl. Re-
ward me, Milo Sturgis."

"It's complicated."

"So what isn't?" Her hand shot out. A
white-gold wedding band circled one of
ten bony fingers. Her nails were short,

unpolished. But for the ring, she wore no jewelry.

Milo said, "Now we shake?"

"We sure do," said Kelly LeMasters. "Seeing as we're going to be warm, nurturing, mutually advantageous buddies."

A car approached from Santa Monica Boulevard. Shiny unmarked, new enough to lack plates.

Milo motioned LeMasters away from the lot entrance, turned his back to the oncoming vehicle.

"Who's that?" she said.

"Doesn't matter. Let's not talk here."

Kelly LeMasters said, "No prob. That Indian place you like?"

He glared at her. "*Nowhere* I like, I don't want to be seen with you. Minty fresh notwithstanding."

"Fine," she said. "If it means you're going to give me something juicy."

"No obligations."

"That's what they all say."

We headed up the block into the residential area south of the station. Milo and LeMasters walked abreast as I trailed two steps behind. A few turns later he stopped in front of a dingbat apartment building. White stucco instead of aqua but stylistically not dissimilar from Melvin J. Wedd's part-time residence.

Milo's idea of a private joke? Nothing about him suggested mirth as he drew himself up to max height, the way he does when he's out to intimidate.

If that was the goal, it failed with Kelly LeMasters. She took a notepad and pen out of her bag and said, "Go for it."

Milo said, "Put that away, we're off the record. If you guys still respect that."

"Milo, Milo," she said. "If nothing's on the record, what use are you to me?"

"This may come as a shock, *Kelly:* Being useful to you isn't my priority."

"Of course not, solving nasty old murders is, yadda yadda yadda. But you know as well as I do that those things go together. How many of your closed files would still be open if you didn't get media exposure when you needed it?"

"I appreciate the value of a free press. But my hands are tied."

"By?"

"Off the record?"

"Regarding that small point?" she said. "Sure."

"Bureaucracy."

She said, "You've got to be kidding. *That's* the staggering secret? We all deal with red tape, you think my employer's all Bill of Rights and no bullshit?"

"Glad you empathize."

"I don't need you to tell me why your stupid, venal bosses closed you up on the second skeleton: politics as usual, the whole Maxine Cleveland real estate thing. You ever meet her? Brain-dead and clueless, should be a perfect fit in D.C. That ploy was stupid, where did it get her?" She removed her glasses. "Your idiot bosses let me get scooped by a *damn student paper.*"

"You want to complain, I can give you some phone numbers."

"How far would that get me?"

"Exactly my point, Kelly. It's like talking to dust."

She studied him. "You're a crafty one, aren't you? Okay, we go off the record, as long as at some point it goes on the record and I don't mean months."

"Nope, can't give you a deadline."

"I don't want a deadline, I just want you to be reasonable." She put her glasses back on. Wrote something in her pad, angling the page so he couldn't see. I've seen him do the same thing with witnesses, trying to kick up the intrigue, establish dominance.

The two of them would make an interesting bridge twosome.

"Define *reasonable,* Kelly."

"Use common sense, cut the crap, however you want to define it. I am *not* going to remain mute for eternity only to have every moron on TV and the Internet going with the story."

Bony hands slapped onto bony hips. "Got it?"

"Got it."

"Fine." Her pen poised. "Shoot."

"Put the pad away."

"You don't trust me to keep it under wraps?"

"You just said your patience couldn't be guaranteed."

"We're wasting each other's time," she said. "This is bullshit."

"Then how about we table the proceedings? Something opens up, I promise to let you know."

"Why would you do that?"

"Because you're right," he said.

She studied him. "You're shitting me. Nice try."

"I'm not. You're right."

"Admitting you made a mistake? Have you checked your Y chromosomes recently?"

"If it was up to me, Kelly, I'd have lots to tell you and it would hit the paper tomorrow. Not because I care about you or your job but because it could be in my best interest. Unfortunately, by pulling that stunt at the parking lot, you made sure anything you write is going to be traced right back to me."

"I . . . maybe that was poor judgment but what was my choice?"

Milo shrugged.

Kelly LeMasters said, "Okay, fine, no notes and I swear to protect your identity." The pad and pen returned to her bag.

Milo said, "Same for the tape recorder you've got in there."

"How . . . fine, you're an ace detective." She produced the machine, switched it off.

He took it, removed a mini-spool that he pocketed, returned the recorder.

Her nostrils flared. "You're going to keep that?"

"For both our sakes."

"Want to check if I've got a nuclear-laser thought-reader in here?"

"Nah, those are so twentieth century. So what do you want to know, Kelly?"

"After all that I have to ask questions? Just tell me what you've learned about those baby skeletons."

"The first skeleton may not be related to a crime."

"What makes you say that?"

"No signs of trauma or injury."

"Maybe it was smothered or something."

"Anything's possible but I need evidence."

"A body buried under a tree is evidence," she said. "If no crime was committed why conceal it?"

"Could've been a death due to natural causes that someone wanted to cover up."

"What kind of death is natural for a baby?"

"Disease."

"Then why cover it up?"

"Wish I knew, Kelly. I may never know."

"Why the pessimism?"

"Too old, too cold."

"I assume you've traced the owners of the house."

"You assume correctly. No leads, there."

"I know," said LeMasters. "I looked into it, myself. Found that old guy in Burbank, the whole John Wayne thing, he had nothing to say. Neither did anyone in Cheviot Hills. Including that kid who blabbed to the SMC paper. Her thing was *I talk to Lieutenant Sturgis, no one else.*"

Milo said, "Power of the press."

"Yeah, we're real popular—so I should just forget about the first one."

"Probe to your heart's content, Kelly. You learn anything, I'll be grateful."

Sounding sincere. Not a word about Eleanor Green, a big blue Duesenberg.

Nothing from me to either of them about Dr. Jimmy Asherwood.

Kelly LeMasters said, "Okay, let's get to the juicy one."

"Once again, Kelly, there's no evidence of trauma but I'm assuming homicide, because of the dead woman who was found across the park. Also, we've done prelim DNA on the bones and the baby was a girl."

Kelly LeMasters didn't emote. "Okay, go on."

"By the state of her dentition two or three months old."

"That's it? What about the woman?"

Milo said, "Does it bother you at all?"

"What?"

"A baby."

Her jaw tightened and her arms grew rigid. "Does it bother *you*?"

"You bet."

"Well, me, too," she said. "So it's settled, we both make our livings off other people's misery but we're still human." She turned to me. "Guess that applies to you, too—the misery part. Tell me,

did you coach him in all this psychological warfare?" She faced Milo again.
"Does it *bother* me? Let's put it this
way: I've got one kid and it took me
three miscarriages to get him, so no, I
don't get a thrill out of dead babies,
don't find them the least bit entertaining. Now what the hell else do you want
to know?"

Milo said, "Sorry."

"Screw the apology. Give me some
meat to chew on."

"We've identified the adult victim.
Nothing in her past predisposes her to
being murdered."

"Name," said LeMasters.

"Adriana Betts, originally from Idaho.
She was religious, had no bad habits,
worked as a nanny."

"She took care of kids?"

"Yes."

"That include babies?"

"In some cases."

"That doesn't sound like a connection to you?"

"Theoretically? Sure, Kelly, but we interviewed her employers and all their

kids are alive and well. No one has a bad word to say about her."

"Religious types can be hypocrites."

"Anyone can."

"What, you're a Holy Roller? Despite what the church says about people like you?"

"Let's stick with the case, Kelly."

"I can't see it," said LeMasters. "Being Catholic and gay." She laughed. "Unless you're a parish priest."

"You're Catholic?"

"Once upon a time."

"Nice to know you've got no biases."

She frowned. "Where will you be taking the investigation?"

"Hard to say."

"No, it's not," she said. "Everyone says you're methodical as well as intuitive, always come up with a plan. So don't hold back on me. What's next?"

"Same answer, Kelly."

She folded her arms across her chest. "I go off-record and you give me generalities?"

"That's because generalities are all I've got. I could feed you stuff that would spark your prurient interest, set you off on a useless maze-run. But it wouldn't help my case, could even hurt it if you printed fallacious crap."

"I thought we were working on trust here."

"We are," he said. "Have we reached our goal?"

"Of what?"

"Mutually advantageous buddy-hood."

"Not even close," she said. "I promised to keep everything under wraps and you gave me squat."

He creased his brow. "I'm going to tell you something else but you have to pledge not to use it until I say otherwise. I mean that, Kelly. It's essential."

"Fine, fine. What?"

"Though of apparently sound moral character, Adriana Betts may have somehow gotten mixed up with bad people."

"What kind of bad people?"

"This isn't fact-based," he said, "but possibly cult members."

"Not fact-based? Then what?"

"Inference."

"Yours or Dr. Delaware's?"

"Mine."

"You inferred from the body?" she said. "Some sort of ritual mutilation? I heard she was just shot."

"Sorry, that's all I can say, Kelly."

"Church-girl in the clutches of Satan worshippers? Any freakos in particular?"

"Not even close," he said. "I'll be looking into that world, would welcome your input on the topic."

"I don't know squat about cults."

"That makes two of us, Kelly."

Her arms relaxed. Her eyes brightened. "Are we talking another Manson thing?"

"I sure hope not."

"This town," said LeMasters, "is Weirdo Central. Can you narrow it down at all?"

"Wish I could, Kelly, and you need to make sure no one knows we had this talk."

"Like I said, I protect my sources."

"I'm not talking legally, I mean total blackout." His turn to move closer to her. Big black eyebrows dipped. He loomed. Kelly LeMasters shrank back. He filled another few inches of her personal space. She tried to stand her ground but the primal fear of something big and aggressive caused her to step back.

"Total," he repeated. "You screw that up, I'll never talk to you again and neither will anyone in the department."

He'd lowered his voice. The resultant half whisper was movie-villain ominous.

LeMasters blinked. Forced herself to smile. "You're threatening me?"

"I'm stating a contingency, Kelly. And here's another one, just to show you what a nice guy I am: If you stick to your part of the deal, you'll be the first one to know if I close the case."

"*If,* not *when*?"

"Appreciate the vote of confidence, Kelly. Either way, you'll scoop everyone. I promise."

"How much lead time will I get?"

"Enough to close everyone out."

"You can guarantee that?" she said. "What about your bosses?"

"Fuck 'em," he growled.

His eyes were green slits.

Kelly LeMasters knew better than to argue.

We walked her back to Butler Avenue, watched her diminish to a beet-colored speck that turned east on Santa Monica and disappeared.

I said, "To paraphrase Persistent Kelly, what's next?"

"I look into Mr. Wedd and you go about your normal life."

"Whatever that means."

"It means have a nice day. Relatively speaking."

CHAPTER
29

Holly Ruche showed up six minutes late. Blanche and I greeted her at the door. She said, "I generally don't like dogs. But I've been thinking of getting one. For the baby."

Worst reason in the world. I said, "I'm happy to keep her out of the office."

"She's like a therapy dog?"

"Not officially but she's got enough credits for her own Ph.D."

She looked down at Blanche.

Blanche beamed up at her.

She said, "What's her name?"

"Blanche."

"She's kind of cute . . . almost like she's smiling. Okay, I guess she can be there."

"Up to you, Holly."

"It's okay. Yes, it's definitely okay, she's well behaved." She took in the living room. "Stylish. You're into contemporary."

After a psychopath burns down your first house simplicity can be a tonic.

I smiled.

She said, "Have you been here long?"

"A while."

"This neighborhood. Must've cost a fortune."

"Let's go to my office."

Seated on the battered leather couch, she said, "Sorry. That crack about a fortune. No business of mine. I guess I'm just hyper about how much things cost. Especially real estate."

"The decorating's at a standstill?"

"Still in the talking stages."

"You and Matt."

She knitted her hands, gazed down. "Mostly me and me."

"Kind of a monologue."

She stroked her belly. She'd put on some girth and her face had grown fuller. Her hair was tied back functionally, tiny pimples paralleled her hairline. "I guess that's part of why I'm here. He's not available. Physically or emotionally. They go together, I guess. He works all the time."

"Is that something new?"

Her lower lip curled. Tears seeped from under her lower lids and trickled onto her cheeks.

"I guess not," she finally said. "I guess that's the real problem. Nothing's changed."

I handed her a tissue. Kleenex should pay me a commission. "Matt's always been work-oriented."

"I respect that, Dr. Delaware. He's super-responsible, that's a big deal, right? He could be a slacker."

"Sure."

"He thinks it's manly. Taking care of business. I guess it is. I *know* it is."

I said, "It's part of why you were attracted to him."

"Yes—how'd you know that?"

"Educated guess."

"Well, you're right, that was a big part of it. It's just—I guess you need to know more about my father. Like the fact that I didn't have one."

I waited.

She said, "I never knew him. I'm not sure my mother knew him." Her fingers closed over the tissue. "This is hard to talk about . . . but I need to be honest, right? I mean this is the place for that."

Her fingers relaxed. She dropped the tissue in a wastebasket. "Being pregnant has made me think about all sorts of things I told myself I'd never have to think about."

"Your own family."

"If you can call it that."

"There wasn't much in the way of family."

"Just me and my mother and she was . . ."

She sat for a while. "There's no two ways about it, Mom was loose. Morally, I mean. Not to me, to me she was just Mom, but looking back . . . she was a cocktail waitress—I'm not saying that was bad, she worked incredibly hard, she took care of me, put food on the table. But she also . . . supplemented her income. By bringing men home, when I was little I thought it was normal. Locking me in my room with cookies and candies."

She bit her lip. "That didn't stop me from seeing some of them. Hearing them. All kinds of men, different ages, races, it was like . . . she called them her friends. 'Time for quiet time with these Oreos and Kit Kats, sweetie. I need to spend time with my friends.'"

I said, "At some point you realized that wasn't typical."

"I realized it when I started kindergarten and saw how other kids lived. My first years were kind of isolated, we lived in a trailer park. Don't get me wrong, it was a nice trailer, Mom kept it up, planted flowers all around, there was a little birdbath where sparrows and finches would come. We were pretty close to a nice neighborhood, working class, solid people, lots of religious types. It didn't take me long to catch on that other mothers didn't do what mine did. I never said anything because Mom loved me, took care of me, I always had nice clothes and good food. The same things other kids had, who was I to be ungrateful?"

More tears. "I shouldn't have said that. Calling her loose, that was wrong, really mean."

Another tissue interlude.

She said, "She's gone, can't defend herself . . . I just feel it's time to be honest, you know? Confront reality. So I can understand myself."

"Now that you're becoming a mom."

"I don't want to be like her," she said. "I mean in some ways I do, I want to be loving, to take care of my Aimee, to give her everything. That's why I married Matt, he's a totally great provider."

"When I talked to you at your house you said you'd worked most of your life, had a career until recently."

"That's true."

"You set out to be independent."

"Yes. So?"

"So even though Matt's maturity and industriousness were qualities you found attractive, you never intended to rely upon him totally."

"I . . . yes, that's true, I guess you're right. You're saying Mom made me tough?"

"I'm saying you're an obviously capable, thoughtful person. Does your mother get some of the credit? Sure, but in the end you made your own decisions."

"I guess I did . . . but I'm still sorry. For saying that about Mom. I miss her so *much*!"

She burst out weeping, took a while to compose herself. "She passed three years ago, Doctor, she suffered so much. I guess I've been angry at her for leaving so young, she was fifty-four. Even though that's not rational. I was being selfish, I'm too selfish, period, I shouldn't have *said* that."

"Did you treat her unkindly when she was alive?"

"No, of course not. When she had to go to hospice—she had ALS, Lou Gehrig's disease—I was always there for her. It was terrible, she hung on for three years. I paid for whatever Medi-Cal and insurance didn't cover. I was there all the time. Her mind was still working but nothing else was, that's what made it so horrible. At the end, she could still move her eyes, I could see the love in them. So how could I *say* that?"

"Your life's in flux, Holly, it's normal for old feelings to come back. You love your mother but some of the things she did frightened and embarrassed you. You've never expressed how you felt about it. It's okay."

"You're telling me it's okay to say things like that? Calling her *loose*?"

"It's a word, Holly. Your actions spoke much louder."

Long silence. "You're so nice. Your wife is lucky—are you married?"

I smiled.

"Sorry, sorry, I need to mind my own business."

"It's not that, Holly. This is about you."

She smiled. "That's sure different. Being the star. Though I guess I was the star to Mom. She never had any more kids. I guess one whoopsie baby was enough."

"You know for sure you were an accident."

"Why wouldn't I be?"

"Your mother sounds like an organized person."

"You're saying she intended me?"

"Did she make any other whoopsies?"

She pulled at the tissue. Tugged at her ponytail. "I see what you mean. She always told me I was the best thing ever happened to her."

"I'm sure you were."

She glanced at Blanche. I gave the *okay* nod and Blanche waddled over to the couch.

Holly said, "Is she allowed up here?"

"Absolutely."

"If you want you can come up, cutie." Blanche leaped effortlessly to her side, moved in close for a snuggle. Holly stroked the folds of her neck. "She's so soft. Like a stuffed animal."

"As cute as a toy," I said, "and a whole lot smarter."

"You've got it all, don't you," she said. "The house, the dog. Maybe a wife— sorry . . . so maybe that's why you think I was a deliriously desired baby. Okay, I'll go with that. My Aimee's wanted, that's what's important. Let me ask you something: Do you think permissive's

the best way to go or keep up the discipline?"

"Depends on the child."

"Some kids need more discipline."

I nodded.

She said, "Matt sure doesn't need
any more, he's the most self-disciplined
person I've ever met."

"How about you?"

"I'm okay . . . I guess I know how to
take care of myself . . . I wonder what
Aimee will be like. Not that I'm trying to
box her in with expectations. I mean
obviously I'd like her to be beautiful and
brilliant—healthy, that's the most important thing. Healthy. So you're saying I
need to get to know her before I work
out my plan."

"You may not need a plan," I said.

"No?"

"A lot of people have good instincts."

"But some don't."

"How about your mother?"

"She had excellent instincts," she
said. "The best." Wide smile. "Now I
feel better. Saying something nice to
make up for the other thing."

She crossed her legs. "That was your

plan, right? To guide me to say something nice."

"Like I said, Holly, sometimes a plan
isn't necessary."

"You knew me well enough to just let
me go on."

"You know yourself."

"I guess I do, Dr. Delaware." She
placed a hand on her belly. "This is
mine, I own it. I'm not saying Aimee's
not a separate person, I get that. I'm
talking about the process. Carrying her,
nurturing her with my body. A woman
needs to feel she owns that . . . I feel
much better now. If I need you can I
call?"

"Of course."

"I don't care anymore about the house
or the remodeling or any material crap,"
she said. "That kind of ownership
doesn't matter."

CHAPTER
30

I made a couple of tuna sandwiches, brought them to Robin's studio.

She said, "The perfect man," washed sawdust from her hands, gave me a kiss. We ate near the pond, talked about everything but work, returned to work. Blanche chose to stay with Robin but she licked my hand first.

I said, "Master diplomat."

Robin held out the half sandwich she'd wrapped in a napkin. "More like I've got the goodies."

"Definition of diplomacy."

◆

I sat wondering what Adriana Betts had done for money and lodging during the months between leaving La Jolla and showing up dead in the park.

Maybe she'd saved up enough to coast. Or perhaps she'd resorted to what she knew best: taking care of other people's offspring. I printed a list of every employment agency in L.A. County that advertised nannies, au pairs, governesses, any sort of in-house staff.

For the next hour, my lie was glib and consistent: I was Adriana's potential employer and she'd listed the agency as having handled her in the past. I must have been pretty convincing because I encountered a lot of outrage at the falsehood. Several people said I was lucky to learn about Adriana's poor character early on. Most made sure to let me know they had far superior candidates.

With a dozen calls to go, I took a coffee break and checked with my service. A family court judge had left a message thanking me for a "helpful" custody report, ditto one of the attorneys on the case. Third was Holly Ruche offering her gratitude, no specifics.

The service operator, a woman I'd never talked to before, said, "You have teenagers by any chance, Doctor?"

I said, "Why?"

"Everyone seems to appreciate you. If you tell me your teenagers do, I may make an appointment, myself."

I laughed.

She said, "You sound cheerful, so that's my answer. You don't have any."

I'd whittled the agency list to four companies when the man who answered at Gold Standard Professionals in Beverly Hills listened to my pitch but didn't reply.

I said, "You know Adriana?"

He said, "Hold on for a moment, please." Deep, mellifluous voice.

As I waited, I examined the company's Internet ad. The pitch featured twenties-style cartoons of butlers, footmen, chefs in toques, maids in lace uniforms, lettering in an angular art deco font. Boldface motto: *The ultimate in classic service, beyond the ultimate in classic discretion.*

Maybe discretion was what kept me on hold for seven minutes before the connection was cut.

I redialed, got voice mail. After fielding more indignation at the remaining three agencies, I gave Gold Standard another try.

This time no one answered.

I Googled the company. A single reference popped up, a piece from the *Beverly Hills Clarion* that could've been a paid ad or least-resistance journalism. Gold Standard's owners were Jack and Daisy Weathers, "former performers, now entrepreneurs in the field of high-end service," who'd parlayed their knowledge of "the unique demands of the industry with post-graduate training in human factors and development."

For Jack that meant a master's degree from a "university" I knew to be a correspondence mill. No educational specs for Daisy. The accompanying photo showed the Weatherses to be white-haired, tan, wearing matching

pink shirts and smiles crammed with
post-graduate dental work.

The smooth voice could easily have
been that of an actor, so maybe I'd
talked to the boss. Gold Standard's address was a P.O.B. in Beverly Hills,
90211. South end of the city, maybe a
mail drop.

Was there no need for an office because clients of sufficient importance
merited house calls? Or did one have to
pass muster before being favored with
private-club status? If the latter was the
case, I'd flunked. Maybe that had nothing to do with Adriana, just disdain for
an obviously undeserving plebe with no
link to "the Industry." But no other
agency had reacted that way.

I put in a call to Milo. He said, "I was
just going to call you. Eat, yet?"

"Had a sandwich."

"That's a snack not a meal. The usual
place."

"No reporter in tow, huh."

"Speaking of Lois Lane, I may have
created a monster. I'm walking over
right now, gonna start grub-festing with-

out you. Seeing as you already had a *sandwich*."

I found him at his usual corner table at Café Moghul, perched like a potentate behind platters of lamb, chicken, lobster, and crab, some kind of meatball big enough to hurl at Dodger Stadium, the usual Himalaya of naan and vegetables, bowls of mystery sauce.

Be nice if synchrony ruled the world and there was a master detective in Mumbai stuffing his face with burgers, fried chicken, and pizza.

Unlike every other time I'd been in the restaurant, the dining room was nearly full. The new patrons were uniformed cops and plainclothes detectives. Everyone chowing down on generous portions but none of the wretched excess left at the Altar of Milo.

I sat down. "Looks like the world's caught on."

"What they caught on to is a special lunch deal, half price on everything."

A detective I recognized waved and brandished a lobster claw. Milo muttered, "Bargain-hunting vulgarians."

The bespectacled woman brought me iced tea and a clean plate. She looked exhausted.

I said, "Busy."

She beamed at Milo. "They listen to him."

He said, "You've got to believe me, it was the flyer you left at the station."

Her smile widened. Knowing she'd encountered a deity and figuring humility was one of his divine attributes.

I said, "What's up, Mahatma?"

He leaned in close, lowered his voice. "Ol' Kelly's digging like a gopher. So far I've received about fifty pages of attachments on infanticides, none of which is relevant. Meanwhile, zip on Adriana, Wedd, or Charlene Chambers as herself or as Qeesha D'Embo. And none of the cult sites I've found seems to fit. Including their photos."

"Cults post publicity photos?"

"You better believe it, they're proud of themselves. Basically, it's a party scene, Alex, lots of nudity and naughty groping. Weirdest thing I found was a Beelzebub-worshipping bunch that gets off by smearing themselves with food, the prime sacramental offering being baked beans. Vegetarian, of course."

I said, "Someone's engaged in truly ugly behavior, why advertise?"

Nodding, he downed half a plate of lamb, wiped his hands and mouth, scanned the room, switched to a low-volume leprechaun brogue. "I *was* a wee bit *impish,* laddy. Gave Ms. LeMasters the name and number of one Maria Thomas and told her it wouldn't displease me if she harassed the brass about going public on selective info."

"Selective as in what you decide."

"Is there another definition?"

"Maria's not going to make the connection to you?"

"The story Kelly's telling her is she's fed up with me because I keep stonewalling her so she's decided to go over my head. If Maria gives her the okay, no problem. If Maria tells her no, she'll publish a follow-up piece on the park murders, anyway. To my great apparent chagrin."

I said, "Impressively devious."

"When in Nome, do as the Ice Queen does. Meanwhile, no cult link to Wedd but I have learned a few things about him, most of it disappointing. Not only does he lack a criminal record, according to his landlord he's a model tenant, pays on time, never complains. As opposed to Surf-Boy Sommers who's chronically late with his rent and bitches about everything and who the landlord sees as a druggie. So I'm not sure he's gonna work as a witness. I also found out that an A.C. company was in Wedd's place to install new thermostats two weeks ago, landlord let them in, the place was neat, clean, nothing out of the ordinary."

"Landlords have to notify tenants about service calls, so Wedd would've had time to clean up."

"In this case the landlord got phone authorization from Wedd the same day. He did say from the look of the place Wedd didn't seem to use it much. Which backs up the dual-crib theory. I was able to get Wedd's cell number and email, as well as the work history Wedd listed on his application."

He pulled out his pad. "Steadily and gainfully employed for over three years at a company called CAPD, Inc. The in-triguing factoid in this whole data storm is CAPD has no listed address. The 'PD' part made me wonder if they're trying to sound police-like, a hush-hush pri-vate security outfit. But there are no business listings in the county under that name and when I called the num-ber Wedd listed I was automatically transferred to a company of the same name on Grand Cayman Island and their answer was an electronic beep that then cut off midsentence. And when I searched for an island address, there was none."

I said, "The Caymans are big on off-shore banking."

"That was hypothesis two, some shady financial scam, and Qeesha be-ing a naughty girl mighta had a history with them. So I called Ray Lhermitte in New Orleans but CAPD meant nothing to him."

"Wedd told Sommers he worked in the industry. I just fielded my own bit of intrigue, based on that."

I told him about my agency calls, the evasive response at Gold Standard.

"Maybe he just didn't like the sound of my voice but my gut says he was hiding something."

A cop across the room flashed a thumbs-up. Milo growled, "Rank conformist." To me: "Gold Standard. Why not Platinum? Okay, let's ditch these bandwagon-jumpers and see what *Gold* Standard's all about."

He threw cash on the table. The woman in the sari rushed over and tried to return the money. "For your commission!"

"Give it to charity," he said.

"What charity, Lieutenant?"

"Something kind and gentle."

"Like you."

He stomped out of the restaurant.

The woman said, "Such a wonderful man!"

One of the cops called out, "Pardon, could we have some more of that spinach?"

CHAPTER

31

As we drove to the south end of Beverly Hills, I thought of something. "Sommers said Wedd avoided conversation. How'd he know Wedd was an Industry guy?"

"Let's find out."

Sommers answered his phone. "He used to get *Variety* delivered."

"Used to?"

"Haven't seen it for a while. Also the way he walked was a tip-off. Full of himself. Like 'I'm a dude who *knows* people.' He do something bad to those girls?"

"No evidence of that, Robert."

"Meaning maybe he did," said Sommers. "Okay, if he shows up I'll let you know."

Gold Standard's address matched a two-story building clad with salmon-colored granite. Quick 'n Easy Postal and Packaging took up the street-level space. The female clerk working the counter was young and cute with doe eyes and a fox-face. Her hair was a red tsunami. Sleeve tattoos and a steel stud jutting from her chin said pain wasn't an issue for her. Neither was discretion.

Milo said, "Where can I find the people who rent Box Three Thirty-Five?"

"Go outside and up the stairs."

I'd been wrong about a mail drop. Was glad to be humbled.

"If their office is right here why do they need you?"

The clerk said, "Hmm. 'Cause I'm cute?"

He squinted to read her name tag. "Well, sure, I can see that, Cheyenne. Is there any other reason?"

She twirled the chin stud. It caught

for an instant, made her wince, finally rotated. "The building owner doesn't provide mail slots for the tenants."

"How come?"

"'Cause that was the deal in order for us to move in. It worked, most of them rent from us. Are those guys in trouble or something? 'Cause they don't seem like the type."

"What type is that?" said Milo.

"They're kinda . . . like old?" She inspected us. "I mean serious old."

"Grandma and Grandpa."

"Not like my Gram-peeps. *They* don't have a clue."

"These guys do."

"These guys are like cool dressers. In an old way."

"These fashion plates have a name?"

"Plates?" she said.

"What are their names, Cheyenne?"

A fingernail pinged the stud. A speck of blood seeped from between steel and skin. A tiny red bubble formed. She flicked it away. "They *are* in trouble? Wow."

"Not at all, Cheyenne. We just need to talk to them."

"Oh. They're Daisy and Jack. She used to act on TV and he was like a musician."

"They told you that."

"Yeah, but it's true, I saw her acting."

"Where?"

"On TV," she said. "One of those movies, cowboys and horses. She was like the girl he loved."

"The main cowboy."

"Totally. He put her on the horse and they did a lip-lock. She was hot."

I said, "Was Jack playing guitar in the background?"

"Huh? Oh, no, he was like into trumpets or something. In a TV band."

"One of those late-night shows?"

Blank look. If I was a network head I'd be worried about longevity.

Milo said, "So what kind of business do Daisy and Jack run upstairs?"

"I dunno."

"What kind of mail do they get?"

"Dunno that either."

He smiled. "You never look?"

"Mail comes in the morning," she said. "I get here at noon. Why don't you just go up and talk to them if you're so interested?"

"They're in?"

"Dunno."

"Okay, thanks, Cheyenne."

"So maybe they're in trouble, huh?"

Stairs carpeted in cheap blue low-pile polyester led to a windowless foyer rimmed by five slab doors. No sound from behind any of them. Gold Standard Professionals' neighbors offered electrolysis, book-binding, tax preparation, and gift counseling.

Milo said, "Gift counseling? What the hell does that mean?"

I said, "Maybe they tell you who's been naughty or nice."

"Next there'll be laxative counseling. 'We open new channels of communication.' Okay, here goes nothing." He rapped on Gold Standard's door. A male voice said, "Who's there?"

"Police."

"*What?*"

"Police. Please open up."

Another *"What?"* but the door cracked. Jack Weathers had added a clipped white mustache and some wrinkles since his *Clarion* interview. He was tall, well built, seventy to seventy-five, wore a white polo shirt under a sea-green cashmere V-neck, taupe linen slacks, calfskin loafers sans socks. His skin was shiny and spray-bronzed, his eyes a deeper tan. A wedding band crusted with pavé diamonds circled his left ring finger. One pinkie hosted a white-gold emerald ring, the other a rose-gold creation dominated by a massive amethyst. The gold chain around his neck was curiously delicate.

He said, "Police? I don't understand."

Milo flashed the badge. "Could we come in, please, Mr. Weathers?"

"Do I have a choice?"

"Of course, sir."

A female voice said, "Jack? What's going on?" Before Weathers could answer, a woman came up behind him and shoved the door wide open.

A foot shorter than her husband, Daisy Weathers had on a black jacquard silk top, cream gabardine slacks, red stilettos that advertised a virtuoso pedicure. Serious bling glinted at all the predictable spots. The white in her hair verged on silver-plate. The style was some cosmetologist's ode to meringue. Her eyes were glacier-blue, oddly innocent. Small bones and a sweet face had kept her cute well beyond the expiration date.

Jack Weathers said, "They're the police."

Daisy Weathers said, "Hi, boys. Collecting for the law enforcement ball? We give every year." Sultry voice. She winked.

Milo said, "Not exactly, ma'am."

Jack Weathers said, "They don't send guys in suits for the ball, Daze. They send kids—scouts, cadets, whatever you call 'em."

Daisy Weathers said, "Cute kids, they're making 'em bigger nowadays. What can we do for you boys?"

Milo said, "We'd like to talk about Adriana Betts."

She looked puzzled. "Well, I can't say I know who that is."

Jack Weathers's face darkened. A fist punched a palm. "*Knew* it—it was one of you who called earlier, right? If you'd left a number, I'd have called you back."

I said, "Got cut off, couldn't get through after that."

His eyes danced to the right. "Well, I don't know about that. Our phones are working fine."

Daisy said, "Jack, what's going on?"

"All they had to do was call, this really isn't necessary."

"He says he did."

"Well, all he had to do was try again." Maybe Weathers was usually truthful, because lying didn't sit well with him. I counted at least three tells in as many seconds: lip-gnaw, brow-twitch, foot-tap. Then his eyes got jumpy.

"Anyway," I said, "we're here, so no harm, no foul."

Milo moved toward the doorway. Jack Weathers considered his options and stepped aside.

Daisy Weathers said, "What was that name, boys?"

Milo said, "Adriana Betts."

"Is that someone I'm supposed to know, Jack?"

The eyes turned into pinballs.

She touched his wrist. He jerked re-
flexively.

"Jackie? What's going on?"

"It's nothing, baby."

I said, "So she did work for you."

"No one works *for* us," said Jack
Weathers. "We're facilitators."

"Ja-ack-ee?" said his wife. "Again?"

Weathers looked away.

"Jack!"

"No big deal, Daze."

"Obviously it is a big deal if the police
are here."

He cursed under his breath.

She said, "You boys better come in
and straighten this out."

The single-room office was furnished
with two cheap desks and three hard-
plastic chairs. The walls were hospital-
beige and bare. A lone window half
covered by warped plastic blinds looked
out to an alley and the brick wall of the
neighboring building. One desk was set
up with a multi-line phone, a modem, a
computer, a printer, and a fax machine.
The other held a collection of bisque
figurines—slender, white-wigged court

figures engaged in spirited nonsense. Daisy Weathers took a seat behind the porcelain and lifted a lute-playing lady in a ball gown. One of her six rings clinked against the doll. Her husband winced.

Then he slipped behind the bank of business machines and eased his long body as low as he could manage.

Milo said, "Tell us about Adriana Betts."

Daisy said, "Yes, do, dear."

Jack said, "She came with good recommendations."

"Did you do the screening, Jackie?"

"It was an urgent one, Daze."

She slapped her forehead. "Bending rules. What a shock." To us: "My sweetie pie, here, has a heart softer than a ripe persimmon." That sounded like a line from a movie.

Jack said, "Someone comes to me in need, I try to help."

"He really does, boys. I wish I could get mad at him but you need to know him, he's a people-pleaser."

Milo said, "What kind of screening do you usually do?"

"Comprehensive screening," said Jack. "Just what you do."

"What we do?"

"Er . . . what I'm sure you do when you hire police officers." Weathers's smile was a pathetic grope for rapport. "To ensure the best fit, right? Everyone knows BHPD's the best."

"I'll pass that along to them," said Milo. "Actually, I'm LAPD."

"Oh," said Jack Weathers. "Well, I'm sure the same applies to you, we used to live in Los Angeles. Hancock Park, lovely, we had a gorgeous Colonial with a half-acre garden, the police were always helpful."

"Great to hear that, sir. So with Adriana Betts you decided to forgo the usual screening."

Daisy let out a prolonged sigh. Jack shot her a look that could've been a warning. Or fear.

"As I said, there was urgency."

I said, "Someone was in need."

"That's what we do," said Jack. "We fill needs."

"In Ms. Betts's case, child-care needs?"

He didn't answer.

Daisy said, "No matter who you are, finding the right people is always a challenge."

I faced Jack. "Meaning someone important. Who'd you send Adriana to?"

He shook his head.

Milo said, "Sir?"

Jack Weathers said, "What exactly are you claiming happened? Because I absolutely refuse to believe it was anything serious. I pride myself on being an excellent judge of character and that young lady had obviously fine character. She was *religious,* had a letter from her pastor."

Milo pulled out one of Qeesha's mug shots. "What about this young lady?"

Daisy blurted, "Her?"

Jack tried to hiss her silent.

She said, "I'm really at sea over this. Will someone please tell me what's going on?"

Jack folded his arms across his chest.

Milo said, "You'd placed Qeesha D'Embo where you sent Adriana."

Silence.

I said, "Qeesha vouched for Adriana.

That's why you didn't feel the need to screen her."

Daisy said, "Normally, we'd still screen. But if it was urgent—"

"They *get* it," said her husband.

She pouted. "Jackie?"

"We're not saying anything more, gentlemen. Not without advice of counsel."

Milo said, "You want a lawyer to answer routine questions?"

"You bet."

Daisy put the figurine down. No visible tremor but the base rattled on the desktop.

Milo said, "You're not being accused of any crime, Mr. Weathers."

"Even so," said Jack.

"You didn't screen Adriana but you did screen Qeesha."

Daisy said, "I've never heard of Qeesha, we knew her by another name— what was it again, Jackie?"

Weathers shook his head, drew his finger across his lip.

"She's a beautiful girl," said Daisy. "The way those black girls can be with their big dark eyes. What *was* her

name . . . something with an 'S,' I believe, I'd have to check the—"

"Shut *up,* Daze!"

Daisy Weathers stared at her husband. One hand bounced on her desktop. The other rose to her face, pinched
cheek-skin, twisted. Her eyes turned
wet.

Jack Weathers said, "Oh, baby."

Daisy sniffled.

He turned to us. "Now look what
you've done—I need you to leave."

Standing, he pointed to the door.

Milo said, "Suit yourself, Mr. Weathers," and got up. "But here's what puz-
zles me. You run a business based on
the ability to judge character. You said
before that whatever happened to Adriana wasn't a big deal because she was
a woman of good character. But from
what I can tell, you're only batting five
hundred, sir. Good for baseball, not so
good for job placement."

"What are you *talking* about?"

"You were right about one thing,
wrong about the other. Yes, Adriana
seems to have been a woman of excel-

lent character. But what happened was a really big deal."

"What happened?" Weathers demanded.

"Your lawyer can tell you. After we return with your friends at BHPD armed with a search warrant for all of your records."

"That's impossible!" Weathers shouted.

"Jack?" said Daisy.

"It's not only possible," said Milo, "it's probable."

"You're not making sense!" said Weathers. "Adriana had excellent character but she still committed some kind of . . . bad deed?"

"She didn't do anything, Mr. Weathers. Something was done *to* her."

"She's hurt?" said Daisy.

"She's dead, ma'am. Someone murdered her."

"Oh, no!"

"I'm afraid yes, Mrs. Weathers."

"I never even knew her, Jack hired her. Poor thing." She cried. It seemed genuine, but who could be sure about anything on the Westside of L.A.

Her husband remained dry-eyed.

Milo said, "Care to fill us in, sir?"

"Not on your life," said Jack Weathers. "Not on one blessed second of your blessed life."

CHAPTER

32

We lingered outside the door Jack Weathers had just shut.

Conversational noise began filtering through the wood: Daisy Weathers's higher-pitched voice, plaintive, then demanding. No response from Jack. Daisy, again, louder. A bark from her husband that silenced her.

Several seconds later his voice resumed, softer, less staccato. A long string of sentences.

Milo whispered, "On the phone, now it's a lawyer game."

We left the building.

◆

Milo drove a block, U-turned, found the farthest spot that afforded a view of the marble-clad building. Red zone but until a B.H. parking Nazi showed up, the perfect vantage point.

I said, "Waiting for Jack to leave?"

"Maybe I stirred up enough for him to meet with legal counsel. I tail him, find out who I'll be dealing with. Without that I can't approach him."

"No warrant party with BHPD?"

"Yeah, right. On what grounds?"

"Jack's demeanor."

"He got agitated? To a psychologist, that's grounds. To a judge, you know what it is." He stretched, knuckled an eyelid. "Any way it shakes out, he's toast. Runs a business based on image and trust and hires one woman with a police record, another who ends up getting killed. And who was referred by the bad girl. Screening my ass."

I said, "Maybe it goes beyond that. Weathers bills himself as a Hollywood insider so maybe he also placed Wedd. At the same client who employed Qeesha and Adriana. Someone powerful enough to shelter income in the Caymans and to scare Weathers straight to legal counsel."

"CAPD," he said.

"Let's try to find out who they are."

"Easier said than done."

"Maybe not."

I pulled out my cell, punched my #1 preset.

Robin said, "Hi, hon, what's up?"

"Got a spare minute for some research?"

"About what?"

"Ever hear of CAPD?"

"Nope."

"Who would you call if you needed info on a big-time showbiz-type?"

"What's this about, Alex?"

I told her.

She said, "Interesting. I'll see what I can do."

Most of Robin's guitars and mandolins are commissioned by professional musicians and collectors who play seriously. A few end up stashed in the vaults of rich men seeking trophies—lucky-sperm recipients, real estate tycoons, Aspergian algorithmers, movie stars.

Plus the lampreys who get rich off movie stars. I rarely think of my girl as a Hollywood type but she's the one who gets invited to all the parties we seldom attend.

Six minutes later, that paid off. "Got what you need."

"That was quick."

"I looped in Brent Dorf."

Dorf was a luminary at a major talent agency. I'd met him last year when he picked up a replica of an eighteenth-century parlor guitar that would end up hanging on a wall. When he found out what I did for a living, he reminisced about being a psych major at Yale, regretted that he hadn't pursued it because his "primary passion" was helping people. My experience is people who talk about being passionate seldom are.

Brent had impressed me as the perfect political type—a mile wide and an inch deep, programmed to banter on cue. His jokes were clever, his attention span brief. Whatever charm he managed to project was diluted by the flat eyes and sanguinary grin of a monitor lizard. At least he paid his bills on time.

I said, "Dorf knew about CAPD?"

"Boy did he, honey. Unfortunately, Big Guy's life is going to get really complicated."

She explained why.

I told Milo.

He said, "Oh."

Then he swore.

CHAPTER
33

Prema-Rani Moon was Hollywood royalty. As is the case with real royalty, that meant a mixed bag of privilege and decadence.

Grandpa Ricardo (né Luna) had been nominated for an Oscar but didn't win the statuette. Grandma Greta's success rate was one for three. Uncle Maximilian's average over a forty-year career was the best: a perfect two out of two.

Daddy Richard Jr.'s star had glittered, then sputtered, with seven forgettable pictures followed by a descent into the gummy haze of heroin addiction. Rick

Moon's final attempt at rehab was a stint at a Calcutta ashram run by a guru later proved to be a rapist. Flirtation with fringe Eastern philosophy led Moon to endow his only child with a hybrid Indian name: Prema, a Sanskrit word for "love," and Rani, "queen" in Hindi.

By the time the little girl was five, all traces of religion in her father's muddled consciousness had been banished and he was living in Montmartre with the little girl's mother, a second-tier Chanel model turned semi-famous by her marriage to the handsome, tormented American film scion.

A coke-induced heart attack claimed Rick's life at age thirty-eight. Lulu Moon claimed she'd tried to revive her husband. If so, the powder she'd crammed up her nose hampered the process. Fourteen months later, she was buried next to Rick at Père Lachaise cemetery after slashing her wrists while her daughter slept in an adjoining bedroom.

Prema, as she was now known, discovered the body. Never schooled, she couldn't read the barely literate suicide note that belied Lulu's claims of attending the Sorbonne.

Shipped back to Bel Air, the child was raised by her grandparents, which translated to a stream of boarding schools where she failed to fit in. The child-rearing ethos on Bellagio Road was less-than-benign neglect. Ricardo and Greta, still working occasionally in character roles, were gorgeous alcoholics and compulsive plastic surgery patients who had no interest in children—in anyone other than themselves. By the time Prema was fourteen her grandparents were pickled in Polish vodka and resembled wax figures molded by addled sculptors. Two years later, Ricardo and Greta were dead and Prema was an adolescent heiress whose considerable assets were managed by a private bank in Geneva.

With no other option, Maximilian Moon, now knighted and living in London, took on the task of serving as his niece's guardian. That translated to a two-room suite on the third floor of Sir Max's Belgravia mansion, Prema enduring her uncle's abysmal piano playing and getting to know the coterie of young lithe men he labeled his "paramours."

When Prema was sixteen, a poobah at a major modeling agency noticed the tall, slender blond girl with the scalpel-hewn cheekbones, the ripe-peach lips, and the huge indigo eyes standing in a corner at one of Max's parties with an unlit joint in her hand. The offer of a contract was immediate.

Prema yawned her way down the runway as a Gaultier clothes-hanger, rented herself a garret off Rue Saint-Germain, never bothered to visit her parents' graves. The combination of passive income and modeling fees allowed her to regularly score chunks of hashish the size of soap bars from Tunisian dealers near the flea market, a treat she shared with her fellow ecto-morph beauties.

Her apathy during Fashion Week made her all the more attractive. *Elle* and *Marie Claire* vied to feature her as the next *jeune fille* sensation. Prema turned them down and abruptly abandoned modeling because she found it "stupid and dull." Back in London, she occasionally ran with a crowd of similarly bored kids but preferred solitary time for smoking weed.

One day, Uncle Max paused long enough in his butchery of Rachmaninoff to suggest his now gorgeous niece attend university. When Prema laughed that off, he offered her a stint as a fairy in a Royal Shakespeare Company production of *A Midsummer Night's Dream* in which he was slated to play Oberon.

Prema agreed.

She loved being someone else.

The rest is fan-mag history.

Donald Lee Rumples was born in Oklahoma City where his father worked as a pipe fitter and his mother stayed home raising five kids. Preternaturally handsome but lacking the coordination for athletics enjoyed by his brothers and the attention span for scholarship displayed by his sisters, he dropped out of high school at seventeen, worked as a janitor, then a gutter at a meatpacking plant, gave that all up and hitchhiked to L.A. where he swept up a 7-Eleven on Western Avenue in Hollywood.

That career lasted four months, at which time he wangled a day job as a golf caddie supplemented by a night-time gig sweeping up a pizza joint in Brentwood. It was there that the wife of a TV producer took a shine to the black-haired, black-eyed kid tidying up the pepperoni and offered him a position as a houseboy at her manse in Holmby Hills.

A year of not-so-clandestine bedding of the somewhat large lady of the very large house led to Donald's being spotted while serving hors d'oeuvres at his host's Christmas party. The spotter was a casting agent and the offer was a walk-on part in a low-budget horror flick.

Once on the set, Rumples caught the eye of a female assistant director. The following day he'd moved into her Venice apartment. Weeks after that, he traded up to the Encino compound of her boss, the male director. Months later he was the toy of a studio executive with a spread in Bel Air who got him an agent. That led to a speaking part in a dog food commercial. The spot sold a lot of kibble and Donald scored a speaking part in an action film and a legal name change. His face and physique were adored by the camera and if he had enough time he could memorize a few lines.

The action flick was marketed to teenage boys but women loved it and marketing surveys revealed the reason: "strong but sensitive" black-haired, black-eyed Ranger Hemos, played by Donny Rader. A curious slurred delivery that would have been judged clumsy in a homely man was labeled sexy by legions of female admirers.

One of those admirers was Prema Moon, now thirty-four and an established star. She summoned the younger man with the strangely appealing mumble to her compound off Coldwater Canyon. Donny had just begun living with his last costar, a sweet-tempered B-list actress with the IQ of adobe. Prema couldn't have cared less about prior commitments. In what *People* termed "a disarming burst of candor" she described the courtship as "the boy was fresh meat. I swooped down like a raptor."

Donny moved to the estate. Bigger and better roles came his way. Two years into their relationship, he and Prema were each pulling twenty million a picture and lending new meaning to the term "power couple." Paparazzi got rich peddling candid shots of the duo. Donny and Prema took it to the next level, costarring in three pictures. Two stylish comedies tanked but the dystopian sci-fi epic *Wizardine* grossed north of two billion internationally.

At age thirty-seven, Prema Moon announced her desire for a quieter life, adopted an orphan from Africa and two from Asia, became the spokesperson for a slew of human rights organizations, caused diplomats to squirm as their shorts rode up when she addressed the U.N. in her trademark sultry voice.

At forty, she added a baby girl to her "tribe."

Donny Rader, ten years his wife's junior, dropped out of the limelight.

The couple's net worth was rumored

at three hundred million. Everyone figured they'd resurface. A hack at *The Hollywood Reporter* termed them "far greater than the sum of their parts," and dubbed them Premadonny.

The sobriquet stuck. How could it not?

Milo said, "CAPD, Creative Aura of Prema and Donny. Sounds like something you'd doodle while zoning out in class."

I said, "Along with goofy drawings of rocket ships. Robin's source says it used to be one of their holding companies but it got dissolved, something to do with changes in the tax code."

"Lord Donny, Lady Prema, top of the Industry food chain. Jack's probably mainlining blood pressure meds."

"Working for them could be why Wedd doesn't use his apartment much. Their compound is ten acres, probably includes staff housing."

His phone played "Hungarian Rhapsody." Kelly LeMasters said, "I feel for you. Having to deal with that bitch."

"Maria was her usual charming self."

"Maria," she said, "is one of those automatons who delude themselves they're capable of independent thought."

"She stonewalled you, huh?"

"She sure tried," said LeMasters. "I told her I'd run a follow-up story hell or high water and would harass you to the point of stalking and she waffled just like you said. The way we left it is she'll call you to work out the 'proper data feed' and get back to me."

"Good work, kid."

"Now we're buddies?"

"Common enemy and all that, Kelly."

Click.

He said, "Ten acres. Didn't know you were interested in movie stars."

"A couple of years ago a man representing them called for an appointment for a 'family member' but claimed he didn't know who. I asked him who'd referred them to me. He had no idea about that, either, was just following instructions, asked if I could make a house call. I said okay if payment would be portal-to-portal. He said money was no object, gave me the address. I was intrigued so I did some research, including Google Maps. The next day, a call came into my service canceling. When I phoned to ask why, I couldn't get through. I tried again, same result."

"They hire another shrink?"

"I have no idea."

"Lucky me," he said. "If you'd actually seen them or their kids, you'd have to recuse yourself. No actual contract or contact, no confidentiality, right?"

"Right, but if someone that powerful wanted to sue me, they'd do it anyway."

"You're staying out of it?"

"Hell, no."

CHAPTER

34

We'd watched the marble-clad building for nine minutes when Maria Thomas called.

"Just had an obnoxious conversation with a *Times* reporter who brags she's been dogging you."

Milo said, "Kelly LeMasters, Olympic gold medalist in the Pest-athlon."

"She getting in the way of the job?"

"If it goes any further, she will," he said. "At this point she's just an annoyance."

"Well," said Thomas, "she's threatening to hound you to the ground unless

you feed her exclusive info and if you
don't give her anything, she'll dig for alternative sources and go public. And
we both know she'll find alternatives, all
those loose-lipped idiots floating around
the department."

"That's my problem, Maria?"

"Now it is."

Milo groaned. Turned to me and gave
a thumbs-up and grinned like a drunk.

"Way I see it," Thomas continued,
"you can neutralize her by being selective."

"Easy for you to say, Maria. You're
not the one getting dogged."

"Yeah, yeah. Anyway, that's the way
it's going to be. You're instructed to
meet with her A-sap and offer her judicious info."

"Define judicious."

"At this point," said Thomas, "Moron
Maxine's real estate deal's totally
screwed so feel free to play with the
Cheviot Hills angle. Give her anything
that doesn't compromise the investigation."

"I've been shutting her out completely," he said. "Now I do a total about-face."

"Flexibility," said Thomas. "It's a sign of psychological strength, ask Delaware."

"I see him, I might just do that."

"Whatever. Now go meet with the bitch and stay in control. Any progress on the case?"

"Not much."

"Then it's no big deal. Feed her a steaming mound of bullshit, press-types are born with taste buds for it."

Click.

I said, "Didn't know Machiavelli was Irish."

He laughed. "When you're in love, laddie, everyone is Irish." His head swiveled toward Beverly Drive. A car had pulled up in front of Gold Standard's building.

Iron-gray Mercedes sedan. A curly-haired, middle-aged man in a navy suit got out and remote-locked the car. Bypassing the mailbox outfit, he opened the door to the second floor, stepped in and up.

Milo said, "Maybe he's someone

needs gift counseling but I'm smelling the musty aroma of lawyer."

He swung another U, got behind the Mercedes, copied the tags. Continuing south into L.A., he crossed Pico, turned left on Cashio Street, parked, ran the numbers.

Floyd Banfer, home address on South Camden Drive in B.H.

A 411 call obtained Banfer's professional listing: attorney-at-law, office on Roxbury Drive just north of Wilshire in B.H.

"Keeping it local," said Milo. "Should I go back in there and confront them or give myself time to plan? I'm leaning toward wait and see."

"Sounds like you know what to do."

"Spoken like a master therapist."

We headed back to the station. He continued past the staff lot, stopped where I'd parked the Seville, kept the engine running.

I said, "Playdate's over?"

"I'd better get the meeting with Le-Masters out of the way. I'd bring you along but she'll probably make a big deal about the cop-shrink thing and I figure you don't want the exposure."

"More important, it'll be good for Kelly to feel she's getting your undivided attention."

"That, too."

"Anything I can do in the meantime?"

"Clean up your room and stop sassing your mother. What can you do . . . okay, here's something: Figure out a way I can get into Premadonny-Land to look for Mr. Wedd."

"Maybe you won't need to," I said. "If he's holed up there, eventually he'll leave."

"Start surveillance on the place?" Out came his pad. "You remember the address?"

"No, but it's easy to find. Coldwater north, about a mile past Mulholland on the west side of the road there's an unmarked private road that leads up to a gate."

"Your research included driving up there?"

"I'm an empiricist."

"Some rep called you, huh? Wouldn't it be something if it was Wedd?"

"It would," I said.

"You've already thought about that."

I wished him well, got out of the car.

He said, "Hooray for Hollywood." Roared away.

CHAPTER
35

My research on Premadonny had involved more than I'd let on to Milo.

After the call from the stars' rep, I'd picked among millions of Web citations. Bios composed early in their careers aired bins of dirty laundry. Everything subsequent was P.R. pap programmed as carefully as a laugh track.

Clips from their films left no question about their physical perfection. A Renaissance artist would've submitted to indignity, if not outright torture, in order to paint them.

Prema Moon came across as a com-

petent, occasionally impressive performer who could amplify or lower her
sexuality as if equipped with an erotic
rheostat. The only mention she made of
her children was on a press release an-
nouncing her "hiatus from film work in
order to concentrate on being a full-time
mom." Donny Rader lent his support to
that move, calling his wife "the ultimate
earth mother, protective as a mama
lion."

Rader's acting was surprisingly one-
note. His default mannerisms were the
slow, theatrical lowering of hooded eyes
and the tendency to slur his words.

The man who'd requested the appointment had begun talking in a
choppy, agitated delivery but had shifted
quickly to mumbly diction.

I replayed a few of Rader's clips,
heard the same elisions, over and over.
If not identical to the man on the phone,
awfully close.

Had it been a worried father phoning
me about his child but choosing to hide
that fact? Because A-list celebs weren't
supposed to do things for themselves?

Or was there a deeper motive for the deception?

Whoever the "representative" was, he'd skated away from naming the child in question, assuring me I'd find out soon enough then hanging up. His tension had been notable, and that could mean an especially worrisome problem.

I'd keyworded *premadonny children.*

Millions of hits on the parents but almost nothing on the kids.

An image search pulled up a solitary photo gone viral: a shot taken a few months before in New York of Prema and her kids attending a Broadway Disney musical.

Red-velvet, gilt-molded walls in the background supported the caption's assertion that the group had been photographed in the theater lobby. But the space was otherwise unpopulated, which was odd for an SRO hit, and the lighting was dim but for a crisp, klieg-like beam focused on the subjects. Maybe Prema and her brood had been let in early. Or they'd arrived on a Dark Monday in order to be posed as carefully as a Velázquez royal sitting.

I studied the shot. Prema Moon, wearing a conservative, dark pantsuit that set off cascades of golden hair, stood behind the four kids. The lighting was gracious to her heart-shaped face and her perfect chin and her beyond-perfect cheekbones.

The oldest child, a boy of ten or eleven, had fine features and ebony skin that evoked Somalia or Ethiopia. A doll-like Asian girl around eight and a grave Asian boy slightly younger flanked a platinum-haired, pouting toddler with cherubic chubby cheeks and dimpled knuckles.

All of them were dressed in matching white shirts and dark pants, as uniformly clad as parochial school students. No names provided, just "Prema and her pretty quartet."

"Pretty" was an understatement; each child was gorgeous. All but the youngest smiled woodenly. The collective posture, again excepting the toddler, was military-rigid.

Prema graced the photographer with the faintest smile—just enough parting of moist, full lips to imply the theoretical possibility of mirth. Her eyes refused to go along; laser-intense, they aimed at some distant focal point.

No physical contact between her and her progeny; her arms remained pressed to her sides.

I searched the kids' faces looking for anything that might tell me whom I was scheduled to see. Not much of anything emotion-wise, which in kids meant plenty was going on.

Intrigued about what I'd encounter once I got behind the gates of the compound, I logged off.

A day or two after the cancellation, I remained curious. Then my calendar booked up the way it usually does and I was concentrating on murder victims and patients who actually showed up.

Now, nearly two years later, I drove home, curiosity re-ignited.

This time the computer was a bit more cooperative and I found a couple of hundred references to the children, including their names.

Kion, thirteen.

Kembara, eleven.

Kyle-Jacques, eight.

Kristina, four.

But not a single image. The theater-lobby shot had been expunged.

A closer reading of the citations proved disappointing. All of them discussed how zealously Premadonny protected their progeny's privacy. A few snarky types bemoaned the couple's "CIA approach to parenting," but most of the chatterers and bloggers and gurus of gossip were supportive of the attempt to prevent the children from becoming "grist for the paparazzi mill."

Maybe so, but there was another reason for isolating children.

Milo was concentrating on Melvin Jaron Wedd's link to the compound on Mulholland Drive. My mind was going in a completely different direction.

I made some coffee, added foamed milk and cinnamon, brought a mugful to Robin's studio.

She put down her chisel and smiled. "This is becoming a regular thing."

Blanche's little flat nose quivered as she inhaled the aroma. I fetched her a bacon-bone from the box Robin keeps at hand. She took the treat from my fingers with her usual delicacy, trotted over to a corner to nosh in peace. Robin sipped and said, "You even girlied it up for me, what a good boyfriend."

"Least I can do."

"You owe me for something?"

"Cosmically, I owe you a ton. When you call Brent Dorf a second time, my gratitude will blossom further. Ask if I can talk to him in person about Premadonny. If he has nothing to offer, maybe he can refer me to someone who does."

"You actually suspect those two of something?"

"It hasn't gotten that far, but a murder victim worked for them and maybe so did a prime suspect. Toss in Qeesha D'Embo, who could be victim or suspect, and it's well beyond interesting."

"Weird goings-on behind the gates," she said. "Maybe they just hired the wrong people."

"Maybe," I said, "but all of this has stirred up something that happened a couple of years ago."

I told her about the canceled referral,

my suspicion that Donny Rader had tried to hide his identity. "Back then my gut told me there was a serious problem with the family. Now I'm wondering if that meant a child disturbed enough to hurt a baby."

She put her cup down. "That's horrible."

"Horrible and worth covering up. Prema Moon gave up her career and recast herself as a devoted, protective mother. Both of them have. Can you imagine the repercussions if it turned out they'd raised a murderous child? Even if the baby's death was accidental—kids horsing around, something unfortunate happened—that kind of disclosure would be disastrous. Any mother would have good reason to go to the cops. But Qeesha D'Embo was no stranger to deceit and working the angles, so she might've put a serious squeeze on. We know she had conflict with Wedd, assumed it was a romantic issue. But Wedd could've been Premadonny's paymaster, so maybe the problem between them was business."

"She wanted more, he said no, she's dead, too."

Her nails pinged the coffee mug.

I said, "Sorry to pollute your day."

"I'm fine—the car scam, Alex. Why would Premadonny stoop to insurance fraud?"

"That could've been Wedd improvising so he could pocket the payoff money."

"Or he really is the only bad guy and they had the misfortune of hiring him. What exactly does he do for them?"

"Don't know, the agency's clammed up."

"A murderous child," she said. "How old are the kids?"

"Four, eight, eleven, thirteen."

"So the oldest," she said.

"Most likely."

"Boy or girl?"

"Boy."

"What else do you know about him?"

"Nothing, they've all been swept out of sight, I'm talking utter invisibility. There are good reasons for keeping your kids out of the public eye. But there are also bad ones."

"Protecting a homicidal thirteen-year-old."

"Protecting the alternative universe that created a homicidal thirteen-year-old. Rob, when I come across unusually secretive, isolated families, there's almost always major pathology at play. The most common factor is abuse of power—a cult-like situation. Sometimes that stops at eccentricity. Sometimes it leads to really bad things."

She drank more coffee, placed the mug on her desk. "Okay, I'll call Brent right now."

"Thanks, babe. Let him know I need him because he's dialed in."

"Brent's all about being Mr. Inside, that's the perfect approach." She smiled. "But of course you knew that."

CHAPTER
36

Brent Dorf had just left for New York on business. His assistant claimed a return date hadn't been set but promised to deliver the message.

Robin said, "Brent'll be interested in what I have for him, I'm counting on you, luv."

She hung up.

I said, "Luv?"

"Charles is British and gay but he likes flirting with girls. Brent's gay, too, for that matter. But he has absolutely *no* interest in girls."

She laughed. "I can just imagine him

and Milo taking lunch at the Grill on the Alley."

"They allow polyester?"

"On alternate Tuesdays."

"We haven't been there in a long time."

"I don't think we've ever been there."

"There's another reason to go," I said. "Tonight sound good?"

"You're in the mood?"

"For time with you, always."

"Meaning you're tired of thinking."

I told her that's not what I meant at all and that I loved her and went back to my office.

Dinner was a two-hour respite and when we left the Grill shortly after ten p.m., I felt loose and content. The night air was clean and warm, an invitation to walk. Rodeo Drive's around the corner from the restaurant and once the tourists go to bed, it's a peaceful stroll. Robin held my arm as we strolled past windows showcasing stuff no one could afford. We made it home by eleven.

Making love was a great next step in the quest for distraction but when you're compulsive and addicted to the bad stuff, you inevitably return to that dark place. I lay next to Robin as she slept peacefully, unanswerable questions eddying in my head.

The following morning, as she showered, I took Blanche outside for her a.m. toilette and retrieved the paper from the driveway. Leafing through, I came across Kelly LeMasters's follow-up story on the park murders.

Page 10, maybe five hundred words, but she'd scored above-the-crease placement.

Milo had lured her with the promise of something juicy but nothing close to that appeared in the article, leaving LeMasters to play with human-interest filler: the mystery trajectory that had taken Adriana Betts from church-girl to murder victim, the impact of two Cheviot Hills murders upon affluent citizens.

Adriana's sister, Helene, and the Reverend Goleman were quoted but their comments were no more revelatory than their station-house interviews. The sad mystery of a "strewn infant skeleton" was noted as was the "eerie parallel" to the bones found under Matt and Holly Ruche's cedar tree. Nothing about the park baby's racial makeup or parentage.

Milo's name didn't come up until the final paragraph, where he was described as "a veteran homicide detective left baffled." The piece ended with an "anyone with information" message and his landline.

I figured he'd be busy all morning fielding leads, was surprised when he phoned at nine.

"Taking a break from the tipsters?"

"Got Moe and Sean on that, I need to roll. Just got a call from Floyd Banfer, Jack Weathers's lawyer. He wants to meet, an hour and a half, B.H. parkway, corner Rexford."

"Right near City Hall."

"Banfer's serving papers at BHPD, said he'd walk over."

"He's suing the police?"

"Some sort of workers' comp deal on behalf of a fired officer. Nothing, he assured me, that I'd find objectionable."

"What's on his mind?"

"He wouldn't say but he's definitely

antsy, Alex. I like that in attorneys. Makes them seem almost human."

Milo and I arrived at ten twenty, found a bench on the north side of the parkway with a clear view of the Beverly Hills government complex. The original city hall is a thirties Spanish Renaissance masterpiece. The civic center complex built fifty years later tried to work deco and contemporary into the mix and ended up looking tacked on. A degraded granite path, Chinese elms, and lawn separated us from Santa Monica Boulevard. Traffic howled in both directions. An ancient man accompanied by a husky attendant inched a walker past us. A trio of Persian women in Fila tracksuits bounced by chatting in Farsi. A young woman who could have been a Victoria's Secret model if the company raised its standards raced past all of them looking miserable.

Directly in front of us was a six-foot-by-ten-foot mound of lumpy chrome-plate.

Milo said, "What the hell is that?"

"Public art."

"Looks like a jumbo jet had digestive problems."

At ten twenty-six Floyd Banfer exited the police station, crossed the street, and headed toward us. When he arrived, he was flushed and smiling, a compact man with a peanut-shaped head, bright blue eyes, and the kind of white stubble that Milo calls a "terrorist beard."

"Punctual," he boomed. "Nice to be dealing with professionals." Compact man with an expansive bass voice.

A hand shot out. "Floyd Banfer."

"Milo Sturgis, this is Alex Delaware."

Shakes all around. Banfer's grip was a mite too firm, his arm remained stiff, his eyes wary. The smile he'd arrived with seemed glued to his face. "Pretty morning, eh?"

"Don't imagine Beverly Hills would allow anything less, Counselor."

Banfer chuckled. "You'd be surprised." His suit was the same dark gray we'd seen yesterday, a slightly shiny silk-and-wool. His shirt was a TV blue spread-collar, his tie a pink Hermès patterned with bugles. Fifty to fifty-five, with thin, wavy hair tinted brown and throwing off red highlights the way men's dyed hair often does, he radiated an odd mix of good cheer and anxiety. As if he enjoyed being on edge.

Milo motioned to the space we'd created between us on the bench.

Banfer said, "Mind if we walk? That piece of shit they call art makes me queasy and any chance to exercise is welcome."

"Sure."

The three of us headed west. The granite pathways are supposed to resist dust but Banfer's black wingtips turned gray within seconds. Every few yards, he managed to wipe the shoes on the back of his trousers without breaking step. At Crescent Drive we paused until cross-traffic cleared. A helmeted bicyclist rounded the corner and sped toward us and Banfer had to step to the right to avoid collision.

"Totally illegal," he said, still smiling. "No bikes allowed. Want to chase him down and give him a ticket, Lieutenant?"

Milo hadn't told Banfer his rank. Banfer did his homework.

"Above my pay grade, Counselor."

Banfer chuckled again. "So why did I ask for this meeting?"

He paused, as if really expecting an answer.

Milo and I kept walking.

Banfer said, "First off, thanks for being accommodating, got a tough week, if not now, it would have to wait."

"Happy to oblige, Mr. Banfer. What's on your mind?"

"Floyd's fine. Okay, let me start with a given: Jack Weathers is a good man."

Milo didn't answer.

Banfer said, "You kind of scared him, popping in like that."

"Not my intention."

Banfer picked up his pace. "Be that as it may, Lieutenant, here's the thing: Jack and Daisy are good people, run a good business, perform a good service—did you know they used to be in the Industry? Small screen mostly, Jack played music and acted, did a whole bunch of *Hawaii Five-O*'s, some *Gunsmoke,* couple of *Magnum*s. Daisy was on *Lawrence Welk* for years. Then Jack did real estate out in the Valley and Daisy did some dance teaching, she was a dancer before she was an actress, performed with Martha Graham, knew Cyd Charisse, I'm talking talent."

"Impressive," said Milo.

"I'd say."

Several more steps. A group of younger Persian women glided past, trim in black velour, wearing pearls and diamonds, listening to iPods.

Banfer said, "What I'm trying to get across is these are decent, honest people, been working all their lives, neither of them came from money, they found a niche, developed it, thank God they've been doing well, can even possibly think about retiring. At some point. Though I don't know if they will, that's up to them."

"Makes sense."

"What does?" said Banfer.

"Making their own decision about retirement."

"Yes. Of course. My point here is that we're talking good people."

"I'll take your word for it, Floyd."

"Good. Anyway, in case you don't know how the Industry works, let me cue you in, it's all hierarchy. Bottom of the pyramid up to the top, we're talking highly structured, who you know determines how you do, things can change in a snap." He paused to breathe. "Who'm I preaching to, this is L.A., you're pros."

We reached Canon Drive. A homeless man shuffled toward us, leaving a wake of stench.

Banfer wrinkled his nose. "No more vagrancy laws. I'm ambivalent about that, would like to see them taken care of properly but you can't just go scoop them up out of the park the way I saw in Europe when I was a student backpacking in the eighties. Made me think of storm troopers."

Milo made no effort hiding the glance at his Timex.

Banfer said, "Time to cut to the chase? Sure, makes sense."

But he offered no additional wisdom as we continued walking.

Halfway to Beverly Drive, Milo said, "Floyd, what exactly can I do for you?"

"Accept the data I'm going to proffer in the spirit with which it's offered."

"Meaning?"

"Jack and Daisy need to be kept out of any homicide investigation, nor will their contract client—the client in question—be notified of their input to the police."

"CAPD," said Milo. "Creative Aura of Prema and Donny."

Banfer's chin vibrated. "So you know. Okay, now you see what I mean."

"You go to court much, Floyd?"

The question threw Banfer off-balance and he stiffened his arms. "When it's necessary. Why?"

"Just curious."

"You're saying I'm long-winded? Would bore a jury? Don't worry, I do just fine. Am I being a bit . . . detailed? Maybe I am, yes, I am. Because I told Jack and Daisy I'd take care of it and darned if I'm going to go back to them and tell them I didn't. They're good folk."

"Which one are you related to?"

Banfer turned scarlet. "Why would you assume that?"

"You seem unusually dedicated but sorry if I presumed."

"Let me assure you, I'd do the same for any client, Lieutenant." A beat. "But if you must know, Jack was married to my mother's sister and then she died and he married Daisy. So technically, Daisy's my step-aunt but I think of her as my full aunt, she's dear to me, she's a dear woman."

"She seemed very nice."

"Jack's nice, too."

"No doubt."

"So do we have a deal?"

"That depends on what you have to offer."

"I have the truth to offer, Lieutenant Sturgis—may I call you Milo?"

"Sure."

"Milo, this can be extremely simple if we go the simplicity route. I give you information and you use it as you see fit in your criminal investigation but you don't draw Jack and Daisy into it."

"I have no desire to complicate their lives, Floyd, but I need to be up front with you. If they've got crucial information, it could find its way into the case file."

"Not true," snapped Banfer. "Just call them confidential informants and everything will go smooth as silk."

"I can do that but I can't promise that at some point a prosecutor's not going to want to know their identity."

"If that happens, you say no."

"It doesn't work that way, Floyd."

"Then we . . . have a problem."

"You may have all kinds of problems if Jack and Daisy don't cooperate, Floyd. I don't need to tell you about all the unpleasant legal maneuvers at the D.A.'s disposal."

"I'll fight each and every one."

"That will toss Jack and Daisy right into the limelight."

Banfer slanted forward, walked faster.

Milo said, "All this hassle just to make sure Premadonny doesn't get mad at them?"

"It's not a matter of mad," said Banfer. "It's a matter of excommunication. Do you know how powerful those two are?"

"A-list."

"Oh, no, no, no." Banfer's hand arced above his head, like a kid playing airplane. "*Miles* above A-list. It's like pissing off the queen of England."

"Last I checked the queen hadn't excommunicated anyone, Floyd."

"Okay," said the lawyer, "perhaps I engaged in a bit of hyperbole, but still. If word gets out that Jack somehow violated a confidence, the results could be professionally and financially devastating."

"Jack and Daisy signed a gag clause."

Banfer frowned. "Standard operating procedure when dealing with clients at that level."

"Maybe so, but we already know Jack sent Adriana Betts to work at Premadonny's compound and we're fairly certain he did the same for a couple of other people who may be connected to Adriana Betts's murder. Did you read today's *Times*?"

"Of course," said Banfer. "That's why I called you."

"The reporter's itching for anything I

can give her. I've been holding her off but that could change."

"You're threatening to leak my clients' identities?"

"You called the meeting, Floyd. I'm letting you know how things stand."

Banfer clicked his teeth. "Lieutenant Sturgis," he said, as if hearing the title for the first time. "Do you by chance have legal training?"

"I'll take that as a compliment though I'm not sure I should. The answer is just what I've learned on the job."

"Well, you're a wily man, Milo. Not what I'd expect. Because frankly most of the cops I encounter aren't what you'd call intellectual giants."

"You encounter a lot of cops?"

"I do my share of workers' comp, have represented several of your compatriots, learned how they tick. Typically their long-term goals don't stretch beyond a brand-new motorcycle and a Hawaiian vacation."

"Oh, those crazy kids in blue."

"It was meant as a compliment. You seem different, Milo. A careful planner."

"Accepted and appreciated, Floyd.

So what is it you'd like to tell me in the hope that Jack and Daisy remain bullet-proof?"

Banfer stopped, took hold of the bulb at the end of his nose and twisted. His breath had grown ragged. He said, "Let's sit down."

CHAPTER
37

Beverly Hills park benches are complex creations, curvy and black and wrought iron with a center divider that makes it difficult for more than two people to sit. Milo motioned Banfer to the left. A flick of his head directed me to the right.

Leaving him on his feet, looming.

Another homeless man shambled by, eyes rolling, stumbling.

Banfer said, "That's probably where they got the idea for that picture—*Down and Out in Beverly Hills.* They prettied it up, but that's the Industry . . . okay, back to business: Jack and Daisy are—"

"Wonderful people. Acknowledged, Floyd."

"Ethical people," Banfer corrected. "Jack made some mistakes, granted, but the basic core is ethical so there's no reason for you to worry about them."

"Mistakes as in hiring Adriana Betts without vetting her."

Banfer rubbed his temples. "Facts can only tell you so much when you're dealing with human beings, Milo. Jack's come to trust his instincts and Ms. Betts impressed him as a decent young woman."

I said, "Plus it was an urgent situation."

Banfer clicked his teeth again. "Allegedly."

"You have your doubts?"

"The origin of that supposition was a call Jack received from another employee at the compound. Someone he'd placed a while back. She—there was an assertion that the clients needed additional child care as soon as possible, Jack was to come up with someone

immediately. This individual knew someone who fit the bill perfectly—the right
training and experience. Jack's a people-pleaser, he got into the business to
fill human need. It seemed like an ideal
arrangement."

Milo said, "Don't see a big problem
there, Floyd. If he had checked Adriana
out he would've learned she was
squeaky-clean."

Banfer crossed his legs, tugged a
sock up a hairless shin. "Well, that's
good to hear."

"On the other hand, Floyd, if the employee who recommended her was
Qeesha D'Embo, that complicates matters."

"I'm not familiar with that name."

"How about Charlene Chambers?"

"Nor that one."

Milo produced the mug shot.

Banfer sagged.

"How do you know her, Floyd?"

"She represented herself to Jack and
Daisy as Simone Chambord. That's the
name Jack and Daisy used to check
her out and she came up spotless."

"When was she hired?"

"Twenty-three months ago."

Soon after leaving Boise.

I said, "What was she hired for?"

The question seemed to puzzle Banfer. "Child care, of course." He tapped the photo. "After you showed that to Jack and he called me in a panic, I took a closer look at her. Specifically, I traced the Social Security number she'd used when she applied for the job. It matches a Simone Chambord, all right, but that person turns out to be an eighty-nine-year-old woman living in a rest home in New Orleans. I called over there and the director informed me Mrs. Chambord had advanced Alzheimer's, had been that way for five years."

"Jack and Daisy's search didn't pull that up?"

"They were focused on relevant criteria. Criminal record, poor credit."

"Good point," I said. "Advanced Alzheimer's would sure inhibit criminality."

Banfer shook his head. "The potential ramifications for Gold Standard are obvious but no harm was intended."

Milo said, "Your clients provided a con artist as a nanny for movie stars' kids, did the same for a woman who ended up dead. Yeah, I'd say those are ramifications."

"That's a tiny proportion of all the wonderful people Jack and Daisy have connected with wonderful clients."

Recited with all the conviction of a gulag loyalty pledge.

I said, "Unfortunately, you're only as good as your last picture."

Banfer sighed. "I've advised Jack to sit tight, but obviously he's on pins and needles. To make matters worse, Daisy knew nothing about any of this."

Milo said, "Unhappy wife, unhappy life."

"It's a mess, all right. By the way, I did check out Ms. Betts's Social Security and it comes back to her. Have I missed something? Because she and Chambord seem an unlikely pairing."

Milo said, "Nothing crooked has turned up on Adriana."

"That baby found at the park—those bones—what's the connection?"

"Don't know yet, Floyd. That's why we wanted to talk to Jack and Daisy."

"Well, they certainly can't tell you anything about *that*."

"Qeesha—Simone—was hired twenty-three months ago. What about Adriana?"

"Recently. Around three, four months ago according to Jack."

"He can't be more precise?"

Banfer stared straight ahead.

Milo said, "He destroyed the files?"

"I can't get into that."

"Your client got rid of potential evidence. If you advised him to do that you could be facing obstruction charges."

"Same answer, I'm afraid."

Banfer turned to Milo. Milo glared and Banfer faced forward again. "Let's put this in context: I've been more forthcoming than I need to be, given the circumstances."

"What circumstances are those, Floyd?"

"No charges have been filed against anyone, you're at the supposition stage, fishing around, and neither I nor my client is obligated to talk to you about anything. However, we *chose* to cooperate volitionally because we're *not* obstructionistic. And in terms of files, I'm unaware of any statute requiring a small businessman to cope with needless paper buildup."

"Fair enough," said Milo.

Sudden switch to an easy, amiable tone. Banfer risked another try at eye contact. Milo smiled.

"Well," said the attorney, "it's good to see we've reached a meeting of the minds."

"I agree. Now how about we talk to Jack, directly."

"You feel that's necessary?"

"Wouldn't ask if I didn't, Floyd."

Banfer sighed again, punched numbers on his cell phone. "Hey, it's me . . . as well as can be expected . . . I told them that . . . they still want to talk to you . . . I'll stay right here, not to worry . . . might as well, you've got nothing to hide . . . sooner's better than later, Jack, let's get it over with and move on . . . we're on the parkway between Beverly and Camden . . . good idea." Clicking off, he studied the traffic. "On his way."

◆

Jack Weathers wore a blue cashmere blazer, a white silk shirt, dove-colored slacks, blue suede loafers with gold buckles. If they recast *Gilligan's Island,* he'd be great for Thurston Howell the Third. Except for the defeated, sagging shoulders, the bags under his eyes, the wrinkles that had deepened during the twenty-four hours since we'd last seen him.

The shuffling gait of an old, weary man.

I got up and vacated the space next to Banfer. Weathers hesitated.

Milo said, "Take a load off, Jack."

Weathers's jowls quivered. Pink capillaries laced the whites of his eyes. A couple of cuticles were rubbed raw, detracting from an otherwise perfect manicure.

He sat down heavily and Banfer filled him in on what we knew. When Banfer wanted to, he could be concise.

Jack Weathers laced his hands together, stared at his knees.

Milo said, "Tell me everything you remember about the woman who called herself Simone Chambord."

"What's her real name?" said Weathers.

"Why don't you let me do the asking so you can do the answering."

Weathers's head snapped back.

Floyd Banfer said, "Let's keep it streamlined, Jack, and they'll be out of your hair."

Weathers said nothing. The group of younger Persian women returned. His attention shifted to shapely rears, and that seemed to relax him.

He said, "Good-looking girl, black but lightish. I figured her for a wannabe actress."

"Because of her looks."

"That and she had a way about her."

"What way was that, Jack?"

"Vivacious," said Weathers. "Theatrically vivacious."

"Like she was playing a role."

"This town, everyone plays a role. What I'm getting at is everything was just a little bit exaggerated." He studied Milo. "You're kind of central-casting yourself."

"So you figured Simone for a wannabe."

"But she had the right credentials for the child-care job. Experience, letters of reference."

"From who?"

"Previous employers."

"How about some names?"

"Don't recall," said Weathers.

"How about checking the file?"

"No file." Weathers colored. "We turn everything over regularly."

"Paper buildup."

Floyd Banfer rubbed one leg against the other.

Jack Weathers said, "Exactly."

"Okay," said Milo, "but when she applied you must've called her references. Any memories of who they were and what they told you?"

"Nah, I've got so many applications, nothing stands out."

"Business is good."

"Can be," said Weathers. "All I can tell you is she checked out."

"Wannabe actress," said Milo. "Guess you see a lot of that."

"I go in assuming the real agenda is advancing their careers. Or so they believe."

Milo said, "Doesn't work that way?"

"Works against them."

"Why's that?"

"Because once someone's seen as being in a service position they tend to be . . . always seen that way."

"They're viewed as inferior?"

"Not inferior," said Weathers. "Different."

"Donny Rader started off as a golf caddie and houseboy for a producer."

"That's the official story."

"Not true?"

Weathers sneered. "I don't know what's true, what's not. I don't know anyone's narrative."

Floyd Banfer said, "It's all a matter of information control. We hear what they want us to hear."

"Stars," said Milo.

"Anyone in power."

I said, "So you have no problem hiring wannabes."

Jack Weathers said, "Not if they learn their proper place and do the damn job."

"Did Simone Chambord learn?"

"Never heard about problems."

"Far as you know, she's still working for Premadonny."

"I'd assume."

"What else do you remember about her?"

"Good-looking," said Weathers. "Extremely attractive. In that fresh way. Great figure . . . she could carry on a conversation, said she loved kids, showed me a child-development book she was reading."

"She was hired as a nanny."

"No," said Weathers. "As a child-care assistant."

"What's the difference?"

"Pay scale, for starts. When the client insists on an official nanny, we hire British girls who take formal training at one of the schools they have over there. They've got the book learning but some of them can be a little uptight. Some clients like that. Others want something more relaxed."

"Prema Moon and Donny Rader have a relaxed attitude."

"I'd assume."

"How many other people have you sent to them?"

"Couldn't say," said Weathers.

Milo said, "Wild guess."

Weathers looked at Banfer. Banfer nodded.

"Wild guess? I'd say half a dozen."

"What jobs did you fill for them?"

"I believe there were a couple of do-mestics. Housekeepers. We don't do that anymore, can't compete with the domestic-specialty agencies, all those ads they run in the Spanish papers. But back then we did, so probably that's it. Couple of domestics."

He turned to Banfer. "This is okay?"

"So far, Jack."

Milo said, "You're worried about Pre-madonny's gag clause?"

"Hell, yeah," said Weathers. "We're talking damn stringent."

"As opposed to . . ."

Banfer said, "Clauses that are less stringent." He smiled at his own obfus-cation.

Milo said, "Educate me, Counselor."

"It's nothing complicated, Milo. De-fault is generally a ban on talking to the media, publishing a book, that kind of thing. This particular clause covers virtually every single syllable uttered about Premadonny to anyone on any topic. Is it legally binding? Probably not, but testing that theory would bring considerable anguish. In any event, Jack's told you everything he knows about the Chambord woman and Ms. Betts."

"Then on to the next topic," said Milo, pulling out the enlargement of Melvin Jaron Wedd's DMV photo.

Floyd Banfer's face remained blank.

Jack Weathers said, "Oh, shit."

CHAPTER

38

Floyd Banfer placed a hand on Jack Weathers's cashmere sleeve. "He's also one of yours?"

Milo said, "Who is he, Jack?"

Weathers wrung his hands. "A guy . . . M.J."

Milo said, "Melvin Jaron Wedd. When did you place him at the compound?"

Weathers muttered something.

"Speak up, Jack."

"Three years ago. Give or take."

"What's his job title?"

"Estate manager," said Weathers. "I'd placed him before, similar thing."

"Whose estate did he manage before?"

"Saudi family, gigantic place in Bel
Air. Four, five years ago."

"And before then?"

"No, that was the first. They had no
problems with him—the Arabs. They
moved back to Riyadh."

"So you sent him to Premadonny."

"Yeah, yeah."

"Who solicited your help?"

"Business manager."

"Who's that?"

Weathers's eyes traveled to the right.
"Not the manager directly, some assistant."

Floyd Banfer said, "Or some assistant's assistant."

Weathers regarded his nephew
crossly. "That's the way it goes with
people at their level."

Milo said, "Who's their business manager?"

"Apex Management. They handle a
lot of the biggies."

"What do you remember about M.J.?"

"A guy," said Weathers. "I think he
had some bookkeeping experience.

444   JONATHAN KELLERMAN

Him I *did* check out. What's the problem with him?"

"Maybe nothing, Jack."

"Maybe nothing but you're carrying around his picture?"

"His name came up."

"Meaning?"

"His name came up."

Weathers waved a hand. "Frankly, I don't want to know. Now can I go and try to pay some bills? I'm no civil servant, got no cushy pension and overtime."

Milo said, "Sure. Have a nice day."

"Sure?"

"Unless you've got something more to tell us, Jack."

"I've got nothing. To tell or to hide or to relate or report. I'm in the service business, I find service people for clients who need service. What they do once they're hired is their business."

Bracing himself on the bench's center divider, he got to his feet, buttoned his blazer. Banfer stood and took him by the elbow. Weathers shook off the support with surprising fury. "Not ready

for a scooter yet, Floyd, let's get breakfast, Nate 'n Al, Bagel Nosh, whatever."

Working hard at casual.

Banfer tapped his Rolex Oyster.
"Sorry, appointments."

"Busy guy," said Weathers. "Everyone's busy. I should be busy."

He hobbled away.

Banfer said, "His blood pressure's
not great, I hope the stress doesn't
cause problems."

Milo winked. "That sounds like prep
for a civil suit."

"Not funny, Lieutenant. Are we
through?"

Before waiting for an answer, Banfer
headed east on the parkway. A curva-
ceous female jogger came heading his
way. He didn't bother to look.

Milo sat down on the bench. "I drove
by that private road this morning. Like I
thought, tough surveillance. The county
registered the compound as eleven
acres, divided into three legal parcels,
all registered to another holding company called Prime Mayfair. Tried a trace-

back, it dead-ends at a paper-pusher who works for Apex Management."

I said, "A lot of plot to thicken."

He looked up Apex's number. Got transferred a few times. Hung up, shaking his head.

"Got stonewalled by an assistant's assistant's walking-around-guy's gopher's peon's underling slave. Not that anyone would tell me anything even if I could get through. Weathers's destroying his files doesn't help, want to take bets he'll be torching Wedd's soon as he gets back from breakfast? And for all the tough talk to Banfer, there's nothing I can really do about it."

"At least you've got confirmation that all three of them worked together."

He kicked a leg of the bench. Unfolded Wedd's DMV shot and stared at it for a while. "I need face-time with this prince but getting into that compound's as likely as being invited to an Oscar after party." He smiled. "Actually, Rick was invited to one a few years ago. After sewing up the DUI daughter of some hoo-hah producer who drove her Aston into a wall."

"Did you go?"

"Nah, both of us were on call that night . . . okay, I'll figure out a way to watch the place. After I recanvass the park, see if the staff or the regulars remember anything."

He checked with Reed and Binchy to learn if Kelly LeMasters's story had pulled up anything solid. It hadn't. Same for the anonymous Crime Stoppers line.

I said, "Breakfast? Nate 'n Al, Bagel Nosh?"

"No, thanks, already ate."

Prior meals had never deterred him before.

I said, "Hope you feel better."

Back home I put in a call to Dr. Leonard Coates.

Len and I were classmates in grad school, worked together for a year at Western Pediatric. I stuck around at the hospital, putting in time on the cancer wards while Len shifted to a Beverly Hills private practice.

Soon after hiring a publicist, Len began getting quoted in the popular press. It didn't take long to acquire a celebrity patient load, and a few years in he'd taken over the penthouse floor of a building on Roxbury, was overseeing half a dozen associates. While suffering from a serious case of Hollywood Sepsis.

It's a progressive condition, also known as Malignant Look-At-Me Syndrome, leading to excessive dependency on public exposure, self-invention, and the narcosis of fame.

Len's addiction had led him to write a useless pop-psych book, peddle countless treatments for screenplays and reality shows, obsess on getting his picture taken at certain parties in the company of eye candy. Tall and slim and meticulously bearded, he plowed through a succession of women. I'd stopped counting his marriages at four. He had two kids that I knew of and the few times I saw them they both looked depressed. The last time Len and I had run into each other was at a hospital fund-raiser. Smiling all the while and checking out the crowd nonstop, he'd spent a lot of time griping about "ungrateful brats. Just like their mothers, you can't fight genetics."

His service operator put me on hold. The audio track was a sales pitch for "Dr. Coates's compelling new book *Putting Your Life in Balance*."

The operator broke back in as a synopsis of chapter 1 was ending. The gist was "Stop and Smell the Roses." I'd never known Len to have a hobby.

She said, "Sorry, Doctor's unavailable but he'll get the message."

I said, "How's the book doing?"

"Pardon?"

"Dr. Coates's new book."

She laughed. "I just sit here in a small room and answer the phone. Last thing I read was a utility bill."

To my surprise, Len called my private line nine minutes later.

"Hey, Alex! Great to hear from you! How's life treating you?"

I said, "Well, Len. You?"

"Off-the-chart busy, it never stops. But what's the alternative? Stagnation? We're like sharks, right? We need to keep moving."

"Congratulations on the book."

"Oh, you heard the tape? We'll see how it does. I calculated my hourly fee writing it. Somewhere south of ten bucks an hour but my agent claims it's a stepping-stone. She's been getting nibbles for a talk show, says I've got more people-warmth than you-know-who, so maybe. What's up?"

"What do you know about Prema Moon and Donny Rader?"

A beat. "May I ask why you'd care about people like that?"

"Hollywood types?"

"Shallow types," he said. "That's my bailiwick, you're not going to encroach on my territory, are you, Alex?" He laughed. "Just kidding, you want 'em, they're yours. Though you have to admit, I'm better suited to that kind of thing because we both know I'm about as deep as a rain puddle in August. You, on the other hand . . . please don't tell me you've sold out, Alexander. I've always thought of you as my positive role model."

Guffaws, rich, loud, audio-friendly.

"You're selling yourself short, Len."

"Not in the least. Know Thyself is my first commandment. Meanwhile, I just bought myself a new Audi R8, the convertible. Tuned it up so the compression's insane, real beast, and trust me, that didn't come from listening to whiny mothers. Bet you're still with the old Caddy, right?"

"Right."

"There you go," he said. "Loyalty and solidity. Maybe one day it'll be a classic."

"I can hope."

"So what's with the sudden interest in the Golden Gods?"

"You know them?"

"If I did, would I be talking about them? No, I don't know them personally but after all these years . . . how can I put this—okay, let's just say if someone told me either of them had Proust on the nightstand I'd figure it was for a drink coaster."

"Not intellectuals."

"*None* of them are," he said, with sudden fury. "They're genetic freaks—bipedal show-dogs able to memorize a few lines. Sit heel stay emote. Even if they start out with some native intelligence they're egregiously undereducated so they never *know* anything. I had one—obviously I won't tell you her name—who came in to talk to one of my staff about a problem kid. But only after she was turned down by the Dog Whisperer. Why'd she go to him first? Probably to get on TV. But the reason she gave us was all animals are the same, right? It just takes the proper vibrations to make everything perfect."

I laughed

"Sure it's funny," said Len, "except we're talking about a five-year-old with enough problems to fill the DSM and Mommy wants to treat him like a pug. Anyway, no, I'm not personally intimate with either Prema or Donny but I have heard that he's borderline IQ and she basically runs things. Now, same question: Why the curiosity?"

"Be my therapist, Len."

"Pardon?"

"I need you to keep this in confidence."

"Of course. Sure."

◆

I told him about the broken appointment two years ago, the surfacing of Premadonny's compound in a current criminal investigation.

He said, "Oh, my. See what you mean about tight lips. And even without the whole ethical thing, no sense getting on the bad side of people like that."

"They're that powerful?"

"That's the town we live in, Alex. You didn't grow up here, right? You're from some wholesome flyover place—Nebraska, Kansas?"

"Missouri."

"Same difference. Well, I was born in Baja Beverly Hills, my dad was an aerospace engineer, back then the studios had their influence but it was mostly about rockets and planes, real people making real product. Not the bullshit-purveying company town it is now. So good luck."

"He's no genius and she runs the show."

"Supposedly he's close to retarded—'scuse me, developmentally disabled. And living with Stupid, she'd need to run things, no?"

"She sounds like the perfect political spouse."

"Ha! There it is—that acid wit Alexander occasionally allows himself to indulge in. I used to dig when you did that in school. Made me feel better about my own uncharitable cognitions. I used to dig our time in school, period. Western Peds, too, Alex. They worked us like galley slaves but we knew we were doing good every day and it was exciting, right? We never knew what each day would bring."

"That's for sure."

"Like the time we were trying to have lunch, I remember like it was yesterday, we've got our tuna salad and our coffee on our trays, are about to finally take ten minutes and you get paged and this look comes over your face and you just leave. Later, I run into you and you tell me some patient's father brought a gun onto the onco ward, you spent an hour talking him down."

"Good times," I said.

"They *were,* man. Especially 'cause I ate your tuna." He laughed. "Imagine that, today—shrink gets a call, handles it, finito. Nowadays there'd be a mass panic, some gross overreaction due to protocol, and someone would probably get hurt. I did some of that shit myself when I was there, Alex. Crisis interventions no one heard about because they were successful. Those were *great* times."

"They were, Len."

"But get real and move on, huh? I *do* love my R8. How many miles on the Caddy?"

"Lost count by the third engine."

"Beyond loyal, we're talking commitment. Well, good for you. And great to hear from you, friend, we need to do lunch."

CHAPTER
39

I trolled gossip sites and the links they sent me to for personal sightings of Prema Moon and/or Donny Rader.

They'd been highly visible until four, five years ago, showing up at clubs, screenings, premieres, charity events, shopping sprees. Audiences with heads of state. But the two hits I found covering the last eighteen months featured Prema only, both times in L.A.: World Affairs Council symposium on African famine, Banish Hunger luncheon where the actress received an award.

Time to give my personal conduit to

Glitz-World another try. Robin was sweeping her workbench. Pads for applying French polish sat in a wastebasket. The flamenco guitar hung drying.

"Gorgeous."

"You can test-drive it for me in a couple of days."

"Perks of the job," I said. "Do you still have a way of contacting paparazzi?"

"I'm sure some of my clients do."

"Could you call one of them?"

"Looking for a lead on the *staaahs*?"

I told her about the sudden drop in sightings.

"Burrowing because they've gotten weird?" she said. "Okay, I'll try Zenith. He's not so big anymore but he hangs with the biggies and his current flame's that actress on the doctor show and she's always good for a cleavage shot."

Zenith Streak né James Baxter professed ignorance of "all that bullshit" but he connected her to his publicist who punted to another rock star's personal manager. It took three additional calls before she obtained the number of a paparazzo named Ali, whom she sweet-talked before passing the phone to me.

I introduced myself.

He said, "Hey, dog, whusup?" in a Middle Eastern accent.

"Haven't seen much on Premadonny lately."

His voice climbed three notes up the scale. "Whu, you know 'em?"

"No. I was just wondering why."

"Aw, man . . . so why you— They pissing me off, man."

"Why?"

"Whu you think? For not *being,* know muh saying?"

"No more photo ops."

"Got to eat, dog, they the meat, dog. We don' hassle 'em, we they friends with the lens."

"So no idea why—"

"They used to *be,* man. Like a clock, we getting the call, they there smiling, waving, smiling, waving. We shooting and booting and sending. Then we spending."

"They orchestrated everything."

"Huh?"

"It was all prearranged."

"Sure, man, what you think?"

"You ever get pictures of their kids?"

"Nah, just them. Pissing me off, know what a baby brings? Hot tot shot's the mostest lot."

"Any idea why they don't call anymore?"

"They crazy."

"How so?"

"They not callin, they crazy. You not there, no one care. So what, you're like a music person's si-nificant other?"

"Yup."

"You know Katy?"

"Sorry, no."

"Taylor?"

"No—"

"Adam, Justin—you know even Christina, that's cool—how bow Bono? You know anyone, I slip you a share of what's there."

"Sorry—"

"You don know *no one,* dog?"

I chose to answer philosophically. "Not really."

"Then we done."

◆

Robin said, "So they really are playing ground squirrel." Her smile was sudden, mischievous. "Or they've just opted for the simple life."

I said, "Growing their own vegetables, and raising hyperintellectual organic cattle. For the milk."

She said, "Don't forget hand-stitched hemp duds."

We both laughed. I tried to put my heart into it.

Holly Ruche had phoned while I was in the studio. I called her back, figuring single-session euphoria had faded, the way it often does.

But when she answered, her voice was fat with pleasure. "Thanks so much, Dr. Delaware. For what you've accomplished."

Not sure what I'd done, I said, "Glad everything's going well."

"Everything's going great, Dr. Delaware. Matt's talking. Really talking, not just the hello how are you we used to do."

"That's great, Holly."

"Turns out what he needed was for

me to *tell* him I valued what he had to say. Because his parents *discouraged* talking, his father actually used to say 'Children should be seen, not heard.' Can you believe that? Anyway, I did. Tell him. It just opened him up. Me, too. About my issues. And he was surprised to know how I felt about my mom. Which makes sense, I never talked about her until you led me in the right path. Anyway, Matt listened, nonjudgmental. *Interested.* Then he told me more about his childhood. Then we . . . everything kind of kicked up to a new level. I'm feeling in control, like I *really* own this pregnancy. Own my entire life."

"That's terrific, Holly."

"Couldn't have done it without you, Dr. Delaware."

My line of work, things like praise from patients aren't supposed to affect you because it's all about healing them, not your ego.

To hell with that, I take what I can get. "I really appreciate your telling me, Holly."

"Sure," she said. "Do you have another second?"

"What's up?"

"In terms of . . . what happened . . . to the baby. I'm assuming they haven't found anything out? Because I did read about that other poor little thing, it made my heart ache, I cried, Dr. Delaware."

"Sorry, Holly, no progress, yet."

"Something so long ago, I imagine it would be difficult to solve. And this probably won't help but that box—the blue hospital box? For some reason it bothered me. Someone putting a baby in something like that."

Her voice caught. "This is going to sound weird but I've been going online and searching for something like it and finally I found it. A box just like it at a collectibles site called OldStuff.net. From the same hospital—Swedish, the seller calls it a bank box, for depositing money, she has others for sale, from other hospitals. I called her up and she told me back in the day they used metal boxes for extra security when they brought cash to the bank. Before the armored cars were safe enough so you could use bags."

"Interesting."

"Could it be important?"

"At this point, any information's valuable."

"Great, Dr. Delaware. Then I feel good about all the time I spent online. Bye."

I logged onto the site. Identical blue box. No additional wisdom.

Robin knocked on my office door. "Going to keep working for a while?"

"Nah, let's have some fun."

She looked at the screen. I explained.

She said, "Never thought of hospitals as cash businesses."

"Place was an abortion mill back when abortion was a felony. Illegal means high profit margins."

I logged off.

She said, "Fun sounds okay." Utter lack of conviction.

I put my arm around her. "C'mon, life's short, let's own ours. How about music?"

"Sounds good."

"Let me check the Catalina . . . here's their calendar . . . Jane Monheit."

"Like her," she said. "If we can get tickets, let's do it."

◆

Monheit was in fine voice backed by a band that never stopped swinging, the food at the club was decent, a couple of generous Chivas pours went down well.

We got home and beelined to bed and afterward I plunged into sleep, stayed out for an atypical seven hours, woke up with an aching head that filled quickly with words and pictures.

When I got to my office my cell phone was beeping and my landline message machine was blinking.

A pair of calls, less than a minute apart. I punched Play on the machine.

Milo's voice said, "Found my boy Wedd. Call."

"Sturgis."
    "Congrats."
    "Hear what I have to say first."

CHAPTER

40

Melvin Jaron Wedd had been found in the passenger seat of his pimped-up black Explorer. Single gunshot wound to his left temple. The entry hole said large-caliber. The stippling said up close and personal, though probably not a contact wound.

Brain matter clotted the back of his seat. A Baggie of weed sat between his splayed knees. A glass bong glinted on the floor near his left shoe. The impact had caused him to slide down, leaving his corpse in an awkward semi-reclining state that wouldn't have been comfortable in life.

His mouth gaped, his eyes were shut, his bowels had emptied. Rot and insect activity said he'd been there days rather than hours.

Masked and gloved, a C.I. named Gloria was going through his pockets. She'd already procured his wallet, pulled out a driver's license, credit cards, eighty bucks in cash. Milo didn't need any of that to know who the victim was. A BOLO-find on Wedd's Explorer had shown up in his office email shortly after six a.m. He'd been online an hour before, "eating futility for breakfast."

Blood in the SUV said the Explorer was the murder scene. The vehicle had been left at the rear of a construction site east of Laurel Canyon, four hundred feet up a quiet street just north of the Valley. Nice neighborhood; a while back, Milo had caught a case not far from here, a prep school teacher left in a bathtub packed with dry ice.

A large, elaborate house had been framed up on the lot. Weathered wood marred by rust streaks below the nails

said it had been a while since the project was active. Care had been taken to
preserve the assortment of mature eucalyptus at the rear of the lot. The trees
hadn't been trimmed and some of their
branches drooped to the ground and
continued trailing along the dirt, shaggy
and green, like oversized caterpillars.
The foliage had served to partially shield
the Explorer but if anyone had been
working on the site, they'd have noticed
the vehicle immediately.

I said, "Foreclosure?"

Milo said, "Yup, last year. Guy who
found the body goes around checking
out bank-owned properties. The former
owners are a nice older couple from
Denver, moved here to be with their
grandkids, tried to build their dream
house, got taxed out of their dry-clean-
ing business. I had Denver PD talk to
them. They've never heard of Wedd and
they come up antiseptic-clean. And
there goes my case on Adriana because
ol' Melvin ain't ever talking."

Gloria called out his name. We approached her, tried to stand sufficiently

back to avoid the wafting of death fumes.

"This was in his jacket, Milo. Upper inside pocket."

She held out a matchbook, white cover, unmarked. The kind you get with cigarettes at the liquor store.

Milo said, "So he had a fuel source for his dope."

Gloria opened the book. No matches left, just fuzzy stubs. Inside the book's cover, someone had scrawled in blue ballpoint. Tiny, cramped cursive.

Milo put on reading glasses, gloved up, took the book.

I read over his shoulder.

This is guilt.

Gloria said, "Can I theorize a little?"

"Sure."

"If we'd found a gun, I'd look at this as maybe a suicide note. Seeing as it's clearly a homicide, either your victim had remorse for something and wrote this himself or someone else thought he should pay for something."

"Have you checked his other pockets yet?"

"Twice. I even looked in his underwear." She wrinkled her nose. "I'm dedicated up to a point. Any idea what Mr. Wedd could be guilty of?"

"Before this I had a few ideas." He shook his head. "Anything else?"

"The driver's-seat adjustment seems to roughly fit Wedd's height, so either he was driving and moved to the passenger side or your offender's around the same size. I guess the weed and the bong are meant to imply a drug party. But with no matches in the book or anywhere else, same for ashes or residue?"

"It looks staged to you?"

"That or there was an interruption before the party got going," she said. "Was Wedd involved in that world?"

"Not that I know," said Milo. "But I don't know much, period."

He stepped away from the stench. Gloria and I followed. She said, "I'll do my best to rush DNA on the bag and the pipe, see if any chemistry other than his comes back. You saw those prints the techies pulled from the car. They've already gone to the lab, maybe you'll get lucky."

He said, "That's my middle name."

"Lucky?"

"Maybe."

A tow truck arrived to hook up the SUV. Neighbors had begun to emerge and uniforms were doing their usual blank-faced centurion thing, easing concerned citizens away from the scene with no thought to reassurance.

Milo looked at the white-bagged body being gurneyed away. "Melvin, Melvin, Melvin, so now you're another victim." To me: "All those women he had coming in and out, there could be a horde of angry husbands, boyfriends." Back at the corpse: "Thanks a bundle for your dissolute lifestyle, pal."

I said, "You see Wedd getting into a car with an angry husband? Letting him drive?"

"Someone with a gun? Sure. Or the offender's a jilted female, hell hath no fury and all that."

"Tall girl."

"Plenty of those in SoCal—what, you don't like the jealousy angle?"

"It's a common motive."

"But you have a better idea."

I told him my growing suspicions about Premadonny, leaving out the possibility of a violent child.

He said, "Creepy-World flourishes in Coldwater Canyon? What's the motive for doing two, maybe three employees, Alex? They're abusing their kids and bumping off the staff to keep them quiet?"

"Put that way, it sounds pretty weak."

"No, no, I take every product of your fertile mind seriously, it just came out of left field. Okay, let me focus for a coo: They bug you because they isolate their kids. Maybe they got tired of the hustle, had enough dough, said screw it."

I said, "That could be it."

"But," he said.

"No buts."

Gathering the flesh above his nose with two fingers, he deepened the fissure that time and age had provided. "Dealing with suspects like that. God, I hope you're wrong."

"Forget I brought it up."

His cell squawked Tchaikovsky. He said, "Okay, thanks," dropped the phone back in his pocket. "Prints from two individuals in the car: Wedd's and an unknown contributor with no match to AFIS. Unknown's was on the driver's side of the center console, Wedd's showed up on the trunk latch and the interior of the trunk. To me that says our movie stars *aren't* involved."

"How so?"

"Someone at that level chauffeuring the help? More likely some disreputable who Wedd pissed off did this. Not that it makes a difference in terms of Adriana and the baby getting icier by the second."

He left me standing there, headed toward the SUV, stopped, returned. "That canceled appointment, any hint about what kind of problem their kid was having?"

"The guy I spoke to wouldn't even tell me which kid it was."

"Okay, they're weirdly secretive. Maybe shitty parents—no shock, given all the money, no one getting told no. But that's a long way from linking them to my murders and I've still got Qeesha, a confirmed criminal and likely a killer herself. And Wedd, a guy who defrauded insurance, and Adriana, who might've had a secret life. Toss in ingredients like that and no telling what'll cook up."

I said, "Felony gumbo."

"You figure I'm in denial. Hell, yeah, sure I am. But aren't you the one says denial can be useful?"

"I love being quoted."

"Hey," he said, "it's either you or the Bible and right now I'm not feeling sufficiently pious to invoke Scripture. C'mon, I'll walk you to your car."

CHAPTER

41

Obsessiveness and anxiety are traits that can clog up your life. But the way I figure, they've got plenty of evolutionary value.

Think of cave-people surrounded by predators. Jumpy, annoyingly picky Oog sleeps fitfully because he's mindful of creatures that roar in the night. More often than not, he wakes up with a dry mouth and a pounding heart.

Easygoing Moog, in contrast, sinks easily into beautiful dreams. One morning he fails to wake up at all because his heart's been chewed to hamburger

and the rest of his innards have been
served up as steaming mounds of car-
nivore candy.

The blessing-curse of an overly developed attention span helped me escape a family situation that would've
continued to damage me and might've
ended up killing me. Since then, over-
the-shoulder vigilance has saved my life
more than once.

So I'll sacrifice a bit of serenity.

Milo was right; denial could be the
right way to go but this morning it felt
wrong and I got home itching to focus.

An hour on the computer gave way
to double that time on the phone. My
pitch grew better with repeated use but
it proved useless. Then I switched gears
and everything fell into place.

By four p.m. I was dressed in a steel-
gray Italian suit, open-necked white
shirt, brown loafers, and hanging near
the southwest corner of Linden Drive
and Wilshire.

Busy stretch of impeccable Beverly
Hills sidewalk, easy to blend in with a
light pedestrian parade as I repeated a

two-block circuit while pretending to window-shop.

The Seville was parked in a B.H. city lot. Two hours gratis, so shoppers could concentrate on consumer goods and cuisine.

I wasn't planning to buy anything; I had something to sell. Or trade, depending on how things worked out.

Apex Management was headquartered in a forties-era three-story brick building that looked as if it had once housed doctors and dentists. A few months ago, I'd read about the Beverly Hills city council wanting to clamp down on medical offices because health care attracted hordes of—surprise!—sick people who took up too many parking spaces and failed to spend like tourists.

Entertainment ancillaries like Apex, on the other hand, churned expense accounts at the city's truffled-up eateries and attracted publicity magnets and the paparazzi and there's no such thing as bad publicity.

I was facing a collection of psychotically priced cashmere sweaters and wondering if the goats who'd donated their hair were having a rough winter when the first human outflow emerged from behind Apex's carved oak doors.

Three men in their twenties and thirties, then four more, all wearing Italian suits, open-necked dress shirts, and loafers. Industry-ancillary uniform. Which was the point.

Next came a man and two women in tailored pantsuits, followed by a pair of younger women similarly but less expensively attired. Those two let the door close on the next person out: a tired-looking older man in a green janitor's uniform.

Three minutes later the prey came into view.

Tall, late twenties, crowned by a thick mop of blond-streaked, light brown hair, he wore black-framed geek eyeglasses that stretched wider than his pasty, bony face. In the firm's Christmas party photos he'd worn wire rims.

He'd also tended to pose standing slightly apart from his co-workers, which had led me to hope he was a loner.

Wish fulfilled: all by himself and looking worn out and distracted.

The perfect quarry.

I watched him stop and fidget. His suit was black with a pink pinstripe, narrow-lapelled, snugly fitted. Cheaply cut when you got close, as much hot glue as stitching in play. A Level Two Service Assistant's salary wouldn't cover high-end threads.

I walked toward him, noticed a loose thread curling from one shirt collar. *Tsk tsk.*

We were face-to-face. He was concentrating on the sidewalk, didn't notice. When my shadow intruded on his, his head rose and he gave a start and tried to move past me.

I blocked him. "Kevin?"

"Do I know you?"

"No, but you do know JayMar Laboratory Supplies."

"Huh?"

I held my LAPD consultant I.D. badge close to my thigh, raised it just enough so he had to strain to read the part I wasn't covering with my thumb.

Showcasing the always-impressive

department seal while concealing my name and ambiguous title.

"Police?"

I said, "Could I have a moment of your time, Kevin?"

His mouth opened wide. So did the carved oak door, ejecting more suits, male and female, a large group buoyant with liberation, headed our way, laughing raucously.

Someone said, "Hey, Kev."

The quarry waved.

I said, "I can show them the badge, too."

His jaws clenched. "Don't."

"Your call, Kev." Walking back to Wilshire, I returned to the sweater display, kept my eye on him while pretending to study my cell phone.

Co-workers coalesced around him. A woman said something and pointed across Wilshire. Smiling painfully, he shook his head. The group continued on, merry as carolers. Crossing the boulevard, they continued toward a restaurant on the ground floor of a black-glass office building.

El Bandito Grill.

A banner proclaimed *Happy Hour!!!*
Not for Kevin Dubinsky.

As I waited for him, he kicked one heel
with the other. Contemplating an alternative. Failing to come up with one, he
removed his glasses and swung them
at his side as pipe-stem legs propelled
him toward me.

When he got close, he mumbled,
"What's going on?"

I said, "How 'bout we walk while we
chat?"

"Chat about what?"

"Or we could talk right here, Kevin." I
pulled out the photocopied order form.

JayMar Laboratory Supplies,
Chula Vista, California

Five hundred dermestid beetles and
a set of surgical tools, including a bone
saw, purchased four months ago.

It had taken me a while to get the
info. Call after futile call using the address of the compound off Coldwater
Canyon.

The pitch: "I'm calling to renew an order for dermestid beetles . . ."

No one knew what I was talking about. Then I realized I'd goofed big-time. People like that didn't do things for themselves. After substituting Apex Management's shipping address—a warehouse in Culver City—I had confirmation by the seventh call, a nice clean fax of the form.

Kevin Dubinsky's name at the bottom as "purchaser."

Facebook and LinkedIn supplied all I needed to know about him. Let's hear it for cyber-truth.

He turned away from the order form. "So? It's my job."

"Exactly, Kev. Your job's what we need to discuss."

"Why?"

"You buy flesh-eating insects and scalpels regularly?"

"I figured it was . . ." He shut his mouth.

"It was what?"

"Nothing." Flash of bitter smile. "I'm not paid to think."

"Are you paid *not* to think?"

No answer.

"What you take home, Kev, you might want to reconsider your priorities."

"There's a problem?"

"Only if you don't cooperate."

"With what?"

"Better I ask the questions."

"Something bad happened?"

"I don't visit people to talk about jay-walking, Kev."

"Oh, shit—what's going on?"

"Like I said, Kev, the less you know the better."

"Shit." He licked his lips, began walking east on Wilshire. I kept up with his long stride. All those years with Milo, great practice.

I said, "Tell me about it."

"I don't remember specifics."

"You buy what you're told, all part of the job."

"That *is* the job. Period."

"Service assistant."

"Yeah, it's stupid, I know. I need to eat, okay?"

"You get a call to—"

"Never a call, always email."

"Buy me bugs."

"I order all kinds of things. That's what I'm paid to do."

"You do all the purchasing for the Premadonny compound?"

"No, just . . ." Head shake.

"Just things they don't want their name on?"

Silence. Wrong guess. I'd try the same question later.

"So how many times have you ordered beetles and knives?"

"Just that once."

"You didn't find it weird?"

"Wondering wastes time."

"Busy guy," I said. "They work you hard."

"Like I said, I like to eat."

"Don't we all."

He stopped. "You don't get it. I don't ask questions and I'm *not* allowed to answer any."

"About . . ."

"Anything. Ever. That's Rule Number One. Numbers Two through Ten say refer back to One."

"That sounds like something your boss told you."

No reply.

I said, "Privacy's a big deal for Pre-madonny."

"They're all like that."

"Stars?"

"You can call 'em that."

"What do you call 'em?"

"The gods." His lips turned down. A sneer full of reflexive disdain. The same flavor of contempt I'd heard in Len Coates's voice.

Perfect opening for me.

"Funny, Kev, you'd think they'd want nothing *but* attention."

"They want it, all right. On their terms." Long slow intake of breath. "Now I'm fucked, I already said too much."

I said, "Service assistant. That could mean anything."

Kevin Dubinsky emitted a high, coarse sound that didn't approach laughter. "It means fucking *gopher.* Know what they actually pay me?"

"Not much."

"Less than that." He laughed.

Resisting the urge to pluck the loose thread from his collar, I said, "That's the way the Industry works. The gods perch on Olympus, the peasants grovel."

"Better believe it."

"So no sense getting screwed on their account, Kevin."

"I like to *eat,* man."

"I'm discreet. Tell me about the job."

"What's to tell? I order stuff."

More eye movement. Time to revisit his first evasion. I said, "Not for the entire compound."

He gnawed his lip.

"Eventually we're going to find out, Kevin, no sense complicating your life by getting tagged as uncooperative."

"Please. I can't help you."

"Who'd you buy that crap for?"

Silence.

I said, "Or maybe we should assume you bought it for your own personal use, that could get *really* interesting."

"Her, okay? I only buy for her, he's got his own slave."

"Who's that?"

"Like I know? I do what I'm told."

"You buy stuff she doesn't want traced back to her."

"I buy for her because she can't dirty her hands being a real person." He laughed, patted a trouser pocket. "I use a Centurion—a black card—just for her swag. Get to pretend every day."

"Must get interesting."

"Nah, it sucks."

"Boring purchases?"

"Boring expensive purchases." He mimed gagging himself with a finger.

I said, "You buy, the stuff ships to Culver City, the paperwork gets filed somewhere else, so if someone goes through her garbage they can't figure out what she's into."

"Maybe that's part of it," he said. "I always figure, it's God forbid they do anything for themselves."

"Do you handle groceries and stuff like that?"

"Nah, that goes through her staff at the compound."

"What do you buy?"

" 'Special purchases.' "

"Meaning?"

"Whatever she feels like."

We walked half a block before he stopped again, drew me to another display window. Manikins who'd have to plump up to be anorexic were draped in black crepe garments that might be coats. Blank white faces projected grief. Nothing like a funeral for selling product.

He said, "I'm going to tell you this so you'll understand, okay? One time—I don't know this personally, I was told it—they actually set up a scene so she could fill her car up and look like a regular person. They picked a gas station in Brentwood, Apex paid to clear the place out for a day, masked it off with those silver sheets photographers use so no one could see what was going on. They gave her a car that wasn't hers, something normal, and she pretended to fill it up."

I said, "For one of those stars-are-just-like-us deals."

Another contemptuous look. "Five takes for her to get the hang of putting gas in a fucking car. She had no fucking clue."

"Unreal."

"Her life is unreal, man. So what'd she need those bugs for?"

I smiled.

"Okay, I get it, shut up and cooperate."

"Do your purchases get audited?"

"Every month a prick from accounting goes over every damn thing. I charge a pencil that can't be explained, my ass is grass. A girl who used to work in the next cubicle, she bought for—I can't tell you who—she got busted for a bottle of nail polish."

I said, "Sucks. So what's the most expensive item you've ever bought for her?"

"Easy," he said. "Last year, time share on a Gulfstream Five. Seven figures up front plus serious monthly maintenance. She never uses it."

I whistled.

"That's the point, dude. Doing stuff no one else can do, to show you're God. One day I'm going to find a real job."

"How long have you been at Apex?"

"Little over three years," he said. "Started out doing messenger shit. Which was basically bringing envelopes from one schmuck boss to another, picking up lunch, all kinds of scut. When I signed up, I figured it would be temporary. So I could save up enough and go back to school."

"What were you studying?"

"What do you think?"

"Acting."

He chuckled. "They taught you to detect pretty good. Yeah, I was like every fool comes to L.A., thought because I was Stanley in high school and my drama teacher loved me I could live . . . atop Olympus." He shook his head. "My crib's a barf-hole in Reseda, I'm barely getting by, and now I got cops talking to me. Maybe it's time to go back and study something real. Like real estate. Or online poker."

He reached for my sleeve, retracted his hand before making contact. "Please don't screw me, dude. All I did was what I was told."

"If that's true, I don't see you as having any liability, Kevin."

"I don't mean problems with you, I mean the job. Rule One."

"I'll do my best to keep you out of it."

"The way you said that scares me."

"Why?"

"It could mean anything."

"What it means, Kev, is that we need each other."

"How?"

"You don't want me talking about you and my bosses can't afford you telling anyone about this meeting because there's an ongoing investigation."

"No prob, I won't say a word."

"Then we're cool."

I held out my hand. We shook. His skin was clammy.

"Thanks for talking to me, Kev."

"Believe me, my yap is permanently shut. But can I ask one thing? Just for my own sake?"

"What?"

"Did she do something bad with that shit? I figured it was for the kids, some sort of science project, you know? She's always getting stuff for the kids."

I said, "Ever hear of the Lacey Act?"

"No, what's that?"

"Protection for endangered species."

"That's what this is about? Those stupid bugs were illegal?"

"Protected." I ran a finger across my lips. "Like this communication. Have a nice day, Kevin."

"I'll try," he said. "Getting harder, but I'll try."

CHAPTER

42

The morning after meeting Kevin Dubinsky, I dressed in sweatpants, a T-shirt, running shoes, and a Dodgers cap, was ready to leave by eight. Blanche, figuring it was time for a stroll, bounced up to me and smiled.

I said, "Sorry, honey," fetched her a consolation strip of bacon that she regarded with sad eyes before deigning to nibble, carried her to Robin's studio, and left the house.

I drove up Beverly Glen, turned right at Mulholland, passing the fire station near Benedict Canyon, stopping once

to pick up a nice-sized branch that had
fallen off an ancient sycamore. Sailing
through pretty, dew-livened hills I
reached the Coldwater Canyon inter-
section, across from TreePeople headquarters.

A little more than half a mile south of
the private road that led to the Premadonny compound.

I drove two miles north of the property, found a patch of turnoff not meant
for long-term stay, left the car there,
anyway. Stick in hand, I returned south
on foot.

Crows squawked, squirrels chittered,
all kinds of animal noises became evi-
dent once you listened. I spotted a deer
munching dry grass then speeding
toward a McMansion that blocked far
too much canyon view, came upon the
desiccated remains of a gorgeous red-
and-yellow-banded king snake. Juvenile, from the size of it. No signs of violence to the little reptile. Sometimes
things just died.

I kept going, using the branch for a
walking stick that I hoped would imply
Habitual Hiker. Nice day to be out walk-

ing, if you ignored the occasional car roaring toward you, oblivious or hostile to the concept of foot travel. Fools texting and phone-yakking and a notable cretin shaving his face made the journey an interesting challenge. More than once I had to press myself against a hillside to avoid being pulverized.

I kept up a steady pace, tapped a rhythm with the stick, pretended to be caught up in pedestrian Zen. In L.A., that makes you strange. In L.A., people ignore strange.

When I reached my destination, I found a tree-shielded spot across the road and had a look at the entry to the compound. A discreet sign warned against trespassing. An electric gate ten or so yards up blocked entry. The road to that barrier was a single lane of age-grayed asphalt in need of patching, shaded by bay laurels and untrimmed ficus. A stray plastic cup lid glinted from the shrubbery. Appropriately secluded but a little on the shabby side; not a hint this was Buckingham West.

I continued walking, searched for police surveillance. None that I could see;

maybe Milo hadn't gotten around to arranging it.

I hadn't heard from him since the meet at Melvin Wedd's crime scene. Probably inspecting Wedd's apartment, locating next of kin, all that logical detective procedure.

Correspondence with Wedd's family would be an exercise in deception: prying out dirt about a victim/possible suspect under the guise of consolation. Milo was good at that, I'd seen him pull it off plenty of times. Later, he'd mutter about the power of positive hypocrisy.

I covered another mile, reversed direction, took a second look at the access road to the compound, repeated the process several times, never encountering another person on foot.

They say walking's the best exercise, if we had time to do enough of it, we wouldn't need to jog or run or tussle with implements of gym-torture. By the time I got back in the Seville my feet were starting to protest and I guessed I'd covered at least ten miles.

It had been a learning experience. Body and mind.

◆

When I was minutes from home, Robin called. "Guess what, Brent's back in town, can't wait to talk to you."

"Eager to do his civic duty?"

She laughed. "More like his un-civil duty. He hates them, Alex. Quote un-quote. He's lunching, guess where?"

"Spago."

"Grill on the Alley. Karma, huh?"

"Last time I was there the company was a whole lot cuter."

"But nowhere near this informative, baby. Good luck."

The Grill bustles pleasantly at dinner-time. During lunch it roars, filling up with Industry testosterone, every power booth occupied by movers and shakers and those too rich to bother doing ei-ther. Each bar stool is occupied but no one gets drunk. Platters of food are transported smoothly by an army of white-jacketed waiters who've seen it all. Sometimes tourists and others na-ive enough to venture in without a res-ervation bunch up at the door like im-migrants seeking asylum. A trio of hosts seems genuinely remorseful when they reject the unschooled.

My hiking duds were far below the sartorial standard but you'd never know it from the smile of the woman behind the lectern. "May I help you?"

"I'm meeting Brent Dorf."

"Certainly." She beckoned a waiter with an eyebrow lift and he led me to a table on the south side of the restaurant, concealed by the center partition.

Far from the see-and-be-seen; Brent's clout was beta.

He was hunched over a Caesar salad, forking quickly as if he needed to be somewhere else yesterday. When he saw me, he didn't stop eating. A millimeter of white wine remained in his glass.

The waiter said, "Cocktail? Or Chardonnay like Mr. Dorf?" and handed me a menu.

I said, "Iced tea's fine. I'll also have a Caesar."

"No croutons, dressing on the side, like Mr. Dorf?"

"Dressing and croutons are fine. Anchovies, too."

The waiter smiled approvingly, as if someone finally had the sense to do it right.

Brent said, "Lay on the calories and the sodium, easy for you skinny folk."

He was thinner than me, had the wrinkles and sunken cheeks to show for it. His head was shaved, his oblong hound-dog face had been barbered so closely that I wondered about electrolysis. Last time I'd seen him he'd been thirty pounds heavier and sported a soul patch.

I said, "You're not exactly obese, Brent."

"Good tailoring, you don't want to see me naked." He looked at the ramekin of salad dressing at his right elbow, considered his options, pushed it away. "I'm under pressure, my friend."

"Tough job."

"Not that pressure, body pressure."

"Honestly, you look good, Brent."

"Yeah, yeah, everything's relative," he said. "Got myself a twenty-eight-year-old dancer with statue-of-David definition, I'm talking physical perfection." He sighed. "Todd claims he loves me but we both know he's out for the good life. By both of us, I don't mean him and me, I mean you and me. Seeing as you're a mental health sage."

My tea came.

Brent said, "How's *your* gorgeous other?"

"Terrific."

"Robin, Robin," he said. "I always thought she was special. A knockout who knows how to use power tools? Sexy."

"No argument, Brent."

His eyelids descended, half hooding irises the color of silt. He looked around the room, bent closer, lowered his voice. "So you want to know about Lancelot and Guinevere."

"Anything you can tell me."

"Funny," he said, "I figured *you* could tell *me*."

"Why's that?"

"Because I sent them to you. Referred them. Figured by now you'd have all the insights."

"That was you?" I said. "They canceled, never saw them."

"Figures," he said. "They're big on that."

"Canceling?"

"Reneging." His hand tensed, gave a small wave and brushed against his glass, knocking it over. The minuscule amount of wine was no threat as it dribbled to the tablecloth, but he flung himself back as if escaping an avalanche. High-strung type.

When the waiter came over to help, he barked, "I'm fine, just bring his food."

"Yes, sir."

I drank tea as Brent checked out the adjoining booths. No one paid attention to his scrutiny.

"So they never showed up," he said. "Well, they fucked me over big-time, that's why I'm happy to give you dirt. But first tell me why you need to know about them."

"Can't."

"Can't?"

"Sorry, that's all I can say, Brent."

"Ooooh, big giant *police* mystery? Got to be juicy if that cop has you on it." He winked. "Another O.J. thing? Blake? Something better?"

"Not even close, I was hoping you'd get me closer."

"I do the giving, you do the taking?" He laughed. "So you've met Todd."

My salad arrived. Brent lifted an anchovy from my plate, chewed, swallowed. "Blood pressure's probably through the roof now, but yummy."

"So how'd you come to refer them to me?"

"I was doing a deal and the issue came up. I think kid-shrink, I think you."

"What kind of problem were they having?"

"How should I know? I never talked to them."

"Your people set it up with their people. Then you took lunch."

"Ha ha ha. As a matter of fact, yes, that's what happened. But high-level people. People authorized to make decisions. We were at that stage by then, I thought I had the deal nailed."

An index finger massaged the empty wineglass. Reassuring himself he was steady. He said, "My house has a wine cellar, I've got twelve hundred bottles, more than I'll be able to drink, and Todd doesn't touch alcohol."

"Embarrassment of riches."

"Yeah . . . anyway, that's it. Someone asked about a therapist, I said I knew someone."

"They asked for a child therapist, specifically."

"Hmm," he said. "I think so—this was what, two years ago?"

"Just about."

His eyes drifted toward the bar, followed the entry of four men in suits and open-necked shirts. And loafers. He started to wave, stopped when they failed to notice him. Or ignored him. They continued to a corner booth. He finished his wine.

I said, "No hint about what the problem was."

"Ri . . . ight." Still checking out the room.

I ate salad as he gave the anchovies an occasional lustful look. "I need to be honest, Alex. It wasn't something I thought much about, I was concentrating on the deal. Besides, I get that kind of thing all the time."

"Requests for referrals."

"Doctors, dentists, chiropractors, masseuses. All part of the job."

"Knowing the right people."

"Knowing the right matches, who fits with who. I figured you'd be okay for them because you have all the right paper, probably wouldn't fuck up."

I smiled. "Thanks for the endorsement, Brent."

"They canceled, huh? So what else is new."

"Why'd they bail on your deal?"

"Not *my* deal, a deal between titans, I'm talking A-est of the A-list, something that could've been *huge.* I set it up elegantly, if it had gone through, I'd never have to think about anything for the rest of my life."

"Blockbuster."

"Blockbuster times a quintzillion, Alex. I'm talking action, romance, long and short arcs, merchandising potential up the wazz, sequels that would've gone on for infinity. I'm talking the biggest thing they'd do together, *wa-aaay* bigger than *Passion Power* and that piece of shit pulled in heavy eight figures with overseas distribution. The upside would've been astronomical. More important, I staked my word on it, staked my fucking soul. Everything was in place, contracts drawn, clauses hammered out, legal fees alone cost more than entire pictures used to rack up. We were set up for a signing, going to make a big thing about it, press conference, photo ops. The day before, they change their mind."

"How come?"

"People like that have to give a reason?" His fist hit the table. The wineglass bounced. He caught it. "Gotcha, you little bastard."

Beckoning the waiter, he brandished the glass. "Take this away, it's annoying."

"Yes, sir."

Flecks of foam had collected at the corners of Brent's mouth. He made claws out of his hands, scratched air. "I put everything into it, Alex. Hadn't taken on another client the entire year and I'm talking names, people pissed off at me. Everything else came my way, I dele- gated to other agents at the firm. So of course, my alleged friends and col- leagues held on to everything after I got . . . after the deal got murdered and I had nothing, was starting from fucking scratch and my credibility's worse than a politician. Everything changed. I got moved to a new office. Want to take odds it was bigger? Don't." Long sigh. "But I'm getting back to a good place in my life, every day's progress."

He shoved his plate to the side. "The deal was perfection, every *meeting* was perfection. And for a bullshit reason like that? Give me a fucking break."

I said, "Thought they didn't give you a reason?"

"I said that? I never said that. What I said was people like that don't *have* to have a reason. Yeah, they gave an ex- cuse. Family matters. And that's *after* I referred them to you, so what the fuck was their problem?"

His eyelids dropped farther. "Here's a confession, Alex. For a while I got paranoid. About you. Did they go see you and you laid some shrink crap on them—spend more time with the kids, whatever—and *that's* what fucked things up? For a while I had . . . thoughts about you. Then I realized I was getting psycho, if I didn't watch out I'd go totally psycho."

He reached across, patted my wrist. "I have to be honest, that's one reason I wanted to meet with you. To find out what the fuck happened. So now I find out you don't *know* what the fuck happened and you're asking *me* what the fuck happened. Funny. Ironic. Ha ha ha. And they're in some kind of trouble. Good. I'm happy. They should rot in hell."

"What kind of people are they?"

"What kind do you think? Selfish, narcissistic, inconsiderate, he's an idiot, she's a controlling bitch. You buy that Super Mom–Super Dad crap? It's just part of the façade, everything about people like that is a façade. You ever hear him talk? Dluh dluh dluh dluh. That's what passes for James Dean, now. Welcome to my world."

The waiter came over. "Anything else, gents? Coffee?"

Brent said, "No. Check."

I paid.

Brent said, "Good man."

CHAPTER

43

I reached Milo at the coroner's.

"Just watched a .45 slug get pulled out of Wedd's head, a weapon ever shows up, it's early Christmas. His apartment was vacant except for a mattress on the bedroom floor and some over-the-counter pharmaceuticals in the john. He used to get heartburn and headaches, now he's passed both along to me. Had the place dusted, sent the meds and the mattress to the lab, located one relative, Wedd's brother, cowboy-type in Montana where Wedd's originally from. No contact with Brother

Mel for years, was appropriately shocked about the murder, said Mel was always the wild one but he never figured it would get that bad."

He paused for breath.

I said, "Wild but no criminal record."

"Minor-league stuff when he was young—joyriding, malicious pranks, neighborhood mischief, a few fights. No criminal record because the sheriff was his uncle, he'd bring Mel home and Mel's dad would whup him. Then Mel got bigger than Dad and the parents basically gave up."

"When did he come to L.A.?"

"Ten years ago, brother's had no contact with him since. He wasn't surprised to know Mel had gone Hollywood. Said the only thing Mel liked in high school was theater arts, he was always getting starring roles, could sing like Hank Williams, do impressions. John Wayne, Clint Eastwood, you name it."

"I've got something. You might even think of it as progress."

I told him about the order from Jay-Mar Lab, my talks with Kevin Dubinsky and Brent Dorf. Leaving out Len Coates

because everything he knew was sec-
ondhand.

Milo said, "Knives and beetles. Her."

"Purchased right around the time the
baby was born. Poor little thing might've
been targeted in utero."

"I need to digest this . . . got time?
My office, an hour."

Midway through the drive to the station,
I got a call from Len.

"Alex, I can't tell you where I got this,
so don't ask, okay?"

"Okay."

"The client we discussed did in fact
opt for a therapist other than yourself.
But the contact was limited to a single
visit so obviously there was some serious resistance going on, don't take it
personally."

"Thanks for the reassurance, Len."

"Well," he said, "we have feelings,
too, no one likes to be passed over."

"Agreed. One visit for what?"

He cleared his throat. "Here's what I
can tell you, please don't ask for more:
Client shows up late, can't seem to ar-

ticulate a good reason for being there, leaves before the session is over."

I said, "Trouble focusing." Thinking of Donny Rader's voice on the line, his reputation as a barely literate dullard.

Then Len slipped and changed all that. "She . . . there was a lot of generalized anxiety, no ability to . . . explicate. Basically, it amounted to nothing, Alex, so I don't see anything you can do with it."

She.

"I'm sure you're right, Len. Thanks."

"Law enforcement issues notwithstanding, Alex, none of this can ever be repeated to anyone."

"I get it, Len. You have my word."

"Good . . . you still taking patients?"

"Infrequently."

"I'm asking because sometimes I get run-over. Good cases, not bullshit ones, things get crazy-busy, I could use backup."

"Beyond your associates."

"They're kids, Alex. We're vets. You interested?"

"Something short-term, in a pinch, I might be able to help."

"Pretty busy, yourself."

"It can get that way."

"Playing Sherlock, huh? Ever think of selling yourself to TV? Make a good series."

"Not really."

"No interest at all?"

"I like the quiet life."

"Think about it anyway, I'd produce in a heartbeat. And don't be a stranger."

I continued toward the station, thought about Donny Rader setting up an appointment, Prema Moon showing up late and leaving early, unable to explain what she was after.

A couple of nervous, caring parents? That didn't fit with the notion of cold-blooded baby killers. Something was off. I was struggling with that when Milo rang in.

"Almost there," I said.

"Change of plans."

He laid them out. I got on the freeway, sped downtown.

CHAPTER

44

The chief had opted to hide in plain sight, designating the meet at Number One Fortune Dim Sum Palace, one of those arena-sized places in Chinatown that still feature gluey chop suey, oil-drenched moo goo gai pan, and sea-food of mysterious origin.

The air was humid with steam, sweat, and MSG. Linoleum floors had been pounded dull by decades of feet. The walls were red, green, more red, raised panels embossed with gold dragon me-dallions and outsized renderings of birds, fish, and bats. Chinese lettering might have meant something. Hundreds of lunchers were crammed into vault-like dining rooms, tended by ancient waiters in black poly Mao suits and tas-seled gold beanies who moved as if running for their lives.

Enough clatter and din to make the Grill seem like a monastery. If there was a caste system behind this seating scheme, I couldn't decipher it, and when Milo asked to be directed to the chief's table, the stunning hostess looked at him as if he was stupid.

"We don't take reservations and we have eight rooms."

We set out on the hunt, finally spot-ted him at a smallish table near the cen-ter of the sixth room surrounded by hordes engrossed in their food. No one paying attention to the white-haired, mustachioed man in the black shadow-stripe suit, white silk tab-collar shirt, gray-yellow-scarlet Leonard tie that screamed *more is more.*

He saw us when we were thirty feet away, looked up from chopsticking noo-dles into his mouth, wiped his mouth and drank from a glass of dark beer.

I looked around for his bodyguards, spotted a pair of cold-eyed burlies four tables over, pretending to concentrate on a platter of something brown.

"Sit down. I ordered spareribs, pepper steak, shrimp-fried rice, and some sort of deep-fried chicken thing, hopefully they won't include the damn feet." Glancing at Milo. "You I know will eat anything." To me: "That sound suitable for your constitution?"

"Sure."

"Easy to please today, Doc? Strange phase of the moon?"

He'd been trying to hire me full-time for years, had never accepted failure with anything approaching good nature.

He returned to eating, chopsticks whirling like darning needles. Excellent fine-motor coordination motivated a huge load of noodles under the mustache. He chewed, had more beer, looked around. "Damn barn."

One of the old waiters brought tea and beer and sped away.

The chief said, "You stirred up a hornets' nest, Doctor."

"Keeps life interesting."

"Maybe yours. Okay, give me a brief summary. And I mean brief. You, not Sturgis. He already went over the basics when he called and made my life complicated."

I said, "At least three people who lived at Premadonny's compound have been murdered."

"Three?" he said. "I've got the nanny and the guy—Wedd."

"The baby found in the park."

"That," he said. "All right, go on. Why do you suspect dark events at Xanadu?"

"A couple of years ago, I received a call from a man I believe to be Donny Rader, requesting help—"

"Why do you think it was him?"

"The way he spoke."

"Like a moron."

"Indistinctly," I said.

"Okay, he needed a shrink for a brat, he's an actor, big surprise. What else?"

"I set up an appointment that was canceled. I didn't think much of it. But the death of one, maybe two child-care workers got me wondering about the family situation and I tried to learn as much as I could. That turned out to be next to nothing because the family's basically gone underground. Moon and Rader used to be ultra-public figures. They peddled their fame. Now they've disappeared. No venturing out in public, no chatter on the Web, and right around the time I got that call they abruptly canceled a major film project due to 'family issues.'"

"Maybe they didn't like the script."

The waiter returned. Platters were slammed down unceremoniously. The chief said, "So they're miserable maladjusts. So what?"

"My experience is that extremely isolated families are often breeding grounds for psychopathology. Three people with connections to them are dead. Something's going on there."

"Sounds like you've got nothing, Doc."

"Until recently, I would've agreed with you. Then I learned that Prema Moon purchased flesh-eating beetles and surgical tools. Right around the time the baby was born."

"Show me the proof."

I produced the form from JayMar,

began explaining the purchasing process.

He cut me off. "They've got peons to
wipe their asses for them, another big
shock." He put on glasses, read,
frowned, slid the form into an inner
jacket pocket.

Milo said, "Only thing missing, sir, is
beeswax. If we can get access to the
rest of their—"

The chief waved him quiet. "Beetles.
Crazy bitch. How exactly did you get
hold of the form, Doctor?"

"I called supply houses pretending to
be someone from Apex, said I wanted
to renew the order. Eventually, I found
the right one."

"Planning on billing the department
for your time?"

"Hadn't thought about it."

"You just do this for fun, huh?"

"I'm a curious guy."

"How long did it take you to find the
right company?"

"A few hours."

"You're a persistent bastard, aren't
you?"

"I can be."

"Deceptive, too . . . no telling how that'll play into the hands of some nuclear-powered lawyer. If you're deemed a police agent, it could open up claims of insufficient grounds, hence illegal search. Which is probably bullshit but with judges you never know. If you're deemed to be a civilian, it could open *you* up to some ball-squeezing cross-examination, not to mention an invasion-of-privacy suit by people who can buy and sell you a thousand times over. That happens, forget any chance of a quiet life for the foreseeable future. These people are like governments, they go to war. You willing to take that risk?"

I said, "Sounds like you're trying to discourage me."

He put his chopsticks down. "I think long-term, Alex." First time he'd used my name. "That separates me from ninety-nine percent of the population. Even at Harvard."

He loved putting down the Ivy League, rarely missed the opportunity to bring up his graduate degree from the iviest of all.

I said, "You think I was wrong to dig up the information."

"I *think* this could get nasty."

"What happened to that baby was beyond nasty."

He glared. "I got a white knight here." Lifting a sparerib with his fingers, he chewed down to the bone, ingesting meat, gristle, and fat. "Take one, Sturgis. You not stuffing your face scares me. It's like the sun stopping mid-orbit."

Milo spooned some fried rice onto his plate.

The chief said, "Not into ribs, today, Lieutenant?"

"This is fine, sir."

The chief smirked. "Establishing your independence? That makes you feel like a grown-up, be my guest." To me: "This is a mess."

He reached for the plate. Another rib got gnawed to the bone.

I said, "Another thing I did—"

"Another thing? Jesus Almighty, you figure you're running your own investigation?" His eyes shifted to Milo. Milo's head was down as he shoveled rice into his maw.

520   JONATHAN KELLERMAN

The chief turned back to me. *"What?"*

I told him about the morning's hike. "None of the principals entered or exited the compound but I did learn that it's a pretty busy place. In the space of three hours, I saw a seven-man groundskeeping crew, a grocery delivery, a repairman from a home-theater outfit, and a plumber. I copied down the tags—"

"Why?"

"I figured it might offer a possible way to get in—"

"Sturgis pretends to be a gardener or a plumber? *Habla español,* Sturgis? Know how to unclog a sink? *I* do, my *father* was a plumber, I spent my summers elbow-deep in rich people's muck. You ever do that, Sturgis? Wade in rich folk shit?"

Milo said, "Frequently, sir."

"Don't like the job?"

"Love it, sir. It is what it is."

The chief looked ready to spit. "Don Quixote and Sancho Panza . . . so, being a psychologist, Doc, you figure a crafty way to gain entry would be to hitch a ride with one of the peasants who services the castle, once you're inside, you just mosey around at random in the hope of stumbling across definitive evidence?"

"I was hoping to catch Moon, Rader, or any of the kids leaving. But when I saw the volume of traffic, it occurred to me there might be an opening."

"If Moon or Rader had left, you figured to tail them."

"Discreetly."

His face darkened. "Dr. Do-A-Lot. You talk to animals, as well?"

"If I've overstepped, I'm sorry."

"Overstepped?" He laughed. "More like you've invented new dance moves. What day does the garbage get taken out at that place?"

Milo said, "I'll find out." He walked to the dining room doorway, talked on his cell.

The chief returned to his ribs, tried some pepper steak. Pincer-grasped a plump little pink shrimp out of the fried rice. "Not hungry, Doc?"

"Actually, I am." I tried a rib. Greasy and delicious.

"Just like you," said the chief.

"Pardon?"

"You're like the damn ribs. Unhealthy but satisfying. Congratulations, Sturgis plodded along but you're the one who learned something."

"He—"

"No need to defend him, I know what he is, he's good at what he does, as good as I'm gonna get. You, on the other hand, are a different animal. You piss me off without trying. You also make me wonder what the department would be like if everyone was super-smart and psychotically driven. Don't tell Sturgis I said that, you'll hurt his feelings."

He and I ate in silence until Milo returned.

"Garbage collection's in two days, sir."

"Be there before the trucks arrive, Sturgis. Wear comfortable clothes and bring enough empty barrels to haul away every bit of trash. Don't be noticed. Separate anything with DNA potential and run a match to the baby bones. Maybe this Qeesha character is still alive and shedding cells, we find an eyebrow pencil, a tampon, whatever, that links her to the bones, we're a step forward. We also get an accurate victim count, two not three, and think of her as a homicidal bitch who killed her own kid."

Milo said, "DNA analysis could take a while."

"I'll speed it through to the max."

"Until then—"

"Until then you and your geniuses try to do what the doctor, an allegedly untrained civilian, was apparently able to accomplish: Watch the goddamn place without being seen. Prema or Donny or Qeesha appear, they get tailed. With finesse. Seduction, not rape, Sturgis."

"Got it, sir." Milo started to rise.

"Where do you think you're going?"

"Getting back to work."

"This *is* work, Sturgis. Amusing the boss. Now don't let me down, I want to see some calorie consumption."

45

Amusing the boss translated to a quarter hour of near-silent scarfing. The chief was a lean man but he had a staggering capacity for intake. We watched him polish off the ribs and pick all the shrimp out of the rice before he shot a French cuff and smiled at his Patek Philippe. On cue, the burly duo got up and headed toward us. The chief got to his feet, buttoned his jacket.

He looked down at Milo. "Who's paying for this repast?"

Milo said, "If you'd like—"

"Just kidding, Sturgis, I don't exploit

the workingman. Or in your case, Doc, the theorizing man."

He threw bills on the table. "Stay as long as you like. Just be gone in ten minutes so you can resume what the city pays you for, Sturgis."

Before his minions could reach him, he race-walked out of the room.

Milo looked at the picked-over rice. "Would your Hollywood buddies call that a good meeting?"

"My buddies?"

"Contacts, whatever."

"Well," I said, "depends on whether the picture gets made."

We left the restaurant, headed to a parking lot across Hill Street.

Milo said, "He talked a good case but what I got out of it was 'let's stall.'"

"Why'd you call him?"

"I didn't, I called Maria. She listened, hung up, two minutes later his secretary informs me where to go for lunch."

I said, "He's got to know he can't forestall the inevitable."

"Maybe, but he'll sure try. So with

Prema getting the bugs and the tools, what's our theory?"

"Maybe competitive culling."

"Meaning?"

"One female eliminates another's offspring in order to maintain dominance and eliminate competition for the desirable male. Big cats and primates do it all the time, and where polygamy exists, humans do it, too."

"Donny's the baby's daddy?"

"Movie star, attractive younger woman with a penchant for manipulation?"

"Yeah, that's a recipe. So what, Donny was big-time naughty with Qeesha—Simone, whatever—but Prema wants to hold on to him anyway?"

"Prema wants to avoid public humiliation."

"Manipulation," he said. "If it's true, think Qeesha planned to get pregnant?"

"Could be. A baby with Donny Rader could kick up her lifestyle."

"If she held on to her life."

I said, "Maybe Qeesha wanted more than generous child support. Maybe she thought she could actually replace the Queen Bee. Unfortunately for her, the Queen figured it out and took care of business. That could explain why the bones were treated so cruelly: deconstructing the competition, reducing the problem to a lab specimen in a coldly efficient way. It would also serve as a warning to Donny. Look what I'm capable of when I'm threatened."

"Where does Wedd fit in?"

"To me he still looks good as Adriana's killer, because even with doping her up, I don't see Prema managing to physically restrain another woman, drive her to the park, shoot her. Plus, Wedd's car was spotted near the scene. Wedd could've also dispatched Qeesha—talk about your efficient estate manager. But at some point he turned expendable."

"Queen Bee tying up loose ends."

"She's a tall woman," I said, "might fit the seat position on the Explorer. Getting Wedd to drive her somewhere wouldn't be a problem. Attending to her needs was his job. And the spot where he got shot isn't that far from the compound. Laurel up to Mulholland, hook west to Coldwater, drive a few miles.

For someone in good shape, no challenge walking back."

"Shoot a guy, mosey on home, do Pilates," he said.

"And maybe ditch the gun along the way."

He phoned Sean Binchy, ordered him to search Mulholland Drive between Laurel and Coldwater for a .45.

I said, "Qeesha was an experienced con. Had enough street smarts to pick up on any growing tension at the compound. She called in Adriana for support because she was unwilling to give up her dream. Figured if she could hold out until the baby was born, Donny would bond with his child and protect her."

He said, "Buzz buzz buzz goes the Queen Bee and the Drone wimps out."

We reached the Seville. He pointed to his unmarked, several vehicles up the row. "Off to garbage patrol."

"When will you start the surveillance?"

"After the trash reap. Why?"

"I'm kind of into hiking," I said. "For the exercise."

He looked at me. "Free country. Hope you get good weather."

I was back on Coldwater by nine the following morning, had added a small backpack. Inside was a pair of miniature binoculars, two bottles of water, a few snacks.

Being noticed wouldn't be a problem, just the opposite, but that was good: I was now that guy who parked his Cadillac on the turnoff and was foolish enough to brave oncoming traffic in the name of aerobics.

I'd also brought a companion: Blanche trotted along happily at the end of the short, pink leash she favors when making personal appearances. I made sure to keep her away from the road and she picked up the drill quickly, heeling and adjusting herself to my pace, breathing audibly but easily.

Nothing like a dog to make you look harmless. Especially a small cute dog and there's nothing cuter than a French bulldog.

And no Frenchie is more appealing than Blanche.

Still, she's not a setter or a retriever and even with cool weather and ample hydration, I knew my time would be limited by her stubby legs and her flat face.

My first sighting of the compound entrance was at nine eighteen. Sixteen minutes later, I used my phone to record a delivery from an organic market on Melrose. Eight minutes passed before the truck exited.

Just before ten a.m., a dry cleaner from Beverly Hills completed a similar circuit, then nothing for the next half hour. Blanche and I settled in a shady, safe spot up the road. Water for both of us. I ate a PowerBar and she made short but dainty work of a Milk-Bone, burped happily, and grew entranced by flowers, flies, butterflies, bees, potato bugs. A small plane that circled overhead for a few seconds.

We were back at ten forty-eight, watching the entrance to the compound. Seconds later an unmarked white Econoline van with blackened windows passed us, rolling down from the east. No livery number that I could see, so not hired transport. No I.D. of any sort. As it turned up the compound road, I got my binocs out.

An arm shot out and punched the call button. As the van idled, I managed to make out the lettering around the license-plate frame.

There was a 323 phone number on the top slat.

Home Sweet Home Schooling on the bottom.

The gate swung open, the van drove in. I called Home Sweet Home's number, got voice mail for Oxford Educational Services followed by a brief description of the mission statement:

Specialized instruction and on-site learning experience provided by alumni of top universities, designed to augment and enrich the educational experiences of homeschooled children.

Did that include anatomy and forensic anthropology?

Nine minutes after the Oxford van had entered, it drove back out, headed south on Coldwater. One of the windows was half open. I caught a flash of juvenile face before the glass slid back up.

On-site learning.

A field trip?

Scooping Blanche into my arms, I ran back to the Seville.

CHAPTER

46

I caught sight of the van descending Coldwater. A Jaguar and a Porsche traveled between us. Perfect cover as we crossed into Beverly Hills.

The cars kept going as the van turned right at Beverly Drive, edging Coldwater Park and cruising slowly.

The park was small but well equipped, with a shallow rock-stream, a playground, and barbered grass. Toddlers frolicked. Mothers nurtured. Nice place for the youngest of the Premadonny brood—the little blond girl—to recreate. The older kids would probably be bored.

Then again, these were children who rarely got out. Maybe swings and slides would be a big thrill.

The van made that moot by rolling past the park. Mansions gave way to small charming houses on narrow lots, as the road grew dim under canopies of shaggy old trees. Potholes appeared. The ambience was more funk than luxe, not unlike the slice of Beverly Glen where I lived.

Fifteen mph signs and speed bumps began to appear every few seconds. No problem for the van; it had been crawling at ten miles an hour, came to a full stop at each bump. I hung as far back as I could without losing visual contact, allowed a gardener's truck to sandwich in. The new convoy continued for another mile before the van veered right and the truck stayed on Beverly Drive.

Now I knew our destination. Good clean fun for all ages.

Franklin Canyon Park is a hidden slice of wilderness minutes from the self-conscious posing and the hypertensive drive of the city. Six-hundred-plus acres of untamed chaparral, skyscraper cedars, pines, and California oaks surround miles of hiking trails and a central hub bejeweled by a sun-mirror lake. A smaller pond is chock full with ducks and turtles and sunfish and minnows.

I knew Franklin because I used to take my previous Frenchie there when he grew restless. A bully, black-brindle heathen named Spike, he loved to explore. Though his affinity for poultry made the duck pond a challenge.

Packs of feral dogs were rumored to prowl the park's upper reaches but we'd never seen them. We did spot chipmunks, squirrels, the occasional late-rising skunk, lizards, and snakes, including a rattler or two that Spike dismissed as unworthy of his attention. A couple of times our presence provoked a chorus of ululation from distant coyotes. It was all I could do to restrain Spike from hunting down the uncouth intruders.

I'd never brought Blanche to Franklin Canyon, probably because she's so content with short strolls, hanging with Robin, and consulting on clinical cases.

As I drove up the mile and a half of sinuous mountain road that led to the park's entrance, she was sitting up, alert, head cocked quizzically.

"First time for everything, gorgeous."

Space for cars was limited and once the van entered, I could afford to hang back. Pulling over at the next turnoff, I retrieved additional supplies from the Seville's backseat, slipped them into my pack.

I rolled into the main lot, a rectangle of dirt bordered by post-and-beam fencing and surrounded by waist-high native grasses. No other vehicles in sight.

Leashing Blanche, I put my pack on and began walking down an oak-lined road. One curve and there was the van, right where I'd guessed.

Just above the fenced hollow that contained the lake. Several yards above the pond.

At this hour, not a lot of people around. Which, I supposed, was the point. An attendant helped an old woman trudge along the pathway. A few other dog-walkers strolled. Everyone smiled at Blanche and a woman with a longhaired dachshund stopped to chat, asking the usual canine-related questions.

Pleasant woman but the wiener dog wasn't nearly as amiable and it began to growl and chuff. The woman said, "Easy, Hansel."

Blanche looked up at me with *what's-his-problem* curiosity.

Hansel lunged.

"Bad boy," said the woman with obvious insincerity. The dachshund barked. The woman smiled, said, "My, yours is quiet," and walked on, the perfect enabler.

My attention shifted to a spot up the road. Two people exiting the front of the van.

The first was the driver, a soft-looking, fuzz-bearded guy in his twenties wearing a blue shirt, jeans, and sneakers. He placed a wheeled suitcase on the ground.

From the passenger side came a bespectacled, curly-haired woman around the same age, garbed identically. She carried a multicolored paisley bag heavy enough to require both hands.

The man slid open the van's rear door and extended his hand. A doll-like Asian girl accepted his help and descended, truing the straps of her own pink backpack. She wore a yellow T-shirt, lavender shorts, bubblegum-colored running shoes topped by frilly socks. Long black hair was held in place by a silver band.

She began laughing as a younger Asian boy leaped out, landed on his feet, and punched air. His hair was spiked, his backpack, black dotted with white specks that were probably skulls. A white T-shirt billowed over green shorts worn long and baggy, skater-dude-style.

Next came an older boy, skinny, smallish, with skin the color of coal. I knew he was thirteen, but puberty hadn't arrived and his limbs were licorice sticks. His purple shirt and yellow satin basketball shorts sported the Lakers logo. On his feet were black athletic shoes with silver trim.

Kembara.

Kyle-Jacques.

Kion.

The youngest boy tried to get Kion sparring. Kion mussed his brother's hair, waved his hands, feinted back, refused to take the bait.

Kyle-Jacques shouted, "Aaaah—you die!"

Kion hooked thumbs to his chest, flashed a *who-me?* grin.

Kyle-Jacques bounced, turned to his sister, began to harass her the same way. She looked at him the way compassionate gods regard sinners. He appeared to settle down. Then he leaped in the air and let out what the non-initiated would consider a martial arts yell. Landing off-balance, he flailed, stumbled back comically, managed to stay on his feet.

The bearded man said, "Good save, K.J."

Kion and Kembara laughed uncontrollably.

Kyle-Jacques scrunched his face, jumped around, stood still as if abruptly sedated.

The bearded man said, "Okay, tribe,

time to learn some science—Julie, we doing the full tribe or is Bunny-Boo still reluctant?"

"I'll check." Julie disappeared around the van, appeared seconds later holding the hand of a little towheaded girl.

Four-year-old Kristina wore a white blouse, a pink chiffon tutu, and sparkly sandals that said she'd picked her own outfit. She rubbed her eyes, yawned.

Julie said, "Still sleepy, Boo? Want me to carry you?"

She began lifting Kristina. The child resisted. Julie backed off. Kristina whimpered.

Julie said, "It'll be okay, Boo, you just woke up—wanna see the turtles?"

Head shake.

"How about the ducks—remember the ones with the funny red heads?"

Silence.

Kristina sat down on the dirt.

Kion said, "Here we go again. Drama."

Kembara said, "*Always* drama with Boo."

Kyle-Jacques resumed shadowboxing.

Julie said, "Sam?"

Sam shrugged. "If she needs to rest . . ."

Julie said, "Okay, Boo, you can rest in the van, I'll take you back."

Kristina began toeing the dirt.

Sam said, "Okay, remainder-of-tribe, Julie will deal with Boo and we will proceed to learn about protozoans and other good stuff."

Julie kneeled by Kristina. The little girl ignored her. Let out an abdominal grunt of protest.

A woman appeared from around the van. Tall, thin, in roomy gray sweats and a broad-brimmed straw hat that shielded her face, she walked over to Kristina, bent her knees, held out her hand.

Kristina shook her head. The woman in the hat swooped her up. Kristina molded to her. The woman said something. Kristina didn't respond. Then she giggled. The woman tickled her chin lightly. Kissed her cheek. Turned Kristina's face gently and kissed the other cheek, the tops of the child's eyelids.

She rocked the child. Said something else. Kristina nodded.

Kembara sang out, *"Draaa-maaa!"*

Still carrying Kristina, the woman in the hat walked to the older girl, kissed her the same way.

Kembara said, "Ugh," but she looked pleased.

The woman in the hat had tilted her face so I could see her jawline.

Clean and defined to begin with, tightened by a broad smile.

She placed Kristina down on the ground, took the girl's hand.

"Time for you to learn, too, Boo. You'll love it."

Kristina considered her options. Nodded.

The procession began.

CHAPTER

47

I'd eavesdropped half turning from the van and its occupants, outwardly focused on canine toilet behavior.

Blanche obliged by taking care of business in her usual dainty manner, sniffing the dirt to find a perfect spot upon which to bestow her natural resources. Upon finishing, she kicked up some dust. One of the strategic implements I'd retrieved from the backseat was a plastic poop bag and I used it to good effect. The nearest trash basket was right on the way. Karma.

Swinging the bag conspicuously, I

sped up and passed the group. The woman in the hat was carrying Kristina again. Julie wheeled the suitcase, Sam toted the plastic bag.

As I got several paces ahead, one of the boys, probably Kyle-Jacques, said, "Cool dog."

Kembara said, "Looks like a gremlin."

"It's a bulldog," said Sam. "They were bred to fight bulls but that was a long time ago, now they're just pets."

Kyle-Jacques said, "That one couldn't fight nothing."

"Anything," said a new voice, adult, female.

Familiar. In another context, sultry. What I heard now was gentle, maternal instruction.

Kyle-Jacques said, "Yeah, whatever."

Blanche and I reached the pond with time to spare.

A couple dozen ducks swam and splashed. Concentric rings on the surface of the water betrayed the presence of fish. Turtles the size of dinner plates lazed on the banks. An old pittosporum tree in the process of dying, it roots decaying slowly, leaned precariously toward the water. A queue of turtles lined its wizened trunk. Half a dozen glossy shells stationed as precisely as marines at roll call, heads and limbs retracted. Arrayed that way, the reptiles looked like exotic pods sprouting from the wood.

Two benches at the far end of the pond were shaded by sycamores and oak. I selected one, placed my backpack at my feet, lifted Blanche and set her down next to me. Checking out the world beyond the Seville's passenger window, walking, and pooping had pretty much exhausted her. She snuggled up tight against my thigh, placed her knobby little head in my lap, fluttered her eyes, and began to snore.

I stroked her neck until her breathing grew rhythmic and slow. *Sweet dreams, Gorgeous.*

The group arrived at the pond just as I retrieved the other strategic object I'd stashed in the pack: the current issue of *The International Journal of Child Psychology and Psychiatry.* The lead article was a survey of pediatric responses to hospitalization. An area I'd studied years ago. I'd been meaning to get to it.

As I alternated between reading and peeking above the top of the magazine, the party of seven stopped at the turtle-clad tree branch. Sam pointed and lectured, motioned to Julie, who did the same. The kids—including little Kristina—paid attention. Kion and Kembara stood still. Kyle-Jacques was a little jumpier and he moved toward the old tree to reach for a turtle.

Julie held him off with a hand on his arm.

He asked her something. Julie drew him closer to the amphibians, pointed to some detail of the turtle's shell.

Kyle-Jacque nodded, backed off.

Sam opened the wheeled suitcase, removed a blanket, and spread it on the dirt. Extricating a stereoscopic microscope, he carefully placed the instrument in the center of the fabric. The scope was joined, in turn, by a fishnet, a ladle, and a plastic vial. Then a small wooden box whose contents glinted when Sam popped the lid. He held something up to the light.

Glass specimen slides.

Julie said something. The older three kids removed their backpacks, laid them down, began unzipping. Kristina held on to the hand of the tall woman in the hat.

I thought: Time for the latest whiz-bang e-tablets.

Out came three spiral notebooks and marker pens.

Wrong, Smart Guy.

About so much.

As Julie lectured and pointed, Kion, Kembara, and Kyle-Jacques sat cross-legged on the bank, sketching and jotting notes. Sam walked to the pond's edge, steered clear of the inert turtles, and ladled water. Transferring the green liquid to the vial, he capped it and brought it back to the microscope on the blanket.

It took several attempts to set up a slide bearing a water bubble. By the time Sam was finished, Kristina's interest had been piqued and she'd pulled free from the tall woman in the hat, stood next to the teacher. Sam focused the microscope, narrowed the eyepieces to fit the little girl's face.

She peered. Looked up beaming. Peered some more.

The woman in the hat said something. Kristina joined her sibs. Julie gave her a pad and a green crayon.

The woman walked a few paces away, stopped, called out, "You okay, now, Boo?"

Kristina ignored her.

"Boo, I'm going to sit down over there." Pointing to the free bench.

"Go, Mommy!"

I continued reading as the woman sat down a few feet away. Out of her purse came a book. *Happiest Toddler on the Block.*

She read. I read. She snuck a few peeks at Blanche, now awake and serene.

I'd canted the journal cover to offer a clear view of the title.

The woman had another go at her book. Looked at Blanche, again.

I pretended to focus on the magazine. Read some of the lead article, began skimming. Nothing had changed much since I'd worked in a hospital.

Blanche stretched, jumped from the bench onto the dirt, stretched some more.

I said, "Morning, Sleeping Beauty." Blanche licked my hand, rubbed her head against my fingers.

The woman said, "Are you just the cutest?"

Blanche grinned.

"Excuse me, but I have to ask. Did she just smile at me?"

"She does that with people she likes."

"Totally adorable. With some dogs it seems like they're smiling but they're putting out a different energy—more of a warning? This one . . . she really *is* something."

"Thanks."

The brim of the hat rose, offering me a full view of the face below.

No makeup. No need. Classic, symmetrical bone structure the camera adored. Fine strands of hair escaped the confines of the hat but most remained tucked in. Mousy brown, now, blow-away fine. Filaments clouded the back of a long, graceful neck.

Impossible not to know who she was.

Today, I was playing the most clueless man in L.A. Offering her the merest of smiles, I returned to my magazine.

Footsteps caused me to lower the pages.

Kristina, running toward her mother.

"Easy, Boo, don't trip."

"Mommy, Mommy, it's a smail!"

Holding out a brown, cochlear shell.

"Is there actually a snail in there, Boo, or is it empty?"

"It's empty."

"So the snail left its home."

"Huh?"

"The shell is the snail's home, Boo. Maybe this one left to find another one."

"Huh?"

The woman kissed the child's cheek. "It's a beautiful shell, Boo."

"It's a smail—aaahh wanna see the doggy!"

"We don't bother doggies, Boo—"

"Wanna *see!*"

I closed the magazine. "It's okay."

"You're sure? I really don't want to bother you."

"Of course. Her name is Blanche and she loves kids."

Hand in hand, the two of them approached. On cue, Blanche assumed the sit-stay. Kristina reached to pet the top of her head.

I said, "Actually, she likes it better when you do it this way." Placing my hand low, in tongue range. Kristina imitated me. I said, "Perfect." Blanche licked. Kristina giggled and moved in for another tongue-bath.

Her mother said, "Okay, that's fine. Thank the nice man, Boo."

Kristina began petting Blanche. Her strokes quickened. Veered on slaps. Her mother took hold of her wrist, guided the tiny hand down.

Blanche licked pudgy fingers.

Kristina squealed.

The woman said, "Blanche. Like in *Streetcar.*"

I smiled. "She likes the company of strangers."

The woman laughed. "I can see that. Great disposition. It's a blessing."

Kristina showed the shell to Blanche and shouted, "Smail!"

Blanche smiled.

Kristina ran off laughing.

The woman said, "Sorry for interrupting your reading."

I said, "Talk about adorable."

Her eyes drifted to the magazine. "You're a psychologist?"

"I am."

"I'm reading something kind of related—hold on."

Her walk to her bench was languid, graceful. She returned with the toddler book.

"I know it's pop stuff," she said. "Would you mind telling me if it's worth anything?"

"It is," I said. "I know the author."

"Really."

"We trained at the same time. At Western Pediatric Medical Center. Your little one's a bit past toddler."

"I know," she said. "I just like to learn." The book dropped to her side. "That hospital, I actually did a— I spent some time there. Not with my kids, thank God. Just . . . I helped out. Years ago, before I had kids."

"It's a good place."

"You bet . . . anyway, thanks for sharing Blanche with Kristina."

She offered her hand. Long graceful fingers, clean nails, no polish.

I said, "Blanche lives to socialize."

Taking a cue with the panache of Streep, Blanche wiggled her hindquarters.

The woman laughed. "I see that—um, do you happen to have a card?"

I gave her one.

She read it. Her eyes saucered.

I said, "Everything okay?"

"Oh, sure . . . it's just . . . I almost . . . this is going to sound totally weird but a few years back someone actually referred me to you."

"Small world," I said.

"I'm sorry, this is kind of awkward . . . the appointment got canceled. I listened to someone else who gave me another name. It wasn't very helpful."

"Sometimes," I said, "it's a matter of fit."

"This was a bad fit—listen, this is going to sound pushy but would you be willing to give it another try? An appointment, I mean."

"Sure."

"Wow," she said, "that's gracious of you. Um, could it be relatively soon?"

I pulled my appointment book out of my pack, knitted my brow.

She said, "You're booked solid. Of course."

I closed the book. "Got a cancellation tomorrow, but it's early. Eight thirty if you can make it."

"I can. Sure, that'll be fine." She looked at the card. "There's no address here."

"I work from home. I'll give it to you."

She produced an iPhone, punched in the info. "Eight thirty it is, thank you so much, Dr. Alexander Delaware—I guess I'd better be getting back to my tribe."

We shook hands. Her skin was cool, dry, thrumming with the faintest tremor.

She said, "I'm Preem, by the way."

"Nice to meet you."

Flashing a million bucks' worth of smile, she hurried to her brood.

◆

I pretended to read another article, slipped Blanche a Milk-Bone. "You earned caviar but this is all I've got."

When she was finished nibbling, we left, passing the kids and the teachers and Prema Moon, everyone busy with an assortment of vials, slides, leaves, illustrated books.

Prema Moon gave me a small wave and held a leaf up to Kembara. "Look at this, honey. Tri-lobar."

The girl said, "Great, Mom," in a voice ripe with boredom.

"Pretty, no?"

"Uh-huh."

"That means it has three lobes—three of these little roundy things."

"*Mo*-om, I need to *draw*."

CHAPTER
48

Hang around L.A. long enough and you're going to spot actresses. I've probably seen more than the average citizen because a few famous butts have warmed the battered leather couch in my office and once in a while I tag along with Robin at the type of party most people imagine to be fascinating but typically turns out to be mind-numbing.

I've learned that cinematic beauty is a funny thing. Sometimes it's limited to the screen and real life offers up a plain face that closes up like a frightened sea

anemone when the camera's not whir-
ring. Other times, physical perfection
transcends time and place.

Prema Moon sat on the couch wearing *couldn't-care-less* clothes: loose
jeans, brown sneakers, a shapeless
V-necked sweater that had begun life
as sad beige and had faded to tragic
gray. Her macramé bag was one shade
sootier, fraying where the fabric gathered into bamboo handles.

Like yesterday, she wore no makeup.
Indoor lighting turned her hair mousier
than it had been at the park. The ends
were blunt and uneven, barely reached
her shoulders. Homemade hack job or
an exorbitant styling meant to look that
way.

If she indulged in Botox, she was
overdue. Fine lines scored her brow, the
space between her eyes, the sides of
her mouth. The skin beneath her eyes
was puffy. The indigo of her irises was
lovely but oddly low-watt. Warm but
sad.

She was gorgeous.

◆

She'd arrived precisely on time, driving a small gray Mercedes with black windows and squeaky brakes. Blanche and I greeted her at the door. Prema stooped to pet. "Hello again, Princess." She did the usual quick-check of the living room, offered the comment I get all the time:

"Nice place, Dr. Delaware. Kind of hidden away."

"Thanks. This way."

When we arrived in the office, Blanche waddled to Prema's feet and sat down.

"Is she a therapy dog?"

"She can be," I said. "But she has no problem waiting outdoors."

"Oh, no, I couldn't do that to her—c'mon, baby, you join us."

She sank into the couch, turned small, the way skinny, high-waisted people do. Leaning to scratch behind Blanche's ear, she said, "I don't want to break any rules, here, but is it okay if she sits up here with me?"

I clicked my tongue. Blanche jumped up on the couch, settled in close.

Prema Moon said, "Well, that was pretty nimble."

I sat back and waited, the calm, patient therapist. Wondered if someone with her training would see through the act.

I'd had a restless night, waking up four times with a pounding head and a racing mind. Wondering if I could trust my own judgment.

Had I dragged Milo's case into a bog destined to sink it?

How would I tell Prema I'd stalked her without scaring her out of the office?

At five a.m., I'd crawled out of bed, padded to my office, scrawled notes.

I returned an hour later. Gobbledygook.

However it shook out, Prema passing through my doorway bought her insurance: From now on I was bound by confidentiality, maybe useless to Milo.

A logistical mess; I hadn't expected it to turn out this way. Had been aiming for a chance to observe the kids. Hadn't counted on Prema being in the van.

Not completely true.

The slim chance the putative Evil Queen might materialize had led me to bring Blanche and the psych journal, a pair of perfect lures.

Even with that, I'd expected small talk at best. Some kind of observational insight I could bring back to Milo.

My clever little plan had worked too well.

I'd been wrong about so much.

Prema Moon kept massaging Blanche. Checked out the prints on the wall. Put on dorky glasses and squinted at my diplomas, returned the specs to her macramé bag.

"Nice," she said. "The feeling, here. What you imagine a therapist office is like. *Should* be like. The other one—the doctor I went to instead of you—that was a cold space. Just screamed *I don't care about people.* Cold and expensive—what's your fee, by the way?"

"Three hundred dollars for forty-five minutes."

"Compared with her, you're a bargain." She counted out cash, placed the bills on a side table. "This place talks softly. Earnestly."

She fooled with her hair. A strand

broke off and floated to her knee. She tweezed it between thumb and forefinger, tried to deposit it in the wastebasket. The hair adhered to her fingertip. She rubbed until it dropped. That took a while.

"As you can see, I'm a little compulsive."

I smiled.

She smiled back. Hard to read the emotion behind it. By comparison, Mona Lisa was blatant.

"Okay," she said, "the thing with therapy is to be utterly honest, right?"

"As honest as you feel you can be."

"There are degrees of honesty?"

"There are degrees of revelation," I said. "It's a matter of what you're comfortable with."

"Ah," she said. "Yes, I suppose you're right. In the end, we're all strangers except to ourselves, that's why your job is so interesting, you try to . . . span the gap." Head shake. "That probably didn't make sense."

"It made perfect sense."

Her eyes drifted back to the paper on my wall. Blanche snuggled closer.

"Never had a pet. Don't know exactly why."

"Four kids," I said, "I'd imagine you're pretty busy."

"I mean even as a child. I could've had a pet if I asked. I could've had anything. But I never asked."

She blinked. "Okay, time for that honesty: The reason the appointment was canceled wasn't because I was urged to see someone else. It was because of you specifically. The other work you do. Do you understand what I'm saying?"

"Police cases."

"Exactly. Someone thought it would be a bad idea for someone like me to get involved with a doctor who did that. No one close to me, just a suit—a person paid to be careful."

A beat. "But here I am, after all. Which leads me to a second bit of honesty, Dr. Delaware. I suspected you were following us the moment you turned off Coldwater onto Beverly."

I took a second to digest that. "You suspected but you didn't sound an alarm."

"If it was me alone, I'd probably have

turned around and gotten the heck out of there. But with the tribe, a trip that had been planned for a long time? I suspected but I didn't know for sure, so no sense scaring them, ruining their day. So I waited to see what you did once you entered the park and you just walked your dog and ignored us and I figured I was wrong, you were just a guy with a dog. Then we met up by the pond and you cleverly ignored me but made sure I'd see that magazine. Even then, I didn't think much of it. Then I read your card and I remembered your name. Remembered that other work you do and started to wonder."

She twisted a thicker clump of hair. Several more strands fell to her lap. She made no attempt to clear them.

"And yet," she said, "I'm here."

I said, "I'd like to help you."

She said, "With what?"

Thinking of Holly Ruche, I said, "Owning your life. Finally."

"Really?" she said, as if finding that humorous.

Then she cried.

◆

I supplied a box of tissues and a bottle of water. She dabbed, drank. I waited for her questions.

The first one she asked surprised me. "What do you think of my tribe?"

"They seem like a great bunch."

"Four gems, Dr. Delaware. Four flawless diamonds. I'm not taking credit but at least I didn't screw them up."

"Prema, a friend of mine says happiness comes from taking all the credit and none of the blame."

She clapped her hands. "I love that . . . but sometimes it's hard to separate blame from credit, isn't it? To know what's real and what isn't. Back when I was a public person, people who'd never met me had opinions about everything I did. One day I was a goddess, the next I was evil incarnate."

"Celebrity's all about love–hate," I said, thinking, as I had a hundred times over the last few days, of the venomous contempt expressed by Brent Dorf, Kevin Dubinsky. Len Coates, who should have known better, because he'd been trained to analyze facts not rumors, had never laid eyes on her.

None of them had.

She said, "I'm not complaining, it's part of the game. But I used to wonder where all that crap was coming from. People so *sure.* Alleged *experts* accusing me of swooping into orphanages at random, bribing officials so I could walk away with the cutest babies. As if building a family was as simple as choosing strays at the pound. Or, worse, I raided Third World villages with a private army and stole infants from poor people."

Speaking in the singular.

She hugged herself. "*True* reality is I went through channels, got screened. Had the kids screened, too, because I'm not that selfless, forget all that sainthood crap they've also tried to lay on me—stupid diplomats at the U.N. making like I'm Mother Teresa. I'm a mother, small 'm.' Didn't *want* an incurably sick baby or a mentally challenged baby. Didn't want to be surprised by bad news. Does that offend you?"

"Not at all."

"I mean I was willing to deal with whatever came up naturally, but why make life harder than it needs to be?"

"Makes sense."

"I mean there's no reason not to make your life as good as it can be, right? To feel *worthy* of happiness."

She crumpled a tissue. "I was clueless. About creating a family. It's a challenge under the best of circumstances. If you do it right, it's daunting, you have to put in time, personal investment, doubting yourself. Educating yourself. You can't just read books or dial it in, you can't just delegate it to other people. So I decided to do it right and changed my life."

She swiveled toward me. "Big insight to a psychologist, huh? But what did I know? Not that I'm some Suzy Housewife baking cookies. Keep me away from kitchens, keep me *far* away if you value your intestinal tract. And I know I'm lucky, I can pay people to do things I don't want to do. But actually raising my children? The real stuff? That's *my* job."

She smiled. "Listen, I'm not some martyr, claiming I gave it all up for them. I lost nothing, gained everything. They bring me meaning every day, the other stuff never did. Now the thought of blabbing someone else's lines makes me want to throw up."

I kept silent.

"You think I'm a burned-out weirdo?"

"I think you've moved on."

"Well," she said, "whether you mean it or not, you say the right things—sorry, I tend to be a little cynical." More hair fluffing, more ciliary rain. "So they seemed well adjusted to you?"

"They did."

"Did you expect spoiled monsters?"

"I didn't know what to expect, Prema."

"Aw c'mon, 'fess up, Dr. Delaware, you had to have a little bit of expectation, no? Crazy Hollywood mom, crazy kids? But trust me, no way that was going to happen. No way they were going to have a childhood like mine. I don't believe—I *refuse* to believe that we're condemned to repeat our own crap."

My personal mantra. When things got low I congratulated myself for not ending up like Harry Delaware.

I said, "If I didn't agree, I wouldn't do this job."

Prema Moon's eyes watered up again.

The tissue had wadded so tightly it disappeared in her fist. "I don't know why I'm getting into this. Why I feel the need to justify myself to you."

I said, "It's normal to feel judged in a situation like this."

"You followed us. That was based on a judgment. What's going on?"

"I've been trying to learn about you and your family. Haven't been very successful because you've dropped off the grid. When families isolate themselves, it's often because of serious problems and that's what I suspected. I know now that you've been trying to take control of your life, are focused on protecting the kids. For good reason. You know that better than anyone."

She bit her lip. "Great monologue, Doctor. You could've made a living in my old business. But you still haven't answered my question."

"You need help, Prema. You know that. That's why you're here."

She opened her palm, watched the tissue expand like a time-lapse flower. Crushed it again. "Maybe you're being sincere, I hope you are. But with the

good ones—the *performers*—you can
never be sure. Meryl, Jack, Judi. Larry
Olivier—I knew Larry when I was a kid,
he was always sweet to me. But when
he chose to be someone else? Good
luck. Maybe that's you, Dr. Alexander
Delaware."

"You're the performer, Prema."

"Me? I'm a hack. I made a ridiculous
fortune doing crap."

"I think you're selling yourself short."

"Not in the least, Dr. Delaware. I know
what I am and I'm okay with it." Her
knuckles were white and shiny as ivory.
"How long have you been *learning* about
us?"

"I did a bit of digging right after that
first appointment was made. Because
the circumstances were odd: The person who called was evasive, wouldn't
even tell me who the patient was. I assumed I'd be seeing one of the kids,
looked for anything I could find about
them. Which wasn't much but I did
come across a photo. You and the kids,
a theater lobby in New York. They
seemed unhappy. Ill at ease. You stood
behind them. You came across de-

tached. Not exactly a happy family portrait."

Her eyes flashed. "Detestable picture,
you have no idea how much time and
money it took to get it offline."

"I'm glad I saw it before you succeeded. Now I understand."

"Understand what?"

"I'd missed the emotional content.
You were scared—all of you."

She flinched. "Why would I be
scared?"

I said, "Not why. Of who."

She shook her head. Closed her eyes.
Sat lower and got even smaller.

I said, "My guess is you—all of you—
were scared of the person who set up
the shot. Someone who doesn't care
about kids, but didn't mind using them."

The eyes opened. New shade of indigo, deep, hot. "You're frightening."

"Am I wrong?"

Silence was my answer.

I said, "You talk about your children
in the singular. 'I,' not 'we.' You're doing
it alone. For good reason."

She crossed her arms. Blanche licked
her hand. Prema remained unmoved.

Her lips set. Angry. I wondered if I'd lost her.

I said, "No matter what you do, he rejects them completely. It must be tough, living with that degree of callousness. Your kids are your world. Why can't he see how wonderful they are? Understand the joy of being a parent. But he doesn't. And now there's a new level of fear and that's why you're here. Because of the other work I do."

Shooting to her feet, she stormed out of the office, made it halfway up the hall where she stopped short, swung the big bag as if working up momentum to use it as a battering ram.

I had a clear view, stayed in my chair.

The bag grew still. Her shoulders heaved. She returned, stood in the doorway, leaning against the jamb for support.

"My God," she said. "The things that come out of your mouth."

Then she returned to the couch.

CHAPTER

49

Another head shake. More hair fell. A woman coming apart strand by strand. She hugged herself. Shuddered. Ten fingers began working like Rubinstein on Rachmaninoff.

I said, "If you're feeling cooped up, we can talk outside."

"How did you know I felt that?"

Because you look like a caged animal.

I said, "Lucky guess."

I told Blanche to stay in the office, paid her with a Milk-Bone.

Prema Moon said, "She can come with us."

"She needs to nap." The real reason: Time to minimize distraction. And comfort.

I walked her through the house, out through the kitchen and down the rear steps to the garden, stopping by the pond's rock rim. The waterfall burbled. The sky was clear.

"Very mellow," she said. "To encourage confession?"

"I'm not a priest."

"Isn't this the new religion?"

"God doesn't talk to me."

"Only Freud does, huh?"

"Haven't heard from him in a while, either." I sat down on the teak bench that faces the water. The fish swarmed.

Prema Moon said, "What are they, Japanese koi? Pretty."

She took in the garden. Robin's studio, softened by trees and shrubs. A whine cut through the waterfall. The band saw.

"What's that noise?"

"The woman I live with builds musical instruments."

"She's going to come out here and see me?"

"No."

"You've trained her to stay inside when a patient's here?"

"Once she's in there, it's for hours."

"What if she does come out?"

"She'll go right back in."

"What's her name?"

I shook my head.

"Sorry," she said. "I'm just . . . I'm jumping out of my skin, this is . . . I don't *know* what it is. Don't know what to *do*."

I uncapped the canister of fish food, scooped a handful of pellets, tossed.

She watched the koi eat. Said, "Well, yummy for them."

Not a word out of her for a long time. When that didn't look as if it was going to change, I said, "Tell me what frightens you."

"Why should I?"

"You're here."

She reached for the koi food. "May I?" Tweezing again, she threw in one pellet at a time. "I like the silver one. Elegant."

I said, "Okay, I'll start. People who work for you seem to die unnaturally."

Her arm shot out. She hurled the rest of the food. The fish feasted. "People? All I know is Adriana. And I only know about her because I heard it on TV and it freaked me out completely."

"Did you contact the police?"

Long pause. "You know the answer. I didn't. Because I couldn't see what I could possibly offer. She worked for me only for a short time. I really didn't know her."

I said nothing.

She said, "What did you mean 'people'? You're freaking me out."

"First Adriana, then Melvin Jaron Wedd."

Her hand flew to her face. *"What! Mel? No! When?"*

"A few days ago."

"Oh, God, no—what are you *telling* me?"

"He was murdered a few days ago. Was he a good employee?"

"What?"

I repeated the question.

"Sure, fine, he was great. Murder? What happened—"

"Reliable? Skilled at organizing?"

"Yes, yes, all that, what does it matter?"

I said, "In addition to all that, he had a special talent. Vocal impressions."

"What? Oh, that, sure, yes, he'd do cartoon characters for the kids. So?"

"He did a pretty good imitation of Donny. When he called me for that appointment on your behalf."

"What!"

"I thought it was Donny. But it was Mel, wasn't it?"

She said, "Mel called for me but—I never told him to do that."

"Guess he improvised."

"Why would he?"

"I thought you might be able to tell me."

"Well, I *can't,* I have no *idea* why."

"Then I'll take a guess, Prema. Subtle hostility. He didn't much care for Donny, because he'd learned what Donny is like. He knew that Donny wouldn't be happy about your consulting a child psychologist. So he mimicked Donny. Mel's little bit of nasty irony."

She stared at the water.

I said, "Mel refused to tell me which kid I'd be seeing because the answer was none of them. The kids didn't need help, they were doing fine. All things considered."

She looked at me. Her eyes were wet. "I'm doing my best."

"I believe that you are. So the question remains: Why did you want to see me? I'm a child psychologist so it wasn't about therapy for you. That leaves some kind of family issue."

She didn't answer.

I said, "Maybe a marriage that's unraveling? A concerned parent wanting to learn about the impact on the children? And how to minimize it?"

She covered her face with both hands.

I said, "You care about everyone and everything. Donny couldn't care less. You always wanted kids, he never did. You convinced yourself his attitude would change once he saw how cute they could be. It didn't, he cut them off completely. And they know it. That's why that picture in the lobby was so stressful. It was his idea, the first time he'd shown any interest in family life, so there had to be an ulterior motive. What was he planning to do with the shot? Use it for publicity?"

She raised her arms, punched air clumsily. "Damn him! For a stupid movie! Big lead role for him, he was going to play a *dad*."

"Typecasting."

Her laugh was bitter. "Caring, bumbling, lovable *dad*. Can you believe the morons who thought of that?"

"Not exactly *Citizen Kane*."

"Not exactly *Citizen* Sane. Piece-of-crap script, piece-of-crap casting, *his* big comedy debut, it was going to open a whole new world for him."

She got up, walked several steps away, returned.

"His *plan* was to sell the photo to *People* for big bucks. He never asked me, knew what I'd say. Instead he sprang it on me as we drove from the airport into the city. He'd instructed the driver to go straight to the theater, his agent had paid to rent the lobby. The whole purpose of the trip was educational. Show the kids the Metropolitan Museum of Art, the planetarium. I was surprised when he offered to come along. Allowed myself to be hopeful, maybe he'd seen the light. Then he pulled that! Expecting them to pose for hours of pictures. Him with the tribe, both of us with the tribe. He wanted them to jump in the air and laugh and hug him and kiss him! *Disgusting!* I killed it. The rule from the beginning was always they *never* got used. For his crap or mine. He knew that and now he's trying to *change* it? Because someone's paying him to be a *dad*? He tried to force the issue, I stood my ground. It got ugly, I told the kids to wait in the limo. By the time I got back to the lobby, he was gone. He drove straight back to Teterboro, chartered a plane to Vegas, stayed there for weeks, doing his Vegas thing. The tribe and I tried to make the best of it. I'd rented a big quiet apartment on Sutton Place, doorman, security, off the beaten path. I managed to take them a few places without attracting attention. They wanted to know where he'd gone. I said he wasn't feeling well but they knew I was lying. I tried to reach out to him, maybe we could talk, work something out. He wouldn't take my calls. Then he texted me a picture of himself and some . . . girls. Let me know quite graphically that he didn't miss me."

Her face tightened. "After that, we moved even further apart."

"Lovable dad," I said. "Don't recall that film."

"Never got made."

"How come?"

"Maybe someone realized how bad he sucks as an actor?" Shrug. "That's the way the business works, mostly it's air sandwiches." Her toe nudged the rock rim.

Time for me to nudge her. "Have you told the kids about Adriana's death?"

"Of course not!"

"How did you explain her absence?"

"I said she went away on vacation. It would only matter to Boo, Adriana was Boo's person, the others don't need anything like that."

"A nanny."

"Not even a nanny, just someone to watch Boo when I'm tied up."

"Four kids," I said. "Sometimes you can get spread pretty thin."

"I manage." She sniffed. "There's nothing else I'd rather be doing."

Out of my pant pocket came a piece of paper. I unfolded, pretended to read.

She pretended to ignore me. But it had been a long time since she'd performed and she struggled with her curiosity. "What is that?"

I handed it over. Fumbling in her bag, she produced her glasses. Scanned the receipt from JayMar Laboratory. The copy I'd kept for myself. "Beetles? Scalpels? What is this?"

"Check the name of the recipient, Prema."

"Who's that?"

"Someone who buys stuff for you through Apex Management. For you only."

Her mouth dropped. "What? That's ridiculous. I've never heard of this place! Beetles? Scalpels—a *bone* saw? What the hell's going on?"

She tried to return the receipt. I kept

my hands in my lap. "Kevin Dubinsky ordered all that stuff for you."

"Mel handles my purchases."

"You wanted something, you'd tell Mel, he'd pass it along to Kevin?"

"Who's Kevin? I don't know any Kevin. Everything's done by email, anyway."

"You'd email Mel and he'd pass it along to—"

"This is crazy." She re-read. "Dermestid—sounds gross. Why would I want bugs in my house? We pay a pest service to get rid of bugs, last year it took two days to clear a wasp nest. Kyle-Jacques is allergic to bees and wasps."

"Dermestid beetles aren't household pests, they're specialists, Prema."

"At what?"

"They consume flesh. Quickly and cleanly. Scientists use them to clean bones."

"That's disgusting! Why would I want something like that?"

Her hands shook. The paper rattled.

I'd given her the perfect opening but she'd made no attempt to weasel out by offering a plausible explanation.

Oh, those beetles. I forgot, they were part of the kids' science project. I'm big on teaching them science, you saw that yesterday.

She said, "Beetles? Scalpels?" She turned white. "You're saying someone cleaned *Mel's* bones? Or Adriana's—omigod—"

"Mel was shot and left intact. Same for Adriana. Is anyone else authorized to contact Kevin Dubinsky on your behalf?"

"I keep telling you, I don't know any Kevin Dubinsky. My life—you delegate, things get . . . away from you."

"Who has access to your email account?"

"No one has access to my personal account. I don't use it much, anyway, try to stay off the computer because the Internet's nothing but mental pollution. I'm into reading. Books. Never had much school, I need to catch up. So I can be smart for the tribe, already they know stuff I don't. Especially K.J., he knows so much math."

"Are there other email accounts at your home?"

"Of course, for the household," she said. "I can't tell you how many or who uses them—I sure don't. We have a computer company, they set it up. For day-to-day things."

"Would those household accounts be used for shopping?"

"For food, toilet paper. Not bugs!"

"Who's on your staff?"

"Total? If you mean people coming in and out, like gardeners, pool service—those pest-control people—I couldn't even tell you, there's always someone around fixing something."

"Who lives on the premises, like Mel?"

"It used to be crazy, we used to have an army," she said. "After I stopped working I began to pare down. Mel is—was the overall manager. I used to have a personal assistant but I let her go a few years back, the only reason most people have P.A.s is they're afraid of being alone. I *relish* being alone."

"Does Donny have an assistant?"

"Always," she said. "They come and go. Girls, always girls. The latest one I couldn't even tell you her name, we live . . . Other than that there's just the housekeepers. Imelda, Lupe, Maria, I need three to keep the place clean, it's a big undertaking, they're lovely. Religious ladies, cousins. That's it. Oh, yeah, a cook. For healthy food."

"Plus Adriana."

Tears filled her eyes. "Plus her. She was also religious. I could tell because she kept a Bible by her bed and sometimes I'd see her praying. Personally, I'm not into that but I respect it. Are you saying the same person who killed her killed Mel?"

"Too early to tell," I said. "Have you moved to replace Adriana?"

"I'm not sure I need to, Boo's growing more independent. More interactive, hanging out with the tribe more."

"Do you have chauffeurs?"

"We used to have two, one for him, one for the rest of us, but that was a waste, we don't go out much, I switched to a car service."

"Did Donny keep his driver?"

"No . . . I don't think so."

"You don't know?"

She exhaled. "We don't exactly live together."

"Where does he live?"

"Next door. The adjoining property. I mean it's one property, I bought it years ago, but it's three separate parcels. I was going to develop it as one big estate but then . . . things changed. The tribe and I use the big lot. Seven acres, a main house, some outbuildings, tennis court, pool, stuff."

"And Donny?"

"He took the middle one, around three acres. The smallest one is a little less than an acre. No buildings on it, no one goes there."

She thrust the JayMar form at me. "Take this back, it's freaking me out."

I pocketed the paper. "When you heard about Adriana, did you talk about it to anyone?"

"No."

"Not Mel?"

"Why would I discuss it with him?"

"People work together, they talk to each other."

"Mel and I weren't like that," she said.

"No socializing."

"We talked when there was something to talk about. Don't get the wrong picture, I didn't snob him out but it's not like—wasn't like we were friends, a friend is someone who likes you for yourself. Mel wouldn't have stuck around for a second if I didn't pay him."

Her smile was grim. "I don't have friends, Dr. Delaware. I have people I pay."

Thinking of all the women Robert Sommers had spotted parading in and out of Wedd's apartment, I said, "How was Mel's love life?"

"He had none that I knew about."

"No girlfriend?"

She smiled. "Mel was gay."

"You know that because—"

"He told me. Like I said, when there was something to talk about, we talked. One time Mel was looking upset and I asked him what was wrong and he told me. I have to admit, I had no idea, he never gave off any gay vibe. What was bothering him was he has—had a brother, some macho cowboy-type, and they hadn't seen each other in a long time because Mel had run from who he was. Now Mel wanted to . . . what's the word he used—*resurrect,* he wanted to resurrect the relationship, was worried once the brother found out it would screw things up permanently. Why is his love life important?"

"Someone gets murdered, it's good to know about their relationships."

"Mel may have had some but I'm unaware of them. Why did you show me that beetle thing?"

"The night Adriana was killed, something else was found in the park. The skeleton of a two-month-old. The bones had been cleaned by dermestid beetles."

She gasped, made a retching sound, bent low. "I'm supposed to be connected to *that*? That's *insane*." She clawed her hair. "This *can't* be *happening*!"

"Who'd want to set you up, Prema?"

"No one."

I said, "One more thing. After the bones were cleaned they were coated with beeswax."

She clutched my arms. Looked me full in the face. Shrieked.

Springing to her feet, she backed away from me as if I were diseased.

Ran toward the house, made it to the kitchen steps but didn't climb them.

Instead, she began pacing the yard. Fast, robotic, tearing at her hair. Great workout companion for Milo.

On her ninth circuit, she sped to the rear of the yard where tall trees blacken the grass. Leaning against the trunk of my oldest coast redwood, she sobbed convulsively.

Just as I'd decided to approach her, she straightened her shoulders, sucked in breath, and returned to the teak bench.

"The park where she—where they were both found. If they mentioned it on the TV, I didn't hear, I really wasn't paying attention until I heard Adriana's name. Was it Cheviot?"

"How'd you know that, Prema?"

"Oh, I know." Gripping her knees with both hands, she put herself in an awkward crouch. As if prepping for a leap off a cliff.

Nowhere to fly. She remained frozen. Moaned. "I know all *sorts* of things."

CHAPTER

50

Milo was at his desk. "You did *what*?"

"It started out as surveillance," I said. "Things progressed."

"You told her everything?"

"I told her enough to get through to her."

"She's your new pal."

"She's not the offender."

"You know that."

"I'll put money on it."

Silence.

I said, "You need her and at this point she thinks she needs you."

"Needs me for what?"

"Keeping her kids safe."

"All of a sudden Devil Princess is a saint?"

"Think of it this way," I said. "You may get out of garbage detail."

"She came to your house alone? No paparazzi in the bushes?"

"Not her style, anymore," I said.

"Just a simple gal. Your new best friend."

"Love to chat, Big Guy, but you need to get over here."

He grumbled. I heard a door slam. "On my way."

"Good man."

"So few of us left."

Back in the office, I poured Prema herb tea, gave her some playtime with Blanche, allowed her to drift into abstract discussions on child-rearing. Then I got back to the questions.

She offered no resistance, was answering freely when the bell rang.

She blinked. "That's him? We really need to do this?"

"We do."

"Only time I've ever dealt with the police was in London, a bunch of us got busted for smoking hash in a park. Rich little twits, everyone had connections, we got off with a warning."

"You've got connections, again."

"Do I . . . ?"

"Prema, there's a reason you decided to come here." I got to my feet. "Ready?"

Standing slowly, she teetered for a second, hooked her arm in mine.

"No red carpet," she whispered. "But here we go."

Introductions were brief. Both of them were wary. When they shook hands, Prema used both of hers, as if wanting to prolong contact. Milo offered only his fingers, pulled away soon.

I led Prema to the living room sofa, sat down next to her. Milo settled in a facing chair. His suit was one I'd seen for years, a baggy green-brown hopsack worn over a white shirt and a muddy blue tie that Prozac couldn't fix.

One thing was different: He'd slicked down his hair. Two-hundred-forty-pound kid waiting for communion.

Prema said, "You look just like a cop should."

Milo said, "You look just like a movie star should."

"I meant that as a compliment, Lieutenant. I find it reassuring."

"So taken." His expression was unreadable. "What can I do for you, Ms. Moon?"

She turned to me.

I said, "Just go for it."

She inhaled. "Okay . . . all right . . . Donny Rader smokes meerschaum pipes."

"Does he."

"Do you know what meerschaum is?"

"Some kind of carved stone."

"It's a mineral, Lieutenant. It washes up on the beach and people carve it into smoking pipes. Donny Rader has lots of carved meerschaum smoking pipes, I don't know how many. He smokes weed in them, not tobacco. He's a compulsive collector, loves *things.* To my mind, it's just greed. Like cars: He's got a dozen, maybe more, even though he hardly ever drives them. He has more clothing than I do." One hand kneaded the other. "He collects women. But we don't need to go there."

"Sounds like your husband leads a busy life, Ms. Moon."

She flinched.

I said, "There's another collection."

"Yes," she said. "There is. He has a closet full of guns. When we were living together I made him lock them up in a big safe. That I paid for. For the children's safety."

"Where are the guns now, Ms. Moon?"

"At his place."

"You don't live together?"

"He lives in the adjoining property. I bought all of it years ago but I only use part of it."

"You know about his gun closet because—"

"I saw it. Not recently, we don't have much . . . I stay at my place, he's at his."

"When did you see the gun closet?"

Her chest heaved. "Maybe half a year, I really can't be sure."

"You went to visit—"

"Not a visit, an obligation. He needed to sign a tax form from our accountant.

Our life is complicated, you can delegate a lot of things but at some point
you still need to sign your name to papers. All the financial forms come to me
because he'd neglect them."

"So around six months ago—"

"Could be seven months, eight, five,
I don't know. What I do recall is he was
still in bed, the place was a mess, as
usual. There was a woman. I asked her
to leave for a moment. So he could sign
the tax form. The safe's in a closet in
his bedroom. The closet door was open,
there were also loose guns. On shelves.
And big ones—rifles—propped up on
the floor of the closet. I got out of there."

"Has he ever threatened you with a
firearm?"

"Not yet."

"You think he might."

"At this point, Lieutenant, I don't know
what to think."

I said, "About the meerschaums . . ."

Milo's eyebrows rose.

Prema said, "Yes, of course. The meerschaums. The lovely meerschaums . . .
when you collect them, the big deal is
to get them to color gradually as you

smoke them. From white to amber. For that to happen, the pipes are coated after they're carved. Then the owner recoats them from time to time."

Her hands clenched. "What's used for the coating, Lieutenant, is beeswax."

Milo's lips pursed. "Really."

"Specifically, confectioner's beeswax, Lieutenant. With all those pipes, Donny Rader must go through the stuff like crazy because he buys pots of confectioner's beeswax. Back when we were living together, I saw it in his workshop. He builds things. Birdhouses, ashtrays. Not very well."

"You've seen him work with beeswax."

Nod. "One time he called me in to watch him work on a pipe. Showing off. He heated up the beeswax, brushed it on, waited for it to cool, then buffed it shiny. About a month ago, he ordered six fresh pots of beeswax. I know *that* because instead of going through his purchasing assistant—a gopher at Apex, our management firm, we each have one—he ordered it online himself. Using *my* personal credit card, the package ended up on my desk. It came from a baking supplies outfit, my first thought was the cook had bought it, someone had screwed up and used my personal card instead of one of the household cards. Then I opened it and realized what was inside and called him to take it. We met at the gate to his place. I asked him why he'd bought it using my name. He didn't really have an answer, was pretty much loaded on weed or whatever. As usual."

"He say anything at all?"

"He mumbled something about not being able to find his own card. Which made sense, he's always losing things. It didn't explain why he hadn't gone through Apex, but I didn't push it, this was wax, no big deal, and frankly the less contact we have with each other the better. I forgot about the whole incident until I learned today that he'd bought something else saying it was for me. Only this time he *had* contacted my purchasing assistant at Apex, probably using one of my email addresses, and bought . . . those terrible things."

"You know the order came from him because—"

"Because *I* didn't buy them, Lieutenant. He's obviously trying to cover his tracks. By casting suspicion on me."

Milo studied her.

She said, "I know it sounds crazy, but, Lieutenant, I will take any lie-detector test you want me to take. I have never once in my life bought beetles or surgical tools. *Or* beeswax. Nor have I ever asked anyone to buy those things for me. Check out every single computer in my house including my personal computer. I'm sure you've got specialists who can do that."

"Do you know for a fact that he bought the wax online?"

"How else?"

"Maybe he got on the phone and ordered."

She thought. "Okay, good point, maybe—so examine our phone records, we've got I don't know how many lines between us, go ahead and trace them all. Then do the same thing for his phones and see what you learn."

Milo rolled his tie up to his collar, let

it drop. "Any idea why your husband would need beetles and surgical tools?"

Her hands clenched. "Do I have to say it?"

She turned to me.

I gave her my best therapist smile.

She said, "Fine, I'm afraid—I'm terrified that it had something to do with that poor baby in the park. And that's another thing. The park. Like I told Dr. Delaware just before you got here, Donny Rader has a connection to that place. He used to work as a caddie at the golf course right next door. Back when he was a nothing."

Milo's bulk inched forward. "This is all very interesting, Ms. Moon. Thanks for coming forward."

"What's my choice, Lieutenant? He's obviously trying to ruin me."

"So you believe your husband is—"

"Could I ask a favor, Lieutenant? Please don't call him that, he's my husband in name only."

"You believe Mr. Rader had something to do with the baby in the park."

"I don't know what else to think, Lieutenant. Those bones were treated just like he treats his stupid pipes. After he sicced those horrible bugs on them."

"Any idea why he'd do such a thing?"

"No," she said. "I mean he's not a caring person, quite the opposite. But I never imagined . . . not until Dr. Delaware told me about the beeswax."

"No idea at all what Mr. Rader's motive might be?"

The question I hadn't gotten to when the bell rang.

Her eyes filled with tears. "I have an idea. But not one that makes sense."

"What's that, ma'am?"

"It's not rational. Not in terms of normal people, anyway," she said. "I mean how can you ever explain things like that?"

"Explain what, ma'am?"

She pulled at her hair. "This is . . . even for him it's—let me ask you one thing, Lieutenant. Was the baby in the park black?"

Milo looked at me. "Why would the baby be black, Ms. Moon?"

"Because the only baby I can think of who lived at my house since Boo—my youngest—was born was black. The mother was someone who worked for us. She went into labor early, actually delivered in her room in the staff house. Needless to say I was shocked. One day she's pregnant, the next she's got a baby. She said she delivered it herself. Her, a little girl. I wanted to get her to the hospital, she said no, she was fine. I thought that was absolutely crazy but she insisted and she *seemed* fine. Even though the baby was small. Not abnormal small, not a preemie. Everything seemed okay. Except for the blood and crud on her bed."

She frowned. "My home, her delivery."

"How long ago was this?"

"Maybe . . . four months ago?"

"What happened after that?"

"The baby was adorable—lovely little thing, great disposition. Cordelia. That's the name the mother gave her. I gave the mother time off to care for her. Gave her some of Boo's old baby clothes. Had Boo's crib set up in her room. She repaid me by leaving without giving notice. That's what I assumed—a flakeout. But now . . ."

"You think something worse happened."

She didn't reply.

Milo said, "Ms. Moon, why would Mr. Rader harm this particular baby?"

Long silence.

Prema said, "Maybe you can do DNA?"

"For what?"

"To find out who the father was."

"You think it could've been Mr. Rader."

Her eyes narrowed. "I know what he is. I *didn't* know he could be that stupid."

"What is he?"

"Anything with a vagina gravitates toward him. He doesn't exactly play hard-to-get."

"You suspect the mother of the child and Mr. Rader had an—"

"I don't suspect, I know. Once, after her workday was over, I saw her go over to his place. After dark. Wearing a minidress. There was no reason for that, she worked for *me.* Watching *my* children."

"Did you mention it to her?"

Head shake. "No big deal, everyone has sex with *him,* it's about as meaningful as taking a drink of water."

"His promiscuity didn't bother you."

"In the beginning—when we started out—it sure as hell did. But later? Just the opposite. Kept him out of my hair. But did I suspect he'd knocked her up? Never, because that had never happened before. And she never got that look *they* always get."

"Expectant mothers."

"No, no," she snapped. "Freelance vaginas thinking they've snagged him. When that happens they get a certain smile, a smug smile. I've fired assistants, cooks, maids. Not because I'm jealous. But don't think you can collect a paycheck from me and give me that smile."

Milo said, "The baby's mother didn't have the smile."

"She had a nice smile, the way a woman gets when she's productive. It's a special thing for women, Lieutenant."

Her hand grazed her belly. Tears filled her eyes. "Or so I've been told—no, no, scratch that, no playing the pity card,

I've got my tribe, they're gems, just as precious as if I'd carried them myself."

She bounded up, hurried to the door, flung it open, ran out.

No footsteps from the terrace.

Milo glanced at me. I held up a restraining palm.

A minute later, she returned. Positioned herself between us.

Center stage.

Milo said, "Please," and pointed to the sofa.

She said, "I know you guys are just doing your job but this is cutting the *guts* out of me."

CHAPTER

51

The police detective strode to the movie star's side, placed his arm around her, guided her back to the sofa.

"I'm sorry, Ms. Moon, I really am. If it makes you feel any better, you're helping achieve justice. For that baby and others."

Prema didn't answer. Milo relocated to a closer chair. Pulled it even nearer.

She said, "Mr. Fuck-everything-that-moves. *Another* collection. That's why my estate manager is—was a man. That's why the maids I have are Church Ladies in their sixties."

"You think Donny Rader killed the baby."

"I never would have thought him capable. I mean I know he couldn't care less about kids. But . . . I guess he's capable of anything if it's in his best interests. She probably became an inconvenience—pressured him."

"For money?"

"Money or emotional commitment—wanting him to step up to the plate. I will tell you one thing: Giving her serious money would definitely be a problem for him. Because he has no control over the finances. Gets an allowance because he's an idiot."

"What's serious money?"

"Anything more than ten thousand dollars a month. If he needed to come up with something like that, he'd have to ask me. Or else start selling his crap."

She turned to Milo. "That's probably the motive, Lieutenant. She got greedy, put him in a bind." She sagged. "But that poor baby. How did it die?"

"That's unclear."

"What do you mean?"

"The skeleton bore no evidence of trauma."

"The skeleton," she said. "Why would he do that?" She turned to me. "What kind of insanity is that, Dr. Delaware?"

I shook my head.

Milo said, "This woman, what was her—"

"Simone. Simone Chambord."

He showed her Qeesha D'Embo's mug shot. In this photo, no concealment of the booking numbers around her neck.

Her mouth formed an oval. "She's a criminal?"

"She had a police record."

"Oh, God, what a sucker I am. She told me she was a teacher's aide, had preschool experience. That's what the agency told me, because of that I hired her to watch over Boo, Boo was just a toddler."

Another stare at the arrest form. "You're telling me I entrusted my Boo to a criminal?"

"Sorry to say, Ms. Moon."

"I must be the biggest fool in the universe."

"Anyone can get taken, ma'am."

"There wasn't a hint of anything off. She was kind to Boo, Boo liked her, and Boo doesn't take to everyone. *I* liked her. That's why when she got pregnant and her energy flagged, I took pity on her and helped her out by hiring another person."

"Adriana Betts."

"You're going to tell me *that* one was an ax murderer?"

"No, ma'am. Clean-living church-girl. How'd she and Simone get along?"

"Fine," she said. "Why?" She shuddered. "Oh, of course. He killed her, too, so *she* was connected." She rubbed her face. That plus the pacing; Milo's spiritual sister. "What was *her* story?"

"I was wondering if you knew."

"Well, I don't. Adriana was . . . there seemed nothing complicated about her. Then again, I liked Simone." She laughed. "To think I helped her with her pregnancy—gave her clothes, books, encouraged her to take it easy."

"Adriana came on to relieve Simone."

"Yes."

"Your suggestion or Simone's?"

"Mine. I used the same agency and once Simone was gone Adriana took over completely, did a great job. Then she walked out on me, too. Or so I thought."

"Did you try to find out why she left?"

She threw up her hands. "My life is hectic, people come and go, you have no idea how hard it is to find dependable help."

"Like Mel Wedd," said Milo. "Did he work for Mr. Rader as well as for you?"

"He was the estate manager and, technically, all three properties are the estate. But his day-to-day job was under my supervision."

"How did he and Mr. Rader get along?"

"He didn't respect Donny. Or so he told me."

"Why?"

"Because of Donny's behavior."

"Promiscuity."

She ticked her fingers. "Promiscuity, being constantly stoned, never taking responsibility. Mostly, not caring about the kids. Mel thought that was unconscionable."

Milo said, "Mr. Rader shut the kids out of his life."

"To shut them out, he'd have to be aware of them, Lieutenant. He acted as if they didn't exist. How do you explain that to a child?"

Her hand touched her mouth. "I guess with that attitude, doing things to a baby isn't so big a stretch."

Milo said, "Back to Mel Wedd for a moment. Any idea why Mr. Rader would kill him? Assuming he did."

Another easy opening, if she was manipulating. Once again, she didn't take it. "No. I can't imagine."

Milo looked at me again.

I shrugged. *Still your play, Big Guy.*

He said, "Was Mr. Wedd involved in any of Mr. Rader's activities with women?"

"Mel? Why would you ask that?"

"Wedd's been spotted in the company of several attractive women. Streaming in and out of his apartment. Including Simone Chambord."

"You're saying Mel *pimped* for that bastard?"

"Or he might have been in charge of the finances."

"What finances?"

"Paying women off when Mr. Rader was through with them. In Simone Chambord's case, that may have included getting a car for her. A red BMW. It once belonged to Mr. Wedd but he reported it stolen and Simone Chambord was seen driving it."

"Oh, this is all too much. What else do you want to drop on me, Lieutenant?"

"That's it."

"Insanity," she said. "Okay, now what do we do about it?"

CHAPTER

52

The plan was logical, meticulous, elegant in its simplicity.

Even in the chief's grudging appraisal. "Assuming you're lucky, Sturgis."

At eight thirty a.m., two days after my session with Prema Moon, the tutors from Oxford Educational Services drove through the stout wooden gate of her estate.

Newly scheduled all-day trip to Sea-World, in San Diego, the kids had visited last year, begged to return. Prema had punted with the classic parental "Soon, one day."

At seven thirty she announced, "Surprise!" to a quartet of sleepy young faces.

"How come, Mom?"

"Because Sam and Julie say you've all been great with your studies."

"Oh."

"Whoa. Cool."

"When are we going?"

"Right now, everyone get dressed. Afterward, Sam and Julie will take you to a great Mexican restaurant and you can all stay up late."

Mumbled thanks. Big smile from Boo.

At ten fourteen a.m. a brown, dust-caked, kidney-punishing Dodge van rolled through that same gate. Entering Prema's spread required a thousand feet of climbing past the wrought-iron barrier that blocked access to the tree-shrouded private road. At the top were three identical barriers of weathered oak inlaid with oversized black nail-heads, each equipped with a call box.

Per directions, Milo drove up to the

left-hand box. As we waited to enter, I
spotted a black glass eye peering from
the boughs of a pine. Closed-circuit
lens focused on Prema's gate. Then another, aimed at Donny Rader's. Maybe
he'd installed his own security system.
Or Prema cared more about his com-
ings and goings than she'd let on.

I pointed the cameras out to Milo. His
placid nod said he'd already seen them.

Four beeps from the call box, the
gate swung open smoothly, we rattled
through. The brown van had been bor-
rowed from the Westside LAPD im-
pound yard. Cheap stick-on signs on
each flank read *Adaptive Plumbers.* The
213 number below was printed in nu-
merals too small to read from a distance. If someone actually called it,
they'd get a disconnect.

I sat up front in the shotgun seat. Behind me was a tech sergeant named
Morry Burns who occupied himself
playing Sudoku online. The slew of
equipment he'd brought, including a
portable dolly, occupied the van's rear
storage area. Behind Burns sat K-9

specialist Tyler O'Shea and a panting retriever mix named Sally.

Milo said, "Pooch okay?"

O'Shea said, "She's awesome. Lives to do the job."

"All-American work ethic."

"El Tee, I'll take her any day over your garden-variety so-called human."

Prema Moon was waiting for us in the parking lot west of her mansion. The area was an easy acre, paved beautifully, ringed by river rock, cordoned by low privet hedges. Space for dozens of cars but only four today, all compact sedans. Three bore the bumper sticker of a Spanish-language Christian station. The fourth had customized plates reading *TRFFLES.*

The mansion hovered in the distance, a frothy, pink-beige Mediterranean that almost succeeded in looking old, perched assertively on the property's highest knoll. Windows gleamed like zircons. Red bougainvillea climbed the walls like gravity-defying rivulets of blood. The hue of the stucco was a perfect foil for an uncommonly blue sky.

Several smaller outbuildings dotted the property, same color, same genre, as if the mansion had dropped pups. North of the structures, walls of cypress surrounded something unseen. To the rear of the property was a black-green cloud of untamed conifer, sycamore, eucalyptus, and oak.

As we got out of the van, Prema strode toward us, holding a sheaf of papers. She wore form-fitted black jeans, a black mock turtle, red suede flats. Her hair was combed out and shiny, held in place by a thin black band. She'd put on lipstick and eye shadow and mascara.

New take on gorgeous.

Milo said, "Morning."

"Morning, Lieutenant. I just called the tribe, they're halfway to San Diego, should be gone until eight or even nine. Is that enough time?"

Milo said, "We'll do our best." He introduced her to Morry Burns.

She said, "Pleased to meet you."

Without answering, Burns laid down a pair of metal carrying cases, returned to the van, brought out the dolly. A third trip produced the flat sides of several unassembled cardboard boxes. He walked up to Prema. "Is there some hub where all your computers feed?"

"Like command central? I don't think so."

"You don't think or you don't know?"

Prema blinked. "No, there's nothing like that."

"How many computers on the premises?"

"Don't know that, either. Sorry."

"You have a smart-house setup? Crestron running the lights, the utilities, your home theater, all your toys?"

"We do have a system, but I'm not sure the computers go through it."

"Show me your personal machine. We'll work backward from there."

"Right now?"

"You got something better to do?" Burns began stacking his dolly.

Milo pointed to the papers in Prema's hand.

She said, "I pulled phone records for the last six months. Every line that goes through this property."

Without looking back, Burns said, "Landlines and cells?"

"Yes."

"Your employees have personal cell accounts?"

"I'm sure they do—"

"Then that's not every line." He made another trip to the van.

"Well . . . yes," said Prema. "I just wanted to help."

Tyler O'Shea appeared with Sally in tow.

Prema said, "A dog?"

Milo said, "While you work with Detective Burns on the hardware, Officer O'Shea will be exploring the property with Sally."

O'Shea, young, virile, muscular, gawked at Prema. When he managed to engage eye contact, he beamed.

She smiled back. O'Shea blushed.

"Hi, Sally, aren't you a pretty girl?" She reached to pet the dog. O'Shea blocked her with his arm. "Sorry, ma'am, she needs to concentrate."

"Oh, of course—concentrate on what?"

Milo said, "Finding anything interesting."

"You think you'll find evidence *here*?"

"We need to be thorough, Ms. Moon."

Sally's leash strained as she oriented herself toward the forest. Her nose twitched. She panted faster.

Prema said, "Sally's one of those . . . dogs that look for bodies?"

O'Shea said, "That's part of her repertoire, ma'am."

"Oh, my." Head shake.

"What's back there in the trees, ma'am?"

"Just trees. Honestly, you're not going to find anything."

"Hope you're right, ma'am." O'Shea clicked his tongue twice. He and Sally headed out at a quick trot.

Morry Burns returned. Tapped his foot. Checked his watch.

Milo said, "Who's working on the premises today, ma'am?"

"Just the core staff," she said. "The maids and the cook. Do you need to talk to them?"

"Eventually. Meanwhile, go with Detective Burns. Dr. Delaware and I will stroll around a bit."

Prema forced a half smile. "Of course. He's a psychologist, anything can be interesting."

First stop: the four walls of cypress. An opening on the east side led us into a flat area the size of two football fields. One corner was devoted to a safety-fenced half-Olympic pool with a pad-locked, alarmed gate. The opposing corner housed a sunken tennis court. Diagonal to that were a regulation bas-ketball court, a rubber-matted area set up with four trampolines, a moon-bounce, a tetherball pole, two Ping-Pong tables, and a sand pit that hosted a plastic slide, a swing-set, a seesaw, and a yellow vinyl tunnel-maze.

Milo said, "Kid-Heaven, courtesy Su-per Mom. What's that, making up for her own shitty childhood?"

"Could be, if you're in an analytical mood."

"You're not?"

"Let's find the maids and the cook."

◆

The interior of the house was what you'd expect: the requisite vaulted rooms, quarry-emptying expanses of marble, enough polished wood to threaten a rain forest. The art on the walls was professionally spaced, perfectly framed and lit: oil paintings biased toward women and children as subjects and the kind of pastel landscape that combats insomnia.

The maids were easy to find. Imelda Rojas polished silver in the dining room, Lupe Soto folded laundry in a white-tiled utility room the size of some New York apartments, Maria Elena Miramonte tidied up a playroom that would thrill a preschool class. All three women were in their sixties, solidly built and well groomed, wearing impeccable powder-blue uniforms.

Milo spoke to them individually.

Easy consensus: Senora Prema was wonderful.

Senor Donny was never here.

Despite that, Rader's name elicited tension but when Milo asked Imelda Rojas what she thought of him she insisted she didn't know. He kept up the

questioning but stepped aside early on
and punted to me. My doctorate wasn't
any help, at first; Maria and Imelda were
unable, or unwilling, to articulate their
feelings about Rader. Then Lupe Soto
opined that he was "a sinner," and when
pressed, specified the nature of Rader's
iniquities.

"*Putas,* always."

"Lots of girls."

"No girls, senor, *putas.* Is good he no
live here. Better for the chillin they no
see that."

"He used to bring *putas* here?"

Lupe said, "You kidding? Always
there."

"His place."

"Yeah, but we know."

"How?"

"The TV in the kitchen."

"Could you show me, please?"

She led us down a double staircase too
grand for Tara through a succession of
big bright sitting rooms and into a tin-
ceilinged, maple-and-steel kitchen easily forty feet long. Mounted on the far
wall were a dozen small screens.

Lupe Soto pointed to one. The image was inert. One of the wooden gates.

"See?"

I said, "He didn't try to hide what he was doing."

"Nah."

I showed her the well-worn mug shot of Charlene Chambers aka Qeesha D'Embo aka Simone Chambord.

"*La negra?*" said Lupe Soto. "Yeah, she, too."

"She went over to Senor Donny's place?"

"All the time. But I don tell Senora Prema."

"Why not?"

"Not my business." She placed a hand over her heart.

"No one wanted to hurt her feelings."

"Yeh."

"What's Simone—this woman—like?"

"Who she like? Him." She sneered. "*Puta.*"

"What kind of person is she?"

"Smile a lot, move a lot hoo hoo hoo." Illustrating with a brief shake of ample hips. "Then she have the baby and she go way."

"When did she have a baby?"

"Mebbe . . . four, fie month ago?"

"And when did she leave?"

"I don remember, senor."

"Where'd she go after she left?"

"Dunno. Now, I gotta work."

We revisited the other two maids, repeated the same questions. More of the original reticence. But Imelda Rojas's eyes were jumpy.

I said, "You're sure you have no idea where Simone went?"

"Nup."

"What kind of car did she drive?"

"Car? Red." Giggle. *Rojo.* Like *mi nombre*—my name." More amusement. "*My* car is white."

"Thought the red car was Mel Wedd's."

"Him? No."

"You never saw him drive the red car?"

"Nup, I see a black one. Big." She shaped a circle with her hands. "Like Senor Donny car."

"Mel and Senor Donny drove the same type of car?"

"Zactly the same," she said. "Senor Donny got a lot of cars." She thought. "Mebbe he give one to Senor Mel."

"He likes Senor Mel?"

"Dunno." No objection to my usage of present tense. No idea Wedd had been murdered.

"Is Senor Mel a nice person?"

"I gue-ess."

"He treats you well?"

"I don work with him."

"Was he friendly with Simone Chambord?"

"Everyone here friendly. Senora Prema the more friendly."

"More than—"

"All peoples. She for the kids."

"Senor Donny—"

Head shake. "I gotta work."

"What about Adriana?"

Sudden flash of smile. "She nice. Read the Bible."

"Have you seen her recently?"

"No."

"Any idea where she is?"

"You know?"

I shook my head.

She said, "Nice lady. She go away?"

"Looks like it."

She shrugged.

I said, "People come and go, all the time?"

"Not me."

"You like it here."

"I like to work."

"Could you show us where Senor Mel lives?"

"Building Two, we all there."

"Could you show us?"

Prolonged sigh. "Then I got to *work*."

Building Two was a pleasantly land-scaped single-story structure due north of the mansion. An eight-by-eight lobby set up with dried flowers in big copper vases opened to hallways on two sides. Like a nice boutique hotel. Four doors lined each corridor. Lupe Soto said, "Okay?" and started to leave.

Evoking additional sighs, I got her to show us her quarters, a spotless, daylit bedroom with a small sitting area and an en-suite bathroom. Imelda and Maria slept in the flanking rooms.

"Same as me. Zactly."

The farthest room was occupied by

the cook, a stick-like woman in her late twenties wearing mini-check chef's pants and a white smock. She answered our knock, filing her nails.

The layout behind her was identical to Lupe's, but festooned with rock posters and oversized illustrations of food. The bed was unmade. The smell of gym sweat and perfume blew out into the hallway.

"Yeah, what's going on?" Her hair was short, yellow, textured like fleece. Bruise-colored tattoos coiled up the side of her neck. I wondered if avoiding the carotid and the jugular had been a challenge.

Milo's badge caused the skin around the illustration to pale. She lowered the nail file. "Police? What's going on?"

"Nothing serious, we're just here to check a few things out at Ms. Moon's request."

"About what?"

"An employee who worked here seems to have gone missing."

"Who's that?"

"Simone Chambord."

"Sorry," she said. "Must be before my time."

"How long have you been working here, Ms. . . . ?"

"Georgie," she said. "Georgette Weiss. How long? Like a month. Make that thirty . . . eight days. She okay? That woman? I mean did something happen to her?"

"Don't know yet, Ms. Weiss. You like working here?"

"Like it? You kidding?" said Georgie Weiss. "This is like a dream gig."

"Easy."

"Cook healthy for her and the kids? No maniac E.C.—executive chef—going nuclear on me, no asshole customers trying to prove they're important by sending perfectly good plates back? Yeah, it's easy. Plus she pays me great. More than I made working twice as hard at restaurants."

"She's a nice lady."

"You bet. Especially," said Georgie Weiss.

"Especially, what?"

"Especially considering."

"Who she is."

"I mean face it, she could get away with anything, right? But she's like a real person."

"What about him?"

"Who?"

"Donny Rader?"

"Never seen him, actually." She looked to the side. "They don't live together— don't quote me, I need to be whatya-callit—discreet."

"Of course. They live separately?"

"He's like next door so I'm not sure what that is. I mean, it's not far, there's like an empty property and then his place." She shrugged.

"You ever cook for him?"

"Never. That's all I know, don't quote me, okay?"

"No prob," said Milo. "What about Mel Wedd?"

"What about him *what*?"

"He easy to work for?"

"I work for Prema, he does his thing, we really don't interact." Another side-ward glance. "Can I tell you something but really please I mean it don't quote me."

"Sure."

"Seriously," said Georgie Weiss.

"Seriously."

She scratched her head. "Mel. He's not the friendliest guy but that's not what I'm talking about. Officially, I think he works for Prema. At least he seems to, he's like here all the time. But . . . I think he could also be hanging with *him.* Donny, I mean. Because I've seen him drive over there. At night."

"After hours."

Nod. "That's another thing. About Prema. When the day's over, it's over. Some of them, they think they own you, it's like slavery, you know? Do for me twenty-four-seven?"

"Not Prema."

"Prema makes the rules and you're expected to keep them but *she* keeps them, too."

"She doesn't exploit the help."

"Trust me, that's rare," said Georgie Weiss. She rattled off the names of two other actresses and a male star. "Spent some time P.C.ing—private chefing—for them. *Slavery.*"

"Nice to know someone's different."

"You bet. Maybe it's 'cause she has kids. She's totally into them."

"Eating healthy?"

"She's like . . . an involved mom. But not crazy-healthy like every anorexic Westside bitch, they see a glass of juice they have a seizure. It's reasonable stuff, just watch out for too much sugar and fat. That's my food, anyway."

"Good deal."

"The best. I *love* it. Hope you find that woman." She began to close the door.

Milo didn't try to stop her physically. His voice was enough. "So you think Mel Wedd is going behind Prema's back after hours?"

She studied him. "You're trying to say *he* did something to that woman?"

"Not at all," said Milo. "Just checking everyone out."

"I just thought it was weird, Mel going over there. Because he works for Prema and obviously they're not—it's not like they're a couple—so what could he be doing over there?"

"Mel's the estate manager," I said. "Maybe the entire property's considered the estate."

"Hmm," she said. "Guess so." Nervous smile. "Whatever, keep me out of it, okay? I just want to cook my food."

The second hallway contained three rooms, instead of four. A utility closet at the rear housed the water heater and the A.C. unit.

The first door was unlocked. Bare mattress, empty nightstand and dresser. A portable crib stood folded in the corner.

Milo gloved up, had me wait as he went in, emerged shaking his head. "Nothing and it's obviously been cleaned. But I'll have it processed, anyway."

The second room was locked. He said, "Stay here, make sure no one goes into Simone's," and left the building. Ten minutes later, he returned with a large ring of keys.

"Stored in the laundry room but none of the maids would tell me that, so I had to bring Prema down."

"She inspires loyalty," I said. "How's it going with the computers?"

"Hard to tell with Burns, he's so damn grumpy."

"How come?"

"You're the shrink." Selecting a key, he unlocked the second room.

Tightly made bed, Bible on the nightstand. Framed pictures on the dresser.

Regloving, he ran through the same solo search. Opened a closet door wide enough for me to view the contents from the corridor.

Sparse supply of bland-looking garments.

He went into the bathroom, called out, "Nothing sexy here, either."

Returning to the dresser, he opened drawers, inspected the framed pictures. Stepped closer and held them out for my inspection.

Adriana and her church group, including the woman she'd known as Qeesha D'Embo but had come to accept as Simone Chambord because friends in need did what was expected of them.

The two women stood heads together, beaming.

Qeesha cradled a tiny brown infant.

The baby had a round face, inquisitive black eyes, a sweet mouth, graceful, long-fingered hands, a full head of dark hair.

Beautiful child.

Finally, the bones had a face.

Cordelia.

My throat clogged.

Milo raced out of the room.

Melvin Jaron Wedd's quarters veered toward messy but smelled okay. Probably the Armani cologne in his medicine cabinet.

The fragrance shared space with Viagra for fun, Lunesta for sleep, five varieties of caffeine pills for energy. Tube of lube in the top nightstand drawer. In the second, a short stack of gay porn.

Nothing interesting in the dresser until Milo kneeled low and pulled a small blue leatherette spiral notebook out of the bottom, right-hand drawer. Stashed under a stack of beefy sweaters too warm for L.A.

The book bore the gold-imprinted legend of an insurance broker with an office in Beverly Hills. Probably one of those Christmas giveaways.

Inside was an appointment calendar, complete with holiday notations, dated the previous year. Wedd hadn't used it to organize his schedule; the pages were unmarked.

Milo leafed through. Toward the end, several blank pages headed *Notes* contained just that.

Mel Wedd's penmanship was impressive. Nice straight columns, too. Two side by side per page.

**Cheryl, Jan 3–7: 1000.00
Melissa, Jan 6–7: 750.00
Shayanne Jan 23: 750.00**

Forty-nine women's names, fifteen of them occurring twice or more. Monthly totals approached ten thousand dollars but always fell slightly short.

"Simone" showed up sixteen times over a two-year period.

First payment: three hundred dollars. An increase to six hundred, then six notations of eight fifty.

Milo said, "Merit raise—whoa, look at this."

Sudden boost on the eighth payment: $4,999.99. Seven more of those, each dated the first of the month.

Milo said, "She takes up a whole bunch of the ten-grand limit, leaving less for other girls. Guy's a superstar, would have to come begging for dough, talk about demeaning."

I said, "He's Prema's bad child."

He looked at me. "Been carrying around that insight for a while?"

"Just thought of it."

"She couldn't raise him properly, moved on to real kids?"

"She's invented her own world." I took a longer look at the log. "Eight big payments conforms to the final months of Qeesha's pregnancy. Up to that point, she was figuring out what to do, by the fourth month she couldn't hide it any longer, decided to take action. Donny told her to abort, she strung him along, kept delaying as he kept paying. Then it was too late and she had the baby and her hold over him was telling Prema. She continued to live here, got Prema to hire Adriana for backup. To serve as an insurance policy if things got ugly."

"Adriana didn't turn out to be much insurance."

"When Qeesha and the baby disappeared, Adriana suspected the worst. But going to the police wasn't an option. Child-care aide makes accusations against mega-celebs, no evidence to back it up, how far would that get? So Adriana decided to stick around and snoop. Then the baby skeleton showed up under Holly Ruche's tree and it made the news and someone heard about it and thought it would be a grand idea to ditch a second set of bones not far from there so the police would think some sort of serial ghoul was at work."

"Fifty years between dumps is a serial?"

"Not well thought out," I said.

"Not a genius," he said. "Aka Donny."

"He's the one with the wax and the knives and the bugs. And the guns."

"According to Prema."

"All verifiable accusations."

"And I'm the verifier."

◆

We left Wedd's room. Milo carried the appointment book away from his body. "Gotta get an evidence bag for this . . . Here's something else to chew on, Alex: Donny dumping his own kid's bones and doing Adriana the same night seems like a challenge for someone supposedly that dumb."

I said, "Agreed. Had to be a two-person job. Donny and Wedd. That way there'd be no need to schlep Adriana across the park. Wedd was Prema's guy by day, but Donny's pimp and paymaster and who-knows-what-else by night. The maids knew about it, everyone knew about it except Prema. Wedd was a wannabe actor, wanted to emulate the star—drove the same kind of car as the star. He wasn't ridiculing Donny when he imitated him over the phone. He was pretending to *be* him."

"Hell, Alex, maybe it was more than that: What if Wedd had a crush on Donny? So when Donny asks him to take care of nasty business, he's fine with it. Unfortunately, Donny grew uncomfortable with his knowing too much and took care of *him*."

I said, "Nighttime drive, weed and a bong. Sure, it fits. Wedd probably figured he'd be partying with his idol."

"Power of celebrity," he said.

"It even got the best of a wily, manipulative woman like Qeesha. If her head had been clear, she'd have known from the way Donny shut out four kids that he wouldn't take well to fatherhood. To being pressured."

"Playing her usual game," he said. "But out of her league."

Footsteps at the mouth of the corridor made us turn.

Tyler O'Shea held a tired-looking Sally at the end of a slack leash.

Milo said, "Anything?"

O'Shea gave a thumbs-down. "Only dead thing in that forest was a really gross, rotting squirrel way at the back, that's what was attracting her. Sorry, El Tee."

"No big deal," said Milo.

"You knew already?"

"I never know, kid. That's what makes the job fun."

"Oh. Okay. So we're finished?"

"Not even close."

CHAPTER

53

We came upon Morry Burns and Prema leaving the big house. Burns walked ahead of her, wheeling his dolly, now piled high with boxes. When he saw us, he picked up speed. Prema stopped, stood there for a second, walked back through her front door.

When Burns reached us, Milo said, "You're really starstruck, Morry."

Burns said, "Huh?"

"What'd you learn?"

"Her system stinks." Burns cocked a head at the mansion. "All that dough, the kids have rooms like a Broadway production, and she cheaps out on crap hardware. I could get technical but it wouldn't mean anything to you, so leave it at crap. Nothing's linked, real pain to go through each machine."

"Same question."

"Huh?"

"Learn anything?"

Burns tapped a metal case. "Nah. But I took her hard drive, will dig deeper. Also drives from other machines they use—get this—to buy groceries. Or-gah-nic arugula. No need to encrypt that."

"What about the kids' computers?"

"Two desktops for four of them." Burns cackled. "Maybe they're learning how to share. She's got them on every parental lock known to mankind, they're lucky to get the weather. Maybe that's why they hardly ever go online."

I said, "Could be they like to read."

Burns stared at me as if I'd talked in tongues. To Milo: "We through here?"

"Not even close."

◆

O'Shea and Burns took a lunch break near the pool. Take-out Mexican Milo had brought along.

We found Prema in her cavernous kitchen, sitting at a granite-topped counter drinking tea. No maid in sight. The CCTV screens remained inert.

Milo said, "Do you have those real estate documents?"

"You need to actually see them?"

"We do."

She left, returned a few minutes later. "Here's the trust deed on the entire property."

Milo read carefully, per Deputy D.A. John Nguyen's instructions.

"As you can see, I'm the sole owner," she said. "I bought it before I knew him."

A divorce lawyer would laugh at that but for Milo's purposes, the deed was sufficient.

He produced a form of his own: Prema's consent to search the entire property. She scrawled her name without reading.

"Okay?" she said, drumming granite.

"You're sure he's over there."

"He drove in late, like one thirty in the

morning, hasn't left since. I saw it right there." Pointing to the bank of screens.

"It records twenty-four-seven?"

"It sure does. Everything feeds into a computer and before you got here, I scrolled through. He has *not* left."

"Does Detective Burns have the hard drive for that computer?"

Prema's perfect mouth formed an O. "Sorry, forgot to tell him about it. But all it does is record feed from the security system and most of that's blank."

"Where's the computer?"

She slid open a drawer beneath the screens, pulled out a small laptop.

"How far back do you keep recordings?"

"Hmm. I really don't know."

Burns's grumpiness turned to outright hostility. "I told you to give me everything. You didn't think to mention this?"

Prema said, "I—it slipped my mind."

He began pushing buttons, muttered, "'Nother piece of crap."

Prema looked to me for support. I gave her a *who-knows?* smile. She returned to her tea as Burns fiddled with the laptop.

"What date do you want, Lieutenant?"

Milo told him.

"Hmmph. Here you go."

Nothing the night of the murders until one thirty-three a.m., when a vehicle passed through Donny Rader's gate.

Big, dark SUV.

"No front plate," said Burns. "Tough luck for you, Lieutenant, the camera angle could pick it up."

From across the kitchen, Prema said, "That's got to be his. He's piled up a bunch of tickets for not putting on a front plate."

Burns mumbled, "Ooh, major scofflaw."

Blocking Prema's view with his own bulk, Milo placed his hand on Burns's shoulder. Burns looked up at Milo. Milo's wolf-grin lowered his head. A naughty child finally disciplined.

Milo pulled out the pages he'd received from DMV: regs on Donny Rader's sixteen vehicles. Four Ferraris, three

Porsches, a Lamborghini, a Maserati, a Stryker, a pair of Mercedeses, an Aston Martin Rapide, a vintage Jaguar E-type.

Two SUVs, both black: a Range Rover and Ford Explorer. "Go back, let's see if we can figure out which it is."

Three rewinds later, the bet was on the Explorer.

Milo said, "Now go forward."

"Sure, Lieutenant."

We didn't need to wait long.

Forty-nine seconds after the first SUV had exited, an identical set of wheels rolled through Rader's gate.

Front plates on this one. Milo said, "Freeze that," and checked the tags against his notes. "Yup, Wedd's."

Prema said, "Mel was there?"

"Any reason he would be?"

She shook her head. Rested her chin in her hand and stared at nothing.

Milo said, "Why don't you relax somewhere, Ms. Moon."

"It's okay, I've got nowhere to go."

Low, morose tone. Burns looked at her as if for the first time. Bland curiosity, no sympathy.

Milo prodded Burns's shoulder with a fingertip. "Keep going."

Twenty-nine seconds after Wedd's exit, a third vehicle, smaller, shaped like a car, zipped through Prema's gate.

Pinpointing the make and registration was easy: brand-new Hyundai Accent, Banner Rental. It took several calls but Milo finally reached a supervisor at the company's corporate headquarters in Lodi and obtained the details.

Adriana Betts had rented the car three days prior from the Banner office on Santa Monica Boulevard in West L.A. Taking advantage of special week-long rates.

Poor deluded woman playing amateur detective.

Milo took the laptop from Burns, fast-forwarded through another ten minutes. Twenty. Nothing. He handed the machine back to Burns, said, "Let's go."

Prema said, "It's happening?"

"In a bit, Ms. Moon."

"Why the delay?"

"We're organizing, ma'am. Now I suggest you go and find a place where you can—"

"Just as long as you do it before the tribe returns. I can't have them exposed to bad things."

I thought: *If it were only that simple.*

CHAPTER
54

We headed for Prema's acre of parking lot.

Burns said, "Fresh air. Finally."

I said, "You don't like actors."

"Don't try to shrink me, Doc."

Milo said, "It's a reasonable question, Morry. Whatever your bullshit is, it came close to obstructing."

Burns turned pale. "I—"

"It's still a good question, Morry."

"Whatever," said Burns. He began to walk ahead of us, thought better of it, stopped, threw his hands up. "My sister was an actor. Did some crap off-Broadway, nothing serious. She killed herself five years ago. Completely ruined my parents' lives."

"Sorry," I said. "The business was too much for her?"

"How would I know about the business?" said Burns. "She ruined their lives by killing herself because she was a narcissistic drama queen, always had been."

Milo said, "Morry, stay in the van, see if you can do anything else with the machines."

"Yeah, sure. I'll get nothing but I'll try."

As Burns loaded his equipment, Tyler O'Shea emerged with Sally. He rubbed Sally's scruff. The dog looked rejuvenated.

Milo said, "We're a go, Ty, let's do it on foot. I'm gonna start with the soft approach, nothing SWAT-ty, because this joker's no genius, he has drug issues and a closetful of guns, I'm hoping the element of surprise will be enough."

"Plus he's famous," said O'Shea.

"What does that have to do with it?"

"More of a surprise, El Tee. Probably no one ever bugs him."

"Famous," said Milo. "If everything works out, that'll change to infamous."

The walk from Prema's property to Rader's took six minutes. Sally would've preferred to run it in two. Milo had the gate code, courtesy Prema Moon: 10001.

"Had to keep it simple, Lieutenant, because he can't remember anything."

He pushed the buttons, the gate cooperated, we continued along asphalt in need of resurfacing. Longer, steeper access than to Prema's estate, an easy quarter mile with nothing visible other than greenery. At some points the trees grew so thick that the sky disappeared and day turned to imposed dusk.

O'Shea said, "Man likes his privacy."

Milo lengthened his stride. O'Shea took that as the *shut up* it was meant to be.

As we kept climbing, Sally's fur rippled in the breeze. Soft but acute eyes analyzed the world at hand. Her posture was erect, her trot rich with pride. Work-dog heaven.

Then she stopped.

O'Shea said, "Would you look at that."

The road ended abruptly at a mesa filled with cars. Enough parking space for a dozen vehicles positioned properly but I counted seventeen sets of wheels stacked within inches of one another, some extending to the surrounding brown grass.

Donny Rader's black Explorer was positioned nearest to the road, slightly apart from the automotive clog. Easy exit for the daily driver. Milo photographed the SUV from several angles, scribbled in his pad.

The other cars, exemplars of high-ticket Italian, German, and British coach-work, were caked with dust, splotched by bird-dirt, fuzzed by leaves. A few tilted on deflated tires.

Sixteen matches to the DMV list. The addition was a red convertible sand-wiched in the center of the stack.

Milo squeezed his way over to the

BMW, took more pictures, made more notes.

O'Shea said, "Can I ask why that one, El Tee?"

"Victim's wheels."

"He kept it? What an idiot."

"Let's hope he stays that way. Onward."

The house was a low, long box that had been stylish in the fifties. My guess was an expat architect from Europe— Schindler or Neutra or someone trying to be Schindler or Neutra. The kind of site-conscious, minimalist design that ages well if it's kept up.

This one hadn't been. A roof meant to be flat sagged and dipped. Stress cracks wrinkled white stucco grimed to gray. Windows were pocked with birdshit. Rain streaks and pits blemished the flat façade. Like Prema's property, Rader's acreage was backed by forest. But everything else was hard-pack.

We approached the house. Internal shutters blocked off the view the architect had intended. The door was a slab of ash in need of varnish. Solid, though. Milo's knock barely sounded.

He pushed the doorbell. No chime or buzzer that I could hear.

Louder knock.

The door opened on a girl-woman in a thong bikini. Her hair was a riot of white and black and flamingo-pink. Late teens or early twenties.

She stared at us with bleary, heavy-lidded eyes. White powder smudged the space between her perfect nose and her perfect lips. The bikini was white, barely qualified as a garment with the bra not much more than pasties on a string and the bottom a nylon triangle not up to the job of pelvic protection. Breasts the size of grapefruits heaved a split second after the rest of her chest moved, the mammary equivalent of digital delay. Her feet were bare and grubby, her nails blood-red talons.

She rubbed her eyes. "Huh?"

"Police, ma'am. Is Mr. Rader here?"

She swiped at the white granules above her mouth.

Milo said, "Don't worry about your

breakfast, we just want to talk to Donny Rader."

The girl's mouth opened. A frog-croak emerged. Then a squeak. Then: "Don-nee!"

No need to shout, Rader was already behind her, materializing from the left, wearing a red silk robe. The robe was loosely belted, exposing a hard, tan body. The pockets bulged. A bottle of something with a booze-tax seal around the neck poked from one. The contents of the other were out of view. Maybe a bag of white powder. Or just a glass. If he bothered with a glass.

He pushed the girl out of the way, did the same eye rub. "Whus happening?"

Big man, larger and more muscular than he came across on the screen. Coarser, with a near-Neanderthal brow shelf, grainy skin, thickened nostrils that flared like a bull's.

Long, shaggy, ink-black hair flew everywhere. His eyes fought to remain open. Described in the fan mags as black, they were actually deep brown. Just enough contrast to see the pupils.

Widely dilated despite the bright afternoon light.

White powder on his face, too, a thick
smear on his lips and chin. Snowy dust
littered the red robe's shawl collar. The
top seam of the other robe pocket.

Milo said, "Police, Mr. Rader."

"Whu the fuh!" Throaty growl. The
iconic slur.

"Police—"

"Fuh!" Donny Rader backed away.

Milo said, "Hold on, we'd just like to
talk—"

"About whu?"

"We'd like to come in, Mr. Rader."

"Whu the fu—hey! You ain't cops,
you're some shit from her, trying to
mess with my mind—"

"Sir, I can assure—"

"Assure my asshole, get the fuh outta
here!"

"Mr. Rader, we really are the police
and we—"

Donny Rader shook himself off hard,
hair billowing, a hyena clearing its maws
of blood. The girl in the bikini had remained behind him, clutching her face
and hyperventilating.

Milo stepped forward, aiming to get his toe in the door.

Howling, Rader jammed his hand into the robe pocket that didn't hold the bottle, yanked out something metallic and shiny.

He faded back, began to straighten his arm.

The last time Milo had faced madness, he'd been caught off-guard and I'd saved his life. That didn't fit the script of seasoned cop and shrink and despite his acknowledgment, it would scar him.

Maybe that's why this time he was ready.

One of his hands clamped like a beartrap on the wrist of Donny Rader's gun-arm, pushing down and twisting sharply as his foot shot between Rader's bare legs and kicked laterally to the left. As Rader lost balance, Milo's other arm spun him around and by the time Tyler O'Shea was ready with cuffs and a now snarling Sally, Rader was down on the ground and the .22 lay safely out of reach.

Rader foamed at the mouth, turned dirt to chocolate soda.

The girl in the bikini whimpered.

Milo said, "Ty, take care of her."

O'Shea checked out the tight, tan body. "You're a pal, El Tee."

He cuffed the girl displaying no particular reverence. Something to the left caught his eye. "El Tee, you better look at this." Something new in his voice. Fear.

Milo hauled a struggling, howling Donny Rader to his feet. "Hold still and shut it."

"Fuh you."

O'Shea walked the girl out of the house. He looked stunned. "You got to see this."

Milo said, "Check it out, Alex."

The house was a sty. Piles of trash blanketed the floor and the furniture. The air was putrid with rotted food, body odor, weed, a medicinal smell that might've been poorly cut cocaine.

A cat-urine stench that might've been cats or crystal meth.

O'Shea had seen and smelled worse, so that wasn't it.

Not wanting to disturb potential evidence, I stepped carefully over the garbage. Then I saw it. Hanging from a low rafter, the feet dangling a few inches from the floor.

A human skeleton, wired and braced by a steel rod running parallel to the spine.

Stripped and clean but for hair left on the head. Long hair. Dark, curly.

Full-sized skeleton. I guessed it shorter than me by at least six inches.

The pelvic arch left no doubt: female.

The jaws had been positioned to create a gaping cartoonish grin. Exaggerated glee that was the essence of horror.

I made my way through the slop-heap, got right up to the skeleton. Sniffed.

New smell.

Pleasant, sweet. Herbaceous.

Honeybees buzzing in the hive.

CHAPTER

55

Milo plastic-tied Rader's ankles and belted him into the brown van's second row. Tyler O'Shea positioned Sally up front as a sentry. She enjoyed snapping and growling at the now cringing, weeping actor.

Allowing himself the luxury of an unlit cigar clenched between tight jaws, Milo played the phone, calling in jail transport, crime scene techs, the coroners.

The chief's office, almost as an afterthought. The boss was out; Milo declined to leave a message.

Tyler O'Shea continued to guard the girl in the bikini.

Barbara "Brandi" Podesky, self-described as a "performer and dancer," had no wants but a warrant did pop out of the database: failure to show up for community service on a first-offense marijuana bust. She'd be heading to West L.A. lockup. The news stunned her and she began whining that she was cold.

O'Shea checked out her body, said, "We'll get you something soon." Not a trace of sincerity.

Milo went to look at the skeleton, emerged seconds later and positioned himself in the doorway. Chewing his lip and wiping his face, he got back on the phone. As he waited for a connection, his facial muscles relaxed and something aspiring to be a smile stretched his lips.

"Ms. LeMasters? Milo Sturgis . . . yeah, I know it has been, but not to fret, how're your ace-reporter chops this beautiful day? And are you still in love with your husband? . . . Why? Because trust me, Kelly, you're gonna dig *me* more than *him,* do *I* have a scoop for *you.*"

Just as he clicked off, the chief beeped in. Milo began to supply details I already knew so I left him there, figuring to walk off some excess energy.

I circled right of the car-crush. Came face-to-face with Prema Moon.

Milo had instructed her to stay behind. Some leading women didn't take well to direction.

"Where is he?" she said.

"In the van, but you need to stay away."

"Why wouldn't I stay away? So. It's over."

For the justice system, it was just beginning.

I said, "Yes."

No response for a second. Then she winked at me. Turned her back and tossed her hair and offered a frisky shake of her perfect rear.

Laughing—a giddy, knowing, brittle sound—she walked off the set.

CHAPTER 56

On TV, it would have been a cinch.

The female skeleton's DNA tracked to Qeesha D'Embo, that of the baby in the park was linked to both Qeesha and Donny Rader. Bloodstains, bone fragments, skin flakes, and hair found in the double garage that Rader had set up as his taxidermic workshop belonged to mother and child.

Several of the women located through Mel Wedd's little blue book confirmed that Rader had often retired to the dark, dingy, space after partying, demanding to be left alone with his "projects."

The bullet pulled from Mel Wedd's brain matched a .45 in Rader's firearms closet. Rader's collection consisted of thirty-seven poorly maintained weapons included an Uzi and a Russian assault rifle.

Milo had hoped that the .22 bullet pulled from Adriana Betts would match the gun he'd taken from Rader. But it didn't, couldn't be traced to any of Rader's armaments. That lent credence to the notion that someone else, most probably Melvin Jaron Wedd, had murdered her.

Most probably at Rader's request, but good luck proving that.

The more I thought about Rader's and Wedd's identical SUVs, the stronger the hero-worship scenario got. But Deputy D.A. John Nguyen didn't like it, was intent upon finding something more ominous and premeditated.

"I need creepy psycho stuff, Alex. Give me Manson, bloodlust, a folie à deux, the works."

Milo said, "Seems creepy enough as is, John."

"Never enough." Nguyen grinned. "Maybe I'll get a book deal out of it."

Reality was, the case would stretch on for months, maybe years. Donny Rader, despite being buttressed by an army of high-priced legal talent, had failed in his request for bail. But the special cell he occupied at the men's jail put him safely away from the gangbangers and the lunatics and the trophy-hunters, and stories had begun to circulate about special privileges for the star, mailbags overflowing with love letters sent by severely disturbed women all over the world, female deputies charmed by the artfully slurring actor.

Kelly LeMasters got a serious book deal from a New York publisher and quit the *Times.* Tough luck, John N.

The smart money had Rader avoiding trial via diminished capacity, serving some time in a cushy mental hospital, maybe eventually getting out.

I wasn't so sure. Then again, I'd been wrong about so much.

At this point, I could live with that.

◆

One month and five days after Rader's arrest, I drove to Western Pediatric Medical Center, looked for Salome Greiner, found her again in the doctors' dining room. Late in the day for lunch. Just her and her Jell-O, cottage cheese, and tea. As if she never left the place.

I sat down across from her.

She said, "The prodigal psychologist returns."

I said, "Jimmy Asherwood was a wonderful man who led a tragic life. I can see why you'd want to protect him. I have no desire to smear his memory. He did nothing to deserve that. Quite the contrary."

She sighed. For all her vitality, an old woman. I felt like a troublesome son. Continued, anyway.

"I know about his war injury, know that any relationship you and he had wasn't sexual."

Anger caused her mandible to jut. "From you," she said, softly, "I'd expect a bit more imagination."

That threw me.

She said, "What exactly do you want?"

Rather than answer, I said, "Jimmy respected the right of a woman to control her own body but he was aware that sometimes women—girls—could be pushed into decisions they really didn't want. Girls from a certain social caste who'd created an inconvenience for their families. Enter, Swedish Hospital."

"Goods and services for cash, darling. What could be more patriotic?"

"When the girls decided to terminate, Jimmy went along with it. But unlike the other physicians, he tried to find out what they really wanted. Stepped in when he felt they were being steamrolled. How'd he convince the parents?"

"You're the expert on human nature."

"My guess is he told them the procedure could endanger their daughter's life. And I'll bet some parents didn't care and found themselves another doctor because for a certain genre of alleged human being, stigma trumps everything."

Her response was to saw a cube of Jell-O.

I said, "When the babies were born,

Jimmy's involvement didn't end. Just the opposite, he took care of everything. With the help of Eleanor Green, a compassionate soul who loved kids. Exactly the type of person who should become a nurse."

"Ellie," she said. A liver-spotted hand rose to her breast.

I said, "Ellie and you. Maybe others."

"Army of the just," she said. "We were a little battalion of . . . idealistic meddlers." She put down her fork. "After Dachau, I felt I needed to."

I touched her hand. She pulled away. "Are you satisfied, Alex?"

"Sometimes Jimmy delivered the babies, sometimes you did. When the infants were up to the journey, they were transferred to Ellie's care. In a big house in a nice neighborhood that Jimmy rented for that purpose. After being medically screened for a few months, they were given to families who wanted them. People who'd been screened. Not official adoptions, everything had to be off the record."

"Thirty-three," she said. "That's how many we placed. People all over the country. Thirty-three adults who have no idea."

"Thirty-three minus one," I said. "What happened?"

Shaking her head, she got up. I expected her to leave but she walked to the hot-water urn, filled a fresh cup, unwrapped a tea bag, watched it dangle.

When she returned to the table, I said, "Salome, I'm sorry if—"

"Crib death. That's what we called it then, later we got fancy, the way we always do, and it became sudden infant death syndrome. That didn't explain what caused it but it sounded more scientific, no? Nowadays we have our theories but we still don't really understand it. We do know how to prevent a significant amount of it."

"Sleeping on the back, never the stomach."

She smiled. "All those babies with flat heads, parents get all exercised, thinking their little gift's going to grow up looking funny and not get into Harvard. I tell them relax, stop worrying about stupid things."

She shook her head. "No sleeping on

the tummy, so simple. That's how she—
how Ellie found him. On his belly, not
moving. A boy, boy babies are more
vulnerable than girl babies. Maybe that
never changes, eh, Alex?"

I said, "You live longer than we do,
that's why we get to postpone our maturity."

Now her hand rested on mine. "You
were always a witty one."

I got myself some coffee. The two of
us drank for a while before she said,
"Ellie thought it was her fault. Jimmy
and I found her rocking the baby, he'd
been dead for a full day, she'd sat with
him all that time, didn't want to let go of
his body." Shivering. "I had to pry it
from her."

"So you allowed her to bury him in
the backyard."

She gripped both my hands, exerted
astonishing pressure. "Why not, Alex?
Her grief was monumental and we
couldn't exactly report it to the health
department."

"Of course not," I said.

"We had a little ceremony. At night.
Nondenominational. Each of us offered

a prayer. Whispering to avoid alerting the neighbors. Jimmy dug the hole. I planted a little sycamore tree I'd purchased at the nursery. And flowers. Clivia. Around the base. They're beautiful orange, love the shade. We wanted Sam—we gave him a name, so he'd be someone—we wanted to place him in a miniature coffin, but we couldn't figure out where to find one without arousing suspicion. So we used . . . something else."

"Metal box from the hospital. Used to bring money to the bank."

"It's what we had, the alternative was, what, an orange crate?"

"I assumed there was symbolism, Salome."

"What?"

"He was seen as having great value."

She stared at me. Smiled. "I like that. I will adjust my memories to include that. Now if you'll excuse me—"

"Did Jimmy and the rest of you continue placing babies?"

"Of course," she said.

"But Ellie stopped."

Nod.

"What happened to her?"

"She moved to another city, I will not tell you where. Married a man who loved her, I will not tell you his name. Had a baby of her own. Died. That's all you need to know, Alex."

I stood. "Thank you."

"You will tell the policeman?"

"No reason to."

"Then why—ah, of course. You were always driven. A little obsessive, maybe?"

I smiled. "It happens."

CHAPTER

57

Ninety days after Donny Rader's arrest, Milo emailed me a link from *Daily Variety.*

His scrawled comment: *No comment.*

Prema's Aura Shines Gallically

Mega-star Prema Moon has emerged from self-imposed retirement to ink a deal with the Feinstein Group for an action-adventure pic featuring a superhero mother struggling to raise her children while combating cosmic evil forces. The mega-budget production, still untitled, will film in Croatia and France, enabling

Prema to travel easily to her newly purchased chateau-cum-organic-farm in the Loire Valley. When asked about the parallels between the story line and her real-life situation in which ex Donny Rader was arrested for multiple murders while she was forced to shield her four-tot brood from his nefarious behavior, Prema's representative declined comment. Chad Zaleen penned the script with Garvey Feinstein producing through his Lighthouse shingle, along with Andrew Bronson, Bill Kander and Dan Elhiani. Ethan White, Barry Urbanovitch and Prema, herself, will exec produce. Filming is slated to begin . . .

Five months later, the mail included a silver-edged pink card in a matching envelope.

> **We are so joyful**
> **And thankful**
> **To the Earth Aura**
> **And the Goodness all around**
> **As we proudly welcome:**

Aimee Destiny

Born beautiful and healthy and brilliant at a whopping 8 lb. 4 oz!

Holly and Matt Ruche

In lieu of baby gifts please donate to Western Pediatric Medical Center

ABOUT THE AUTHOR

JONATHAN KELLERMAN is the #1 *New York Times* bestselling author of more than thirty bestselling crime novels, including the Alex Delaware series, *The Butcher's Theater, Billy Straight, The Conspiracy Club, Twisted,* and *True Detectives*. With his wife, bestselling novelist Faye Kellerman, he co-authored *Double Homicide* and *Capital Crimes*. He is also the author of two children's books and numerous nonfiction works, including *Savage Spawn: Reflections on Violent Children* and *With Strings Attached: The Art and Beauty of Vintage Guitars*. He has won the Goldwyn, Edgar, and Anthony awards and has been nominated for a Shamus Award. Jonathan and Faye Kellerman live in California, New Mexico, and New York.

jonathankellerman.com
www.Facebook.com/
JonathanKellerman